Also by Clare Leslie Hall

Broken Country

Days You Were Mine

Pictures of Him

A Novel

Clare Leslie Hall

Simon & Schuster Paperbacks

NEW YORK AMSTERDAM/ANTWERP LONDON
TORONTO SYDNEY/MELBOURNE NEW DELHI

Simon & Schuster Paperbacks
An Imprint of Simon & Schuster, LLC
1230 Avenue of the Americas
New York, NY 10020

Originally published in Great Britain in 2018 by Orion Fiction, an imprint of the Orion Publishing Group Ltd., as *Him*.

First Simon & Schuster trade paperback edition September 2025

Manufactured in the United States of America

10 9 8 7 6 5 4 3 2 1

Library of Congress Control Number: 2025940469

ISBN 978-1-6682-1051-2
ISBN 978-1-6682-1052-9 (ebook)

For John, with love

Pictures of Him

Now

It's my favorite nurse, the one who brushes my hair gently, taking care never to catch the bristles in a knot, and who dabs at my face with a warm flannel rather than the vicious wiping that some of the others indulge in. I could react. I never do.

She talks to me constantly as she works, lifting my upper lip so that she can scrub my teeth with delicate little circular motions, raising a glass of water to my mouth and telling me: "Take a big swig now, my darling, and swill it around."

She calls me "beauty" or "darling," never Catherine. Sometimes I can focus on her words for a little while before the tug of dreams pulls me back to you.

"Your family are coming today," she says.

My little girl will be patting my face with her small, soft hands, my boy standing silently by my chair, watching with his grave eyes. My husband will talk to me, telling me about his day with the note of self-consciousness that is always there. Who can blame him? Bloody embarrassing talking to a brick wall, day after day.

"Hello, Catherine," he'll say, always my name now.

Beauty. Catherine. Just labels that hold no meaning. I am whoever they want me to be. Mostly I sit still while the words whirl above me, dancing golden specks of dust caught in the sun.

"Recovery"—this word is said a lot. By Sam, who says it in a tense, passive-aggressive kind of way, and by the psychiatrist, whose pronouncement is more hazy, more hip-swinging, easy come, easy go. Who's counting? he seems to say. Sam is . . . Sam is counting. He wants to know how much longer he has to wait: a week, a month, the rest of his life? How much longer before his wife comes back to him?

But I am drifting, drifting. I am a girl again, nineteen, almost twenty. I am loved, wholly, with a passion that has flooded my bones and my blood and my brain. There is only this, this warmth, this light, this fierce, pin-bright happiness. And it is so good to be here, if I can just hold it, just freeze it right at this moment.

"I won't ever leave you," I say, and you pull me tighter into your arms and we fall asleep that way, wrapped up like a parcel, and I won't wake all night. But then I do wake, and just like that, the axis spins and everything changes.

The nurse is back. She has an accent, but I have yet to be able to concentrate long enough to work out where she's from.

"Here they are, beauty. Here's your family come to see you. She's lost in her world of dreams today, aren't you, my darling? Talk to her, won't you, she hears it all."

Daisy is kneeling by my chair, her head in my lap. I feel Sam lift up my hands, first one, then the other, and place them on top of her tight dark curls. I feel Joe's presence, standing as he always does just to the right of my chair. Joe doesn't speak to me anymore.

When he first came he would say, "Hello, Mum," the tersest of greetings, nothing more, and in those two biting words all I could hear was my son's quiet fury. I can't help him, I can't help anyone.

Sam is standing by the window, a blur of dark clothes, his tall, thin body blocking out half the light, obscuring the view of my tree. I'd like him to move. Just a couple of feet would make all the difference.

"Talk to us, Catherine. Please. Show us that you can."

I hear the desperation in Sam's voice more than the actual words, and beneath it, several layers down, I can hear his frustration. He is the kindest man, Sam, he is here, after all, day after day, with no promise of my return, no date set for us to squeak our way across the hospital floors, out into the tarmac gloom of the car park and away from my lonely tree. But I also hear the words he will not say, the silent accusation of willfulness, of selfishness.

"So she could speak if she wanted to?" he asks Greg, the psychiatrist, with his New Balance trainers and his side-parted hair.

"Not exactly," Greg tells him. "Physically, yes, she's capable of it, but she has lost the power of speech. It's not something that can be reversed at will. We have to look at all the reasons why she's stopped speaking. Most likely it's an unconscious avoidance strategy. It's her way of refusing to absorb intolerable information. Catherine shut down because she couldn't cope with what happened at Shute Park that day. She can't process the trauma of it, so instead she represses the memory. Not talking is her defense."

Greg blinds Sam with some medical terminology, describing the dissociative disorder that is supposedly afflicting me; he even alludes to Freud.

"In the nineteenth century this kind of behavior was much more common, especially in women. You might have heard of the hysterics?" he says, upbeat and conversational, like he's at a dinner party. I feel rather than see Sam's resentment. "Often those afflicted might experience numbness or fits or amnesia. In Catherine's case she is unable to speak; to her it's literally as if her vocal cords have been frozen. We call it elective mutism."

Later on it's Greg who squats down beside my chair, knees cracking, and gives me an idea, something to work with, something that will allow me to spend more time with you.

"I think I know where you are in your head," he says, and I feel the insistence of his eyes even though I'm looking out at the garden, focused on my tree. "You're stuck there, aren't you? Right at the end. And I wonder if it might help to go back to the beginning, to put everything that happened in some kind of order. I know it's hard, Catherine, but you do need to get it straight in your mind."

You could think of it as a story, he tells me in a soft, lulling voice, the kind I always used when the children had nightmares. Think of someone you can tell it to, he says, and this bit is easy.

It's our story, yours and mine, and so, of course, I will tell it to you.

Fifteen Years Earlier

Do we start with once upon a time; is that how we'll do it, my love? Once there was a girl who knew nothing of love or lust or the peculiar sense of freedom you bestowed upon her. She had arrived at university with her brand-new Samsonite suitcase and her matching Cath Kidston bedding, an only child, indulged, adored, who'd existed in a helium-pumped triumvirate for all of her eighteen years. She began to make friends, one of them her future husband, as the story goes. Everything came easily: a fellow English student who metamorphosed seamlessly into a best friend, a position on the student newspaper, a trio of A grades that exempted her from exams. Six weeks into her second year, just as the trees were beginning to show off with their golds and crimsons and banana yellows, a boy blew into her tutorial, unexpectedly, earth-shatteringly. The boy was you.

There were five or six of us in the tutorial that day in a circle of shabby, mismatched armchairs, listening to Professor Hardman describe Milton's portrayal of Satan as a military hero. He had a flat, soporific voice, this professor, and the blue-white skin of the exhumed, and he spoke with his eyes closed, one hand cradling his left breast as if he suspected an imminent heart attack.

The door flew open and you came through it wearing yesterday's crumpled clothes and with your hair standing on end, though nothing could hide your beauty. Every single student in the room knew your name.

"Ah, Mr. Wilkes. Good of you to join us. Perhaps you'd like to sit next to Miss Elliot," the professor pointed to the empty chair next to me, "and then you can start reading for us."

Your voice was deep and beautiful, and you read with the preternatural self-assurance that always seems to belong to your kind. Professor Hardman closed his eyes again as he listened to your unhalting description of Satan, and it was a full five minutes before he raised his hand and said, "Beautifully read, thank you. But what do these opening pages tell us about Satan?"

I could feel the rest of the group collectively willing you to stutter or stumble or come out with the same kind of vague inanities that they would produce under pressure, but instead you said you found Milton's portrayal of Satan as a hero unconvincing. You outlined his flawed descriptions of the devil in Books IV and V, which showed that, unlike the rest of us, you'd read the entire poem and made your own judgment on it. In the moment's silence that followed, I knew that the whole room hated you, for your looks, your confidence, your rumored wealth, and now for this display of fierce, unfettered intelligence. But even then, right at the beginning, I felt the first tug of admiration.

Afterward we filed out of the tutorial, across the courtyard, and onto the street to the satisfaction of seeing a traffic warden writing out a ticket for the pale-blue Austin-Healey we all knew to be yours.

"Oh shit," you said, and then you grabbed hold of my arm. "Will you wait here for a second while I deal with this? Please? There's something I wanted to ask you."

Your eyes, the first time I looked properly into them, were jade-colored, pale and piercing at the same time.

I couldn't hear what you said, but I watched in amazement as the traffic warden listened to your defense, a slow smile spreading across her face. As you walked back toward me, she ripped the parking ticket in two.

"Next time I won't be so kind," she called, and you waved your thanks, though your eyes never left my face.

"Do you always get your way?" I said.

"I try to. Talking of which, I'm taking you for lunch. Right now. Mystery location, prepare to be amazed."

"Sorry, I can't."

I began to turn away, but you caught hold of my arm again.

"What's wrong? Why are you being so"—you struggled for the word, then found it—"standoffish"? You were so surprised, I couldn't help smiling. I doubted girls turned down your invitations to lunch very often.

"People to see, places to go, work to do. The usual."

"Oh come on, you can spare an hour or two for lunch, surely?"

"The thing is, I've just started seeing someone."

I felt foolish saying it, and my cheeks flamed. But you just laughed.

"Well, I don't know what you had in mind, but I was only thinking of lunch. Some seafood, maybe a glass of wine. Where's the harm in that?"

I stood there immobilized, wanting to go but knowing I shouldn't. Thinking of Sam but wanting to be with you, the shape of my future if only I'd known it.

"Not today," I said, as if I were refusing dusters from a door-to-door salesman.

You'd read my internal struggle, I saw that with your final smile before you walked back to the pale-blue car.

"Let's try again tomorrow, then," you said.

Four Months Before: Catherine

Our first summer in the country has been dry and hot, each morning the sky relentlessly blue, the earth so thirsty you can almost hear it panting. Sam tells me we chose the perfect time to escape, with the whole of the long summer holiday free to explore the hills and beaches and crackling, dried-up woods of our new habitat.

"We have each other and the kids, and now we have this beautiful wreck of a house. What more could you want?" he says whenever I worry about the sudden, dramatic slashing of our regular income. "My new job starts in September, and until then we've always got your money to fall back on."

My money, compensation for losing my mother to breast cancer fourteen years ago and my father to a new wife in New York. He's living the dolce vita just like us, except his dream involves sushi and high art and a woman who wears matching silk underwear.

We left London in a rush, six weeks from Sam handing his notice in at his reliable, well-paid prep school job to the removal vans rattling up in front of the ramshackle Hansel and Gretel cottage in Somerset.

"It's pretty, I'll give you that," I said the first time I saw the place, with the wisteria curling decoratively around its rusty front gate and an explosion of roses, red, pink, and white, across its front.

I thought it looked like a child's drawing of a house, with its mismatched roofs—one thatch, two tiled, all at different heights—its windows of varying sizes, peeling stable doors, and thick, fur-like covering of ivy. We made an offer there and then, and when the surveyor's report came back revealing wall-to-wall damp and poor insulation, we bought it anyway.

"We're going off to Frome to buy paint," Sam says, kissing me and herding the children at the same time. "We'll get a cake from that shop you like."

I know what he's doing, of course. He's giving me space, freedom to moon and mope and mourn the fact that we no longer live in London, my hometown for thirty-four years, the place where my mother lived and died, that last point the most crucial in my mind.

The minute the door closes behind them, this is what I do. I go up to our bedroom, open the wardrobe door, and from the very back, hidden behind a jungle of unworn boots, I retrieve a box full of letters, photographs, and cuttings, my secret dossier on you. Today my hands close around a piece of lined A4, covered in your distinctive blue-Biro scrawl. I know this letter so well that I could close my eyes and recite it to you right now. I know where there are commas and brackets and a missing full stop. I know where you double-cross your t's and where you don't; I could construct a perfect counterfeit if I wanted to.

You're not coming back to me, are you? I used to tell myself that you would, but as the weeks pass, the time we were together begins to feel like a dream. Are you even real? I look for you in the streets, in every pub I go into, in the library, that funny little Portuguese café where we ate custard tarts and the old lady called you Audrey Hepburn (she was right, it's your eyes). I can't find you anywhere, but somehow the sense of you never leaves me. The feel of your hair brushing across my face, the weight of your hand pressing into mine. I wake in the night and still hear your soft breathing next to me. You are gone, and yet you're always here.

This first letter—there are five—is the one I like best. I can read it and imagine that we are still that girl and boy, sitting in an empty café in Bristol on a pale, quiet Tuesday, a bit like this one. There was no one else there apart from a woman who sat at the table right next to us, hunched over her cup of tea. You offered her one of our custard tarts.

"Will you have one of these?" you said. "We bought too many."

It wasn't true, we'd only bought two, but neither of us had touched them; we were too busy holding hands and smiling at each other.

"You're very kind," she said, and when she turned to face us, we saw that she was very old, her flesh a concertina of a thousand lines.

"She's Audrey Hepburn, isn't she, your girl?" she asked, and we laughed.

You said, "Yes, she is," not knowing if she was confused or really meant it, this old, old woman.

I can read this first letter and I can be you and me again and I don't have to explain. I don't have to say sorry, sorry, sorry, that endless echo that reverberates through my dreams. Instead I sit here, your letter in my hands, and for a little while, I can pretend. You and me in the café or on the beach, our rose-colored beginning, no thought of the end.

The slammed front door signals the end of my world of dreams, the shoebox stashed hastily in the bottom of the wardrobe. I hear the rhythmic slapping of Daisy's trainers running along the hallway, her yell from the bottom of the stairs: "Mum! We're back!" as if there could be any doubt. I meet them in the kitchen, newly painted by Sam and me, where the midafternoon sun bounces in sharp little daggers from the brand-new show-home whiteness—walls, ceiling, floor, fridge, cooker. Daisy unpacks a cake from a brown cardboard box and puts it on a large flowered plate that once belonged to my parents, and Joe fetches mugs from the cupboard, and Sam fills the kettle and catches my eye and says, "OK?" and I nod because mostly I am.

"Beach tomorrow," he says. "There's a little wooden dinghy for sale at Lulworth Cove. I thought we'd go and see it."

While I pour tea into mugs and Sam slices the cake and slides a piece onto each plate, he talks about where we'll be able to sail the boat if we buy it and what color we might like to paint it. He's an expert at reinvention, my husband.

When the phone rings and it's Liv on the other end, Sam walks to the fridge and pours me a glass of white wine.

"Take it in the sitting room," he says, still hooked on the mission to appease. "We're going down to the stream. Take your time."

He hopes that these impromptu phone/bar sessions will make up for the fact that I no longer live five minutes down the road from my closest friend, the girl I met on our first day of university and have spoken to pretty much every day since. Liv asks me what I'm doing, the same question, day after day, as if she expects by some miracle that our lives in the country will somehow have metamorphosed into something more interesting.

"We've just had tea and cake," I tell her. "And Sam's taken the kids down to the stream."

"Sounds like paradise," she says, but I catch the note of boredom in her voice, and I imagine the afternoon taxis that rattle beneath her windows, the red buses slamming on brakes at the corner of her street to disgorge commuters and shoppers and tired, toddler-weary parents. I miss it, is what I think, as I listen for London to thrum down the telephone line.

"Can I come and stay the weekend after next? I've just had an invitation to Lucian's. You know that big summer party he always has?"

At the mention of your name, everything slows, as it always does, the air cools, and momentarily I lose all sense of speech, words, meaning. And perhaps this is where it starts again, our story, after a fifteen-year interlude, with your name, startling, unexpected, surfing the distance between us.

"Catherine?"

"Yes, great, you can always stay, you know that."

"Are you OK with it? Me seeing him?"

Whenever Liv sees you she always asks me if I mind, waiting, I think, for me to tell her what she already knows. Yes, I mind, Liv. I mind with every particle of air that's left in my lungs. I mind that you see him and I don't. I mind that you've continued your friendship with him through all these years even though you suspect it crushes me. When I say nothing, she feeds me bits and pieces of information: "He's having an exhibition in Bruton," she'll say, or "He's just bought a flat in Oxford Gardens." The rest I glean from the papers, which still love to write about you and your tight, impenetrable little circle of friends. There's often something in the diary pages of the *Daily Telegraph* or the *Evening Standard*, a picture of you smoking outside a club or grasping a glass of champagne and the waist of a well-groomed blond, eyeballing the camera with that mixture of defiance and disdain that hasn't faded over the years. You never smile, nor do the blonds.

I could tell Liv about my afternoon spent upstairs with your letters, dwelling as always on our ending, wishing I could twist it or color it or rewind or fast-forward, wishing that I had Sam's skill for reinvention, wishing, always wishing that I could have changed the outcome.

I know that I will spend the night of your party with a head full of poison, drugging myself to sleep, probably, and then waiting until morning for the carefully sanitized snippets Liv chooses to reveal.

"He was lovely," she'll say. "He asked after you," and my heartbeat will slow right down.

I won't ask her what she said, for I already know the answer. She'll tell you I'm fine, that my kids are getting so big now, perhaps that I've moved to the West Country, to a village just twenty miles or so from yours. We share a county, if nothing else.

She will be careful not to talk to me about Jack, whom I dread, or Rachel, who triggers the kind of bone-freezing jealousy I despise in other people. I wish everyone else would be as cautious and sensitive as Liv, but they're not. They firebomb Jack's name into the conversation—the starkness of blood scattered into snow—oblivious to the meltdown that takes place inside me. Even Sam does it sometimes.

"Look, there's that twat from university," he'll say, holding up his newspaper and flashing your handsome, white-toothed friend at me.

"Catherine?"

From the shifting, quieter cadence of her voice, I know what she's going to say.

"You know you can talk to me, don't you?"

Liv has never let go of the idea that you and I should have stayed together, probably because I could never bring myself to tell her the reasons why we fell apart. Even on the morning of my wedding, she tried to make me change my mind.

"It's far too late for that," I'd told her, and I'd asked for a few moments alone.

I'd tried and tried to summon an image of Sam, freshly shaved and handsome in a morning suit. But all I could see was you. Where were you? I'd wondered. You'd inherited Shute Park, your great big house, by then, and I pictured you sitting by the lake, clutching a bottle of whiskey, thinking about our beginning, remembering that lunch, that cold winter's day on the beach. Self-indulgent? I'd say so. You were probably still asleep, wrapped around one of the picture-book blonds. But at least I had my dreams.

Four Months Before: Lucian

I find out my mother has died while another excessive Friday rages all around me. No easy time to receive news of this kind, but one in the morning, off your face on tequila, is an especially awkward fit. I am numb from champagne, vodka and tonic, and, latterly, three hefty shots of tequila, and perhaps this is why I cannot react to the news my sister gives me.

"Lucian?"

"Yes?"

"It's Emma."

Emma. Just hearing her name feels like a rain cloud dispelling its contents from a great height.

"Mummy died this afternoon. An unexpected heart attack; it was instant."

The infantile use of "Mummy" from a woman of forty. This and other inappropriate thoughts punch at my brain and rob me of my power of speech until the pause on the other end of the line becomes impossible to ignore.

"God," is all I come up with.

"The funeral will be in London. Will you come?"

Through the tequila fug I register that no is not an option.

"Yes, of course I'll come."

"Lucian?"

"Yes?"

"I know we haven't been in touch these past few years, but I wanted to say . . ."

A silence that deepens. I realize my sister is crying.

"You'll always be family."

Emma hangs up and I stand immobilized, phone pressed to my ear, listening to the dial tone. My mother's death, my sister's conciliation—it is almost too much to take in.

I threw tonight's gathering to welcome Harry's new wife into the fold. Or at least that was the intention. Truth is, few have ever managed to penetrate the closed circle of friends I tend to think of as family. (With family like mine, you're going to look for alternatives.) There's Jack, whom I've known for most of my life, since boarding school at eight, through public school, university, and the turbulent love-and-drugs fest that we called our twenties. We met Harry at thirteen and eventually carted him off to Bristol University with us, where we were joined by Rachel and Alexa.

By the time I return to the library, my friends are sitting completely upright on the ancient chesterfields. I feel the heat of their eyes as I announce my news through compressed, wooden lips.

"My mother died this afternoon. A heart attack, apparently."

Jack and Rachel hurtle toward me and I find myself being squeezed from both sides, Rachel's thick, blond, tangerine-scented hair swiping across my face like a horse's tail. This is too much. I take a step backward.

"Guys, please. You know we didn't get on. I'm just a bit fazed, that's all."

We sit back down on the chesterfields, and everyone starts behaving like a caricature of themselves. Rachel picks up the half-full tequila bottle, waves it at me, and starts refilling the empty shot glasses. Alexa walks over to the sound system, and moments later the sweeping, funereal strains of Sigur Rós filter across the room. She has a sixth sense for always picking the right tune; I often think she missed her vocation. She's a writer, a relatively successful one, but we should probably have pimped her out in Ibiza. Harry knocks back his tequila shot caveman-style, no salt, no lemon, and his wife, Ling, whom none of us knows, sits right on the edge of the sofa, looking shell-shocked, which is pretty much how she's looked all evening, dead mother or not.

"Ding-dong, the witch is dead," says Jack, raising his shot glass to mine and squinting at me with fierce blue eyes.

My mother the witch. Beautiful, frozen-hearted tormentor of men, literally unto death, in the case of my father. She was nice enough in my early years, but it was all about my father for me back then, trailing around the farm after him, mending fences, chopping down trees, learning to shoot rabbits with his shotgun. That gun, a slam dunk to the heart.

"So. Are we going to the funeral?"

"I guess so. But it's not going to be pretty. The last time I saw my mother and sisters was at my uncle's funeral thirteen years ago."

"Which was anything but pretty."

The one and only time I have seen Jack shocked was when my mother spat her venom amid a room of half-drunk mourners because my uncle made me his sole heir. I think the word "cunt" may have been used, and more than once. They are nothing like you'd expect, my family.

I look across the room at Ling, quietly elegant in her city clothes, and realize we have forgotten the real purpose of the evening. I find myself watching her now, and I see how often she glances at Harry, for reassurance or from incredulity—who knows? She must be stunned by the extraordinary and unexpected turn her life has taken. One moment working in a hotel in

Bangkok, the next married to one of the richest men in England and shackled to his monstrous great house.

It's past four when the party finally wraps up, Harry drunk driving home, Alexa disappearing off upstairs to sleep in her favorite bedroom, Jack on his new fold-up bicycle, a tactical move on Celia's part when her husband had stayed over one night too often.

That just leaves me and Rachel by the dying embers of the fire. Above the hearth there's a huge great beam that came from an old merchant ship; it's got the rusting hooks and nails to prove it. There's one nail that protrudes so far from the beam we call it the devil's finger, and Alexa has wound purple fairy lights around it. They flash on and off, on and off, annoying at first, but I'm used to them now. The library would look wrong without them.

"One for the road?" Rachel says. With us this is often a euphemism for something else.

She looks beautiful in her emerald-green dress, with her bright hair and her carefully made-up face, and it wouldn't be the first time we've ended up together, far from it. But tonight my heart is bleak.

"Rach," I say, shaking my head, "I kind of need to be on my own tonight. The Blue Room is made up for you, as always."

"I understand," she says with a sad little smile that almost makes me change my mind. We have our own set of rules, my friends and I, nothing textbook, but we do like to look after each other.

I take a full tumbler of brandy to bed, knowing I won't sleep yet. It is almost five now, and the morning's half-light is peering around the thick velvet curtains. My bed has been turned down by Mary, my housekeeper, a fresh decanter of water and a clean glass laid out on the table, and the sight of it comforts me, these small, sweet, maternal gestures of concern. If I'd had a mother who was more like Mary and less like my own, well, who knows how things might have turned out?

I sit on the end of the bed, looking around the room that was once my uncle's and has changed very little since those days. The furniture in here is heavy and old and unapologetically masculine, though my uncle, it must be said, veered more toward the effeminate. My father's elder brother, he was overtly gay from the age of eighteen, out and proud, which was unusual enough in the seventies. There was talk of disinheriting him, I believe, but it didn't happen and the house under his ownership became a byword for debauchery, the hub for parties that might last a week. It's certainly made my life easier with the locals: you mention the goings-on at Shute Park and no one bats an eyelid.

I use the vast, and vastly old-fashioned, mahogany wardrobe—I think the correct term is "armoire"—that once belonged to my uncle, now filled with a color-coded array of my shirts, white and black at the front, and blues, greens, pinks, and yellows behind them. I have lined his bookshelves with my books, and two of my paintings hang on the walls. There is one of the view from the hill that sits at the edge of my land; I've painted it hundreds of times, but this version, a monochrome in varying shades of blue (I was trying, and mostly failing, to emulate Picasso), is still the one I like best. The other is a portrait of my father, copied from a photograph when I was nineteen. He'd been dead almost ten years by then, but I still missed him, I still tried to reinvent the landscape of my dreams so that he was there in his holey cashmere jumper and his blue silk spotted scarf, chucking a box of freshly laid eggs onto the table and saying, "Let's make omelets, kiddo."

Two parents, two singular emotions, love and hate; my upbringing was staunchly black and white.

It is properly morning now, and sleep is nowhere close. I could get into bed and read the volume of Raymond Carver stories Alexa gave me for my birthday; I could pick up my sketchpad and draw something, anything, to keep myself from thinking about my mother. The thought that looms is the impossibility of forgiveness, that neither of us will ever be able to say sorry. We fell out spectacularly when I was sixteen and spoke infrequently ever afterward. The final nail was my uncle disinheriting my mother and sisters—not just the big house, which she'd lusted after from the first day of her marriage, but every last coin to go with it. I'd have been more generous if I hadn't hated her so, if I hadn't blamed her exclusively for my father's death, a childlike response I clung on to for reasons I am only now beginning to understand. To think on all this is to concede the weight of regret, the great gray cloud that has been hovering mere inches away since my sister's late-night phone call.

In the end, I do the only thing guaranteed to quell the demons and flip me back into the light: I walk over to the armoire, open the top drawer, and take out an old pencil drawing of the girl I once loved. It was a long time before I could look at this portrait, hastily drawn yet somehow perfectly capturing the blend of innocence and eroticism that marked our all-too-brief months together. The relationship finished in tatters, a cold and heartless ending that tore my heart in two and was worse than anything I'd ever suffered at the hands of my mother. I never understood how someone as sweet and lovely and guileless as her—and I know to this day I was right about that—could have abandoned me so carelessly. I spent months examining all the things I might possibly have done wrong—was I too rich, too arrogant, just too goddamn obtuse? But none of this made sense, not after the way we'd got beneath each other's skin and heart and soul. So I settled for the only explanation there was: she loved the other guy more.

Nowadays I can look at her picture almost objectively. I managed to get her eyes right. I think that's why I like it so much. Those incredible dark screen-siren eyes, a classical otherworldly beauty, the kind that makes you stop and stare. I wonder where she is now, if she's sleeping curled up against her husband, her feet pressing against his, her breathing soft and shallow. Has she cut her hair, does she look older, are there wrinkles on that beautiful face? I've looked for her online from time to time, but there's never anything there, no Facebook or Instagram accounts, no presence at post-university parties. I still see her friend Liv, and I know that she understands my yearning for knowledge of Catherine. Readily she passes on information, usually about her children, a girl and a boy. She never mentions the husband, the man she left me for, though his name, unspoken, hovers between us.

I retreat into my bed, propping up the sketch against Raymond Carver, held in Catherine's solemn gaze until at last my eyelids begin to close.

Fifteen Years Earlier

You began leaving notes in the library cubicle where I worked. I'd go off to look for a book, and when I came back I'd find a folded piece of paper on my desk, emblazoned with your spiky blue scrawl. *Lunch?*

I wondered how you had found out exactly where I was, my preferred spot in the library, away from the second-floor socialites and the back-and-forth traffic by the loos. I wondered if you were hidden in another cubicle close by, watching me open your note with your arms folded and that down-turned smile. How was I meant to find you even if I was considering having lunch with you—which, I told myself, I absolutely wasn't. There was Sam to consider, after all, and I knew your kind, the decadent, excessive crowd you ran with; I knew to steer clear. But still, each new note made my heart beat a little faster. *Is today the day?* read one. *Do you like oysters?* asked another.

Without acknowledging it to myself, I was spending a little longer getting dressed these days, casting aside one jumper in favor of another, bothering with makeup, intensive brushing of hair.

The next Milton tutorial came and went, but the chair next to mine remained empty; the hour, the professor's weak voice, the decoding of Book IV were interminable. I was desolate walking back to the library, desolate. Get a grip, I told myself, you have a boyfriend. Well, almost, an almost boyfriend. Sam and I had been taking our time, friends first but always with that suggestion of something more, smiles meant only for me, his dark-eyed gaze watching me when he thought I wasn't looking. Finally, at the beginning of our second year, a moonlit walk around the harbor, where we'd tentatively held hands, and then, a few nights ago, our first kiss. He was all I thought of during my first year at university, this tall, football-mad, stargazing scientist, until you crashed into my medieval English tutorial and tipped my world on its head.

There was an edge of magic in the way the next note materialized, while I was working, studying my Milton text, head bent over my books. I must have been concentrating hard, for I saw and heard nothing; gradually I became aware of another foreign piece of paper in the corner of my desk. This one was different. I opened it up to find a pencil drawing so detailed and atmospheric I gasped in the formal hush of the library. A restaurant, one with walls made of wood like a ski chalet and tables covered with gingham cloths. Jam jars of flowers so accurately drawn I knew they were gerberas, I could picture the intensity of their petals, cerise or tangerine orange, I thought. One of the tables had a bottle of wine and two glasses filled almost to the rim, and beside it you had written, *Ours?* And just that simple pronoun filled me with an illicit blood rush. At the bottom of the drawing, an instruction: *I'll be outside the library at one o'clock.* Your blue script was familiar to me now; I recognized the loops at the top and bottom of your l's, the curlicue y, the aesthetic, I understood, of an artist's handwriting. This drawing of yours had given me an unexpected insight; it had propelled me forward into a place of less resistance.

There was an oversize white clock on the wall, and I glanced up at it. Ten to one. The world tilted with possibility as I watched the minute hand click through its passage of time, looking down at the intricate sketch—posters on the walls I saw now, miniature forks with all four prongs in place—and back up again at the countdown to my future.

At exactly one o'clock, I picked up my books and left my desk.

Now

Sam and Greg are talking about me again, standing here, right in front of my chair, as if both of them have begun to believe that those who do not speak also cannot hear.

"We can pinpoint the exact moment of dissociation," Greg says. "The question is, how much does she remember about what happened?"

Sam says, "You honestly think she doesn't know?"

I don't like the way his voice sounds; these words of his slither around the base of my stomach, they stick like an air lock in my throat.

"Until she speaks to us or finds some other way to communicate, it's impossible for us to be sure of what she does and doesn't remember. This is all conjecture at the moment, but in cases such as these—and they are rare—the patient often wipes out the exact moment of trauma because they are unable to process it."

"It's been almost three months, Greg."

Sam's voice is earnest, angsty, I can hear his frustration with the doctor. Why can't you sort it out? That's what he's thinking. Why don't you know exactly what's wrong with her? Why can't you fix it?

"You've made your diagnosis, you've told us she has dissociative disorder. Why aren't we seeing any improvement? Why doesn't she want to get better? It's as if she doesn't care."

"Have you heard of *la belle indifference*? Freud again, he coined the term. He used it to describe people who apparently didn't seem to care about their symptoms. But really, this indifference is just another tool to avoid an unbearable feeling or memory. Catherine's shutdown, if you like, is simply her means of forgetting what happened at Shute Park. And making sure it stays forgotten."

"So what now, Greg? What now?"

Sam's voice is calm, but his quiet anger is spray-painted on my brain.

"Is she going to get better? Are you going to cure her?"

"I know it's frustrating, but right now we just don't know what the outcome will be. The most important thing is that you don't give up hope, Sam. And you have to give her more time. That's the only thing you can do."

After Greg leaves, I hear Sam sitting down in the chair next to mine, and I know without looking that he is crying. He doesn't bother to talk to me at first, none of his usual stream-of-consciousness chat, relentless and forced, an enormous effort for a man who was famed for his brevity. I almost forget that he's there, it's such a long time before he starts speaking again.

When I tune back in, I understand that he's talking about a day we spent at the beach. Lulworth Cove, he says. The one with the cliff, the one with the famous door. Durdle Door. Jurassic arch. Geological wonder. There's something in his voice as he says this, and it takes me a while to work out what it is. Do I remember what happened that day, he's asking, the last time we went there? He doesn't mean the obligatory climb to get the best view of that ancient rocky door hooping up from the water, a Caribbean turquoise when viewed from the top. He doesn't mean the little wooden dinghy we ended up buying, a small, shabby boat that captured all our hearts. He wants to know if I remember what came afterward, and I do. The day when everything changed, the precise moment, as it turned out, when I was able to start working my way back to you.

Four Months Before: Catherine

Lulworth Cove, a day of endings and beginnings, though I don't know that yet as we arrive at the famous shell-shaped beach, with its clear, brochure-blue water arcing into shore. Sam strides ahead, picking his way over buckets and pale English limbs, loaded up with backpack, hamper, rug, and towels. We trail behind him, Joe with his earbuds in, not yet thirteen but already in every way a teenager; Daisy carrying books and buckets and the grubby, bobbly Eeyore that at nine she is really too old for. The minute we're settled on a rug, on the farthest, loneliest corner of the beach, the kids race at full pelt into the water, diving beneath its surface and sending white jets of spray up into the air.

"Go on," I say to Sam, who is sitting anxiously beside me, watching me rub sun cream into my face, "go and swim."

He hates sunbathing, sitting still a slow torture to him. What he likes is to swim out as far as he can, pushing himself harder and harder with his labored crawl until he feels the blood pumping in his lungs. He likes to swim to the diving platform with Joe and dive over and over again into the cold, murky depths of the Channel. Or climb over the rocks until he finds the perfect rock pool with Daisy, where they will lie on their stomachs waiting for crabs.

My eyes are shut, and I am drifting in and out of memories, good ones, perfect ones, when an ice-cold hand lands without warning on my stomach. I let out a tortured, horror-movie scream. It's Sam, laughing as he squats down next to me and shakes drops of seawater from his thick black hair. Sometimes I think we're more like siblings than anything else, just an older extension of Joe and Daisy. We are and we aren't, I decide, as Sam slides briefly on top of me, trapping me beneath his cold, hard body, slipping one hand dangerously between my thighs.

"Family beach," I say, pushing him off. "Daisy heading our way."

We lunch in the sun on cheese rolls and crisps and little bottles of Orangina, and afterward Sam forces us on a walk, right to the top of the cliff, where we'll have a perfect view of Durdle Door. It's an easy climb, ledges worn into a staircase over the years, and at the top a covering of grass that has been scorched of its greenness by our long summer of sun. We sit by a cluster of stones, looking out at the sea, and Sam takes two beer bottles from his pockets, a surprise, chipping off their tops cowboy-style against the rocks.

The beer is cold and I'm about to take a sip when he says, "Wait. A toast first. To your mum." He raises his bottle skyward, waiting for me to do the same.

"To Mum," I say, checking myself for the ache that is always there.

It is fourteen years since she died, or fourteen years since she lived—whichever way you look at it, a great big gap of missing and mourning, an absence, a silence that is louder in my head than anything else. I worry that my children are growing up without knowing anything about the grandmother they never met. They do not know, because I cannot bring myself to tell them, that her favorite flowers were peonies and when they were in season she gifted them to herself every week. Peonies and Rodin and Eau de Rochas perfume. Mozart and spaghetti vongole and tailored white shirts from Paul Smith (we found fourteen almost identical ones in her wardrobe after she died). Easy to list her loves, impossible to recount the loss, the moments I had with her, thousands and thousands of them stacked up and compressed into a flat little pillow of sadness.

My children, used to this sort of thing, to their father's impromptu parental toasts, say nothing; they just stare out at the whirls of bright foam breaking at the shoreline.

Afterward we go to look at the boat, an old-fashioned beauty painted white on the outside and sky blue within. She's called *Pandora*, which wins Daisy's heart immediately.

"Best thing is to find a mooring at a lake near you," says the old man who is selling her. "That way you'll use her all the time."

Pandora is more than we can afford, but Sam barters good-naturedly and the old man knocks off fifty pounds, and on the journey home, just over an hour in summer-holiday traffic, we talk of nothing else. Eventually Daisy falls asleep and Joe sticks his headphones on, and Sam flicks through the radio channels, stopping when he finds a program about beekeeping. He cocks his head to one side, the way he does when he's concentrating, and when I start to speak, he shushes me.

"My God, you're actually enjoying this, aren't you?" I say, and he laughs and grabs my hand and doesn't let go for the rest of the journey; even when he changes gear he takes me with him, up, across and down. So I stare out of the window at the colors and curves of the Dorset landscape, still new enough to hold my interest, shrugging myself into our regular country life, and I think that it's really not so bad after all.

By the time we get home it's almost seven, and the kids are tired and cross when I make them go upstairs to shower before supper.

"I'll put some pasta on," Sam says, disappearing into the kitchen, and when the doorbell rings I go to answer it with no thought or preconception in my head at all.

I find Julia Wright, a teacher friend of Sam's, in the porch of our funny tumbledown cottage, and for a moment I'm so surprised that I don't think to ask her in. She came to our house in London once; she brought Smarties for the kids.

"Smarties," Joe said in disgust at the time, "like we're babies."

"Julia," I say, "what a nice surprise," though my heart sinks as she follows me through the hallway, walls lined with our smug happy-days gallery of family photographs: Sam, tall and heart-stoppingly young in a morning suit, laughing down at his bride; Joe and Daisy in their matching car seats, marooned in the middle of a festival; then at school in cobalt-blue sweatshirts, Joe with a forced, serial-killer grin, Daisy with her hair scraped tight into unfamiliar bunches. How depressing, our mellow Wednesday evening will be ruined by interaction with a stranger. I picture the bottles of wine we'll have to drink, the adult supper we'll have to cook, the absence of television and papers and an early night.

"We were just cooking pasta for the kids," I say, leading her into the bright white kitchen, and then I see Sam's face as he turns around from the hob and catches sight of Julia, and my heart catapults and crash-lands on the floor. What can I tell you about those first scorching moments while he semaphores his shame, while our world begins its slow and agonizing landslide?

"Sam?" I say, uncertain for a second or two, but that is all. I can read the horror in the blackness of his eyes and the miserable slope of his mouth. No words are needed; his guilt is rushing from every pore. In a heartbeat I've understood it all.

Julia says, "Hi, Sam," but neither of us reacts.

Sam is staring at me with his dark eyes, the children's eyes, and he looks so, so sad, and I find that I am shaking uncontrollably. This is it, the end or the beginning, I'm not sure which, but I'd do anything to turn back the clock and freeze it on five minutes ago.

I whisper, "How could you?" and Sam sort of howls, "I'm sorry,

I'm so sorry," and Julia, who by now is beginning to understand the dark exchange of information that has taken place between husband and wife, takes a step closer to Sam, and, in a tone of familiarity that makes me want to roar like a caged wild animal, says, "I've tried calling you so many times, but you never call back. How could you treat me like that?"

"What do you want?" I scream, oblivious to the children upstairs, who can probably hear me through the thin cottage floorboards. I *am* the wild animal now.

But Julia ignores me and speaks to Sam instead.

"Can't you understand why I'm here, Sam?" Her voice is unbearable, soft, knowing. "Can't you understand why I couldn't leave it, why I couldn't stand it to be over?"

But Sam is still watching me, a look of utmost sadness printed on his face, printed on my soul, the final moments of our before as the dial flips to after.

Four Months Before: Lucian

Rachel is in the kitchen, eating kedgeree and staring at her phone.

"Morning, darling. Well, technically it's the afternoon. I just got a text from Max. He wants to meet up! I'm so happy."

Ah, yes. Max. The kid. We co-parented for a few years, my friends and I, albeit in our rather haphazard, unconventional way, then Rachel lost custody when he was seven. It broke her, of course, though she never admits it, but I see the tiny etchings of regret around her eyes and I worry that one day they will remold her face into a full-blown mask of despair. She left her husband, Hugo, hedge-funder party boy turned teetotal marathon runner, when the baby was just two. Drugs drew them together and blew them apart a few years later. Hugo is a reborn puritanical: kale smoothies, hot yoga, the whole thing; Rachel a shoo-in for rehab. I paid for her to go once, three thousand notes just for her to walk through the door, not that the money matters. She discharged herself three days later, turning up at Soho House, where it was someone or other's birthday, responding to our shocked expressions with typical flamboyance: "My name is Rachel, and I'm *not* a drug addict."

I look at her now. "Rach, I knew he'd come round in the end," I say.

I put my arm around her and she leans her head on my shoulder, and this is how Alexa finds us when she wanders into the kitchen with wild-woman hair and big panda rings under her eyes.

"What's going on? Why the lovefest?"

"Max texted me this morning. He wants to meet."

"Amazing! Of course he wants to see you. You're his mother."

She slides onto the barstool next to Rachel, kisses her cheek, and begins heaping a plate with kedgeree.

The phone rings.

"Bound to be Jack," says Alexa with the undercut of hopefulness that is always there. She and Jack were a couple right the way through university, unless you count the blood-bitter spats, his incessant flirting, her reckless revenge, the splits and reunions, which became almost pedestrian to those of us who lived through them. Three years ago, on a break from Alexa, Jack met Celia, and a line was drawn under the history of histrionics. I do wonder, though; I see the way Alexa looks at Jack sometimes and I fear that she still loves him.

But it's not Jack on the phone, it's Harry inviting us over for Bloody Marys.

"Thought they might be in order," he said. "Filip is making a batch up right now."

Filip is Harry's Polish butler, who looks after the estate with his wife and their two grown-up sons. His Bloody Marys are immense.

Harry hesitates, a weighted silence while he chooses his words. "Are you OK?"

Harry knows, better than anyone, my capacity for falling apart. We are bound together in our two decades of friendship by the lows as much as the highs, and in my case, a spectacularly bad low.

"Fine," I say automatically, though I wonder as I put down the phone if this is the case. My mother has died, almost a quarter century after my father, making me officially the thing I have felt all along—an orphan. Somehow fine doesn't quite cover it.

Eastcott Grange, Harry's house, is just five miles down the road from my own. It's a great gray pile of a house, an early Victorian manor rebuilt after a fire destroyed the original and handed down through the generations gift-wrapped in tweed. It is a total misfit in Somerset, cider-soaked land of druids, apples, and cheese, with rolling green hills and houses the color of clotted cream. I sometimes think that the grim-faced austerity of Harry's home, prison chic at best, is partly to blame for his incompetence with women. Repression, architectural and otherwise, were his touchstones growing up.

Filip opens the door, and across the hall—marble floors, Romanesque statues, the whole ostentatious shebang—comes the sound of Harry playing the grand piano. I love it when he plays; upbeat ragtime is his specialty, and it never fails to fill me with unexpected optimism. The sound of the piano, the reassuring presence of my friends—in these moments, I feel a sort of contentment.

We find Harry and Ling in the drawing room, sharing the piano stool. She is laughing up at him as he knocks out "Pinetop's Boogie Woogie," a nod to his classical upbringing, though with a cigarette hanging from his mouth, eyes squinting to avoid the smoke and the lock of hair that falls into his face, there's little left of the boy I once knew.

"Don't stop, don't stop!" cries Alexa, and I know that she is feeling the same as me, a kind of thrill at catching Harry and his new wife engaged in a moment of behind-doors joy. There is something about Harry, the definitive big-hearted, broad-shouldered friend, that has always made me crave his happiness above my own.

"Drinks," he says, getting up from the piano and walking over to the cabinet where two jugs of reddish-brown liquid stand ready.

He passes around tall glasses of Bloody Marys, pausing to

kiss Ling on the cheek when he reaches her; a man obsessed. I am a little obsessed with her myself, quite frankly, this young woman we have known less than twenty-four hours. I notice the quiet confidence with which she greets us, quick hugs rather than kisses. "It's good to see you again," she says in her perfect English.

I find I'm watching Ling as we take our drinks over to the sofas. I see how she sits next to Harry with her bare feet tucked up beneath his thighs, how he clasps her foot for a second—nails painted shocking pink—and I catch the half laugh that passes between them.

"Any news on the funeral?" asks Harry. "Or is it too soon?"

"Actually, it's all sorted. You know my sister, nothing if not efficient. St. Luke's next Friday, then back to Flood Street afterward."

"Obviously we'll all come," says Rachel. "Safety in numbers. How bad can it be?"

"You'd be surprised. Though my mother loved a party, so who knows?"

Harry looks over and smiles, a reference for only me. I can still remember his shock at my mother's morning screwdriver. His home life was immensely conservative; short on love, same as mine, but regimented, upright. The first time he came to stay—he can only have been thirteen or fourteen—he picked up her orange juice by mistake and spat his mouthful of scarcely diluted vodka all over the kitchen floor.

"How are you finding life at Eastcott?" I ask Ling.

"Obviously it's very different to anything I've ever known, but . . ." She breaks off to laugh. "Actually, I love it."

Rachel and Alexa, like me, are fascinated by Ling today. Last night, with all the boozing and the drama of my mother's unexpected death, we missed our chance to talk to her properly. They were married in Bangkok with a couple of strangers as witnesses; I think we're all feeling a little excluded by that.

"Where did you grow up, Ling?" asks Rachel.

"In a village in northern Thailand, about an hour from Chiang Mai. It takes a whole day to get to Bangkok."

"Which is where you were living when you and Harry met?"

"Yes, I was working at the hotel Harry stayed in."

"She's being modest," Harry says. "She was pretty much running the whole show."

Ling laughs and rolls her eyes. "Ridiculous man," she says, patting his hand affectionately. To us, she says: "I was the receptionist."

"I tell you, one snap of her fingers and people came running. Me included."

Harry's phone pings with an incoming text.

"That's Ania," he says, "asking if we want lunch."

"Definitely," says Alexa. "Carb heavy, please. I need to eat my way out of this hangover."

Ling unwinds herself from the sofa and stands up.

"Why don't I go and talk to her and see what there is," she says. "Maybe pasta would be good?"

I know we're all watching Ling leave the room and marveling at her calm, unhurried confidence as she goes off to instruct the housekeeper after only one week of living here.

"You were right, Harry. She's wonderful," Rachel says.

Harry's face lights with joy.

"Isn't she? I know you were all worried it happened too fast but, the truth is, I couldn't bear the thought of coming home without her."

He turns to me.

"Come down to the pool for a second? I'm thinking of putting in a new one and wanted to ask your advice."

Of course when we get to the swimming pool, which seems

rather basic and old-fashioned now I look at it, with its bright turquoise tiles and white plastic steps, Harry turns his back on it straightaway.

"You know you could do something really amazing here," I say.

Harry pulls out his cigarettes and offers me one.

"Sod the pool," he says. "It's you I want to talk about. I want to make sure you're all right."

This is a reference to my father's untimely death; no need to spell out what he's thinking. He died when I was ten, three years before Harry and I met. Harry knows, though, how I locked my grief inside myself, just a little savage pinching of my wrists when the pain became too much—self-harming, you'd call it now. He also knows what can happen when my grief is allowed out. There was a time, one we choose never to discuss, when my life spun out of control. I lost my way, let's leave it at that.

I rest one hand on his shoulder.

"This is not going to affect me in the same way. I promise you."

"All right," he says, and we stand beside his archaic pool, finishing our cigarettes in silence.

As is often the case in our friendship, it's the things we don't say that sound loudest. Harry, I fear, would have done anything for me to get the ending I wanted. She might be very much in the past, by fifteen years or more, but at times like this, Catherine has never felt more in my present.

Fifteen Years Earlier

You weren't expecting me to come, I saw that in the flash of hastily concealed surprise as you leaned against your blue car.

You opened the passenger door for me, and I laughed at your old-fashioned chivalry.

The drive to this mysterious destination of yours took more than an hour. I remember looking out of the window, listening to the background wash of the Rolling Stones, your all-time favorite band if you had to choose, you said, while the sweeping plains of the Quantock Hills faded into the high hedgerows and narrow lanes of south Devon.

"Are you abducting me?"

You smiled that peculiar down-turned smile, each corner of your mouth tugged south, the face of an inverted clown.

"I haven't decided yet. Let's see how lunch goes."

We fell into silence. I was thinking about Sam, thinking how he'd hate to see me sitting next to you in the low-slung car. Everything you stood for, Sam stood against, a simple equation of fundamental opposites. Sam's politics had been handed down from father to son like a genetic injection; one of the few things they always agreed on was their utter derision for anyone of privilege.

Finally you brought the car to a stop in a small graveled car park looking out across the sea. I can still picture my first sighting of the Beach House, a battered old hut with peeling blue paint stationed right above South Milton Sands. But then you opened the door to the restaurant, and it was as if we'd stepped inside your drawing; nothing before or since could capture the romance of that moment. It was identical: the wooden walls of a ski chalet dotted with film posters, the red-and-white-checked tablecloths, the jam jars filled with flowers. Outside, the day was cold and gray, but inside the hut it was perfect, a fire burned in the hearth and there were candles on every table. Nowhere in the world could have been better suited to a drawn-out secret lunch.

There was no one else there apart from a mother and daughter who were leaving as we arrived. It occurs to me now that perhaps the restaurant was closing, but you knew the owner and he took your grandiose "We'll try everything" at face value, bringing oysters, crab, whitebait, and grilled sole, a leisurely sequence of dishes that lasted for hours and remains the best seafood I've eaten to this day. There was a bottle of cold yellow wine, and you filled our glasses almost to the brim, just like the drawing. *Ours?*

I'd been secretly observing you throughout the drive, little sideways glances that took in your long, slim fingers on the steering wheel, the frayed wrist of your navy jumper. Now you were opposite me, front on, lit up by candles, and there was nothing to do but look. What was it about your face, I wondered, that made you more beautiful to me than anyone I'd ever seen?

You saw me looking and smiled.

"I didn't think you'd come. What made you change your mind?"

"The drawing."

"You liked it?"

"I loved it. It reminded me of one of my favorite books as a child. You know those old-fashioned pen-and-ink drawings that make you feel as though you could disappear inside them? It was just like that."

You nodded, pleased. You told me drawing and painting were the only things that mattered to you.

"Why are you at university, then, reading English?"

You laughed. "I don't know. Maybe a last-ditch attempt to please my mother. Not that it's working."

You told me your father had died when you were a kid, and your voice as you said it was airy, practiced. But I knew, even then, how this death had changed you.

"Tell me your life story, then," you said.

I rifled through my experiences for a while and could come up with nothing but contentment. When I pictured my home life, it was always Sunday, *Desert Island Discs* on the radio, newspapers spread across the table, the smell of roasting chicken in the air. Conversation that usually focused on me, the full beam of my parents' attention, the warmth and insularity afforded by being a team of three. I was their miracle child, born after nine years of trying, after countless doctors had given up, and they loved me with the zeal of those whose dream comes later.

"I'm not sure my life has begun properly yet," I said, and your mouth curved upward for the first time.

"Perhaps it begins right here."

Four Months Before: Catherine

We don't talk until the children are asleep, tired out from pasta (Sam cooked after Julia had flounced off; I don't know how he managed it), sea air, and perhaps the surfeit of suppressed emotion that pollutes the atmosphere. My voice, hard as metal, razors into the silence.

"You had an affair?"

"No. God, no. Just once. It was stupid, I was drunk. I hate myself."

"When did it happen?"

"The staff party, end of the Easter term."

"Just once? A one-night stand"—I spit the words—"and she's fallen madly in love with you? Bullshit. I don't believe you."

"I'm sorry. I'm so—"

I hold out my hand to cut him off.

"Where? Where did it happen?"

"In the staff room."

"Where? On the sofa? On the floor?"

I'm frantic for details, I don't know why. Sam turns away from me, shoulders curved with despair.

"Answer me, Sam, I need to know."

"Against the wall," he says finally, his voice so quiet I can hardly hear him, and then that image, my husband, his lover, the woman who was in my house less than an hour ago, fills my brain and I sink to my knees, hands covering my face.

"That's so bad, Sam. You wanted her . . ."

Sam kneels down in front of me, takes each of my wrists, and forces me to look up at him.

"All I've ever wanted was you," he says, but I yank myself away.

Minutes pass; it feels like an hour. I am on the floor, curled into a ball, weeping hot tears into our brand-new carpet bought just three weeks ago from a showroom in Frome. And then I am hiding in our bathroom, behind a locked door, Sam on the other side of it, his voice low so as not to wake the kids, but fierce, desperate.

"Please come out. Please let me explain."

Oh, the boring predictability of it all, the wretched cliché of our lives. A messed-up marriage at thirty-four, an infidelity, a stalker for a lover, our own bunny boiler to add into the mix. Worst of all is the sickness I feel, not at Sam or Julia but at myself. For deep down, I always knew this would happen, and I knew that when it did, it would be my fault.

I am thinking of one night on our honeymoon (two weeks in a villa in Antibes, a present from my father) when Sam drank too much brandy after dinner. We were in one of those white-tableclothed, over-waitered restaurants, where two men in tails watched our every move. All of a sudden, Sam started crying—Sam, who had never shed a single tear in the four years I'd known him, not even when my mother died.

"God, what's wrong?" I asked him.

"I'm not sure it's me you really love," he said, his voice thick and brandy soaked. No mention of your name; there never is. He told me he'd found a photograph of him and me, taken during our final year at university. We were sitting around a table, a birthday party for someone or other, and everyone was laughing or smiling except me.

"You looked so sad," he said. "And yet we'd only been back

together a few months by then. If it really was me you wanted, why were you so sad?"

"My mother was dying, Sam," I said, unnecessarily. He of all people understood the fallout from that.

"Obviously I know that. But the look on your face, I don't think it was to do with her. It's your eyes. They looked haunted in that picture. They still do sometimes."

My memory of that particular photo is hazy, but I can just imagine the way my eyes might have burned, not with sorrow but with shame and regret. After I left you, a car wreck of guilt and self-hatred, Sam took me back and made it his life's ambition to rebuild me piece by piece. I wouldn't have survived without him. I needed his goodness to sustain me, I needed to feed on his high opinion of me, and more than either of these, I needed him to keep me safe. It was selfish in the extreme, but he allowed me to do it, he allowed me to build a cocoon around us, hiding away in his rooms, lost to the outside world. We lived that way, absurdly insular, for a whole year, and after university, we got married straightaway and started on our perfect, pared-down, cardboard-cutout life. But underneath it all, right at the heart of things, there was always you.

I realize now, as I steel myself for the conversation that must happen on the other side of this bathroom door, that Sam has been dealing with the specter of you for just as many years as I have.

I find him sitting on the foot of the bed, head in hands. He looks up at me.

"I'm so sorry."

"I know you are." I sit down next to him. "Christ, Sam, she's in love with you. Julia is the reason you made us leave London, isn't she?"

"I thought we could start again, and I could pretend it had never happened. But that wasn't enough for Julia; she refused to accept it was over. Of course I ignored her phone calls. I just wanted her to go away."

"Really just once?"

"Yes. I'm an idiot."

"I don't understand it. Why her?"

"I was pretty drunk. And angry with you. It was during one of our nontalking phases, when you seemed to spend all your time moping in the bedroom. You know how I hated that; I felt so cut off from you. I know it's because of your mum, but you just disappear sometimes, you don't deal with things. I'm not blaming you, I hate myself for what I've done, but I was lonely and Julia was right there. She made me feel good about myself. She wanted me, really wanted me, and that felt so different, like you were when I first knew you, right at the beginning, before . . ." He falters here and your name drapes itself through the atmosphere, but he manages to carry on. "But then she became obsessed. She started following me around at school, at weekends. I was in Sainsbury's with you once choosing wine and I saw her standing just meters away, watching. It's why we had to move. I couldn't take it anymore."

"You're the one person I've always trusted. You know that, you know how much I've needed you."

My voice is cracking, and Sam reaches out a hand toward me, but I ignore it. We sit for a minute or so in silence. I am thinking it was always going to come to this. I am thinking that the strain of living up to you is what killed our marriage, killed Sam, at any rate. I am thinking that Sam, poor, unfaithful Sam, is not really to blame.

"We've been through so much, you and I. Two kids. Your mum . . ." He trails off, no need to say more. She died when I was still reeling from the travesty of losing you. Rapid-fire breast cancer, ten months from diagnosis to a funeral for three hundred at our local Blackheath church. Sam married me pretty soon afterward, a tiny wedding in that same damned church, a gesture of such limitless kindness I cannot quite believe we have got to here.

"Look," he says. "We're going to Cornwall tomorrow; my parents will take the kids off, and you and I can talk."

"I can't come to Cornwall now. How can you even think that? I can't stay with your parents, not with this between us."

"But they'll be so disappointed if we don't go. The kids too."

"Oh God, Sam, I don't know what we should do. I didn't know this was going to happen. But maybe we need time apart to think."

"What are you saying? It was a mistake, it will never happen again. We don't need to do anything except try to forget it ever happened."

This time it's me who extends my hand, and Sam grabs at it, and there we are, flesh against flesh, as we've been so many times before, except now it feels different.

"You and I, we're so good at burying our heads in the sand. But now this has happened, and we have to ask ourselves questions. Like, are we happy together, really, deep down? You slept with someone else, Sam. And you did it because you were unhappy with me."

"Christ, why did that witch have to turn up here? Why is she trying to wreck our lives?"

"Because she's in love with you. Is that so hard to believe?"

"You loved me once."

"I still do."

But always you more. He knows it and I know it, and right now that seems more important than anything, including this love affair with Julia that has blown into our lives with the velocity of a force 10 gale.

Four Months Before: Lucian

We're gathered at Colton House marking another limbo day before my mother's funeral. A word about this den of iniquity, better known as a private members' club, that was so cool, urban, and emphatically un-country it caused a media furor when it opened ten years ago and has drawn a steady stream of musicians, media personalities, and cocaine-addled aristos ever since. People either love or hate Colton. To join, you must fill out an elitist ten-page application form that is known to enrage. Do you know the right people and wear the right clothes, do you have enough cash in your bank account, and talking of cash, whom do you bank with, we do hope it's Hoares.

"How lovely, a club just for knobs," Rachel once said, though she didn't complain when her own membership was rushed through the approval committee. Jack is on the board, needless to say. Everywhere we go, people want a piece of him. He has his own personal army of fans: not just Alexa with her scarcely disguised heartbreak, or Celia, who still wears her infatuation like a teenage hot flush, or me, Harry, and Rachel, who always feel at our best when Jack's around. It's the maître d' at Colton, the bar staff, the postman we share ("He makes you feel ten feet tall, doesn't he?"). But it's our friendship, mine and his, which goes back the furthest.

We met on my first day at prep school, one of those prestigious behemoth places once attended by members of the royal family (my mother's sole selection criteria), and for the occasion my parents and I had arrived in my grandfather's car, this big black fuck-off beast, not quite with an ambassadorial flag but almost. My mother was dressed for a drinks party, very high scarlet heels, I remember, with some kind of trailing dress, and she had made us more than an hour late. Even then, at the age of eight, I understood for her the significance of the arrival, how she craved attention while effortlessly eschewing it. Out of the car like a visiting princess, all eyes upon her—that's everyone: all the mothers (especially the mothers), all the fathers (especially the fathers), the headmaster flapping down the gray stone steps in his Big Bird gown, the teachers, the boys. I knew and didn't mind that my first day at boarding school was a theatrical event; what I was worried about was how I was going to say goodbye to my father without breaking down. On the journey my mother had offered advice.

"Absolutely no tears or hugs. Handshakes only, if you want to fit in. You want to be like the other boys, don't you?"

When it came to it, of course, I'd put out my hand and my father said, "To hell with that," scooped me up, my face pressed against his scratchy wool jacket, and said so everyone could hear it, "Anyone does anything to you that's not nice, then you call home, OK, and I'll come and get you."

He was like that, my father, he didn't give a damn what anyone else thought.

A boy my size, the brightest blond hair, the sweetest of smiles, came right up to us as we said goodbye.

"I'll look after him," he told my parents. "I've been here a term, I know how it works."

That, of course, was Jack, and from that day on we became almost interchangeable. We wore the same clothes (rather, he borrowed mine, sometimes putting on a shirt or pair of trousers I'd discarded the day before). We played the same games—backgammon, blackjack, pontoon. I learned to shoot, he learned to shoot. We fished, we swam, we partnered each other in tennis. As we grew older we chose the same university and shared a house throughout our three years, each day and night, each weekend spent together, drinking the same wine, listening to the same music, sharing food, clothes, my bank account. Was I him or was he me? It didn't much seem to matter.

When he arrives now, holding the hand of his blond toddler, who is taking his first tottering steps, you see the heads turn. And you see Celia, following closely behind, noticing them. There's nothing smug about Celia; I think she counts each starstruck gaze as a potential threat. She weathers the storm of her showstopper husband, but she never seems entirely happy with it.

The problem is that Jack is knockout handsome—Rachel's description—and funny with it, and he dresses like a rock star, today wearing shades, a white shirt fresh from its packaging, and a leather jacket from Christian Dior.

"What we need," he tells the waiter who has rushed over, "is something to blow our minds. What would you recommend? I'm thinking a Margaux or a Montrachet? Red or white, girls?"

He turns to Celia and kisses her cheek.

"You'll drive back, babe, won't you?"

She laughs. "Back to Lucian's later and leave you with your bicycle, you mean?"

Jack shrugs. "Extenuating circumstances. Dead mother and all."

The truth is, I'm never sure how easily this new domesticity sits with Jack. He makes a great show of it, high-profile nappy changing, the changing bag casually slung over his Helmut Lang suit. But he manages to spend almost as much time in my house as he does in his own.

Interesting dynamic at Colton today. Ling and Harry are rather appropriately sharing what I think is called a love seat, one of those half-size sofas, Rachel and I are next to each other on one side of the table, Jack sits between Alexa and Celia on the other side, a pictorial representation of the foibles and transgressions that thrum beneath the existence of our tight-knit circle. I look across at Ling and wonder how much Harry has told her about us. Does she know, for example, about me and Rachel and our on-off affair, which began at university and still reignites at least once a year for three days of frenetic sex before one or the other of us calls it off? Or that Alexa is probably still in love with Jack, and when Celia is not around, the way they flirt and look and laugh, you might think the marriage belonged to them?

Today, though, Jack is in domestic god mode. There's an extended game of peekaboo with Freddie, who sits on his knee: sunglasses up, sunglasses down, each perfectly timed reappearance triggering an adoring chuckle from his baby. He changes his facial expressions—surprised, exhausted, deranged—and the baby laughs even louder. He's good at the dad thing, and you feel the eyes upon him: not just Celia, Alexa, and Rachel, but half the women in the room, who gaze at this blond-haired performer.

"Here, I'll take him," Celia says eventually. "I know you're desperate to go and have a cigarette with Lucian."

Rachel, Harry, and Alexa have just come back from the smoking area, so Jack and I go out alone. The moment we're outside, we hug. It started as a joke, this over-the-top back-slapping man hug, but it sort of stuck. Brotherly love, I guess you'd call it.

"You freaked about the funeral?" Jack asks.

"Yes and no."

While we light up, I contemplate telling Jack how I really feel. That my mother's passing has ignited in me a primal, Munch-like howl of regret. That I can never say sorry, never make peace, never know what it is like to be on good terms with her (we fell out a few years after my father died and spoke little ever since).

But I cannot tell him these things, because he has always hated her for not loving me enough. It was Jack I turned to when I left home at sixteen without any clear idea of where I should go. It was him and his parents who invited me to stay for all the remaining school holidays (I split my time between their house and my uncle's), rustling up another stocking on Christmas Day, an extra egg at Easter, even if I was growing too old for these things. Jack's family lived in a knackered old farmhouse, and his father was always in and out of jobs, new dreams swamping old ones. They'd given up everything to send him to Eton, and then they ran out of money. I'm not sure he thanks them for it—growing up among the super-privileged without any dough himself is at the root of all his insecurity, I'd say. He once said to me, all flashing blue eyes, "I've got to be rich," and I made the mistake of laughing at his earnestness and the note of fervor in his voice.

"It's all right for you," he'd said, the only time he's thrown the money back in my face. But what he didn't understand was that I'd have swapped it all for parents like his. Their consistency, their kindness—it amazed me. There was never a day when Jack and I weren't woken up for bacon sandwiches and a heart-busting walk up a vertical hill; at night, cards were played around the kitchen table with a kind of religiosity. And the food, my God, I've never been one to place much importance on eating, but Jack's mother could really cook. She used to produce pine-nut-crusted lamb from their clapped-out Aga, broken door wedged shut with a chair; potatoes that tasted like they'd been roasted in caramel.

"Worried about the witches?" Jack asks, grinding his cigarette underfoot. Ever since I left home, he has always referred to my mother and sisters as the Three Witches. We were studying *Macbeth* at the time.

"The witches, the friends, the uncles, the aunts. It's been a long time since I've seen them."

A girl we know comes out, clutching a packet of Silk Cut.

"Hi," she says, with an extra smile for Jack. "Your baby's screaming his head off, by the way!"

"Thanks for that," Jack says, and the girl laughs, and he looks her in the eye for a moment too long. Not smiling, just looking. He'd help himself if he could; she's his type exactly.

We walk back into the bar to the sound of Freddie yelling—who knew a small child could make this much noise?—while Celia jiggles him over her shoulder, looking frantic.

"He's tired," she says. "I've got to get him back. You stay."

There's something in her voice, a flatness, a hint of frustration, but Jack ignores it.

"Well, if you're sure?" he says, scarcely looking at his wife as he reaches for the bottle of wine. It's Alexa who taps his wrist and, when he looks up at her, mouths, "You should go," nodding her head over at Celia. I watch my friend's face through its swift passage of emotion: disappointment remolded to resignation.

"You know what, babe? Why don't I come with you," he says. "I'll make us something for lunch if you like."

The transformation is instant. Celia is already grinning as she passes Freddie to Jack, who immediately begins a sort of jazz-hands motion with his sunglasses, up and down, up and down. Within seconds the baby is laughing but with a few outraged sobs in between, as if he's furious to find himself so easily amused.

"Wow, that was intense," says Rachel when Jack and Celia have left in a swirl of car seats and changing bags.

"He's pretty good at it, though, isn't he?" says Alexa. "He's a brilliant dad." Her voice is completely level as she says it, but I know that we all—Rachel, Harry, and I—pick out her regret. She still loves him; I understand why.

"Shall we order some food?" I ask, and Alexa says no, she's going to drive back to London.

"I've given myself this completely unnecessary deadline, I'll be writing all night like an essay crisis."

Alexa is on her third historical novel. She writes romances set in eighteenth-century England, a bit like an edgy Jane Austen. If you had asked me at university to pick a career for Alexa, this would have been the last thing I'd have chosen, but she's good at it; her books are selling well.

The party breaks up. Harry and Ling are still in honeymoon mode, clearly preferring their own company to ours, the dissolute friends.

It's Ling, not Harry, who turns down my invitation to lunch.

"Not this time, thank you," she says, her manner frank and easy. "Harry and I are still brand-new. We have a lot of catching up to do."

And off they go, arm in arm, along the cobbled path, laughing together as they walk away.

That just leaves me and Rachel back at Shute Park for the final countdown to the funeral. We sit in the kitchen for a while, chatting to Mary and eating omelets she makes for us. I'm glad Rachel has stayed; it helps me to hide from the demons.

"Are you sure it's OK for you to take all this time off?"

She waves a dismissive hand. "Of course it's OK. What is this job of mine, anyway?"

In the loosest possible way, Rachel works in PR. Her main employer is a peripatetic art gallery for whom she fires off press invitations and wears her beautiful dresses to openings in places like Weston-super-Mare. She's funny about it.

"I travel a lot for work," she'll tell someone we've met at a party. "Loughborough last week. Tomorrow Melton Mowbray."

"Let's drink a really good bottle of wine. You put some music on."

In the cellar, I think of Jack, briefly, and how much he would like to be here. He loves my uncle's cellar, which is fanatically well organized and stocked with an absurdly large wine collection. For people who care about such things (I can't say I'm one of them), apparently it's one of the best cellars in the country.

I choose a Meursault, Rachel's favorite, a premier cru from 2007, and make my way back to the library, completely unprepared for her choice of music. "Wild Horses." Not just the album—*Sticky Fingers*—but the song. I can never hear it without thinking of Catherine, without seeing her, so young and so beautiful, dancing with her eyes closed and her arms held high above her head. The last time we were together.

The change in me is instant, and of course Rachel sees it.

"Oh Lucian," she says, and when I sit down next to her on the sofa, I see that her eyes are full of tears. "You've never managed to get over her, have you?"

Fifteen Years Earlier

After lunch we sat next to the fire, finishing our wine, and I told you about my dream of being a journalist. It was more than a dream, really; I'd been working toward it since I was twelve years old, writing for the school magazine and the local parish newsletter, and the thing I was most proud of, a string of articles that had been accepted by *The Independent* about life as a London teenager. I'd joined the university newspaper in my first week, and secretly hoped to be editing it in my final year. Then a graduate trainee scheme at *The Times* or *The Guardian*, a stint in the newsroom, after which I'd become an arts correspondent, all working toward my ultimate goal of editing one of the weekend supplements by the time I was thirty.

"You've got it all worked out. None of my friends have a clue what they'll do. We don't even talk about it."

Privately I thought that might be because your friends were the kind who didn't need to think about it, the kind for whom money actually did grow on trees.

You were reluctant to talk about your painting at first. I asked if you wanted to become a professional artist, and you waved your hand dismissively.

"I'll never be good enough."

It was the first time I'd seen a chink in that smooth public-school armor of yours, a glimpse of insecurity.

"You are. More than good enough, if that drawing is anything to go by."

"I'm better when I commit the time, by which I mean all day and all night. Painting isn't something you can fit round a life. You have to do it nonstop if you really want to get somewhere."

"What kind of things do you paint?"

"It varies. Landscapes mostly, but recently I've started doing portraits."

That's when you told me about a portrait you'd made of your father, working from an old photograph.

"It was like bringing him back to life for a bit," you said. "His eyes, his smile. Suddenly I could remember exactly. And not just from the photograph."

I registered how your voice changed whenever you spoke about him, quieting, softening. I thought about asking you how he'd died, but I didn't have the courage, not then.

"I'd like to draw you. Will you let me?"

I shook my head. "Maybe one day."

"Why not now?"

I shrugged. I was still trying to resist you at that point, my own private tug-of-war. The start of a longing that would never cease. You smiled your minimal quarter smile.

"You're not making any of this very easy for me, are you?"

Four Months Before: Catherine

Saying goodbye to the children almost broke me. I didn't want them to pick up on the tension between us, so I'd cobbled together an excuse about Liv needing me to go and stay.

"She's feeling a bit low. I'm going up to London to look after her," I said while the children looked at me in disbelief.

"You're missing our holiday?"

How I hated to see Daisy's quick tears.

"Liv needs me, darling," I said, holding her hard little body against my own. "And you'll be fine with Dad and Grandma and Grandpa, you know you will. It's only a few days."

It doesn't feel good lying to your children, but the truth is so much worse. Your father has been unfaithful to me; that woman who came to our house yesterday, the one who gave you Smarties, the one who wears halter necks and dark-colored lipstick, was his lover.

When Sam dropped me off at the station—a wordless journey, no hand-holding on the gearstick—he pleaded with me to change my mind. We stood waiting for the train to draw in to the platform, my overnight bag at my feet, staring at each other while I turned over the possibility of going to Cornwall, pretending to his parents that everything was fine. But Julia was there, right there, my husband pressing her against the wall, the two of them locked together in their treacherous embrace. He tells me it meant nothing; I think the opposite is true. We can't undo it and we can't bury it either. How can we not examine the fact that Sam was so unhappy he chose to sleep with someone else? Or that it's me who makes him miserable, me with my endless obsession over you? If he and I are to make it work, then somehow I must close the book on you. No more cuttings. No more letters. The end of my dreams.

Liv meets me off the train at Clapham Junction and carries my bag to a nearby café while I talk. She expresses all the right emotions, incredulity and bewilderment at the unexpected turn of events, Sam's shocking infidelity, Julia's arrival on our doorstep, but it is her silences that say the most. Always with Liv there's the specter of you.

"I think he still cares about you," she told me not so long ago, after you'd both been at a wedding together.

"I doubt it," I said, ending the conversation before it could begin.

But I can see the thoughts running through Liv's mind as we sit in this blue-and-white-themed café with our Lapsang Souchong and carrot cake, which neither of us eats. Sooner or later she won't be able to stop herself mentioning your name. So I don't tell her that right now what I would like most is to be lying on the beach on a sunny August afternoon, watching Sam and Joe diving from the platform into the sea, or kneeling on the sand to make one of the seaweed-and-shell pictures that Daisy loves—a mermaid with green broken-bottle eyes, a flat gray nose, and a perfect row of white pebble teeth. I'd like to be sitting in my kitchen watching Sam flipping pancakes, his Sunday-morning party piece, while I work my way through our chipped brown teapot and Daisy sits next to me drawing or reading or playing with her wagon full of little gray rabbits. I chose Sam because he made me feel safe, this tall, strong, football fanatic with his unbreakable, shatterproof morality. How can it have gone so wrong?

"It was only a matter of time before this happened," Liv says eventually. "You've often said so yourself."

"I know, but that doesn't make it any easier."

We are circling each other, the way close friends do, biding our time, waiting for the right moment to spring. Liv wants to dive back into my past, I see it, I feel it; I want to run as fast as I can in the opposite direction.

I met Liv on my first day at university, wafting around the freshers' fair in a Victorian nightie and big clumpy boots, a paper flower stuck in her hair. We got talking as we queued up for the Debating Society.

"You don't have to do any debating," said the society secretary with their innate selling skills, "and we always serve cocktails."

We both paid our five-pound joining fee, and neither of us attended a single debate in three years, but the conversation we struck up in that queue has lasted almost half my lifetime.

The atmosphere changes when Liv reaches down for her handbag and places it on the table between us. She extracts a ripped piece of paper, a newspaper cutting, by the looks of things, and slides it across the table toward me.

"Have you seen this?"

I know just from the look on her face—expectant? nervous?—that it's got something to do with you.

"What is it?" I say, scanning the Births, Marriages, and Deaths column from *The Times*. For a moment I can't see what I'm looking for; it's just a blur of celebrations, engagements, marriages, and new births with names like Otto Atticus and Hebe Summer, never anything normal, never Sarah or Elizabeth or James. And then suddenly a surname, in block capitals, springs out at me as if it's lit up by flames.

WILKES: Serena Elizabeth, died peacefully at home on August 1, aged 60. Much-loved mother of Emma, Joanna, and Lucian.

"Lucian's mother," I say after a pause. "He didn't get on with her, I remember."

"They haven't seen each other for years. But he'll be at the funeral, I would think. It's on Friday."

"No, Liv." I don't need her to spell out what she's thinking.

"Why not? I'm going, and you could come with me. I think it's time."

Heart racing, mouth dry, I look again at the announcement. An open service, to be held at Saint Luke's Church, Chelsea, at 3 p.m. on Friday, August 7. I push the newspaper cutting away from me as if it's infected. There are so many reasons why I can't go to this funeral, not least the fact that I have never met your mother. I haven't seen you for fifteen years, have no idea whether you ever forgave me for the way I left you, suddenly, harshly, without any explanation. And then there are all your friends, who hated me for breaking your heart.

"Jack and Harry will be there."

"Yes, but so will I. We can face them together. It won't be as bad as you think."

"Why are you going, anyway? You don't know Lucian all that well; isn't it a bit weird for you to turn up? You never met his mother."

Dread has made me vicious. Dread, fear, self-hate, call it what you will. What I'd like most right now is for Liv to promise she'll stop seeing you, stop reminding me constantly of this ache, this loss, this absence of you. I know that my reaction to the past twenty-four hours of emotional chaos has been muted and strange. If anything, dealing with the fallout from Sam's unexpected betrayal, I felt half dead inside. But not now. Now the sorrow is instant and overwhelming; it's like being shaken violently awake.

"For Christ's sake, Liv. Please don't ask me to think about Lucian. Or Jack. Or Harry. Not on top of everything else."

My voice is much too loud in this place full of toddlers and buggies and mothers with freshly highlighted hair. My tears, which fall without warning, are an embarrassment.

"Catherine."

Liv extends a hand across the table, but it's too late. Now that I've started crying, I won't be able to stop. Crying for you, crying for me, for Sam and the kids. Crying for the crossroads, bleak and damned, that must rear up over and over again, haunting me with my choice.

Four Months Before: Lucian

In times of crisis, I often turn to Jack. He waits with me outside the church until we see the hearse arrive, and just behind it the funeral car that carries my sisters and their monstrous husbands. They always hated me the most, the husbands, something to do with the fact that they slave in their city jobs Monday to Friday while I—my brother-in-law's words, not mine—"arse about all day in your little Somerset empire."

"Primogeniture," I might have argued. "It's what you get with families like ours."

But it seemed simpler to cut myself off.

Jack manages to take the edge right out of this first meeting. Behind their backs he calls them the witches, but the truth is, he has always seemed to prefer my family to his own, dysfunctional or otherwise. When he channels his charm, older women in particular seem to melt. He does it now, wheeling my sisters into a long-lost embrace. By the time they get to me, both of them are smiling. Joanna, shorter, plumper, and always that little bit nicer, greets me with open arms.

"Hello, stranger," she says.

There's even a mild camaraderie between the three of us as we watch the pallbearers take their places behind the coffin, lifting it to their shoulders in one practiced move. Dead parents will do that. The knee-jerk shock of a coffin will do that. Momentarily we stand united in the face of this new truth, the woman who gave birth to us trapped within a shining wooden box.

As we process down the aisle, I search the pews for my friends and find them sitting together near the back of the church. There's Jack in his sharp black suit, Celia next to him in neat navy blue. Alexa catches my eye as we pass. She is wearing huge, glittery earrings and I love her for it, the disco element to the funeral. We three siblings sit in the front pew, my mother's coffin stationed unnervingly close, just to our left. Try as I might to concentrate on the vicar's words, I am tugged right down to the ghost train of memories I wish more than anything to avoid.

The gloom was all mine after my father died. I wandered, desolate, through a house that seemed unfathomably celebratory. My mother and sisters, always exclusive, were now permanently together, laughing and gossiping in the kitchen, while the contents of the ashtray rose higher and the empty wine bottles behind the bin grew into a glass army. Food was generally an irrelevance: my teenage sisters were always on diets and my mother rarely ate, not that I saw, anyway. When my father was alive, he would peer into the fridge and fling eggs, cheese, ham, and tomatoes onto the table.

"What shall we make, kiddo?"

It was omelets mostly, or toasted sandwiches, but he took the snack repertoire to the grave with him, and after he died I lived on toast. I was bewildered by my loss, the senseless, raging pain. The parasitic loneliness. That's when the pinching began, pinching and pinching, harder and harder, hidden away in my pale-blue bedroom until a network of bruises had spread across my inner arms. It wasn't a cry for help—far from it; all I'd ever wanted was to escape my mother's notice. It was more an addiction to physical pain, the delicious feeling of hurting yourself until your eyes stung and all other thoughts faded away to nothing. I can remember that feeling even now.

I found out the truth about how my father died hours before I was due back at school. My mother was with her friend Marianne, midway through another long lunch. I could hear them talking, laughing, clinking glasses as I approached the kitchen: *Salut!*—the toast Marianne always made, whether they were on tea or vodka.

I was about to go in when I heard my name.

"Darling," Marianne said as I loitered by the kitchen door. "I do think Lucian's a bit of a worry. He's so thin and he seems, well, desperately unhappy."

"Of course he's unhappy. He just lost his father."

I heard the metal click as my mother flicked open her Zippo. I imagined her lipsticked mouth drawing in the smoke, eyes closed.

"It's dreadful for you all, I know. But Henry and Lucian were so close. I wondered if it might help him to talk to someone. You know, a professional."

"And what's a shrink going to say to him?" The anger in my mother's voice seared beneath the door.

"'Your father killed himself, did he? How do you feel about that?'"

The shock realization was as if someone were holding my head beneath a torrent of icy water. Not a heart attack, as I'd thought, but a choice. He chose to leave me. Sitting here between my sisters two decades later, it occurs to me that they would have known exactly how my father died, and that perhaps not telling ten-year-old me was an act of kindness. I realize that my mother, who now lies meters away, as lost to me as he was, must have been hurt by his death, must have felt her role in it, and was perhaps, in some way, ashamed.

The wake has the surrealist tinge of a nightmare, a champagne-soaked party for four hundred in my mother's thin, tall brown-brick four-story. I was last here at sixteen and I am knocked back by its familiarity, the permeation of Acqua di Parma and venom sprayed like blood into the soft furnishings.

My mother's so-called friends, a conveyor belt of age-defying sexagenarians, queue up to greet me.

"The black sheep returns," they crow, one after another, and it's a while before I get to my friends, crammed into a shrunken circle in the farthest corner of the drawing room.

"How's it going?" Jack asks, embracing me for the second time today. "Anyone called you a cunt yet?"

"All right?" asks Harry, gripping both my shoulders and looking into my eyes for a moment too long. He is dressed in a black velvet suit and handmade snakeskin shoes, like a 1970s pimp. Alexa once told him they made him look like Keith Richards in his South of France heyday, and he's been wearing them on repeat ever since. Beside him is Ling, in a narrow black dress and high shoes, dark hair coiled in plaits on top of her head. She looks beautiful and somehow much older than her twenty-three years.

"I'm sorry about your mother, Lucian," she says in her quiet, formal voice.

I'm about to make my standard quip—better off without her—when a wave of regret rolls over me, here in my dead mother's house, a place where I once lived too. The memory comes, as it always must, of the last time I stood in this drawing room, painted lemon yellow back then.

My mother, drunk, wavering on heels, a fierce rage in that feted face: "How dare you blame his death on me? How dare you?"

And me, with the certitude of a sixteen-year-old: "Because you betrayed him. You cheated on him."

She never forgave me; I never tried to understand.

"Me too, Ling," I say instead. "I'm sorry too."

Harry ensnares a passing waitress and takes two bottles of champagne.

"Grieving son right here," he says, pointing at me by way of explanation.

He refills our glasses, and there are moments of reprieve now, whole minutes that could almost pass for any other day. The usual tensions are there—Alexa looking too pretty, too seductive in a dress that, now she has removed her jacket, turns out to be backless. Celia, another pretty girl, but with a tendency to dress like her mother, tries so hard to blend in with us, and it is always the act of trying that sets her apart.

She is asking Alexa about her book, which the rest of us understand is the last thing Alexa wants to talk about.

"It's going fairly well," she says, trying—and partially succeeding—to keep the hostility out of her voice. No writer I've ever met has wanted to discuss the writing process at a party.

"But what's your average day like?" Celia persists. "How much do you write? Do you have a minimum word count or something like that?"

"Babe." Jack wraps his arm around Celia's shoulder. He kisses her cheek. "Alexa is freaking out. You're reminding her of deadlines she'd rather forget."

He's a master at distillation, Jack.

"Sorry, Alexa," Celia says, and then she moves on to Ling.

I think with Celia it's partly an incompetence at small talk and mostly her discomfiture among our friends.

"Are you in touch with your family much?" she asks Ling.

Rachel and Alexa have begun another conversation, but they abandon it to hear Ling's answer. All of us, I think, are fascinated to find out more about Ling.

"We write letters and talk on the phone. But I haven't seen their faces for a couple of years."

"You could Skype them," Celia says. "Or FaceTime."

Ling laughs. "The first thing Harry did was buy me a laptop so I could Skype them. I told him it will take another hundred years for Wi-Fi to reach our community. My family live in a rural farming village with little modernization. Hardly any electricity, cooking over fires, washing clothes in the river." She shrugs. "I don't expect you to understand. If you were to visit my family, you would feel like you'd gone back in time. It's a very poor part of Thailand and a simple life, but it was a lovely place to grow up. Peaceful, slow."

I see the way Harry watches Ling, and it breaks me up a bit. There is no trying to hide his pride; it's pouring out of him.

I remember the text he sent from Thailand when he first got to know her.

Smitten with a woman I've met out here. She is dazzling. And she seems to like me too. Trying not to blow it!

One of us has found love, at last.

I catch sight of my sister Emma on the other side of the room, dutiful eldest child, surrounded by an adoring posse of my mother's friends. Joanna is talking to the vicar while her husband waits obediently beside her, one of those pitiful types who marry their mother and spend the next thirty years waiting for permission to fart. My eyes move from group to group and my heart jolts, painfully, when I recognize Catherine's best friend. Why did no one tell me she was here? I've kept in touch with Liv over the years, but never quite enough to dislodge the uncomfortable memory of the two of us in a pub in Bristol soon after Catherine and I had broken up. I was drunk, morose, possibly crying; she must have been desperate to get away.

"Why did she leave me?" I asked her. "Why does she love him more than me?"

I've never forgotten her response.

"I don't think she does," she said, eventually. "I don't think she'll ever love anyone the way she loved you."

When Liv catches me looking, she waves and walks over to our side of the room, where she is engulfed immediately by my friends. Hugs and kisses and exclamations of regret all round—"It's been too long!"

"Amazing dress, Liv," says Jack, which it is. Liv is wearing a turquoise dress with a sticky-out skirt, a tiny cardigan draped around her shoulders. With her bright peroxide hair and her lightning-strike earrings, she looks like a futuristic prom queen, a rock-and-roll Sandra Dee. I'd like to photograph her and invert those colors in a portrait later, the dress electric blue, her hair a glowing Egon Schiele red.

Harry introduces Liv to Ling. "Meet my wife," he says, trying and failing to suppress the grin that sweeps across his face.

"You got married?" she says, miming shock, but she is effusive with her congratulations. "Let me see that ring," she says, and Ling holds out her finger with its diamond the size of a quail's egg.

"Bought in Bangkok. Rather obscene, isn't it?" says Harry, simultaneously refilling Liv's glass.

Talk turns to my summer party, which I host every year without exactly knowing why. It has become a slightly ridiculous affair, each one focused around some new talking point: multicolored sheep on the horizon one year—how silly was that—then a group of trapeze artists strung up in nets high above the dance floor, and this time a fleet of brightly painted rowing boats on the lake. I always send Liv an invitation, but she rarely comes, and I was surprised when she emailed last week to accept.

"You must stay," I tell her now.

"Actually, I've arranged to stay with a friend who recently moved to Somerset. She's in London with me at the moment."

Her eyes are communicating something, I'm not sure what, though I suddenly have an idea of the subtext and my heart squeezes a little just contemplating it.

"Come outside for a cigarette?" I say, taking hold of her elbow and leading her through the crowds. We use a back exit through the kitchen, which my mother has clearly had interior-designed since my day: it's all dark-gray slate and chestnut wood, more downtown New York than Chelsea blue rinse. Once outside, we huddle beneath the cherry tree where I skulked and sulked and smoked illicit cigarettes back in the day.

"I hope you don't think it's strange me being here," Liv says. "I didn't know your mother . . ." She tails off, an apologetic shrug.

"It's great that you came. I appreciate it. The more friendly faces, the better."

Liv and I stand beneath the tree, looking at each other while I light a cigarette and exhale the first jet of smoke. I am going to ask her about Catherine. I know it, she knows it, and the question sits between us, letters forming in the ether.

"How is she?" I say eventually, and Liv nods, once, twice, before she answers.

"I'm so sorry to do this to you, Lucian, especially at your mother's funeral. But that's the reason I'm here."

Now

They like to measure my improvements here, inch by inch, or is it millimeter by millimeter? Since talking is not an option and they've all come to accept that, there's a new campaign to make me respond in other ways. Eyes are good, a nod is brilliant. I haven't managed one of those yet. Greg says—threateningly, it seems to me—that I will be going home soon.

"It will help so much if you can communicate with your children in some way. Don't you want that, Catherine?"

Underlying message: shit, selfish mother—and this guy is meant to be a shrink.

Here is what they don't understand. Not talking is much harder than talking. The effort required to never respond is immense; it sucks up all my energy, which is exactly what I want. I know what they are thinking: willful, stubborn, obstinate (though they couch it in different terms: traumatized, damaged, mute). And in a way, they are right. I don't talk because I want to stay with you, and that matters to me more than anything. I want to go back to where I left off, another beginning, the promise of a new start, flesh against flesh, your hand in mine.

Today Sam and Liv visit together, and though they have been told, constantly, that I understand every word they say, they seem to have forgotten.

I'd like to be left alone. I'd like them to leave so that I can get back to thinking about you, but their conversation seeps through my dream world, grit upon snow.

"I do think you're amazing. The way you've stuck by her."

"Well, of course. She's my wife."

Always with Sam now this edge of fury. And when Liv says nothing, all this anger, months and months of it—Sam's frustration at me not speaking, his devastation at the loss of his wife, his children's mother—just seems to erupt out of him.

"For fuck's sake, don't pity me, Liv. At least spare me that. I know what you're thinking. Why does he bother to come when she's in love with someone else? It was you who set them up together again after all this time, wasn't it? Don't you think you should bear some responsibility for that? Trying to play fucking God. And look where that got you."

Sam rages right out of the room, visitor's chair squealing across lino, Liv collapsing, head bent right over her knees, crying, crying. And not responding to Liv, my dearest, darling friend, not reaching forward to put a hand on her shoulder, not finding the words to say, "It's not your fault," will be my toughest challenge yet.

Fifteen Years Earlier

After the monthly editorial meeting, we always went for drinks at the Criterion, a crusty old pub that was popular with students, who wore these things like a badge of honor—the hottest curry, the dingiest pub, the cheapest cup of coffee in town. The editor was a tall, thin Jarvis Cocker type, without the glasses or the charisma. He seemed to exist in a permanent kind of simmering rage, furious about injustices big and small, even the fining system at the library. Privately Liv and I called him Angry Jeff. I didn't enjoy these drinks much, but I always went for at least one, partly out of politeness, partly to keep my eye on the prize—an editorship before my second year was out.

I was halfway through my drink, plotting my departure, when the door opened and you came in with your friends. I knew all their names: Jack, Harry, Rachel, Alexa. My heart cartwheeled and I looked down quickly at my drink. I'd been avoiding you ever since our lunch by the sea without really knowing why, working in my room instead of the library, even missing the weekly Milton tutorial. I couldn't have explained the need to avoid you, only that the thought of bumping into you unexpectedly pumped me up, as it did right now, with an overwhelming surge of adrenaline.

"What on earth are that lot doing in here?" asked Angry Jeff.

"They'll leave when they realize they don't sell champagne or Chablis," said Melanie, a second-year history student whom I was beginning to like.

But you didn't leave. You sat down in the opposite corner of the room, the glossy girls an incongruous sight with their highlighted hair and their cashmere scarves and glinting gold watches.

I kept my focus in a narrow gaze, head movements restricted from my drink to my table of earnest friends, so I didn't see you approach.

"I've been looking for you."

I tried to be casual.

"I've been studying in my room. Less distracting than the library."

"And the tutorial?"

"I overslept."

You rolled your eyes, irritated.

"I don't think so. You're not the oversleeping type."

You leaned down, elbows on the table, face close to mine, voice loud and clear. We hadn't even touched at this point, but the close proximity of you was doing dangerous things to my stomach, my chest, my groin.

"I don't want to play games with you," you said, shockingly forthright in front of the student journalists, who were gazing openly at this exchange.

"Nor do I."

You looked at me for a moment, then stood back up.

"We're going to a party later. Will you come?"

I shook my head. The prospect of a night with your friends was intolerable.

"I don't think so."

"No, you won't come to the party? Or no, you don't want to spend the evening with me?"

"The party," I managed to say. Full sentences and regular breathing were beyond my grasp right then.

This time, a rare full-strength smile that reached up to your eyes.

"In that case," you said, "I have a bottle of very good wine at home that has your name on it."

Four Months Before: Catherine

I am meeting Liv at the Serpentine Café in Hyde Park, always one of our favorite places back in the day. We would meet here on a Sunday morning, recounting tales of the night before over weak cappuccinos, while the health nuts ran by in their neon Lycra. Now she's the girl in Lycra, insisting on a trip to the gym before she meets me. She exercises in a kind of religious fervor these days, half-marathons at the weekend, 6 a.m. trips to the swimming pool.

This has always been my favorite park. I love it for the green-and-white-striped deck chairs, for the blow-dried Kensington mummies buttoning up their toddlers, for the Rollerbladers who whiz around the lake, insolently weaving in and out of walkers, too confident and too fast to care about reproach. I love it for the trees—oaks, chestnuts, and planes, sycamores and limes, a whole color chart of green and yellow, with sudden bursts of cherry and crab-apple pink in springtime. When I was young, my parents used to bring me here, in my own buttoned-up navy-blue coat. We'd walk hand in hand, the three of us, to the lake, where we'd feed the ducks with crusts of bread my father had saved up during the week.

Our children loved it here too, shifting between the paddling pool and sandpit at the top of the Lido to the little playground by the barracks. Standing against the wire netting, transfixed as a troop of guardsmen galloped by on their way to Buckingham Palace, an everyday occurrence if you timed it right. Joe and Daisy are everywhere as I cross the park today, and I long to talk to them, but they are in Cornwall now, surfing or crabbing or mackerel fishing or perhaps parked up in a sand dune with one of their grandmother's mammoth picnics.

"Call the kids whenever you want," Sam told me last night, as though all of a sudden I was the one in the wrong. "But you are right, we need space to think. Let's not talk for a bit."

When I think of the alternative—Sam holed up in some shitty two-bedroom flat in Frome, the kids going off to stay with him every other weekend—all I want is to run back to him and lock the doors behind us. I chose Sam—or rather, I chose to go back to Sam, after you—and I taught myself to love him with an intensity that could not be challenged. I've hidden within our marriage for thirteen years. And though I continue to look for you online and in the papers (as bad as Julia, in my own way, with my closet stalking), I do it to reassure myself that you are happy, or perhaps some less-trite approximation of that word, and that I did the right thing in leaving you and not forcing you to choose between me and your oldest friend. The choice I made was stark and uncompromising, just like the two worlds that you and Sam inhabit: one veined with danger, it seems to me, the other as white and blameless as a glass of milk.

As I approach the café, I see no sign of Liv. There's a couple with a baby in a high chair, the mother holding out torn bits of croissant, which the baby grabs and drops to the floor. Two girls are talking intensely while their coffees cool, untouched, in front of them, and right by the entrance three cyclists swig from bottles of Evian. I am about to sit down at a table when I notice, on the perimeter of my vision, a tall man leaning up against the wooden fence that circuits the lake. My whole body lurches with the instant, feverish blood rush of recognition. My instinct is to run, but it is too late, too late. You turn, see me, and wave, a casual, noncommittal wave that reminds me of our beginning. I am frozen here looking at you, the real you, not just the two-dimensional photographs that have become your replacement over the years.

The shock must be written on my face, because as soon as you are close enough, you say, "Liv didn't tell you, did she?"

"She knows I wouldn't have come."

And those are my first words to you in fifteen years. I watch you incline your head. A look of resignation flits across your face.

"I didn't mean that as it sounds."

"Is it really so bad seeing me again?"

"The opposite of bad."

You smile then, the same trademark smirk, corners down.

"What about a coffee, at least?"

I want to, oh I want to, but I am so afraid of the questions you might ask. I hold out both of my hands, and we inspect them shaking.

"Not sure I can hold a cup."

"Come on, I'll carry it for you."

I follow you into the café, where we queue side by side for our coffees. You are wearing a denim shirt, black jeans, and a pair of once-white Converse. With your back to me, I can look at your hands, long, slim, tanned fingers, nails cut short. And your hair, which still curls over the collar of your shirt. How long have we got? I want to look at you properly, to examine your face for any change: day-old stubble almost as thick as a beard, new lines around your eyes. Our thoughts must be running in parallel, for you turn to me and say, "You look exactly the same."

"I don't feel the same, that's for sure."

"Two kids," you say, missing the point. "So grown up."

"Did Liv tell you what's happened?"

"She did. I'm sorry."

You have balanced our coffees on a black plastic tray, and you carry them outside to the table nearest the lake. There's a moment of silence, both of us searching for the right thing to say. I watch you pick up your cup and put it down again without taking a sip.

"You're in pieces, aren't you? I'm sorry, perhaps this was the wrong thing to do."

"I'm not sure I am. In pieces, I mean. I think, underneath it all, there's a feeling of relief that at least we've started talking honestly."

With me and Sam it was always the things we didn't say that sounded loudest. Try as we might to ignore it, beneath everything, there was always the memory of you.

You lean a little closer toward me, only an inch or so, but enough to send shock waves through me. Your face—a little older, it's true—is still stupidly handsome, though it was never about that for me. Unthinkably, I want to reach out and touch your hand.

"I can't quite believe it's you," you say, like you're reading my mind. "I'd given up hope of ever seeing you again."

My heart is beating wildly. It's hard to breathe.

"Me too."

I think how much easier it has been for me to keep tabs on you, checking the papers or surfing the net for new photographs and almost always finding them. With me there's no Facebook, no Twitter, no Instagram. I wanted to disappear, and that's what I did.

You push your cup to one side as if you mean business, and now I'm coiled inside, sensing the question, counting the seconds until you ask it. I know it's coming. I see it. I see it.

"I've been trying so hard not to ask you this, but it's no good. I have to know. Will you tell me what happened? Why you ran away?"

The wash of coldness is instant, the feeling that there's nowhere to run. Memories I don't want crowding my brain.

I stand up abruptly and my chair tips over, rattling to the ground.

"Catherine?"

You stand up too.

"I can't do this."

You reach out to take my hand, and we stand there on both sides of the table, connected by this strange, extended handshake.

"Why not?" you say, tightening your grip. "How can it matter after all this time? I know something must have happened. Something I don't understand."

"I can't talk about it."

You let go of my hand and it feels cold and lifeless without yours.

"Do you want me to go?" you ask.

I feel the grip of panic, a tightening in my chest.

You leaving now, after all this time apart, is the last thing I can bear.

"Could we just walk for a while?"

We leave our coffees and begin to walk slowly, in silence, around the lake. The things I want are impossible. I'd like to find a tree and lean against it and press myself into your arms, not to kiss, just to feel you against me, the warmth of your skin, your stubble on my face, your breath against my cheeks, and then I'd like to freeze the moment for an eternity. Impossible not to remember the first time we kissed, in your student bedroom so many years ago. We'd toppled onto your bed, and you kissed every bit of my face: eyes, nose, throat, finally my mouth.

"I've wanted to do that for days," you said.

"Have you? But why?"

"Why do you think? Because you're beautiful and I haven't been able to get you out of my mind."

"I'm not beautiful," I said, and I remember how you laughed.

When I looked in the mirror I always noticed the pallor of my skin against the darkness of my hair. I thought I looked washed out, insipid, ghostly. You led me over to the full-length mirror in the corner of the room.

"Can't you see how lovely you are?"

You stood behind me, lifted up my hair, and kissed the back of my neck, and the sensation of your mouth on my skin was almost more than I could bear. You drew your fingers slowly across the features of my face, the length of my nose, the breadth of my lips. We locked eyes in the mirror as you unbuttoned the top button of my shirt, then another and another, until it swung open and I was standing there in my pale-blue bra. We didn't speak, not one word, just the blood rushing in my ears as you removed every piece of my clothing, barely even touching me, until I stood there entirely naked. I can recall exactly the sharp shock of eroticism, pressing my bare flesh against fully clothed you, your hands reaching up to touch my breasts, your mouth warm against my neck. My first taste of sexual adventure, and I was hooked.

I am blinded by longing, breathless with it. Sam flashes into my mind, Sam and then Julia, and I know this will be my excuse.

We are halfway around the lake now on the opposite side to the café, and as we approach it, an old man stands up and vacates his bench. I take your hand and pull you toward it, and just that brief touch of flesh on flesh is a current running through my bones. We sit down and look at each other. This is it. My chance to overturn fifteen years of regret.

"I've thought of you every single day since I left," I say.

Four Months Before: Lucian

I am hungover (parental funerals will do that) and depressed (ditto), and from the look on Catherine's face—horror-struck, no other word for it—it seems the whole thing has been a massive setup. Why am I putting myself through this when it's clear that her feelings toward me haven't changed, not one bit, in the last fifteen years? Because I'm an idiot, that's why.

She looks overwhelmingly beautiful and a little sad, just as I remember her. I have stared at her drawing so many times, that sketch I made more familiar to me than anything else I have ever drawn, and now here she is, standing before me in the flesh. Beautiful. Sad. Frightened. She looks like she wants to run away.

"Is it really so bad seeing me again?" I ask, and she smiles suddenly and says, "The opposite of bad," and call me a bloody fool, but I just want this moment to go on for a little longer.

I suggest coffee, and she follows me into the bland white space of the Serpentine Café, and now all I really want is to look at her. Over the years I've forgotten how dark her hair is, that deep black-brown, the color of earth after rain; and her eyes wider and a little rounder, I see now, than I made them in the sketch, but essentially the truly jaw-dropping feature of her lovely face. I see her surreptitiously watching me, and it makes me smile, to think of us both here transfixed by the ghosts of our past. How could it be any other way? I am thinking of a night when we lay together on my bed, listening to the Rolling Stones, *Black and Blue*, one of my favorite records. When "Fool to Cry" came on, I walked over to the window and lit a cigarette, blowing plumes of smoke into the damp night air. The song always reminded me of my father and his desperate end, and though I said nothing, Catherine knew I was thinking of him.

"You still miss him, don't you?" she asked.

The astuteness of her question and the gentleness of her voice overwhelmed me, a dangerous sea of sorrow rising in my chest. I didn't turn round to look at her when I told her about the way he'd died, a shotgun wound to the head, not a heart attack, as I'd thought at the time. Finally I spoke the words I had been too ashamed to say.

"I feel somehow responsible that I wasn't able to make his life worth living."

"You were ten. It wasn't your fault, you can't think that. It had nothing to do with you."

"We were a team of two, my father and I, him and me against the world, or at least against my mother and my sisters and their little club for three. But he left me anyway."

Catherine didn't say anything, not then; she just walked over to the window, wrapping her arms around me from behind, face pressed into the space beneath my shoulder blades, waiting for me to turn. But later, just as we were about to fall asleep, I remember her voice in the darkness.

"I won't ever leave you," she said.

But a few weeks later, that's exactly what she did.

The question that is tattooed eternally beneath my skin rises up and out of me before I'm able to stop it.

"Will you tell me what happened? Why you ran away?"

It's obvious that I am going to ask this question, that even after all this time I still need to know what went wrong. The way she left me, just a note scrawled on my sketchpad, with no explanation—*I've changed my mind. I can't do this. I can't see you anymore*—her stark refusal to ever see or speak to me again, drove me mad, I think. And I have lived in the shadow of that madness ever since. But this Catherine, the one who claims to be different, this mother of an almost-teenage boy, stands up so violently that her chair tips over, and I see a real horror flash across her face.

"I can't talk about it," she says, and I think, my God, she's actually going to run out on me again. She is hiding something, I realize it instantly, and I wonder why it has taken me all these years to understand. But what? What could possibly be so bad she wasn't able to tell me at the time; what was it that made her refuse to ever see me again? I've tormented myself with this question over the years, and now, looking at her stricken face, listening to her tortured voice, I realize that she has never told me the truth. But I can't push her any further; if I do, she'll run, and that's the last thing I want.

We walk all the way round to the other side of the Serpentine without saying a word, while Rollerbladers glide in between us and joggers pass and toddlers crouch beside the water to drop their torn scraps of bread. We sit down on an empty bench, and she looks at me and says, "I've thought of you every single day since I left," and I understand how hard it is for her to say those words, her version of an apology. I understand that what she is really saying is Please, can we start again? So I'll spend a little longer here, absorbing her loveliness, this girl who once shattered my heart.

The conversation becomes easier. I ask about her children, and she shows me photographs on her phone. The little girl, Daisy, a miniature version of her mother except for her wild curly hair, is dangling upside down from the branch of a tree, an inverted gap-toothed smile.

"She looks funny and brave," I say.

"She is brave. Worryingly so sometimes. A risk-taker. The opposite of me."

I think, yes, that's true. You hid away in a small-time life. You weren't prepared to take a risk on me. The photograph of the boy, Joe, and his father stops me in my tracks. They are playing cards and drinking from matching blue-and-white-striped mugs. I remember Sam, the husband, as I look at this older version in the photograph. I'd hide in the shadows sometimes and watch the two of them walking through town, his arm slung around her shoulders, her long dark hair swinging against her back. I used to wonder what it was about him that made her love him more.

"He looks nice," I say, and I know she understands I mean Sam, not the boy, when she says, "He is nice."

"How did it go so wrong?"

Catherine doesn't answer to begin with, but once she starts speaking she seems unable to stop, words and phrases and broken sentences that tumble over one another and amaze me with their content.

"It's my fault, really, all of it."

When I begin to protest, she waves me silent with an impatient hand.

"You see, I shouldn't have married him, and we both knew that. Because even though he tried so hard to convince me, to convince both of us, that we were meant to be together, somehow it could never quite match up to you and me. And it killed Sam, trying to prove it was him I loved and knowing, really, that it wasn't. I mean, I did love him, I still do, we've had two kids together, we've been married for almost thirteen years, but it wasn't the same and it never could be. And I've thought about you so much, every day, sometimes it felt like almost every moment. It was torture, really, thinking and wondering and remembering with no hope of ever seeing you again. I used to will myself never to mention your name, but sometimes Sam would see something about you in the papers and he'd show me and I'd have to try so hard to act normal, like it didn't matter, like you didn't matter, when deep down we both knew you did. That's why he went off with Julia in the end, I'm sure of it, and I can't blame him. I pushed him into it."

She is crying now but I daren't interrupt or reach out to take her hand or do anything to stop her, for every word she speaks is a revelation. I cannot believe it. It cannot be true. The way she left me was so heartless, so final, as if she hated me, as if I'd done something wrong. And here she is telling me the exact opposite is true, that she's thought about me, yearned for me, longed for me just as I have always longed for her. It changes everything.

"I married Sam," Catherine says, "because he loved me. And because he helped me so much when my mother died. All I wanted back then was to hide away and bury myself where no one could find me. I tried so hard to forget you, but of course I couldn't. You remember how we loved each other, understood each other, how we used to communicate without talking? Mind reading, we said. As though we were living inside each other. How could I ever forget that?"

I'm nodding at her because these are the things that made our breakup so impossible for me to accept. One moment I was understood by this girl, by this woman who is now sitting next to me, in a way I'd never been understood before; the next moment she was gone. My despair was overwhelming.

"I thought you'd forgotten about me," I say, and she rolls her eyes.

"Forgotten about you? There's barely a day when I haven't looked for you. It's been like a curse. Every town or village or shop or restaurant I go into, I think, 'I wonder if he's here.' Every time I'm on the internet I find myself looking for pictures of you. And you're always there; I couldn't get away from you even if I wanted to."

"I don't understand. If you loved me so much, why did you leave?"

I think she is close to telling me the truth; in her seconds of hesitation, I see her weighing it up: what would happen if I told him the real reason after all this time? I'm staring at her lovely face and I see something like fear flash through those dark eyes.

"What was it, Catherine? Did something happen?" My voice is low.

But Catherine sighs and shakes her head.

"Is it enough to tell you I made a terrible mistake and I've regretted it ever since? Every single day."

I'm not even sure who reaches for who, but she is in my arms, her hair brushing my face, our mouths pressing together. We are kissing, kissing, and quickly it becomes fierce, and I know she's still crying because I feel the wet of her tears on my cheek. She pulls away.

"This is madness. No good can come of it. But I need you . . ."

She's in my arms again, and this time the kissing is all wrong in a public place. We need to stop, we have to stop . . .

"Can we go?" Catherine says.

We walk, clamped together, from the park, a long walk, past joggers and schoolchildren and elderly couples, none of whom I really see, onto Queen's Gate, where I flag down a taxi almost instantly and we sit inside, not talking, not touching, while smart white stuccoed London flashes past, until we reach my street, my flat. We step through the front door into overwhelming whiteness, and in the sudden grave quiet we are drawn together, free at last to hold each other, skin on skin, mouth against mouth, bodies that burn like molten flames.

Fifteen Years Earlier

Your house was empty; your friends were all at the party. We were alone, luxuriously so, and I knew, as my heartbeat ripped through me, what would happen next.

"This is the bottle I was talking about," you said, flashing the label at me. Puligny-Montrachet, lyrical-sounding words I'd never heard before. You poured two glasses and said, "Shall we take them to my room? In case the others come back?"

It didn't feel like a seduction scene, sitting next to you on your double bed, not even when you took my glass from my hand and set it down on the floor. When you undressed me, piece by piece, both of us looking into the mirror, my body started shaking even before you'd touched me. You carried me back to the bed and laid me down, your mouth moving dangerously slowly across my body; you took off your own clothes, still kissing me, and then there was only the feeling of you finally naked in my arms. There was something I needed to say but it was too late, too late, and though I didn't mean to, I tensed and cried out as you pushed inside me. You froze instantly.

"God, Catherine, why didn't you tell me?"

We stayed there, completely still, just looking at each other. Neither of us had any words.

"Don't stop," I whispered eventually, and I began to move against you very slowly, and soon the pain shifted into something more bearable, better than that, and all the time you gazed down at me with an expression I can still recall exactly, a look of utmost intensity, a seriousness that made me burn. I began to move faster, pulling you into me, grabbing your hips and urging you to keep going, keep going until this newly delicious, dragging, pulling sensation reached some kind of conclusion.

"You should have said something," you told me afterward, as I lay in your arms, waiting for my heartbeat to slow down.

"I meant to. I was going to, then, I don't know, we got carried away."

"You can say that again. But why now? Why me? What about Sam?"

I could have told you what you had already said to me. That I found you beautiful, overwhelmingly so, that all I wanted right now was to press my body against yours and start all over again. But I was careful back then never to bolster your over-bolstered ego, conscious of all those girls waiting to drop like flies, never wanting to be one of them. Always wanting to be different. Instead I told you about an afternoon with my mother a few days before I'd started at university.

"I've made an appointment for the doctor," she told me as we sat together in the September sun of our little London garden. "I thought it might be an idea to sort out some contraception before you get to Bristol. Maybe you'd like to go on the pill?"

We looked at each other and laughed. I could talk about anything with my mother, sex or the lack of it or, more to the point, my complete lack of interest in it.

"I haven't got a boyfriend. Why on earth would I do that?"

She shrugged. "It's meant to be good parenting these days to put your daughter on the pill. Forward planning, disaster management, something like that?"

I didn't tell her what I now told you. That I was beginning to doubt there would ever be anyone I liked enough to pop a daily pill for; that I'd always thought someone would arrive in my life one day and I would just know, finally, this was it.

"I think I was waiting for you."

Four Months Before: Catherine

Years ago, fifteen of them to be precise, we lay in a bed just like this, bodies tangled, hearts racing. You couldn't get over the fact that you were my first lover; you were shocked and, I think, secretly pleased.

Sam and I had been taking things slowly, friends first, a whole year of drinking coffee and talking late night after night and taking moonlit walks around town. Then finally, for the first time, a few days before, we had kissed. It was the slowest-developing relationship on the planet, and until that morning when you bowled into my English tutorial with your hair standing on end, it had suited me perfectly.

"We were taking our time getting to know each other. And then you came along and everything just exploded."

"Do you mind?"

Mind? I was ecstatic, euphoric, obsessed, possessed. All I wanted was to press my body against yours, to start again, to feel the hot burn of your fingers and mouth and tongue trailing across my flesh. And now the clock winds forward and I am in your bed again, trapped in some bizarre reshaping of the past.

"What now?" you say, your first words in a while.

It is a question I cannot easily answer. I want my now, this now, to be infinite, to stretch out in front of me; I want to be you and me, dark thoughts strung up out of reach, in a safety net above our heads. There is so much I'm trying not to think of, not least my calculated betrayal of Sam, allowing myself to use the excuse of his deceit to have the one thing I've always wanted, even if it's only for a few hours. I know how much this would hurt Sam, far more than Julia could ever hurt me, and yet from the moment you first touched me—earlier than that, right back to my first sighting of you by the lake—I longed to have all the years of private fantasy turned into reality. You and me in each other's arms, flesh against flesh, once more.

"Just this," I say, and you get it immediately.

"This is perfect."

Your mouth against my hair, the warmth of your palm resting on my thigh, your soapy, lemony smell still the same all these years later.

"There is one problem, though. I'm going home today. Back to Somerset. It's my summer party at the weekend, and I should really be around to oversee things. But you could come with me. Couldn't you?"

The safety net bursts as I knew it would. I sit up, swaddling myself in the duvet.

"No. I couldn't."

My voice is harsher than I meant it to be, my response unguarded, instantaneous. Can you see it, do you feel it, can you see what it is that I dread so much? You're watching me, head tilted a little to one side, and the look on your face is the same as before: resignation mixed with disappointment. I'm not surprised after the way we just took each other apart; that wasn't sex, that was longing, fifteen hard years of it, stored and then released in the most electrifying way. And now this, back where we started in Hyde Park a few hours ago.

"There's the kids," I say, trying to explain. "I can't just disappear."

"But aren't they in Cornwall with Sam? Why would they even

need to know? I'm not talking about forever here, just for a day. A few hours even. Wouldn't you like to come? Wouldn't you like to see Shute again? It's hardly changed at all. You could see Mary, she's still there looking after me. Remember Mary?"

Of course I remember her, of course I remember your beautiful house. Never before or since have I stayed anywhere like it. Oh, the glut of vicious memories: you, me, Jack, and Alexa on that most perfect weekend.

Sam and the children are in Mevagissey, a kiss-me-quick harbor town that Joe and Daisy love. Tiny, slanting cobbled streets, shops selling crab lines and boxes of fudge and hundreds of little china ornaments, which they find irresistible. And of course it is true that with the three of them away, there is no reason why I couldn't be in Somerset with you for a bit. Except for the real reason, and I am trying my hardest to keep that where it belongs, locked down inside of me, compartmentalized again and again over the years until it lurks within a labyrinth of boxes, a shiny little bullet of shame. But it surfaces right here in your beautiful London bedroom, in your hotel-like bed with its tower of pillows and cushions. The early-afternoon light is slicing in through the windows—a normal world outside, shoppers and newspaper sellers and coffee drinkers—and I am no longer thinking of you and me but of Jack.

I'd known who he was almost from my first week at university; everyone did. Jack had been gifted the kind of superior looks that made him stand out, easily the most handsome guy at Bristol. At least half the girls were in love with him. He dressed better than anyone else (or rather, exactly like you, a carbon copy in many ways), his hair was blonder, his eyes were more piercingly blue, he had that clean-cut all-American thing. And he was so kind to me when I first got together with you—where Rachel was standoffish and jealous at times, he always made a point of including me, making me feel welcome. How many times did he interrupt a conversation to make sure I understood?

"Hang on," he'd say, stopping Rachel or Alexa in their tracks. "Catherine doesn't know who we're talking about. Back up a bit."

Other times he'd make a great show of giving me the chair closest to the fire, the right amount of ice in my drink, the first helping of a shared takeaway. He was overtly charming but not in a sickening way, and anyway, there was always the sharp undercut of his humor to balance things out. It felt lucky being his friend, like you'd been chosen.

And yet the thought of seeing him again now, fifteen years later, fills me with a dread I cannot explain.

"Look," you say, irritated though you are trying not to show it, "it was just a thought, forget I mentioned it."

You throw back your side of the duvet and stand up. Beautiful body, slim and tanned and toned; your muscle definition reminds me of a classical Greek statue, the kind I've shown Joe and Daisy, the pair of them snickering, in the British Museum.

"Where are you going?"

"To make some coffee. Stay there, I'll bring it back to bed."

It feels strangely intimate watching you dress in your discarded clothes, underwear, then jeans, then shirt, as though I haven't earned the right, so I roll onto my side and look at the books on your bedside table instead. *The Long Firm* by Jake Arnott. I remember Sam reading it once when we were on holiday in France. On top of the Arnott is a bright-blue book called *The Art of Mindfulness*. How surprising.

"You meditate?"

You swivel around and see me examining your books.

"Oh"—the twist of a smile—"that one's not mine."

As the door closes behind you, I am wondering who the mindfulness book belongs to, Rachel or someone else, and the sudden, sharp tug of jealousy makes me giddy. I am in danger of the past catching up with me. Rachel, Alexa, Harry, and Jack, your unchanging circle of friends: the prospect of seeing them is impossible. It cannot happen. It must not happen. If I go off to Somerset with you—and how I yearn to be able to do that, even for a few hours—then sooner or later you'll find out exactly what kind of person I am.

Four Months Before: Lucian

I am a typical male in some ways. Lava-hot sex, like we just had, Catherine sitting on me but with her back turned so that I could hear rather than see her contorted cries, so that I could feel rather than know that she was close, so close, and that when she did finally succumb (shouting my name in such an intensely sexual way, all I can think is how much I need to hear it again), after all these years of us both, probably, fantasizing about this moment, then the walls would collapse and the ceiling would fall in and it would feel as though our whole lives had been leading to exactly this. Afterward, though, literally minutes afterward, I'm back feeling confused and a little paranoid. I ask Catherine to come away to Somerset with me, just for a day or even a few hours, and she reacts as if I've slapped her. This lovely face of hers, one that I've drawn and worshipped and craved at times, is also more expressive than any I've ever seen. And right now, what I'm getting is horror, unveiled, raw, exaggerated. I sympathize with what's happened to her and Sam, of course I do, although it would be fairly easy not to care too much. She left me for him a long time ago, she broke my heart so dramatically, so effectively, it took a long time to recover.

We are so connected, she and I, physically, yes, to an extent where it's almost impossible to look at Catherine without her clothes curling into flames, but also exactly as before, we talk without speaking, we know the same things, we feel the same things, we are in some unfathomable way like the same person.

Already I understand what it was that made it so hard to be apart last time. We see each other, that's it. We see each other in a way that no one else does.

I convince Catherine to have lunch before we go our separate ways, and when we arrive at the restaurant, a favorite of mine, she says, "I'm sorry I've been so on edge. Please can we start again."

I want just as much as she does to forget the hell of our ending and the big question of why, why, why and the fact that we probably should always have been together and we never will be. Of course I want to know what it was that drove her away, but I also feel relief at her suggestion of a reprieve. Yes, we'll go back to the beginning. Yes, we'll pretend, we'll be like any other couple in this tiny, little restaurant, eating some of the best sushi you'll find in London. And while we eat, I'll learn about her life, some of the gaps from all those years that are missing, and perhaps in this way I'll be able to forgive her for the way she left me, and this time, when we say goodbye, we'll both get the full stop we always needed.

She speaks quietly so that I have to strain a little to hear above the clatter of the restaurant, and occasionally I catch a slight inflection that I'd almost forgotten.

"My father is Scottish," she says. "Not so you'd notice these days, just the odd word; if anything he sounds more American."

Catherine's father lives in New York with a woman he married a year after her mother died. I can tell she still hasn't forgiven him.

"What's your stepmother like?" I ask, and her eyes flare with indignation.

"Carol? She's not my stepmother in anything but name. I am an adult with my own family. She just happens to be married to my father."

Right.

"It must have been so hard on you when your mother died," I say, and she nods, a tiny, sharp little nod, and begins talking in a rigid, clipped voice. If I didn't know that she was holding back tears, I'd think she was furious.

"It happened so fast. Every time I said goodbye, I thought, is this it, am I going to see her again, and then, only a few months after her diagnosis, it was."

"I'm sorry I wasn't there for you," I say, and Catherine says, "Don't. Please don't."

Catherine's mother fell ill almost immediately after she and I split up, a grim coincidence that kept her hidden from view for the remainder of her time at Bristol. And no one better placed than me to understand what early bereavement felt like.

Her eyes are full of tears.

"I know that you would have helped me, that you wanted to."

"Sam was there for you. He was better at it than I would have been."

Catherine sighs. "Sam's made it his life's work to try and get me to grieve, but I'm still not sure I've managed it. I'm scared of pain, that's the problem."

"Aren't we all."

There was a time in my life when I was so scared of it I wasn't sure I could carry on.

"What about *your* mother? It came out of the blue, didn't it? A heart attack, Liv said. Do you mind me asking about it?"

I look at this girl whom I have always loved and I decide to risk the truth.

"I didn't get on with her, you probably remember. Now she's dead I worry that guilt will get the better of me." I pat my chest. "It's here, beneath everything. I should have patched things up with her and I didn't. I should have shared my inheritance with her and I didn't. I should have forgiven her for her infidelity—perhaps I should have understood the reasons why she was unfaithful in the first place—but I didn't."

"You're right, there's usually a reason," Catherine says, with the astuteness I remember of old. She looks sad as she says it, as though she has sympathy for my mother. And perhaps she is right.

"I didn't find out about my mother's affairs until a few years after my father died, but I knew she made him unhappy. I was just waiting for a reason to blame her. My uncle told me she'd had a sequence of lovers but that there was one around the time of my father's death whom she seemed to have fallen in love with. I don't know if that's true; whoever he was, they didn't end up together. But it gave me all the ammunition I needed. I hated her for the way she'd cheated on him. In my adolescent mind cheating became synonymous with suicide, simple as that."

Catherine sighs, a long, trembling sigh. She seems a bit broken, hardly surprising. I'm feeling pretty broken myself.

"Did she ever love him?"

"She must have done at the beginning, but they were completely different. Glamour was the thing that drove my mother, clothes, parties, the flattery of others. I think my father's tastes were much too simple; she married the wrong guy, basically. Her greatest disappointment was not winding up in Shute Park. If my father had lived, he would have inherited it instead of me, and that was her pipe dream, swanning around in the big house, holding huge parties. She thought she was marrying the Great Gatsby, only it didn't turn out that way. She never forgave me for living there instead of her and she didn't visit. Not once in the last thirteen years. I could have tried harder to see her; the truth is I didn't try at all. Now I find myself wishing we'd made up."

"I'm sorry," Catherine says, showing yet again that she understands. There's no point trying to put a positive gloss on the situation, as Rachel or Alexa might. All that can be done is for me to find a way of accepting my regret.

I ask Catherine about her life, not just the big poster-sized events but the normal everyday, and as she talks, telling me of school runs and supermarket shops, of washing and ironing and cleaning and baking cakes for children's playdates, I am struck by the contrast between this Catherine, thirty-four-year-old mother of two, and the girl I used to know.

"I thought you were going to be a journalist," I say, and a shadow glides across her face but she carries on talking.

"I became a mother very young. There wasn't room for anything else."

I keep quiet because instinctively I know that Catherine is thinking about this and whether what she said is true.

"Maybe I wasn't brave enough. You need a lot of confidence to work in the media. Not just interviewing people and getting them to talk about things they don't want to talk about. But standing up for your ideas, making out you're better than everybody else. It's a pretty aggressive profession, I've decided. I'm not sure I was cut out for it."

"You were so confident when I first met you. You knew exactly what you wanted, don't you remember?"

I leave the unasked question hanging in the air. *What happened to change you?*

Catherine smiles, but there's no warmth in it.

"I think that's called being nineteen," she says.

Of course what happens throughout this lunch is that I'm looking as well as listening and I'm seeing the curve of her long, smooth neck and the jut of her clavicles and the way her necklace, a silver C on a long chain, stops just at her heart, and I'm thinking that if I was to press my lips there and work my way outward, first left, then right, I would be able to kiss a direct line across to her pale-pink nipples and they would harden quickly under my tongue.

Back at the flat, there's sex again, slower this time. I undress her, moving her hands away when she tries to reach up for my clothes, until she is entirely naked, and then I gently press her back against the wall and stand there looking at her while the cool, cold wall seeps into her flesh. I want the luxury of it, just the looking and then the touching, and so I reach out with my fingers and draw slow, light circles on her neck and her shoulders and her collarbone. And she is shaking but I know from the memory of last time that she'll wait. Hands first, that's what I'm thinking, and then my mouth, and then my tongue. I'll hear her cry my name again. And I'm focused on that.

Yet this second time around, the perfection that is Catherine and me naked together, the almost violence of our lovemaking, her passion more vehement even than mine, will make our parting difficult. We don't talk on the drive to Liv's house, but I'm pretty sure her thoughts are the same as mine. All this longing finally realized; how is it possible that we can leave it here? I'm waiting for Catherine to speak, to say something, anything that might make sense of what has happened between us today, but of course, she doesn't. Silence is her security blanket and she swathes herself in it.

Catherine lets us into Liv's house, a Victorian terrace in Clapham, which is stark white inside but with flashes of brilliant color: a trio of lemon-yellow vases, a shocking-pink sofa, floor tiles an acid-house orange. We find Liv at the kitchen table in her gym clothes, laptop opened up in front of her.

"Well," she says, standing up, grinning, as we walk in. "This looks interesting."

Catherine and Liv embrace and behind the hug Liv catches my eye, a question mark. So-so, I convey back with a sideways nod, almost imperceptible but I see her reading it.

"I've asked Catherine if she'll come down to Somerset with me. Just for a day or even a few hours, but she's not keen."

"Tea?" says Liv, releasing Catherine.

Her gym clothes are a bit like the house—a bright-yellow Adidas vest, purple leggings with flowers splashed all over them, lime-green-and-purple trainers. I feel a rush of affection for Liv. There is something so unfailingly optimistic about her, and the effect she has on Catherine is instantaneous. She's laughing as she takes mugs out of a cupboard and fills a jug with milk from the fridge. She tells Liv about the Japanese restaurant where we had lunch but obviously omits the finer details of our day (sex before, sex afterward, all of it mind-blowing, the kind of sex you'd happily die on). Liv knows, though, I can see her watching us as we drink our tea, watching, thinking, What now, what now? I'm wondering the same thing.

"Have you spoken to Sam?" she asks.

"Not since this morning. In fact he's asked me not to call. For a few days at least, he thinks we need a complete break to work out what we're going to do."

"True enough."

"They're in Cornwall anyway. The kids are happy."

"Well, that's a good thing. Doesn't mean they don't miss you."

I watch the interplay between these two old friends who talk in subtext, and it reminds me of Rachel and Alexa. Perhaps all girlfriends are this way; perhaps Jack, Harry, and I are too, beneath the posturing and sarcasm and the refusal to take anything seriously; perhaps this is the real backbone of friendship, the two-tier conversations, say one thing, mean another, a private language strictly for the initiated.

Liv says, "I don't see what harm it would do going to Lucian's for a while. You'd be on your own, wouldn't you? Or would all your friends be there?"

I catch the look that passes between them. So it's the thought of my friends that bothers her.

"Jack and Harry do live close by. The girls are in London; they come down at weekends. But you wouldn't need to see anyone while we're there, if that's what's worrying you."

"Yes, it's worrying me," she says, and then tries to qualify. "I don't really know what's happening with me and Sam. It would be awkward to try and explain."

"Look, the last thing I'm going to do is force you to come away with me. But at least let me tell you what it would be like. We'd have the whole place to ourselves, just Mary there during the day and a few gardeners whom I literally never see. We could do whatever we wanted. We could swim, we could go down to the lake, like we did before. Do you remember?"

"I remember it was wonderful," she says. "One of the happiest weekends of my life."

"Do it, Catherine!" says Liv, and she reaches forward and takes both her hands. "Chances like this hardly ever come along. No one needs to know that you're there."

Catherine says, "What about the children? What will I tell them? I can't lie."

"You won't need to tell them anything. They won't ask where you are, why would they?"

"It's much worse than anything Sam has done," Catherine says, and Liv just nods.

"I know."

Catherine turns to me. "Can you really promise me that we're not going to run into your friends? I couldn't face that right now."

"It's a deal. No friends. Just the two of us, I promise."

"All right," she says, "I'll come. Just for a bit." She puts one hand to her chest, and I imagine her heart there beneath it, pulsing, pulsing.

Fifteen Years Earlier

You were good at surprises. Surprises were your thing. First those notes appearing out of nowhere on my desk, then that lunch by the beach, in our private ski chalet for two. We'd only been together a few weeks when you woke me early, as dawn was gathering in the long, thin Victorian windows of your bedroom. You kissed my face repeatedly, swiveling over to the other side of the bed when I shifted away from you.

"Surprise."

I opened my eyes to you grinning, one of your rare full smiles.

"We're going on a trip," you said.

The city was scarcely awake as we drove through it, not a student in sight, just early-morning commuters, a paperboy getting blown about on his bicycle, a milk float up ahead. The kind of hour you'd only expect to see if you stayed up all night.

"We're going to your uncle's house, aren't we?" I said as the city faded into the thick farmland of north Somerset, all those high hedgerows and bleak winter fields.

You just shook your head. "Nope."

It can't have been long before we saw the first sign for Bristol Airport, and I turned to you, my face a question mark. Seriously?

"I thought we'd go to my favorite restaurant for lunch. Which happens to be in Paris."

The orchestration behind this surprise blew my mind. You had called my mother, scrolling through my phone to find her number, and asked her to send my passport.

"You spoke to my mother?"

"She was very nice. Very much in favor of our educational trip."

"Actually," you told me, as we nursed our plastic cups of coffee on the airplane, "there's something else I wanted to show you. Aside from the restaurant."

At Charles de Gaulle we took a cab straight to the Museé d'Orsay. My parents had taken me to Paris for my sixteenth birthday, and we'd spent hours in this gallery, my teenage heart drawn to the easy sentimentality of Degas's dancers. But you walked straight past the traditional checklist of Degas, Monet, and Gauguin, taking me to the second floor, where we bypassed the swirling strokes of Munch, until you stood still in front of a picture of a woman leaning forward in a gilt-edged box at the theater, a bouquet of flowers beside her. I thought it classic Impressionist fare; if you'd asked me I would have hazarded a guess at Renoir. But the artist was Eva Gonzalès, someone I'd never heard of, the painting dated 1874.

"Unusual for a woman to be an artist at that time," I said, wondering why you were looking at me so intently. Expectantly.

"You can't see it, can you? The woman is you. Her eyes, her brows, her nose, even her chin. When I first saw you in that tutorial, you reminded me of someone, and afterward I realized it was her."

You made me stand next to the painting while you took a photograph.

Eva Gonzalès was taught by Manet, you said; the bouquet in the picture was almost exactly like the one offered to Olympia in his portrait of the famous courtesan.

"How do you know all this stuff?"

"Too much time moping around galleries when I should have been on the lookout for girls like you. I moved out of my mother's house when I was sixteen. Irreconcilable differences," you said with that airy voice I now understood you used to conceal pain. "I spent a whole summer holiday in Paris, hours and hours here and in the Louvre, staring at paintings, trying to work out what made them so great. And not so great. That was the summer I started painting."

We lunched in a brasserie near the Place des Vosges, a Parisian pastiche of gigantic mirrors and art deco chandeliers, waiters in tails running back and forth across the black-and-white-tiled floor. We had steak frites and red wine that came in a little glass jug.

Perhaps it was just the wine, or perhaps it was the way you ate with your left hand so you could keep on holding my hand with your right, but I had a dizzying sense that this moment, you and me here in this beautiful restaurant, was perfectly preserved and I would remember it exactly, the sense of it, the feel of it, forever.

I found the courage to ask you about your mother, whom you always described in scathing terms.

"She's a drunk," you said. "And like many drunks, she can turn. She says bad things."

You paused, and I watched you being drawn back into a recollection, the sudden crease of a frown.

"She said my father was a coward for dying the way he did. And I flipped out. Told her it was her fault he'd died. That she'd pushed him into it with her serial infidelity. All the love affairs she had and didn't bother to hide."

"That must have been hard for her to hear."

"Not as hard as it was for me to live without my father."

Your voice was raised, momentarily. You apologized and let out a long, shaky sigh.

"It still upsets me to think about it. But the facts don't change.

I'll never forgive her for cheating on him and she'll never forgive me for blaming his suicide on her."

"Sorry," I said, the only word I could think of, and you smiled and squeezed my hand.

"It doesn't really matter anymore."

We heard music as we crossed the Place des Vosges and found an old guy playing his violin, a small crowd gathered round him. There was a café right there on the corner of the square, one of those dark-brown places where you would spend hours just watching, you told me.

"The French know how to live. Those small daily indulgences," you said. "Businessmen knocking back an espresso in a minute flat. Beautifully dressed women arriving at six o'clock for a solitary glass of wine. The English make a virtue out of drudgery and self-sacrifice. I can't stand that."

The Marais was your district; you'd lived just a few streets from the square for a whole summer. You showed me the ornate wooden doors that led to the seventeenth-century apartment you'd rented. You told me about the worn steps, so lethal you almost broke your neck one night falling down them.

I was about to say how lucky you were to live in Paris on your own at sixteen, but then I caught the edge of loneliness and I said nothing.

It was your idea to go into the Jesuit church of Saint-Paul-Saint-Louis, where there was a Delacroix you wanted to see. But it was my idea to light a candle.

"Let's light one for your father," I said as we reached the nave with its statue of the Madonna and the little iron holder where a dozen or more candles burned.

You looked astonished, then broken. I understood then that you had never been shown how to grieve, never been given permission. I wanted to grab hold of you and say, It's not too late now, but I couldn't find the words.

You dropped a few coins into the donation box and selected a skinny white candle, looking back at me questioningly as you lit it and placed it in the holder, as though you were indulging in some bizarre pagan ritual.

We sat down in a pew to look at the candles for a while, and I wondered what you were thinking. I thought about the thousands of other candles burning across the city, the millions and billions of them flickering at the same time around the world, a kind of collective energy keeping alive the memory of all those dead souls. I told you this as we waited outside the church for a cab to take us back to the airport. Death was unknown to me then and my vision of it was purely romantic.

"You're the only person who has ever understood me," you said after a moment. Your voice sounded thin and still, I thought, a little devastated.

Apart from my father, you could have said. But you didn't need to.

Now

I would have no idea how much time passes in here if Sam didn't mention it almost every time he visits.

"It's been four months, Greg," he says, just about holding back the "fucking," though I sense the gap and supply the word myself. Four fucking months.

"The slower we go, the faster we'll get there," Greg says, or some such platitude, dripping petrol onto the fire of Sam's indignation.

Sam wants results. He wants me locked up in trauma therapy sessions twenty-four seven. It's not that he wants me to suffer—the opposite is true; just that he wants his wife back. He wants his old life where he had a lover and his children had a mother. He's chasing that.

Sam's also become an expert in dissociation disorder, and as we know, a little knowledge is a dangerous thing. He has been told that there are three proven moments of my dissociation—the day I left you (the first time), the night my mother died, and my final visit to Shute Park, where I splintered off from my reality so drastically that I have not spoken or connected with anyone else ever since.

I've had this dramatic response explained countless times, and Sam has the details down pat, a user-friendly diagnosis that he trots out to anyone who'll listen (Alexa most recently; I recognized the jangle of her jewelry even before she sat next to me in the visitor chair, crying and then apologizing about crying for what felt like forever before she jangled off again).

Sam likes to compare my dissociation to the freeze response in animals; this is how he's explained it to the children too. In times of extreme trauma, dissociation helps protect the mind, he says; it offers an escape when it seems like there is no escape. The problem is when the dissociation becomes permanent, as it has with me, so that it seems I have no memory of events and little or no connection to the people I'm supposed to know best. Throw mutism into the mix and you have a hellish, complex condition that has baffled my psychiatrist and infuriated my husband.

In our trauma therapy sessions—one person talking (Greg), one person listening or not listening (me)—there has been a great deal of emphasis on creating my safe place. Since I don't speak, my safe place has been selected for me and it's our cottage, the pretty little Hansel and Gretel house with ivy-strewn walls and the long, straggling garden with a stream at the bottom. Greg becomes really quite lyrical when describing the cottage, although I imagine he's only seen photos; he talks about the glint of minnows in the stream and the way the early-morning light slices into the kitchen, creating pools of warmth on the oak table. He asks me to imagine sitting at that table watching Daisy making one of her grand-scale felt-tip drawings, looking out of the window to see Sam working in the garden. It's true these were once treasured points of familiarity and reassurance for me, the old me. It's just that in my head I have a different safe place. In my head I am always with you.

Four Months Before: Catherine

I'd forgotten how Shute Park appears quite suddenly after a bend in the drive. You turn a corner and there it is in front of you, this magnificent vanilla-colored building, a miniature palace with its turrets on either side. It is absurdly grand and quite the loveliest house I have ever seen.

"It's so beautiful," I say, and you look over at me, smiling.

"As you remembered it?" and I nod, too full of the moment to speak, for the ghosts of you and me are everywhere now. Fifteen years earlier, driving from Bristol in Jack's knackered old Golf, him and Alexa in the front, you and me in the back, the four of us swigging from a bottle of champagne. My heart beating wildly as we climbed the steps to the front door, you squeezing my hand before we went inside.

"Don't worry about my uncle. He'll love you. And anything goes, there's no judgment."

Just behind the house I can see the lawn where we lay on a rug with Mary's lemonade and the weekend papers. Glinting in the distance is the lake where we swam, the four of us floating on our backs, the archetypal "before" shot, a Polaroid to happier times.

The house is beautifully symmetrical in that staunchly Georgian way, three rows of windows running across it in perfect graduation, small at the top, then medium, then longer ones across the bottom. Exactly in the center of the facade is a triangular roof; it reminds me of the doll houses that Daisy and I used to love in the

Museum of Childhood, the ones with a panel that pulls away to reveal an ornate Louis XIV interior with tiny little rooms full of spindly gilt furniture.

I am dumbfounded all over again by the wonderfulness of your life.

The thought fills my mind that if we had stayed together all these years, then this house might also have been mine. We would have had a family together by now, a little row of Lucians and Catherines racing around all this grandeur. Do you think it too? I wonder, as I catch you watching for my reaction.

In the entrance hall, which smells just as houses of this kind should—cool air, seasoned wood, an inherent dampness passed down through the ages—we examine the family paintings. There is your grandfather, mustachioed in a tweed three-piece, all set to go out and butcher a skyload of pheasants; your grandmother with curlered hair, dark lipstick, and a choker of thick cream pearls. You stop at the portrait of your father, painted a year or so before he died, you tell me. I remember this painting well; I remember searching it for traces of the boy I loved and noting the eyes, an emphatic green the same as yours, and the mid-brown hair with its tendency to curl out at the ends. What strikes me, though, is how in the fifteen years since we last saw each other, you have become identical to this painting. You are your father. I wonder if you see it too.

"He's so handsome," I tell you. "A cross between Jeff Buckley and Mick Jagger. Same mouth. And hair."

"He'd have been happy with that."

I don't tell you that you look the same but even more so, even more beautiful to me. I am remastering the art of understatement. Always with you in a world of women who were ready to drop at your feet, I wanted to be the one who held back. We have moved on to a painting of your uncle that I haven't seen before, very Liberace in a voluminous silk shirt, martini glass held in a hand that glints with rings, when Mary appears from nowhere, shoes clipping across the parquet floor.

"There you are," she says to Lucian, and then she realizes who I am.

"Catherine! My goodness, what a surprise."

"Mary, it's so nice to see you again."

I offer my hand, but she pulls me into an unexpected hug, and I find myself fighting against a sudden punch of emotion.

As we walk toward the kitchen, Mary asks you about the funeral.

"Was it all right?" Her voice is low and concerned.

"Better than I thought. At least the wicked witches seemed happy to see me this time."

Mary smiles, and I remember that she knows all your secrets, the tribulations of growing up with an adulterous mother, absent sisters, and a suicidal father. You told me once that you cared more for Mary than you did for your own mother. You told me about the cakes she sent you back to school with, the food packages that arrived unheralded throughout the term. The one-sentence postcards just so you could have something in your pigeonhole.

We follow Mary into the kitchen, which has been redesigned since I was here last and looks as if it has jumped straight out of an interiors magazine, with walls of exposed brick, steel worktops, and those fashionable pendant lamps. Now all I want is the space and freedom to look. I'd like to slow the film right down, gliding my finger against the reel so that I can take in every still, each room, each piece of furniture, photographs, paintings, the low leather sofa at the far end of the room. Full-length windows looking out across the lawn. A long oak table with a curve of today's newspapers placed at one end. Most of all I'd like the invisibility to observe you leaning against the sink, talking to Mary while she fills the kettle and begins to lay a tray with cups and saucers.

I watch her handing you a stack of post and you chucking it back down on the little wooden table—"Thanks, Mary, I think I'll look at it later"—without even a cursory glance. So this is you, actually you, after all the years of trying to imagine your life, scrutinizing those two-dimensional images and bland nothing-stories in the press and reconstructing all the gaps. I pictured long lunches by the swimming pool. Barbecues on the lawn. Boating on the lake. But I always came unstuck when I began imagining the friends: Rachel, your on-off lover; Harry and Alexa, who were my friends too once upon a time; and Jack, the full stop to my dreams.

The tea is good. Sitting on the sofa holding your hand is good. Being back here in this most wonderful house is good. But when Mary calls out casually, "Will you be staying for the party, Catherine?" an innocent enough question, my fear of confrontation swamps me, a toxic surge that makes me breathless.

I know all about your party, as anyone with a fixation on the diary sections and society pages of newspapers and magazines would. I wasn't always this way, almost obsessively interested in the foibles of the rich and famous, but it was the only means of finding out what you were up to. I wanted to know what you were doing and who you were doing it with, and more than anything I longed for the day when I might discover that Jack had dropped out of your life. But no, more often than not he was there, right beside you, in his shades, with his Colgate smile, still tightly gripping his position as best friend slash honorary brother. A couple of years ago Sam caught me reading a double-page spread about your annual summer party in the *Daily Mail*. Beautiful girls in shimmering drop-waisted dresses, men in wing collars and tails, those obligatory coupe champagne glasses. The theme must have been 1920s; the headline ran, "Somerset's Not-So-Great Gatsby" (the media have always portrayed you and your friends as hedonistic, good-for-nothing wastrels). Sam, I remember, leaned over my shoulder and said, "Come the revolution . . ."

Now I keep my voice light and even as I tell Mary, "I won't be able to stay that long, sadly."

But I see you watching me, and it seems to me that you are beginning to understand.

Four Months Before: Lucian

If it is surreal for Catherine being back in the house where we were once at the pinnacle of this shared, derailing passion, then it is equally so for me to have her here. I wonder what my friends would think if they could see her here now. The girls would be all right, I think, or at least Alexa would. With Rachel it's always a little complicated, particularly when other women are involved, especially when the woman is Catherine. I'm not at all sure Harry would understand, Harry who oversaw my collapse—I don't exaggerate—about a week after she left. And Jack? Well, Jack is different. He's more like a brother than a friend in many ways and he likes to come first.

When Catherine and I were together, all those years ago, I sometimes wondered if he was jealous. She was astonishing to look at, though she didn't seem to realize it, the kind of face that demands a silver screen: huge dark eyes; a perfect nose, long but slim, elegant; and then her lips, of course, which were full enough to make most men's blood pump faster. I thought that perhaps Jack was jealous of how hard I'd fallen in love, for Catherine and I, after our faltering start, were never apart. And I also wondered if he was a little bit in love with her himself. I wouldn't have blamed him. There we were, the two of us, noodling around in our Clifton townhouse, and all of a sudden Audrey Hepburn moved in and claimed me as her own. So it is probably just as well I have promised Catherine we'll be alone here, that I will keep my friends at bay. I'm ignoring countless texts and phone messages, a typically charmless email from Jack, subject heading: **WHERE THE FUCK ARE YOU, you fucker???**

Meanwhile I get a real kick out of the way Catherine reacts to seeing the house again.

"It's the loveliest house," she says. "I thought I might have over-romanticized it in my memory. But I haven't. It's even better than I remembered."

Most people who come to Shute Park are either too used to it or too entitled themselves to express much enthusiasm for its grandeur. Even after all this time living here alone, though, the house still blows me away. I can remember coming here when I was very young and standing in front of it with my father and uncle, counting the white shuttered windows that ran across the breadth of its facade (eighteen in each tier, the same at the back).

"This could be yours one day," my uncle said. "But it will be your father's first."

"What about when you have children?" I'd asked, and my father and uncle laughed.

"That's looking increasingly unlikely," my father said.

He was ahead of his time, my uncle, unapologetically parading his young, flamboyantly dressed lovers (there was a time when they all seemed to look like Adam Ant) through our small, uptight village and hosting wild gatherings that might last for days. Shute Park under his heritage was never out of the papers. He was hated and abhorred by the *Daily Mail*, another thing to be proud of, and by my mother, who decided (around the time he named me his sole heir) that he was the embodiment of evil. He died of lung cancer when I was twenty-one, and I still miss him.

When my uncle was alive I'd come over from Bristol with my friends most weekends, fueling mad twelve-hour drinking sessions from his open-door-cellar policy, beginning with champagne and the palest of French rosés and finishing sometime after dawn with brandy and sodas, his favorite, lying on the sofas in the library, listening to the Rolling Stones. My taste in music was crystallized in those days; I've been working my way through his extensive collection of the greats—Dylan, Cohen, Van Morrison—ever since. He was a weird fish in many ways but he was my father's brother and my sole supporter, and thirteen years on, I'm still half hoping that he will reappear, that his death, and my legacy, was just another of his twisted jokes.

As we move through the house, now scented with the smell of a roasting chicken, it seems that Catherine is looking for evidence of how I live. She dismisses the drawing room, a dreadful place of swagged curtains and brown furniture and far too much pink, as soon as she sees it and laughs at the incongruous Francis Bacon on the wall. But the library, with its battered chesterfield sofas, drink-splashed sideboard, and boxes full of vinyl, she seizes upon.

"I remember this room," she says, and I'm sure, like me, she's picturing a long night of hard drinking with my uncle, him and Alexa taking turns to play DJ, Catherine, Jack, and me lying on the floor, playing a half-hearted game of Jenga.

Catherine loves the flashing lights—new since her day—that Alexa draped around the nail above the fireplace and gasps at the extent of the tequila collection on the sideboard. Bottles of the stuff, and not your standard student Jose Cuervo either. I learned to drink tequila properly when I was in Mexico, painting by day and sipping the purest white spirits by night. One hundred percent agave is what you want, pricey stuff but it often comes in exquisite bottles. Catherine picks up my favorite one, which is shaped like a skull; I brought it back on the aeroplane wrapped up in a cashmere scarf.

"Quite a tequila habit you've got." Her voice is off and I'm not sure why.

"This stuff is pure indulgence," I say, starting to tell her about it. "To be sipped very slowly, room temperature—" but she cuts me off.

"I never drink it."

She doesn't seem overly impressed with my uncle's cellar either, though there are thousands of bottles, different grapes and vintages all neatly ordered in their custom-made sliding oak drawers. Burgundy and Bordeaux, mostly, though he flirted with New World in his later years.

"How can you possibly get through all this?" Catherine asks.

I shrug. "I can't."

"So what will you do with it?"

"I don't know. I haven't given it any thought."

She opens her arms to take in the cellar.

"All this money. It just seems . . . bottomless." She shakes her head; I sense her disapproval.

"My great-grandparents made a fortune in the stock market and tied it all up very carefully. I know I'm lucky. You're making me feel like I should apologize."

She breaks into a smile. "Sorry."

"You were reminding me of that feisty student journalist."

"Too many years absorbing Sam's indignation. Self-made wealth is fine, obviously; he has a pathological hatred of inherited. Just ignore me."

We embrace between the 2007 Rully and the 2008 Saint-Bris.

"Any preferences?" I say, and she shakes her head.

"You choose. I won't drink much."

I select a Gevrey-Chambertin from 2001 for sentimental reasons that I keep to myself (the year we first met).

Mary has laid up a table for us in the small Chinese drawing room and she has really gone to town. Candles burning everywhere—there must be at least twenty or thirty across the mantelpiece, in the alcoves and on either side of the fireplace—champagne cooling in an ice bucket, and the table heavy with glass and silver. Frankly, I am thinking, she's slightly overdone it—there's a sense of a soft-porn seduction scene, or is that just me?—but Catherine cries, "Oh Mary, this is so, so beautiful," and Mary looks thrilled. That's my housekeeper hooked again, and Catherine has been here less than an hour.

Mary has brought in the roast chicken, hands down my favorite thing to eat; we have a glass of cold champagne and the Chambertin warming by the fire. Opposite me, in some weird twist of fate, is the woman I've loved like an illness for most of my adult life. It's hard to believe she's here.

We used to say that we swapped thoughts, that they crossed somewhere in midair, and it's still exactly the same, for Catherine leans forward and says, "I keep thinking how I should be in bits because of what's happening with me and Sam. I should be feeling so guilty. And instead I feel, I don't know, just elated. To be with you again. To be back here, even for a short while. Is that so wrong of me?"

I think we both know her husband would say yes, very wrong, but I'm not him and I'm also not about to chase that smile from her face. When Catherine smiles, it's really something, I'd like to whip out my phone and record it, then work on a portrait later. Smiling Catherine. You don't see it very often.

It reminds me of the sketch I made of her, the one where she's dressed in one of my shirts, mouth curved into a knowing smile. It was one of the last days we would spend together, as it turned out, a time of such euphoric intensity that I really believed I'd come to know her better than I knew anyone. We talked almost ceaselessly during our waking hours, all the time, whenever we weren't making love. Incredible to think I was Catherine's first lover, for in the space of a few months the sex had become fast-tracked and experimental; to think of it right now—the things we did, the things she did—would be to implode. It was the middle of the afternoon when I picked up my sketchpad and decided to draw her, just as she was, naked in the middle of our lived-in bed.

"Not like this, surely?" she'd said, suddenly prudish.

"How can you possibly mind after everything we've just been doing?"

"Imagine if it fell into the wrong hands," she said, snatching up my white shirt, and that's how I drew her, kneeling up on my bed, the shirt falling almost to her knees. I rather liked the way she looked in it; I liked the sense of possession, the wearing of my things. She's hardly altered, this woman who sits on the other side of the table, lit by Mary's candles, this flesh-and-blood Catherine.

"I still have that sketch of you," I tell her, and instantly the smile fades.

"I remember," she says. "We . . . broke up soon afterward."

Broke up, is that what you call it? Desertion and abandonment are closer to the truth.

"Do I look very different?"

I shake my head. "Exactly the same," I say, but it strikes me, as she asks this, that the real difference between then and now is in her eyes. I captured our euphoria in that sketch; I think that's why I like it so much. The woman opposite me, same huge, expressive dark eyes, cannot mask her sadness.

There's a sense tonight that we're filling in the gaps, a decade and a half of them. We swap histories, edited versions, with careful revisions. She tries to keep Sam out of the conversation, I manage to avoid name-checking my friends, both of us trying to answer the unasked question, the only question: how did your life turn out without me in it?

She wants to know all about the house, what it's like to live alone here. The truth is, I'm hardly ever on my own. Jack comes over most days to play tennis, swim, or shoot, Harry is only a few minutes down the road, and the girls come down at weekends and whenever they're not working (which is most of the time in Rachel's case). But I'm not about to tell her that.

"I'm good at being on my own."

I wonder as I say this if it's true. I can spend hours, whole days, whole nights, down at my studio, and when I'm painting I can forget everything else. But there are nights when Jack is forced to stay at home with Celia, when Harry is in Bangkok or nowadays with Ling, and the girls are in London, when a listlessness comes over me. I drink too much, I smoke a lot, I listen to music, I pass the time, but it feels exactly like that, a mapping-out of hours.

"Did you always know you'd inherit this place?"

"From the age of about six, but I thought my father would inherit it first. I never imagined he would die so young."

Catherine reaches across the table for my hand.

"You once told me you felt responsible for his death. Do you remember?"

I nod as the memory of that night sears between us, the night she promised she would never leave.

"Do you still feel like that?"

"No, I don't think so. I was ten, how could it possibly have been my fault? I just wish it hadn't taken me all this time to realize it probably wasn't my mother's fault either. I've always been so black and white about infidelity. To me it's the lowest crime. You're attracted to someone else? Then you break up and move on. I've spent my whole life hating my mother for betraying my father. But I've come to realize there must have been two sides. Maybe he wasn't so easy to live with. Maybe that's why she looked to other people to make her feel good. You can't go round blaming everyone else. Ultimately it was his fault and no one else's."

Catherine is watching me with an expression of unutterable sadness and I assume she is thinking of ten-year-old me, the victim of parental suicide. Or perhaps she is thinking of her own mother, dead at forty-six, yet another bizarre parallel between the two of us. I want to say something to chase away the gloom, but before I can speak, she says, "You see, that's exactly what I feel. You always have to take responsibility when things happen, the bad as well as the good."

And though I know she's probably thinking about Sam and his affair and the possibility of them separating, there is something about her voice and her eyes, which are sorrowful and somehow haunting, that jars me and reminds me of the past. We keep coming back here, no matter how much we both try to avoid it. This secret of hers, whatever it is, right now, it feels so close I could almost touch it.

Fifteen Years Earlier

You and Jack had a dinner party, a grown-up one supposedly, though it certainly didn't end that way. You had pushed together a couple of tables, covered them with white linen cloths; there were flowers and candles and cute little cellophane wraps of Belgian truffles. Your uncle sent a case of expensive wine. Alexa arrived and scattered little gold stars across the table. She was wearing a bright-pink dress, a tiny thing, and her skin even in the height of winter was smooth and golden.

You had gone to so much trouble. Oysters from the fishmonger, a beef casserole you'd paid someone to make, chocolate tarts ordered at crazy expense from Fortnum & Mason. It was your idea to have the dinner party and I understood why you were doing it. We'd been together for a few months by then and this was your way of telling your closest friends I was here to stay.

Jack, who saw me on a daily basis, went out of his way to be nice to me. He might have been jealous—after all, until I came along, he was without question your number one; you were, you often told me, closer than most siblings. But he was bigger than that. If you and he ever went off to the pub, he made sure to invite me along, and when you and your friends visited your uncle's house one weekend—I'd refused to come, battling an essay crisis, secretly glad of a little time alone—he had tried hard to make me change my mind. Alexa, who, like me, stayed over most nights, had also become a good friend. But there was resistance to our relationship, mainly from Rachel and her girlfriends. Charlotte Lomax in particular, another manicured blond, loved to voice her dislike.

"Everyone knows she's in love with Lucian," Liv said whenever Charlotte's spitefulness rattled me.

I wasn't surprised that Rachel and Charlotte were fighting for your attention that night. You were wearing one of your father's old suits with a black T-shirt and trainers, the first time I'd ever seen you in something formal, and you looked almost shockingly handsome. Jack did too, of course, the undisputed university pinup. He was wearing an identical vintage suit (his taste, I always thought, was an exact replica of yours) with a white shirt and narrow black tie and he was at his most charming, bringing Alexa and me glasses of champagne to drink while we changed, loitering on the edge of the bath talking to us while we jostled for space in front of the mirror.

You and Jack were good at parties, even back then. There were twelve of us, high on champagne cocktails and just the luxury of the thing; it was the absolute antithesis of any student party I'd ever been to, no cut-price Valpolicella, no pasta bake, no one passed out in the bathroom.

I hoped we would be sitting next to each other. Privately I'd had a little fantasy about you sliding your hand beneath the tablecloth and working your way up my bare thighs—if I'd told you that, you would have changed the table plan instantly. But instead I was sitting between Jack and Harry, while you had Rachel and Charlotte, your vixen adorers, slugging it out to left and right. They left no room for anyone else, your attention monopolized right through the casserole and the chocolate tart and even when the plates were cleared away (by paid, uninvited students from the same year; no one but you and Jack would have had the audacity), you remained a tight little cluster of three.

Most people were smoking and drinking glasses of Vin Santo, which your uncle had sent along with the wine. Harry, whom I'd found it hardest to get to know ("It's nothing personal," you told me whenever I mentioned this. "He's never been able to talk to girls."), was opening up to me about his home life. It sounded like something out of a Grimms' fairy tale. A huge house that was so cold in winter he had to wear socks and two jumpers to bed. A nanny who had been passed down through three generations.

"She's in her nineties now. I used to have to tie her shoelaces because she was too stiff to bend down. I think she slept through most of my childhood."

A father who drove a horse and trap to town when he lost his license for drunk driving. A mother who used to read *Racing Post* cover to cover several times through, a dressing gown over her clothes to keep warm.

I told Harry it reminded me of *Cold Comfort Farm*, all those eccentric characters living together in a damp old house.

"Nothing so interesting, I'm afraid. They're fantastically dull, my parents. They only care about grouse and salmon. And their animals. They love their dogs and their horses. That's about it. No other interests. No more topics. Dinners are so boring and so bloody long. The only good times are when Lucian or Jack come to stay."

I began to understand that night what bound you so tightly to your friends—both you and Harry had parents who had disappointed you, your teenage years characterized by a lack of love. Once you'd cut yourself off from your mother and sisters, you lived between Jack's parents' house and your uncle's during the school holidays. The three of you, I saw now, had formed your own family, only recently allowing Alexa and Rachel to join the clique. No wonder you were going to such lengths to have me accepted.

Someone had brought a bottle of tequila with them and it was traveling the length of the table with accompanying chunks of lemon and a little silver dish of salt. When the bottle reached Jack, he poured out a shot and handed it to me.

"No thanks."

Jack shook his head slowly from side to side. When he grinned, all I could see were his perfect straight white teeth. Film-star teeth that had cost a fortune; you told me he'd blown an entire legacy fixing them. My stomach lurched a little when he smiled at me, at his most irresistible.

"No?" He put his head on one side. "But I think you mean yes?"

"I tried it once, it tastes like paint stripper."

Jack folded his arms. Another wide, tooth-flashing smile.

"I'm wait-ing."

It was a challenge and we gazed at each other, his bright eyes boring into mine. I remember thinking how Jack used his poster-boy good looks like some girls use their beauty to get whatever they want. Poor Alexa, was what I thought as I knocked back the tequila shot with a grimace. He was flirting with me openly, no matter that his girlfriend and my boyfriend were seated around the same table.

The party began to get wilder. Alexa put on some music and most of us started dancing. I was a little drunk by now, and when you came up behind me, wrapping your arms around my waist and kissing my neck, I thought I'd never felt happier. I turned around and whispered into your ear, the words that were permanently in my head but I hadn't yet been brave enough to say.

"I. Love. You."

You looked at me with such delight, your whole face transformed by pleased surprise.

"Me too," you said, whispering back into my ear. "Catherine Elliot, me too."

Now

They have brought proper clothes for me to wear, which means someone other than Sam and the children must be coming to visit. Normally it's a tracksuit, elasticized waist, trousers pulled up, slippers pushed on, a look I would have hated in a different lifetime. But not here. Anything goes here. Today it's a shirt, one I recognize, with white-and-gray stripes and tiny black dots; the pattern, harshly geometric, dances before my eyes.

"Let me help you with those buttons, darling," says Alison, who often breaks the rules, brushing my hair or moisturizing my skin when I am meant to be doing these things for myself now. "Let's brighten you up a bit today," she says, unzipping a little red leather cosmetics bag that used to belong to me. I suppose it still does, but I feel no connection to it, this dead girl's purse.

Alison dabs moisturizer onto my face in four places—forehead, both cheeks, and chin—and smooths it in with wide north-to-south circles. My mother used to do that.

"What about a bit of this foundation? It would look lovely on you."

More squeezing, more cream, more dabs. A soft brush paints stripes on my cheekbones. Not the apples, which are lower down, not like they tell you in the magazines.

"Last thing, beauty. Lip gloss. There. Pretty as a picture, aren't you?"

The hiss of a zip being done up, rubber soles on lino walking away from me, then silence for a while. I turn my made-up face to the window and examine the tree, my stalwart friend, now in with its bare wintery branches. I am thinking of you, of course, and that time we had, so precious, so short, an unexpected little burst of rewritten history. Did we treasure it, did we? I know I tried to stay awake in the nights just to hear your breathing or to press myself against your warm skin. I tried to keep my thoughts narrow and focused, on you, on the now, not worrying about our future, not fretting about our past. I didn't manage very well at that, did I?

Alison's shoes are squeaking toward me, and just behind them, something louder, clumpier. Clogs with wooden soles. I know who will be wearing them.

"Here she is, my darling, here's your friend come to see you."

And then a voice I've always loved.

"I gave her that shirt, Alison! Thank you for putting her in it."

"I know how it upsets you when she's in her tracksuit. She used to care about how she looked, didn't she? We'll get there again, darling. Little by little."

When Alison has gone, I feel Liv sitting down in the chair next to me. She takes my right hand and holds it in hers; she squeezes my fingers against her rings. It hurts a little.

"Hey," she says, after a while. "I've brought some things to show you. Things you can touch. And smell. Things you might remember."

This is not a new tactic, but it is one Liv hasn't tried before. I've held Daisy's Eeyore and Joe's Man U football shirt, and an old cashmere scarf of my mother's that used to live under my pillow. And I've expressed nothing each time because nothing is what I crave. The trouble is, my nothing is running out. They keep telling me so.

"Sooner or later, Catherine, we're going to discharge you and you'll be back at home. And we won't be there to help you."

I'm aware of this deadline—it looms, it looms—just as I'm aware of the need to start communicating with my family. If I were able to speak, I'd tell them so. I'd tell them I love them, that deep down inside somewhere, I know I'm a mother and I guess I'm still a wife and I'm working my way back to that. But I can't speak; there are no words, just my dreams and the interruption of others.

Liv turns my hand over and sprays something onto my arm, cool and wet. I don't like it. She holds my wrist against my nose, strong, floral, foresty. I want to move my face away but I endure it, eyes ahead, nostrils flared against the assault.

"You must remember that smell, Catherine? It's Chanel No. 5. I wore it at university and you always stole it and it drove me mad. In the end I bought you a bottle for your birthday. You wore it every day until it ran out. That bottle lasted for years."

We sit together, me doused in perfume, saying nothing, until the silence breaks.

"Won't you talk to me, Catherine? Please. Won't you do it for me, for us?"

Not speaking to Liv, the person I've probably said the most words to in my life, is hardest of all. Sam leaves his anger in the room whenever he visits, but with Liv, every time, I feel her sorrow.

Time passes, I'm not sure how long, and then Liv places something between my hands, a sheet of paper, larger and thicker than a standard piece of A4.

"It's a drawing of you. I know that you can see it, Catherine. And I'm sorry if it hurts. But I want you to look."

I don't need to look to know what it is; I can tell by the weight and thickness and the swirls of darkness, charcoal gray. I'd like to be left alone now. I am ready to disappear, sinking into the warmth behind my eyelids, sucked into the whirlpool of dreams.

What can I see? A bright, light room that is made of glass on three sides. A workbench littered with brushes and paints and pencils. And you. I can see you, brow furrowed, that hard, cold stare as you examine me, your slim, tanned hand streaking across the paper, the rapid back-and-forth movement as you shade my hair. And I am happy here, in the light, where no words are ever needed. If I could speak, I'd ask Liv for two things. Could I keep the drawing, could I hold it here against my heart? And could she leave, please, right now, before the light disappears and you are gone again.

Four Months Before: Catherine

Am I still dreaming? I feel as though I must be, waking at first light, my naked body pressed up close to yours, the man I have spent most of my adult life mourning and regretting. I lie in the half darkness, registering the unfamiliar shapes of the room's old-fashioned furniture. The armoire—not a wardrobe apparently, nothing so pedestrian here—with its molded top that curls up at both ends like a waxed mustache. The bookshelves, which run right across one wall and are crammed with an unlikely mix, half yours, half your uncle's: art books, a complete set of Dickens that look like they've never been opened, several Stephen Kings—"I read them when I can't sleep," you told me—various pictorial odes to the male form including a devastatingly graphic Robert Mapplethorpe.

I love this new, updated knowledge of you: your house, your habits, your daily life. I love opening up the armoire and seeing the neat rows of pressed shirts (so many white ones, it reminds me with a stab of my mother). I like seeing your toothbrush (electric) in the chrome tooth mug and your shampoo in the shower (lime and basil; so that's where the citrus smell comes from). I have spent so many years craving information about you, and gleaning only the smallest, most unsatisfactory snippets from the papers, that being here in your house feels like a sensory overload. I listen to the steady flow of your breathing and feel a little rush of contentment. I'm glad I am awake, I wish I didn't have to sleep at all, that I could inhabit each moment of the day and night and store it up, but for what? For when I am back in the cottage with my sad little box of letters and memories? How can that ever be possible again?

You reach out and put a warm hand on my thigh.

"You're awake."

It was always like this when we were first together, the two of us so tuned in to one another that we even shared our sleeping rhythms. I remember waking to you kissing me and slowly making love in that magical, trancelike way so that afterward I was never quite sure if I'd been dreaming or if it had really happened. You roll over and wrap your arms around me and I feel your lips brushing against the back of my neck. You run a palm slowly from my neck down to my chest to my stomach, where it rests, lightly, a few inches above my groin. Always with you the instant flicker of lust. You shift position so that you are lying exactly on top of me, leaning up on one elbow, tracing the outline of my face with your forefinger, touching my chin, my nose, my eyes.

"It's very early," I whisper.

"Let's not waste any more time sleeping," you whisper back. You are kissing me, your tongue flicking lightly against mine, and your hand has worked its way between my legs and I can feel the hardness of you pressing against the top of my thighs. Hands, fingers, tongue; I know what comes next and there is nothing to do except melt and burn.

An hour later and we are on your hill, sharing coffee from a stainless-steel thermos. It is a little cold and I am huddled into an old blue jumper of yours, which I have stretched over my knees to keep warm. We have caught the last moments of sunrise, a burning deep-orange sky with the great gray mass of Wells Cathedral and the Glastonbury Tor set against it. From up here you can see how the county is all curves, a backdrop of hills—the Mendips, the Quantocks, and Blackdown: you point them out one by one. It makes me think of a giant nude Rubens woman lying on her side, and when I tell you this, you laugh.

"All I can see now is breasts and hips and a potbelly."

You tell me that you come up here most days to take photographs on your phone.

"You'd think I might get bored of the view, but I never do. The mood changes completely depending on the light and the weather; I think that's why I paint it so often. And it's only really by making lots of versions of the same thing that I can get at the essence of it. Sometimes it works, sometimes it doesn't. But I come up here all the time anyway, whether I'm thinking about painting or not. When I'm here, I know I could never leave Somerset."

"But surely you couldn't leave Shute Park even if you wanted to? You couldn't sell it, could you?"

"The estate is meant to stay in the family, passed down from father to son. But it turns out neither my uncle nor I have been very good at breeding. Different reasons, obviously."

"Why didn't you marry?" The question is out before I can stop it.

"I've no idea. Never fancied it, I suppose. Why did you marry Sam?"

My stomach dips at the mention of his name.

"I think because he made me feel safe."

"And I didn't?"

I have fallen into a trap of my own making. No, I wasn't safe with you, but not for reasons you could imagine. I cannot look at you now; I feel sick and ashamed and bone cold suddenly, winter cold. I needed Sam for his black-and-white morality, his high opinion of me. But how can I tell you such things without revealing the truth about why I left?

I force myself to breathe slowly, quietly, in and out, in and out.

"Catherine?"

I'm in a state, you can tell.

"It wasn't that. It wasn't that you didn't make me feel safe."

"Then what was it?"

The blackness is there just on the perimeter of my vision. If I concentrate, if I keep calm, I can push it away.

"I felt I didn't deserve you."

Again the words seem to rush from me almost before I'm sure I want to utter them. You see the truth in this, I know you do, because you stand up and wrap your arms around me and I rest my head against your chest, inhaling your citrusy smell.

"Silly girl," you say, while we watch the colors of the sky fade from orange to palest pink. "How could you possibly think that?"

We spend the rest of the morning in your studio, an old flint cattle shed surrounded on three sides by a purpose-built glass-and-steel box. Inside, the light is so fierce it is almost too much, and the walls and floor have been painted a dazzling white. It is completely bare, this studio, stripped down to the essentials and nothing more—a workbench covered with tubes of paint and sketchpads, a holder filled with pencils, a butler's sink with a jug of soaking brushes, its interior still spattered with specks of rust and cobalt blue. There are canvases stacked everywhere: in piles on the floor, propped against the walls five or six deep, and in one corner a whole tower of blank ones that lean threateningly like an installation.

Even though I've read reviews of your most recent exhibition and tracked down several of your paintings on the internet, it has taken until this moment for me to realize how serious you are about your work. This is not a hobby but a career. I suppose I've been guilty of believing the media hype: the hedonistic rich boy hell-bent on pleasure at all costs. I have spent so many years re-creating an image of you in my head that I have lost sight of who you really are.

The art is good, I think. Aside from the landscapes—four of them the same view from the hill, the cathedral picked out in a slightly depressing gray against a sky just like this morning's, frozen as it turns from pink to orange—there are several woodcuts, the black silhouettes set on intensely colored backgrounds of lime green and shocking pink. The one I like most shows a faceless girl with a fringed bob leaning against a bull, his horns outlined in orange as if on fire from the ball of sun behind him.

"Who's this?" I ask, and you describe how the image came to you almost exactly as it is now, when you were watching *The Minotaur* at Covent Garden.

"It doesn't happen like that for me very often, but I got straight in the car and drove to Somerset and worked in my studio all night."

There is no choice about your drawing me again; you just begin sharpening pencils and clipping paper to an easel and you tell me to sit down and relax however I like.

"Are you going to keep the jumper on?" you ask, and I am sure we are both thinking of the parallels between then and now, me wearing your white shirt and kneeling up on your bed, not long before the night I left forever. This time I am sitting on the floor, cross-legged, looking up at you, and I'm glad I've chosen this position, for it gives me the chance to study you properly. You are lost almost immediately, staring at me with a stern look in your eyes. So this is you, I think, as you streak pencil across the page, eyes narrowed, your hand moving in tiny tight vibrations as you shade something—my hair? My eyes? The navy of my jumper? There are so many questions I'd like to ask, but I know not to break your concentration and I also want to take this moment of looking for myself. When I am back at home, back in my real life, I will try to recall exactly this—the feeling of being regarded, again, at last, by the boy who has lived inside me for the past fifteen years.

Four Months Before: Lucian

The sketch is nearly finished. I am just shading the ends of her hair, trying to get right the way it kinks rather than curls, a slight curve that finishes the smooth, straight sheet of almost blackness. I am wondering if I will turn the drawing into something else, an oil probably; I am thinking how the blackness would work well as a violet or blue, but then what would be the right color for her skin? I am so lost in thought that at first I don't notice Catherine has become bored and uncomfortable. She stretches her legs out in front of her, shifting her weight from one hip to the other. She sighs.

"Get up and walk around if you like. I've almost finished."

She moves around the studio, stopping to look at some canvases, bypassing others, not uttering a single word. I rarely invite anyone into my studio and I don't like people to look unless they are going to look properly. The anodyne over-flattery, I hate that.

"Oh wonderful, darling," Alexa says whenever she comes here, and it's nice of her, of course it is, but it also means nothing. I prefer someone to say I like the way you've done the clouds but I don't really get that tree, it feels too brown, too blocky. Because that's how it is for me too. Maybe I overemphasized the tree, maybe instead of hinting or suggesting, I sledgehammered it onto the canvas. Painting for me is like one long, uninterrupted lesson even though I'm not sure I'm always learning very much or I'll ever be entirely happy with even one piece of work. A while ago I realized that all I had to do was show up in the studio every day and that eventually I would get somewhere; there would be moments when it worked, when I felt at peace. And those moments of utter absorption, a self-contentment I cannot find any other way, well, it's the only reason for doing it.

I am just about to call Catherine over to look at her drawing when she spies a stack of canvases in the corner. The one facing us is a slightly grotesque Baconesque nude, a male, full frontal, intentionally anatomical and unforgiving.

"He's pretty full-on," she says, her first words in a while.

I tell her about the model in my life-drawing class, an old guy who always seems to catch my eye when he's rearranging his testicles.

"Perhaps it's love," she says, casually moving the canvas to one side. And there, hidden away behind Mr. Testicles, is an oil painting of Rachel, her blond hair messy, up-all-night smudges beneath her eyes, a cigarette trailing smoke off canvas. *Smoking (Hot) Nude*, we jokingly titled it at the time. So now Rachel is on the agenda. For a few seconds the air stills and I wait for Catherine to say something, but she doesn't.

"Do you mind?"

"How can I mind?"

She still hasn't turned around to look at me, and I detect a slight shakiness in her voice. She minds.

"Catherine."

I'm up and over to her corner of the studio in seconds.

"Look at me."

She smiles, shamefacedly, but I catch the sheen of tears.

"Pathologically jealous," she says. "Sorry."

"Says the woman who is married with two children. Look. If there was a way for us to be together, to give it a chance, at least, then that is what I'd want. I don't need to question it, even after all this time apart. I'd want to give it a go. But you have two children, we know the obstacles. And if you go back to Sam, my life will carry on as it always has. And that involves Rachel, as a friend first and foremost. Really, there's nothing to be jealous about."

"Does she know about us?"

"I've been avoiding my friends. Like you wanted. They're calling and texting me like crazy."

"I feel you should tell her, at least."

"I will."

We go back to looking at the painting.

Catherine says, "She looks beautiful but a little sad, which is how I always think of her somehow, I don't know why."

"More than a little sad. She's heartbroken but in denial. She just keeps going to the parties and taking the drugs and fighting her way through the hangovers and pretending that everything's fine; more than fine, it's great. But of course we all know it isn't."

I tell Catherine about Max, Rachel's son, eleven now. I tell her about the day she lost custody, her sobbing on the floor of my London flat, fat rivers of tears that left patches of wet on my Moroccan carpet. I tell her about Rachel's five-minute rehab, her shock arrival at Soho House, martini glass in hand, when we'd just been discussing her detox.

Through all this Catherine listens, and when I'm finished, she says, "She'll get there eventually, and when she does, she'll be able to work it out with her son, make him understand. You can't stop until you're ready."

"I think he's starting to come around," I tell her. "She's meant to be seeing him sometime this week. I'm pretty sure it's tomorrow."

And it occurs to me that Catherine is the opposite of Jack's wife, Celia, who cannot help leaking silent judgment whenever

Max is mentioned. You see it in her eyes, her mouth, her shoulders. She can exude disapproval from the back of her head. It's not that she's unkind; more that she is so obsessed with her own small son and with mothering in general that Rachel's "dysfunction"—she actually called it that once—horrifies her.

We stand in front of nude Rachel—funny, really, how wildly personal and inappropriate this portrait seems when you begin to analyze it: her smooth, pale-brown nipples, the deep beige shadows marking out the undercurve of her breasts, the neat strip of hair—seeing but not seeing, for Catherine is in a trance, the two of us caught on a staircase of memory.

I think we'd been together only a week or so, holed up in my bedroom for almost the whole of that time, in the Clifton townhouse I shared with Jack. He brought us a takeaway once, I remember, and apart from that we lived on tea and toast and bottles of very expensive wine my uncle had given me.

Rachel's sharp, impatient knock on the door startled us, post- or precoital as we always were in those days, and I threw Catherine one of my T-shirts and wrapped a towel around my waist. Rachel came in and stood by the door, looking around the room—the rumpled bed, the tangle of Catherine's clothes and mine on the floor, a litter of mugs on my desk—and her pretty face was tense with disapproval. We'd slept together after a drunken party the very first week of term—an unmemorable scuffle on the bathroom floor, as I recall—and never since, but I knew she was in love with me. Or thought she was, at least.

"Hi, Rach," I said. "You know Catherine, don't you?"

It wasn't the smoothest of introductions, not the best setting, the two of us half naked on the bed, Rachel, even back then, too well dressed for a student, with her gold jewelry and her expensive clothes.

Catherine said, "Hi," but Rachel didn't respond with even the most cursory of glances.

"When are we going to see you?" Her voice was plaintive. "Are you coming out with us tonight? There's a party."

"I doubt it," I said. "Unless Catherine wants to."

I looked over at Catherine, but she had shrunk right into the corner, as if she could make herself invisible under Rachel's disinterested gaze.

"I'm going to have a quick coffee with Jack before I go to the library," Rachel said. "Coming?"

I tried to persuade Catherine to come with me as I threw on a T-shirt and a pair of jeans.

"Rachel's just a bit jealous of you, that's all. She'll love you once she gets to know you. They all will."

But Catherine shook her head. "You go," she said. "I'm fine here."

In the kitchen, Rachel and Jack were standing by the sink clearly talking about me, and I walked into a hostile atmosphere of things half said.

"Sometimes you can be so unfriendly, Rach. You made Catherine feel really bad back there."

"I don't think she's the girl for you. Sorry, but I have to tell you."

I looked at Jack, who had annoyed me by saying nothing.

"Presumably you disagree?"

"Of course I like Catherine. You know I do. I think the point Rachel is trying to make is that we don't really see you anymore. It's as if all you care about is her."

The two of them, standing there, all po-faced and sanctimonious. Anger made me thoughtless; I didn't care about Rachel and the pain of her unrequited love, or the way Jack had supported me through the hardship of my teens, and now I was dismissing him like a jealous kid.

"I guess neither of you know that feeling when all you want is to be left alone with someone. Can't you just be civil to her, Rach? Is that really too much to ask?"

Up until that point we had formed a pretty tight group of five: Jack, Harry, and I, who'd been friends since school, and the girls, Rachel and Alexa, a new addition, all of us addicted to good times at the exclusion of pretty much everything else. We had money and time and youth, I guess, and an unconscious desire to fritter it all. Rachel from the outset had insisted on exclusive friendship; she managed it with her noli me tangere reserve and pinpoint put-downs and with the simple fact that she was basically more fun than anyone I'd ever met. If she wanted us to herself, she could have us, was my view. And then I met Catherine.

I feel ashamed now at the way I turned away from them, especially Rachel, whose eyes were vivid with tears. But I'd found love, after a decade of intense loneliness. Erotic love. I hadn't known it could consume in this way, so that all I could think about, the only thoughts I had, were what we had just been doing to each other and what we might like to try next. That she was a virgin when she met me and yet had matched, sometimes even exceeded, the extent of my passion had tipped me over the edge. I was hooked on her, addicted, obsessed, and nothing and no one else mattered.

"She didn't like me, did she?" Catherine asks, fifteen years later, as we stand here in front of beautiful, naked, thirtysomething Rachel, and I know that, as usual, our thoughts are running side by side.

"More, I think, she liked me too much."

"And now? Does she still like you too much?"

She does and she doesn't, is what I think. Sometimes I know

that Rachel's obsession with me—there, I've admitted it—is really just another rung of her drug addiction. She thinks she loves me, but the truth is it's the idea of me and perhaps my unavailability that she loves, in the same way she craves hedonism and rule breaking. Drugs are an empty experience ultimately, and every time she wakes, or rather fails to sleep, through the slicing grittiness of dawn, she knows that. Loving me is an escape, a front, a screen to hide behind, and it's exactly the same with her coke habit. An out-of-control, drug-addicted life is easier to deal with than the harsh issues that lie beneath it: perhaps that she doesn't feel capable of being a mother, perhaps that she doesn't like herself enough to warrant the love of someone else. But enough of the cod psychology. Like Catherine says, Rachel has got farther to fall.

"She thinks she still loves me, though believe me, it's not based on anything real." We stare at each other for a long moment, and then I turn Rachel's portrait to the wall and we kiss.

Fifteen Years Earlier

We became something of a four, you, me, Jack, and Alexa. Most nights she and I would come over, and we ordered a takeaway or occasionally cooked and quite often went out to a party. I drank back then, which was probably just as well, because your lives were awash with booze—Chablis and claret and champagne and expensive brands of Russian vodka I'd never seen before. After the first fortnight spent almost exclusively in bed, I always got up the next day and went to the library or my weekly tutorials while the rest of you slept. I was a slogger, a habit I was unable or unwilling to break, while you had that casual, irritating intelligence that enabled you to read a text at the last minute without doing any background research and come up with an original, incisive commentary that always blew our tutor away.

One Friday I was hard at work in the library when a piece of paper fluttered down onto my books. I looked up and found you leaning over the top of my cubicle, grinning.

"Hello," you said in a voice too loud for the library.

"Hello," I whispered back.

Another drawing, pen and ink again, but this time a grand house with pillars and turrets and three rows of long, thin windows. My heart began to race. I knew instantly that this was your uncle's house, Shute Park, somewhere I'd secretly been desperate to see. Above the drawing you'd written, *Road trip*?

"Really?" I said. "When?"

"Now. Jack's driving, more room in his car."

Jack's car was more studenty than yours, a beaten-up bottle-green Golf that smelled of stale tobacco and spilled beer. Alexa was sitting in the front beside Jack, and when we got into the back seat, she popped the cork off a bottle of champagne.

"Here she is!" Jack said. "Let's get this weekend started."

He pressed eject on the CD player, lifted out a disc, and hurled it into the back. The bright red-and-yellow *Screamadelica* slotted into its place.

"We wanna get loaded!" he cried, putting his foot on the accelerator so that we shot past a group of earnest-looking students on their way into the library.

"It's Friday, losers!" Jack yelled out of the window.

The journey seemed to take only minutes, though perhaps the champagne was blurring my sense of time. One moment we were on the outskirts of Bristol; the next we were turning in between two stone pillars, and my stomach began to flutter with anxiety.

The drive was long and tree lined, which I'd sort of expected, but the house—we turned a bend and there it was, quite suddenly, like a mirage—was even more incredible than your drawing.

I gasped, and Alexa laughed.

"Magical, isn't it?" she said.

What was I doing in a relationship with someone who lived in a house like this?

"One day, my child, all this will be yours," said Jack, making his voice thin and old and wavering.

It was as if he'd read my mind. I felt like an impostor in the face of all this grandeur, and he knew it.

He slammed the car to a stop in front of the house, punching the horn once to announce our arrival. I was in awe of Jack right then; to me his confidence seemed out of reach and overwhelming.

The front door was opened by a small, dark-haired woman whom you introduced as Mary.

"Hello," she said. "Your uncle's in the library, waiting for you."

In the hallway, both you and Jack sniffed the air.

"Mary!" Jack said. "Don't tell me. You've made the pie, haven't you, you amazing woman," and she laughed.

"Yes, of course you're having chicken pie."

I recognized the music before we got to the library: Bob Dylan, *Blood on the Tracks*; you played it all the time. There were no books in the library, just a huge fireplace at one end with leather sofas in front of it, and a sideboard stacked with decanters of spirits: liquids of amber, gold, and brown, bottles of gin and vodka lined up beside them. Your uncle was stretched out on one sofa with a glass balanced on his stomach, but he stood up the moment he saw us. He was tall and thin and surprisingly handsome; I don't know why I hadn't expected that. He wore a blue paisley shirt with jeans and embroidered velvet shoes.

"The reprobates are here. Good. About time."

He hugged you first, then Alexa, then Jack, and finally he offered his hand to me.

"So you're Catherine. I was beginning to wonder if you might be his imaginary friend."

He pointed to an ice bucket on the table in between the sofas.

"We're having champagne in your honor," he said, smiling at me, and in that instant I relaxed.

Here I could be whoever I wanted to be.

Everything was perfect about that weekend. Your uncle treated us like equals, the first adult I'd ever known who did that. Over supper in the kitchen—Jack was right, the pie was incredible—we talked about music and parties and art. Your uncle was a collector; he took me into the drawing room, an old-fashioned room with sprigged wallpaper and highly polished furniture, and there on the wall facing us was a naked man sprawled across a snooker table, poised to take his shot. Eye-watering nudity aside, it was a feat of geometry, this painting.

"Francis Bacon," I said.

"Hideousness is something I like in a picture," he said. "Do you?"

We sat up late in the library that night, playing through your uncle's record collection, and I began to understand your obsession with blues and rock and roll; it came from him first. We must have listened to at least three Rolling Stones albums throughout the night—*Exile on Main St.*, *Black and Blue*, *Sticky Fingers*. But there were some Elvis ballads too, and early Leonard Cohen, and quite often Alexa segued in with something unexpected. I remember her choosing "Piece of My Heart," Janis Joplin, which your uncle loved. I've never been able to hear it without thinking of him since.

"A woman of taste," he told Alexa. "I thought as much."

I was struck by your closeness to your uncle. Quite often I'd find myself straining to overhear conversations between the two of you, filtering out the music or Alexa's incessant chatter to pick up on what was said. I heard him telling you about his lover, how they'd split up and were now back together again. He seemed to be asking your advice.

"You're happier when he's around," you said. "He's good for you."

"Same back at you," your uncle said. "She's good news, your girl."

You laughed and looked over at me and I felt a sharp little thrill at being the cause of your newfound happiness.

I remember thinking, Good, you've got someone who loves you, someone other than me and your friends. It seemed important.

The next day was hot, and we lay on rugs in the garden, reading the Saturday papers and drinking homemade lemonade that Mary brought out for us. Jack had driven into the village to buy the *Mirror*, and he was reading out its most ludicrous stories.

"Listen to this," he'd say, and we'd all look up from our own papers and take notice of him instead. That was the weekend when I began to realize how much he craved your attention. Everything he did was designed for your amusement. I felt a little sorry for him; it looked exhausting.

It was Jack's idea to go swimming.

"Not in the pool," he said. "Let's go down to the lake."

"Good luck with that," your uncle said. "It's freezing cold and choked with weeds. You'll last about five minutes, I reckon."

We took blankets and towels, and Mary packed up a picnic: homemade Scotch eggs, I remember, with bright orange yolks, and coronation chicken sandwiches. Your uncle produced more champagne.

"The only thing to drink at a picnic," he said without irony.

The lake, on the edge of your uncle's land, was like entering a secret wilderness, an oasis entirely screened by poplar trees. There was a little wooden jetty, with a rowing boat tied to it.

"Look. We could go out in the boat," I said, but Jack shook his head.

"Good try, Catherine," he said. "But we're going to be swimming."

None of us had bathing suits, and after lunch, fueled by champagne, Jack and Alexa stripped off easily, not a moment of embarrassment as they ran naked into the water, Alexa shrieking at the cold.

"I can't take all my clothes off," I'd said to you, urgently, when you began to undress.

You leaned over and kissed me.

"Fine," you said. "Keep your underwear on."

Even so, I felt self-conscious walking into the lake in just my bra and pants; you, out of deference to me, I suspected, had also kept your boxers on.

"Prudes!" Jack shouted. "Hurry up. It's fucking freezing."

Alexa kicked her feet, sending up great white arcs of spray to splash us.

The water was cold, that deep, cutting, bone cold, but after a minute or two of hard swimming we'd warmed up enough to float on our backs, the four of us in a row. I remember looking up at the clear blue sky and thinking that I had, finally, been accepted by your friends. Our remaining years at university stretched ahead, a glittering view of unhampered paradise. If only I'd known what was to come.

Now

It's all about dissociation these days. The whys and the wheres and the how-tos, as if I'm a floating balloon that has simply snapped its string. Greg seems to think he can fit all my pieces back together by taking me into the past, those times when I was known to disconnect. No easy task when you're dealing with a mute.

He talks. I listen or don't listen. But his words are in my bones, a slow-burning arthritis; they cut with the clarity of a scalpel.

He's talking about my mother; he has a photograph of her that Sam must have given him, and he asks me to look. One quick glance is all that's needed; this picture lives beside our bed at home. She's suntanned and laughing, head thrown right back; Sam used to say it reminded him of me.

"I think you're scared of pain," Greg says. "Lots of people are. You think that if you barricade yourself into this shell, into this wall of silence, you won't feel the pain. Trouble is, you won't feel anything else either.

"When you lose someone you love," he continues, "their absence is everywhere. Every room you go into, every house you visit, every shop, every street, every park is marked by the fact that they are not there. But that doesn't stop you searching for them."

He lowers his voice.

"I think you're still searching, Catherine, aren't you?"

Idiotically slow on the uptake, the day my mother died, I

understood what absence meant. No more. Ever. No talking, no telling, no listening, no touching. My aloneness was infinite.

She died in the middle of the night, and on some instinct I woke up and walked out into the corridor to see my father putting her pillows and duvet against the wall. So I knew. Her bedding was no longer needed.

I went to see her, not breathing, perfectly still. No chance to say goodbye. To say, Don't go. Stay a little longer. Another hour, another night.

And then I was gone too, Greg's snapped string, perhaps. There was a girl who floated somewhere, watching the drama of this person in her father's arms. "Catherine, Catherine, Catherine." He called her name, but for a moment she could not hear him. For a moment she could not see, hear, listen, or feel. For a moment there was nothing.

Four Months Before: Catherine

We are just leaving the studio when my mobile rings and Sam's number flashes up, sending me into a spiral of panic. I let the phone ring on to voicemail and then I go off on my own to the rose garden and sit down on a bench, waiting for the message to come in, smiling with relief when I hear it.

"Mama! It's me. We miss you. Call us!"

Daisy on Sam's phone. This I can handle. I love the way the kids sound much younger than they actually are whenever you hear them on the phone. When I call back, she picks up all breathy and excited, sounding about five years old.

"Where are you, Mama?"

The question I've dreaded.

"Sitting in a beautiful rose garden at a friend's house."

"Which friend? Is it Liv?"

"No, someone you haven't met yet. Liv is here too, of course."

My heart beats a little faster as I spin this version of the truth, and I quickly follow it with something else. "Tell me about your day. What have you been doing?"

They have been crabbing at Mevagissey, sitting on the harbor wall, dangling lines studded with cubes of bacon. Cornish pasties afterward, and ice creams from a shop that had thirty-two flavors. I miss them suddenly, with a sharp, savage ache. Their smooth, suntanned skin, their high voices, their black-soled summer feet. Daisy's laugh, surprisingly deep, a gin-soaked fishwife's cackle, we always said. Joe's obsession with absurd random facts and talking-dog videos.

"I miss you," I say.

"Then come and see us, silly."

"But you'll be home soon. Only another day or two."

The conversation is over, apparently, for Daisy hands the phone to Sam and I have no preparation, none at all, just his voice on the other end of the line with its faintly northern intonation.

"Hey."

He sounds distant, from another lifetime almost. This man I am supposed to love. There is so much to say that for a while, perhaps a whole minute, we say nothing. I sit here on the stone bench, heart racing.

"How are we going to work it all out?" Sam asks eventually.

"We'll talk. When we get home, we'll talk."

"You must have been thinking about it."

A wave of guilt breaks over me. Of course I've been thinking about Sam, but not as much as I should have done. For the past twenty-four hours, I have been completely taken over by my love, lust, obsession—all three, probably—for you.

"The truth is, I'm trying not to think about it too much. But whatever we do and however we do it, we'll make sure the kids are OK and that we're OK, you and me. As much as we can be."

"Do you think you can forgive me?"

"Oh Sam, I already have. I know why you did it. I understand. It's not about that anymore, not about Julia, I mean."

"It never was, not really."

"No."

Your name again, there between us, a ceaseless silent echo, just before we end the call.

"Do you want to talk about it?" you ask when I come to find you a little later, but I shake my head.

What would be the point? Neither of us wants to face reality when our time together is so short. Neither of us wants to talk about the fact that I'm married with two children, and the thought of leaving them or forcing them to live without Sam is inconceivable. The truth, the one we try our hardest to avoid, is that I married the wrong man. But there was a reason for that.

In the afternoon you decide to take me to Colton House for a late lunch. I'm pretty interested to see this notorious shrine to decadence after the years of reading about it: the media frenzy in the papers when it opened; the outrage from those who don't get through the censorious selection process, the gloating from those who do. I'm not at all surprised that you are a member, a favorite tabloid bad boy not so long ago, the fucked-up posh kid everyone loved to write about.

"So," I ask, "is Colton House really as horrible and pretentious as people say?"

You smile your usual smile.

"Yes. You'll love it."

Three or four times a week you'll come here, you say, for a session with a personal trainer, to use the gym or the indoor pool and then have breakfast with the papers. Sometimes it's an extended lunch with your friends, or dinner in the private dining room for someone's birthday.

"Most days Jack or Harry will call and say, breakfast? Lunch? Bloody Mary? And even if they don't, there's always someone I know if I feel like company."

The temperature change is instant. Do you feel it as I shoot my head around and stare out of the window at the speeding green, the curving, dipping landscape of your paradise? Always it will be like this, those names enough to choke me. Jack, especially Jack; every time I hear his name I am taken back to a place where I don't want to go. Instead I try to focus on the landscape, the hedgerows already burgeoning with red and purple, forced by summer's extended heat into a new season. I catch glimpses of rosehips, sloes, blackberries, and I can think, more calmly now, of my daughter, who loves little more than a blackberry-picking expedition, filling her Tupperware box with the blackest, ripest berries, which I would then turn into a crumble (or, quite often, throw into the bin a few days later). With each of my children, especially when they were small, there was something so touchingly optimistic about gathering fruit, trailing scooters or tricycles as we worked our way along the hedgerows; those were moments of pure innocence for me, regained, relived, utterly absorbed.

Your phone pings with a sequence of arriving texts, one after the other, and eventually you pick it up from the side pocket and drop it onto my lap.

"Switch it off for me, would you?"

"Someone's keen to get hold of you," I say, and as I click the little button on the side of the phone, I catch sight of the message on the screen.

CATHERINE?!! Surely some kind of joke? Rx

"Nice text from Rachel," I say, and my throat seems to close over, just mentioning her name. Over the years, I have known about you and Rachel; I couldn't not have seen the pictures, the two of you staring out from some glitzy backdrop or other, champagne glass in hand, you a few inches taller than her, both bored and unsmiling, as if willing the photo to be over so that you could return to your superior private world. But it was the nude portrait that really undid me, reinforcing the fact of your togetherness in a way I simply wasn't prepared for. Her nakedness, of course, your knowledge of her body, the way she looks out at you with the faintest smile, a lover's joke.

You, I realize it now, are the kind of painter who can effortlessly portray emotion and mood; it separates you from all those amateurs who can render a perfect poppy-stippled cornfield with their A-level brushstrokes and still leave you thinking, so what? I remember staring at an oil painting of your favorite view, and quite apart from the landmarks, the hills, the cathedral, the tor, it felt as if I could actually touch the weather; there's a sense of grimness as the light begins to fade, but also your melancholy as you painted it. With the painting of Rachel, it wasn't so much the nudity—breasts, bush, nothing spared—but the visceral sense of sex, good sex, probably fantastic sex, that actually killed me. I know all too well how good that sex would have been.

"I sent Rachel a text," you say now. "The news is out, they are all going crazy. You can probably imagine."

"But I haven't even told Sam."

"It's all right, I've asked them to keep it quiet. They won't say a word."

They. Does that mean you also told Jack? The last time I saw him was at a party in my final year. My mother had died a few months before; I was in so much pain and I didn't know what to do with it. I locked it away and tried to impersonate the girl I'd once been; I don't think I managed very well. It was rare for me to go out, but for once, just a few weeks before exams, Sam had insisted.

"Come on, a last fling before finals."

Jack caught me alone, waiting for Sam to come back from the bar. I stood frozen in the headlamp of his gaze. Big, overdramatic kisses on my cheeks, rapturous greeting.

"It amazes me that we share the same university town and yet I never see you," he said, as though bumping into me was the best thing that had ever happened to him.

I said nothing while my heart pulsed the drama of my mind. It didn't last more than thirty seconds. Sam came back with two glasses of wine, took my elbow, and led me away without even bothering to acknowledge Jack.

"Catherine?"

Your voice nudges me from bleakness.

"You're worrying about things that aren't going to happen. We're not going to see Jack or Rachel or Harry. I've promised you that. And we don't have much time left. Don't you think we should just enjoy it?"

"I'm sorry."

You smile as if it doesn't matter, as if we can step over my demons and pretend we're the people we once were. And I tell myself to try harder.

Colton House is every bit as impressive as the papers would have me believe. You arrive via a long, tree-lined drive to the house, with its famous Georgian exterior of honey-colored stone. It's a beautiful building, a Jane Austen dream, but in comparison to your place it's nothing, that's the funny thing about it. The bar has been raised so high I feel almost disappointed.

On the way to the main house, we pass the swimming pool—a long, slim, infinity-edged affair filled with shrieking children and surrounded by tanned, toned mothers reading magazines or chatting idly to friends: another day of the summer holidays ticked off with glorious ease. Oh, it's a different life, this one, no catching a bus to the germ-filled leisure center, no trailing ten deep round the V&A, no squeezing onto the only square of sand available as far as the eye can see. Even so, I'd rather be us, I think, but then

I remember—there is no us, not really, not anymore. There's my children, my boy and girl, mackerel fishing or rock pooling or any of the other impeccably chosen, wholesome activities their father has organized, and there's me, strolling toward this infamous headquarters of elitism, byword for excess, for everything that Sam most despises, on the arm of my secret lover. I hate myself for my deception, but that doesn't make it any easier.

We're greeted by a tall man wearing the kind of intensely fashionable high-maintenance beard that Sam loves to hate.

"Matt, this is Catherine," you say, introducing me, and we follow him through the bar—windows looking out across parkland scattered with deer, two well-known musicians drinking beer at a circular bar—and out onto the terrace to a table that has been laid for two. The fabulousness of this place, I'm getting it now.

Most of the tables out here are full with holidaying families, teenagers glued to smartphones, parents slightly tipsy on their almost-empty rosé, a trio of men talking over beer and discarded laptops, a young couple, sharing pre- or postcoital oysters—do you notice as I do, for they are the ghosts of you and me back in the day. There's a pretty, dark-eyed mother and her friend, working their way through a bottle of champagne while her small daughter plays with a puzzle, and a loud table of mixed ages and genders, all of them smoking and drinking, unanimously dressed in black. It feels like the ultimate hideaway, quietly luxurious in that every single detail, from the blue linen daybeds to the smoked-glass ice buckets, has clearly been agonized over, and discreet in the sense that staff appear just when you want them and disappear when you don't. Even at this hour there's an air of wrongdoing, of rule breaking, a hedonism that that seeps from every corner. Anything might happen here, you feel, anything at all, and it wouldn't matter because no one would breathe a word.

Matt is back with a bottle of champagne, which he opens expertly and pours into two glasses.

"*Fruits de mer*?" he asks, disappearing again before you can answer. When you see me looking at the champagne, you tell me it's vintage Pol Roger and that Matt knows to bring it without being asked. You tell me this without a glimmer of irony, and the disparity between us suddenly seems vast. This life you lead, is what I'm thinking. This fabulously indulgent life. What can it be like to have everything you want, all the time? Is it enough?

One of the reasons why I followed you through the years, with my bloodhound instinct for a new feature or diary piece, my feverish late-night searches online, was that I wanted to know if you were happy. I'd made my choice, or rather I'd had it forced upon me, and there was no going back; no amount of rubbing out or coloring in could change that. But had I done the right thing for you? I wondered, as the years passed and the dust settled and the wound grew if not less, then less obvious. Were you and Rachel happy, the way you and I once were? I'd ask myself as I pored over some new photograph, drinking in her professionally blow-dried hair, her beautiful unsmiling face. But of course the photographs could never answer that, just as my catalog of family life, the endless mobile phone snaps, the videos and scrapbooks I make for Sam each Christmas, doesn't tell the full backstory either.

An ease falls across our afternoon. There's good warmth in the sun, the champagne is perfectly cold, and the seafood is even better than our first lunch in that salt-streaked blue hut. While we eat, you tell me about Harry and Ling, the only girl ever to have made an impression on him.

"It was instant, a love-at-first-sight thing, for Harry, anyway. Ling took a bit of convincing, I think. But they were married within a month."

"Doesn't that worry you? How can you know someone properly in a month?"

"I was worried until I met her. Then I understood. She's exactly right for him. She's smart and funny, and he's much happier with her around. And they seem to be besotted with each other."

You tell me about Harry's twenties, "a loveless and pretty lonely decade, I'd guess on reflection, though none of us realized it at the time. It wasn't that girls weren't interested in him and his great big house and his title, because they were, but something, somewhere stopped him. Repression, I guess. This winter he decided to go traveling. He wanted to do it properly, so he bought himself a backpack and flew to Malaysia. He traveled through Indonesia, Cambodia, Vietnam, the hippie trail. And he sounded so energized and full of life whenever he called up; the trip really changed him. Thailand was the last stop, where he met Ling. He sent me a text. 'I got married today.' I asked him why he decided to marry her, and he said, 'I knew I couldn't be without her. And luckily, she felt the same.'"

"So it's a proper love story," I say, and you smile your funny smile and I know you're thinking about us, about our love story and the parallel universe we once inhabited so briefly.

I'm trying to keep myself away from that crossroads, the wrong turning I could never get back from. When you and I were together I was happier and more alive than ever before or since. Anything seemed possible, and then, suddenly, nothing. My world literally shrank overnight.

I begin to tell you about my children, trying, I think, to anchor myself back into my real world.

"Joe seems pretty serious when you first meet him," I tell you. "I was still grief-stricken when he was born, and his babyhood was quiet; we didn't mix much. But he's funny, he can do these pitch-perfect impersonations within minutes of meeting someone. He'd have you straightaway, voice, mannerisms, everything. Whereas Daisy is his complete opposite. She's incredibly confident and self-assured. She always speaks her mind, whether you like it or not."

You reach for my hand.

"You were like that when I knew you," you say, but your voice is kind; there's no judgment. I know the question you want to ask: What happened to change you? And I also know that you're not going to ask it.

"Are you ready to go?"

You press your thumb into the center of my palm, and now I know exactly what's on your mind. You're thinking of this morning, remembering how it was me who took control this time, teasing you, making you wait, until you could no longer bear it. I want to do that again, I want to make you feel the way I feel, desperate, erotically possessed, so much so that I might just rip off all my clothes and lie down here in the middle of the terrace, pulling you down on top of me. The thought of it is making me smile, and you say, "What?" as you reach into your jeans pocket for your wallet, although your own smile tells me that you've probably guessed. Our eyes are fixed on each other, the corners of your mouth turning upward this time, when a shadow falls across the table, and a voice—loud, look-at-me, public school remodeled as estuary—cuts right across the last fifteen years and plunges me into gloom.

Four Months Before: Lucian

"There you are!" says Jack, coming up to our table just as we're about to leave. Celia is right behind him, without her baby for once, and dressed for nighttime, it seems, in big, bold earrings and a low-cut top.

"Catherine! Great to see you again, it's been so long," says Jack, stooping down to kiss her on both cheeks. She stares up at him in wordless confusion. I feel a little confused myself. Pleased to see him, guilty that I've somehow broken my promise to Catherine.

"This is Celia, my wife," Jack says. "All right if we join you?" He's already scouting the terrace for extra chairs.

"Actually, mate, we're just leaving," I tell them, hating how cold I sound but also aware of the look on Catherine's face. Not quite horror, but something close. "Catherine and I haven't got very long together, so we sort of need to spend it on our own. Don't mean to be unfriendly."

"You are joking. The girls are on their way down, Harry and Ling are coming over. We're all meeting at yours. We popped in just now, and Mary said you were here."

"We booked a babysitter," Celia says. "We did try to let you know, but your phone was off."

"It's meant to be a surprise. A good one."

Jack laughs, but Catherine doesn't. She's staring down at the table; she hasn't said one word. I take her hand in mine, but it's like holding a dead fish. I'm not sure what to do. I watch as Jack leans forward, shouldering his way into Catherine's line of vision, forcing her to look at him.

"Catherine?" he asks, with his calculated, fail-safe smile. "Surely it's OK if we come over for an hour or two? The girls really want to see you. We all do. It's been so long."

"Sure. It's fine."

Her voice is flat and unenthusiastic, kind of rude. She doesn't smile back.

"Let's make it a quick one," I say, and Jack looks at me and rolls his eyes.

"Like that's going to happen," he says.

Jack and Celia follow us home in their Land Rover, and though the journey takes fifteen minutes, Catherine barely speaks.

"Honestly, it doesn't matter," she says, when I try to explain that I had no idea my friends were coming over. "It's nice that they want to see me. But I can't stay long. I'll have to get home."

"Just give me an hour and I'll get rid of them," I tell her, and she nods.

"Of course," she says, but the afternoon's color has faded. I'm not even sure what happened. It's as if there is a barrier between us, a paper-thin sheet of something dark and unformed.

The library is empty, so we head on to the kitchen and hear the girls' voices, a wall of noise and loud, shouty, overindulgent laughter. I do love them. It does thrill me to hear them, even after all this time.

"Think of it as a reunion," I tell Catherine just before we open the door. "Which is what it actually is."

She pulls off a weak smile. "Rather than the lions' den, which is how it actually feels?"

We walk in to a shattering volume increase, mainly Alexa screeching at Catherine.

"Catherine! Oh my God. I can't believe it!"

They were once so close, Catherine and Alexa. I feel a sharp little moment of grief at the way it all ended, not just our love affair but the friendships too.

She grabs Catherine into an intense, bosom-crushing hug and I love her for it, but it leaves me and Rachel eyeing each other on either side of the island, and ten seconds later, which comes as no relief whatsoever, we are dealing with the arrival of Jack and Celia. We are all connected by sex, is what I find myself thinking, somewhat inappropriately, and suddenly the age-old foibles and indulgences, the background wallpaper to our comfortable, me-centric lives, begin to feel awkward, ungainly, wrong. Me, Rachel, and Catherine. Jack, Celia, and Alexa.

"Cocktails?" I suggest. "Library?"

I'll make cosmopolitans. Vodka, cranberry, a little grenadine, a dash of lime. Ingredients, I hope, with the power of change. In the library, Celia hijacks Catherine onto one of the sofas while Jack, Rachel, Alexa, and I loiter around the bar like a circle of misfits. So much to say and none of it sayable: it's often this way with us.

"Make them fucking strong, darling," Rachel says, which is enough.

"Aren't you seeing Max tomorrow?" I ask her, remembering now the long-awaited lunch.

"Yeah. And I'm meant to be in the office. Crazy to come down, probably, but I needed to take my mind off it."

The three of us run with this reasoning, even though we all know she is here because of Catherine.

"Where are you meeting him?" asks Jack.

"Byron Burger. Hugo's choice; I can't stand the place—all those nasty wipe-down tables. But Max is a burger fiend these days. Apparently."

Hugo, Rachel's ex, is a good guy, basically, whose drug intake tailed off once Max was born while Rachel's seemed to escalate. Rachel couldn't hack it, her onetime party partner metamorphosing from ally to judger, but the thing that really derailed her was her son's decision to separate from his mother. I hate the way Rachel hurts. This buried wound, guilt and shame branded into her soul. I'd change it if I could; I have tried, though perhaps not as hard as I might.

The drinks are made and Harry arrives with perfect timing, a bottle of Don Julio tequila held high above his head and his wife clinging to his arm. I want to laugh just to see them: the mind-bending wonderfulness of my awkward friend finding love long after we had all given up hope. Ling accepts a drink, which surprises me. In the few times I have met her, she has asked for Coke or water.

"I thought you didn't drink?"

"Hardly ever. He's been corrupting me," she says with a small smile.

"In other words, she's realized she'll die of boredom in this godforsaken backwater unless she gets a habit like the rest of us."

Harry takes his drink and pulls Ling in the direction of the sofas, leaving me alone with Rachel for a moment.

"So," she says, that one tiny word apparently a summation of all that has happened between Catherine and me. "I'm guessing this is Liv's doing and that's why she came to the funeral?"

"How did you know?"

Rachel shrugs. "Obvious, really. Why else would she be there? It's not as if she knew your mother. What about Catherine's husband? What about her kids?"

"He had an affair and they're taking a break to work out what they should do. I don't know what will happen."

"Just hope you don't get hurt, that's all."

"Me too."

The faintest, slightest fragment of a smile from Rachel, and my heart pulses a little at this shared realization, this information swap, my decade and a half of loving the wrong person, or perhaps the right one, just not this one, not Rachel. I watch Rachel take a deep slug of her drink.

"I'll always be your friend, Lucian," she says, though she turns away from me as she says it and I know, without seeing them, that her eyes are filled with unshed tears.

"Same," I say, but Rachel is already walking away to the other side of the room.

Catherine seems safe enough in her place on the sofa, still cornered by Celia and now with Ling on the other side of her. I watch her from across the room and try to work out what she's thinking, how the close proximity of my friends feels after all these years. Her long hair falls across her face and I cannot easily see her expression, but she sits, as if perched, on the edge of the sofa, listening to Celia and, less frequently, talking. Are my friends really so bad? I don't think so. I understand that my long-running on-off affair with Rachel makes this first meeting uncomfortable; I saw her coolness with Jack just now at Colton. And him so pleased to see her. It makes me wonder if she disliked him all along.

People often get Jack wrong. He's loud and overconfident in that rather public-school way; he gives the impression of having been born to wealth, though of course, I know differently. I remember his parents begging to be let off the last year's school fees, the lack of holidays (Jack didn't go abroad until I took him to Paris at eighteen), their despair at not being able to fill up the oil tank. The thing about Jack, which most people don't get, is that he is rampantly insecure. There is a splinter of dissatisfaction running through him, the sense that whatever he has is never quite enough. For some reason I can't even begin to understand, he wishes he were me, pure and simple. He actually said it once, even with the dipso mother, dead father, and indifferent sisters. "I wish I had your life," he said one night when we were up late drinking. "Fill your boots," I told him. "What's mine is yours, brother."

As to the others, well, Harry is the definitive Mr. Nice Guy, with his old-fashioned charm and Edwardian manners (perhaps Ling can bring him into the twenty-first century; none of us ever managed it). And Alexa, high-octane, over-the-top Alexa, only wants to be Catherine's friend again. How hard can it be?

"Who's up for tequila?" calls out Rachel to the room in general, and there's a heartbeat of quiet while we all realize at the same time that she's slurring.

"Careful, Rach," Harry says. "Remember you're seeing Max tomorrow. Maybe save the tequila for another night."

"Don't be ridiculous! Who do you know who can handle a bit of a party better than me and still cope perfectly well the next day?"

"Yes, but it's Max, and you'll have to get up early, and you're going to want to be feeling good for it."

"Oh fuck it," Jack says. "For God's sake, let's have one. I know I need it."

He heads over to the sideboard to fetch a bottle, and on cue Celia looks up from the sofa.

"Jack? I told the babysitter we'd only be a few hours at the most."

The room falls silent, as it so often does when Celia draws attention to herself. It is partly, I think, because she tends to misjudge the mood and tone of an evening. She'll ask Rachel about Max when it's clear to everyone but her it's the last thing Rachel wants to think about. She'll try to engage Harry in a conversation about politics when he just wants to get wasted. Also, we know—better than Celia, it seems—where her husband's priorities lie. I couldn't ask for a more loyal best friend, but as a husband? I'm guessing it's tough. Yes, he's still remarkable looking, that blond-haired, blue-eyed thing that seems to make most women swoon. Yes, he probably loves Celia in his own way, but what of the nights spent here, drinking too much vodka while Celia waits in her designer farmhouse for a husband who may not return before daybreak?

"Why don't you go on ahead," Jack says, adding "sweetheart" as an afterthought. He looks over at the sofa. "I haven't really had a chance to catch up with Catherine yet."

Catherine, who must surely have heard this exchange, doesn't turn her head or break her conversation with Ling.

Celia relents. Relief buzzes around the room.

"So long as we're home by eleven," she says.

The tequila is poured, eight shots lined up like medicine on a Chinese lacquered tray. The evening is gathering pace.

Four Months Before: Catherine

I am in a fish tank, that's what it feels like, submerged beneath a constant flow of water, barely able to comprehend the one-way assault of Celia's relentless talk. She has clung to me with a certain desperation, the outsider at the party, the girl no one wants to talk to, least of all her husband. If it weren't for my preoccupation with my past—and the way it has been hurled unceremoniously into the heart of my present—I would be feeling more sorry for her.

Jack stands beside you, talking while you mix our drinks, telling you about some film venture he's involved with, every phrase he utters weighted with self-belief.

"They loved the treatment, now it's just a question of getting the funding. But I don't see that being a problem with a project of this kind. Everyone's going to want a slice of it."

It occurs to me that perhaps you, with your limitless wealth, are his funding target. I wonder if you realize? And how much money you might have given him in the past.

When Jack moves over to the fireplace, you are left alone with Rachel, your heads bent toward each other, brown against blond as you talk. I can imagine your hands on her body, I can imagine her pretty, lipsticked mouth brushing across your skin. She is beautiful, in that carefully put-together way, with a glossiness, a sheen I could not even aspire to. Everything about Rachel seems to shine: her hair, her skin, her jewelry, her top—a T-shirt made from bronze and khaki sequins, which would be drab on anyone else. She is at ease in this life. I watched as she greeted Mary with a hug, I saw her taking bowls out of a cupboard and filling them with olives from the fridge, pistachios from the larder, the house and its way of life as familiar as her own.

Alexa is the same. I see the way she crouches down beside your uncle's vinyl collection, boxes and boxes of them, flipping through albums until she finds the perfect choice. Blur's "Girls & Boys," as it turns out, a direct bullet from our shared university past. How many times did we dance around the kitchen of your Clifton house, singing every word of every song on the album? There was a moment when Alexa was almost as close to me as Liv. She was infectiously upbeat, easy to love. And she was besotted with Jack. Their love story, like ours, was all-consuming. Glancing at her now, I catch the way she watches Jack at the fireplace and I see that she is still in love with him. Alexa and I, trapped in the vortex of our past.

Celia, when I can concentrate for long enough, is a revelation. Overenthusiastic and a little naïve, she seems like the exact inverse of Jack. It's hard to imagine them together. I know she has money, barrels of it, because you told me so, and I can just imagine him scanning parties, headlamp tuned in to rich heiresses, the clock ticking, his bank account draining.

"We met at a party two years ago," she tells me. "I noticed Jack the minute he walked through the door. Everyone did. They always do. And when he made a beeline for me, I just couldn't believe it. We talked to each other all night and got married four months later. It was a complete whirlwind, very romantic. My parents were worried we didn't know each other well enough, but Jack soon won them over. He can be so incredibly charming. When he wants to be."

There's a tiny pause, a minimal falter; I might not have noticed if I weren't so attuned to Jack's dark side. Celia's whirlwind ran out some time ago, I'm guessing. She leans forward, voice lowered. It's as if she's reading my mind.

"If I'm honest, Jack doesn't seem so interested in me and Freddie anymore; all he really wants to do is spend his time with Lucian and Harry."

"Not much has changed, then. At university they were inseparable. They didn't need anyone else."

"He didn't want a child, he did it for me. He's very good with Freddie, when he wants to be, but he can switch it on and off."

I think of Sam, a father at twenty-two, before he was ready, probably, but God, how he rose to the challenge. The thing about Sam is that he prefers fatherhood to anything else, not in a saccharine way—he just gets children, he likes being with them, it's his escape, his chosen indulgence.

"Lots of men are like that," I say, to make Celia feel better, although I'm not sure it's true. A generation ago, perhaps. The fathers I know are exactly the same as the mothers, rising in the middle of the night to administer Calpol, changing nappies as a matter of course. Why wouldn't they be?

"How long have you been married for?" Celia's question—unexpected, disarming—startles me.

"Me? Oh. God. Thirteen years, fourteen in April."

"You must have been so young."

"Yes. We were both twenty-one."

"And you're not together now. Do you mind me asking about it?"

Do I? The thought of Sam and the children cloaks me in panic. I am so far away from them, or that's how it feels as I sit in the heart of this glittering world, where cocktails are drunk and sequins worn almost as a prerequisite on an otherwise random Thursday night. Right now I crave my old life, my real life, quiet, measured, the opposite of this.

"Sam and I are having a break from each other; we're trying to work out what to do. I'm not sure how we'll handle it."

She leans forward conspiratorially, voice lowered.

"Jack says Lucian has been in love with you all these years. That he never got over you."

"Really? Jack said that?"

Celia smiles unexpectedly. "And obviously Jack likes to be Lucian's number one at all times. He doesn't take competition well."

"I remember," I say, though I want to push this knowledge away, the memory that must always come with it.

"Lucian and Jack, they just, well, really love each other. It's that three-people-in-the-marriage thing; sometimes I can take it, other times I can't."

Harry arrives now brandishing a bottle of gold-colored liquid, his free arm wrapped around his wife. My heart lurches just to see him again. The swooping vertigo of time travel, the sharp jab of the past. Harry standing in the doorway of my university flat, his voice loaded with emotion.

"I'm asking you, please, to stay away from him."

You may have forgiven me for the way I abandoned you with a cruelty and coldness that shocked everyone at the time. But that doesn't account for your friends. I was hated, despised, denigrated in certain quarters of university life for the rest of my time there. The heartless girl who'd brought you to the brink of a breakdown, refusing to explain why I'd left or to see you ever again. I remember the rumors that reached me in those god-awful weeks after we'd broken up. It was said you were drinking yourself to death, drinking right through the day and most of the night, vodka on waking, empty bottles of brandy littering your bed. Liv had found you alone and incoherent in the pub one night; the only words she could understand were my name and the tortured questioning over why I had left. Even she found it hard to defend me back then.

"You broke his heart," she said. "And then you ran off home without even trying to explain. All anyone wants to know is why, and I don't know what to tell them."

People spoke about your estranged mother, an adulterous drunk whom you blamed for your father's suicide. Suddenly you, who had been envied and feted, were a subject of pity and concern. And me? Well, I was universally abhorred for bringing about your downfall.

Despite my trepidation, I can't help feeling curious at this first sighting of Ling, the young woman who has captured Harry's heart. She is pretty and slight, the top of her head resting at Harry's shoulder, long hair that almost reaches her waist. What I notice, in the seconds before Ling and Harry reach me, is how they cling to one another in that slightly frantic way of new love. The incessant touching, the reluctance to be parted for even one moment. I remember it well.

When Harry smiles and says, "Catherine, I'm so happy to see you again," I remember how much I liked him, how much I wanted him to like me. At the time, losing his approval felt like the harshest blow.

He puts a hand on each of my shoulders and looks into my eyes. "It's been too long. This should have happened sooner."

It feels intense, this, a sort of apology, a smoothing-over of our checkered past.

"Yes, it should," I say, forcing myself to smile back at him.

He keeps hold of Ling's hand as he tells me about their naught-to-sixty love affair.

"We were married within four weeks of meeting each other," he says. "Lots of red tape, but we got it sorted."

"Harry loves to bribe people," Ling says, laughing at him. "He's very good at it."

"I was determined not to come home without you, that's all."

There are minutes of relief now, if you can call it that, when Harry goes off to join you and Jack by the fire, leaving Ling, Celia, and me, the outsiders, alone on the sofas. I watch them in their separate corners—Rachel and Alexa conferring in their expressive silent-movie language; Lucian, Harry, and Jack laughing and smoking by the fire—and it seems to me that they are connected as if by an invisible string.

There is so much I want to ask Ling, who sits beside me, still and composed, seemingly with no need to fill these first moments of silence.

I want to know what it's like being married to Harry, thirty-something aristocrat with his legendary twenty-three-bedroom house. What's it like living in Somerset, land of fields and sheep and druids, after her existence in one of the most frenetic places in the world? How was it leaving her family, when does she think she'll see them again, will they come here, have they even met Harry yet? But somehow all these questions feel too intrusive, and I struggle to find the right thing to say. In the end it's Celia who breaks the ice.

"Tell us how you met Harry, Ling."

"You know he was a guest in my hotel, right?"

She breaks off to laugh.

"When I say 'my hotel,' I mean I was on the front desk. And one day Harry walked in, Panama hat, great big baggy shorts, face glowing like a lobster from sunburn. And without thinking, I said, 'English?' And he laughed and pointed to his scarlet face and said, 'How on earth did you guess?' We got talking and we just sort of clicked."

"Did your parents mind you leaving Thailand?" I ask.

"They're used to me making rash decisions. I left home at fifteen to find a job in Bangkok. Started out as a maid in the same hotel and worked my way up. I was lucky, the owners are good people, they treated me like family, even gave me a room for a while. When I told my mother I was marrying a man I'd known only a few weeks, she laughed and said, 'Why does that not surprise me?'"

"But *who* you were marrying, wasn't that a shock to her?" Celia says.

It's something I've been wondering myself but didn't like to ask.

"I didn't know what I was walking into back then. Only that Harry lived alone, somewhere in the southwest, which meant nothing to me. On the plane to England he said, 'There's something I should probably tell you.' And I thought, here we go, here comes the dark past. He's killed a man. He's got some weird sexual fetish. But he said, 'My house is embarrassingly large. It might be a bit of a shock.' And when we drew up at the Grange, we both started laughing and couldn't stop. And eventually I said, 'I'll try to put up with it.'"

I'm so entranced by the story of Harry and Ling it comes as a shock when Jack's voice cuts across our conversation, clear and strong, a statement of intent.

"I haven't had a chance to talk to Catherine yet."

Yet. In his words—a surface pleasantry—I hear a smile that is meant just for me. I know what it would be like to look into those bright-blue eyes; I know exactly what I would find in them.

Something must be showing in my face, because Ling reaches out and places her hand on my arm. On her wedding finger is the biggest, brightest diamond.

"Catherine," she says, "would you mind showing me Lucian's

swimming pool before it gets too dark? Harry is going to put in a new pool, and he wanted me to have a look at it."

Outside, away from everyone, even you, for a moment I have the urge to cry. And Ling sees this, I think.

She says, "You don't like Jack, do you?"

I look at her, surprised. "Is it that obvious?"

She shrugs. "When he came over, I saw how tense you were. That's why I suggested coming out here."

"Thank you."

"I've only met Harry's friends a few times and I always have the feeling they'd rather be on their own."

"When Lucian and I were together it took a long time for them to accept me. And when we broke up I hurt him very badly, and they hated me for it. Even Harry, who doesn't hate anyone."

"We've all done things we're ashamed of," Ling says. "No one ever knows the whole story."

We have reached your beautiful swimming pool now and we stand in front of it, staring at the smooth sheet of water, which looks almost emerald green in the evening light.

I can see why Harry refused to leave Thailand without Ling. There is something about her that is instantly calming, and as we stand together in the darkening night, my fear of five minutes ago begins to dissipate.

Four Months Before: Lucian

While Ling and Catherine are out of the room, Harry corners me over by the sideboard, where I'm mixing more drinks.

"You know what I'm going to say, don't you?" His face is passive, but I know him so well.

"Yes. You're going to warn me about getting involved with Catherine."

"Words to that effect."

My friends know how drastically I fell apart when Catherine abandoned me—over-the-top expression, but that's how it felt at the time. I didn't simply fall apart. I took an overdose. It wasn't just the misery of our breakup; there was more to it than that. Let's call it a decade of childhood heartache, my father's suicide, my mother's lack of interest, a pervasive loneliness that had followed me through school and the first year of university, and that, despite the almost claustrophobic circle of friends, constantly threatened to overwhelm me. I'd bolted this stuff down inside myself and then Catherine came along, and the only way I can describe it is that it felt like I'd been traveling my whole life to meet her. She cured me, that's what I thought, in my hopelessly naïve twenty-year-old mind; she released me from the bitterness of my past, from that boy brutalizing his wrists in his bedroom, from the raging sixteen-year-old who left home without any clear idea of where to go. When she disappeared, literally vanishing without a backward glance, the darkness crashed over me.

I tried to find her, of course, staking out her flat until her best friend, Liv, took pity on me.

"She's gone home," she said. "You could try her there."

Her parents were kind but they wouldn't let me speak to Catherine.

"She doesn't want to speak to you. And she doesn't want to be in a relationship with you anymore," her father said on my third and final phone call. "I'm sorry, but there it is. I'm going to ask you to leave her alone now."

Leave her alone. I wasn't sure I could. What, never again talk to the girl who had finally made sense of my life? Never touch her again, never kiss the soft skin on the inside of her thighs, never hold her hand as I fell asleep? Never surprise her with breakfast when she woke? Never draw her, never undress her, never watch her eyes darken or hear her half gasp as I pressed myself inside her?

Harry saved my life. He'd seen me in the evening, vehemently drunk, violently morose, and though he'd gone home and got into bed, he had lain awake worrying. Eventually he got dressed again, walked over to our house, and found me unconscious on the bed, thirty minutes from fatality, apparently.

It wasn't Catherine I was thinking of when I popped out two strips of temazepam (stolen from my uncle's house for recreational purposes) and ground them into powder. It was my father, who had chosen the same route to escape. In those final moments I understood with piercing clarity what had made him do it. It wasn't that he wanted to die; simply that he no longer knew how to live. I felt the same.

When I came to in the hospital, weak, sick, appalled at what I'd done, Harry was sitting in a plastic chair pulled up close to the bed. He saw that I was awake and started to speak, then couldn't.

"Harry," I said. "Sorry." My throat was raw and my voice just a whisper.

"No," Harry said, eventually. "I'm sorry. For the pain you're in."

"You saved my life, Harry. What made you come back?"

He dragged one hand across his face. He looked shattered, a whole night without sleep.

"I just knew," he said. "I don't know how but I did. I couldn't sleep, I had this feeling that you were right on the edge."

"I'm an idiot."

"I'm going to get you through this," Harry said. "We're going to break it right down. We'll take it minute by minute to begin with."

A thought occurred to me, something that seemed so horrific I tried to sit up in my hospital bed.

"Can you promise me something?"

Harry rested a hand against my chest, pressing me back down. "Take it easy. Yes, of course. Anything."

"Catherine can never know. No one can know. Promise me that."

He did promise. But he also made me see that I couldn't keep it from Jack.

"Jack is like your brother," he said. "He has to know."

Harry didn't leave my side for the next few weeks. He moved into our house and sat with me through the days and nights like a mother nursing a sick child. He kept telling me I was better even before I was. He kept a log of each hour we'd got through, then each day.

"Two and a half weeks since you've seen Catherine," he'd say in his upbeat nurse-like voice. "I'd say that's something of a record."

We had an agreement: no one other than the three of us would ever find out what had happened, not even the girls. Jack, of course, directed all his concern over me into vitriol at Catherine.

"How could she leave you? How could she do that to you?"

He called her names I couldn't bear to hear, and in the end Harry asked him to stop.

"Let's just agree never to mention her again," he said.

And now Catherine is back, in the midst of my friends, sensing their wariness, their defensiveness, without knowing the real reason why. It's a little unfair on her, I guess.

"It was all a very long time ago," I tell Harry. "No matter what happens with Catherine, I'll never do that again."

It's the first time we've spoken of "that" in a long time.

"OK," Harry says. "I'm sure you can understand why I worry."

At the other end of the room, Jack, Alexa, and Rachel are shooting their way through Harry's tequila, watched by Celia, who sits hunched up on the sofa. She seems to be having a miserable time.

"Let's go and rescue Celia," I say.

Rachel, in particular, is wildly drunk. She's leaning against the beam above the fireplace, breasts jutting upward, a sort of inverse downward dog. Too drunk to stand, by the looks of things.

"Rach," I say, "what happened? You're completely wasted. You need to get your head down. Big drive tomorrow."

"I'll take you up, if you want," says Harry, moving toward her, but Rachel wobbles to upright.

"Just a quick sharpener first," she says, reaching into her pocket and pulling out a cellophane wrap of cocaine.

"Oh no, Rach." Harry, Alexa, and I swoop down on her, a cartoon dust ball of pleading and chastisement and recrimination. And then, above the maelstrom, Jack's voice.

"Just what the doctor ordered, I'd say."

The room slides. We could stage a countdown. Ten, nine, eight, seven, six . . .

Celia shrieks, no other word for it, and hurls herself up from the sofa.

"No way, Jack! Don't even think about it. You're so selfish. I've been waiting here for over an hour, we're late for the babysitter. We have to go."

I don't know what gets into Jack; it's so clear that Celia is in a meltdown.

"We?" he asks with a half smile that even I find infuriating. "You could go on ahead, couldn't you?"

Alexa tries to intervene. "Jack," she says, "you really ought to—"

But Celia shouts, "No!" and holds up a hand, a policewoman halting traffic. Less of a scene, more of a volcanic eruption.

"I've had it. You never think about me or Freddie. It's always about you. Everyone thinks you're such a great dad, they don't know what you're really like. You turn it on and off whenever you want to."

And still Jack isn't getting it.

"Oh come on, babe," he says. "Don't overreact. I can come home a bit later, can't I? You don't normally mind."

"Actually I do mind," Celia says quietly.

Her words linger in the air. There's a coldness and a determination in her voice that we've never heard before. Jack has the sense to rush over and wrap his arms around her.

"God, I'm sorry," he says. "You're right. You're absolutely right. I'm a thoughtless, selfish dickhead. Why do you put up with me? You should definitely trade me in for someone else."

He kisses her cheek, once, twice, three times, and scores a reluctant smile. He has a gift for his own repatriation; we've seen it many times. Jack and Celia leave, arms around each other, crisis averted, while the rest of us focus on getting Rachel into bed.

I haven't seen Catherine since she disappeared outside with Ling, and I am clenched with dread when I finally reach my own bedroom. Will she be here? Or has the pressure of seeing my friends caused her to flee? In the darkness I almost fall over her blue trainers, kicked off by the door, and I follow a trail of her clothes to the bed, euphoric with relief. "You're still here," I whisper into the blackness, but Catherine is asleep.

I reach out a palm and place a hand on her thigh, lightly, just for reassurance; I won't wake her.

I'd like to ask her how it felt being back among my friends after all this time. Did she feel the tension, the way it clung to the atmosphere, a density that at times made it hard to breathe? I'd like to tell her about the dark secret that binds Harry and Jack and me together, but I know I can't. A stupid, stupid thing that happened a long time ago. A moment of madness like my father's before me. I'm deeply ashamed of it.

Now

Alexa is here again, talking to Greg about me, about you, and the dramatic intertwining of our pasts. They are not quite out of earshot, and though they speak in lowered voices, I can hear every word. I try not to listen, I try to fixate on the garden outside, the greens and grays and browns, the unchanging backdrop to my newly tiny world. But your name, each time I hear it, cuts through with the clarity of ice.

"Catherine was hated at university. It must have been so hard on her."

"For breaking up with Lucian?" Greg says. "Surely breakups happen the whole time."

"Not like this one. She didn't explain why she left him and she refused to ever see him again. He just lost the plot. And everyone stopped talking to her, all our friends, lots of other people too."

Yes, I remember it well. Doors closing on me, one by one, another shrinkage of my world. In the library, I couldn't bear the stares and the whispering so I simply stopped going there. The old union coffee shop was obviously out of bounds, a mecca for you and your friends despite the dreadful coffee. I couldn't risk pubs or parties, not that the celebratory environment of either suited my permanent heartbreak. There was no respite anywhere and I existed within the walls of our little house in Saint Paul's, watched over by Liv first and later by Sam.

"Catherine just retreated," I hear Alexa say. "None of us ever saw her again. I thought it might somehow be important. For the way she is now . . ."

I hear Greg saying something about the events preceding my descent into mutism. Some of them I recognize, some of them I don't. The word that electrifies, though, like a lethal administration to the heart, is "suicide."

Four Months Before: Catherine

This morning, cocooned by the knowledge that we are alone again, I feel relief, almost optimism. I escaped this first meeting with your friends, the one I've spent so many years avoiding, without any acknowledged judgments (other than a few eye-watering looks from Rachel), no calamitous revelations to wreck the night.

You are still deeply asleep and I go downstairs alone to boil a kettle for tea. Earl Grey, loose leaf, without milk or lemon; I know all your daily habits now. While I'm waiting for the kettle, I wander through to the library, thinking I'll bring in some of the glasses and wash them up. I stop in front of the portrait of you in the hallway, a child of eight or nine. Your hair is lighter and combed into a center parting, and you kneel on the floor, bare-legged in high-waisted shorts, shirt tucked in, one hand resting on the collar of a black Labrador. It's sweetly old fashioned and hilariously unlike the boy I came to know a decade later, but the thing that strikes me is the way the artist has painted your eyes. You could say it's the glory-days simplicity of being nine years old, but I would tell you that these are "before" eyes; there's a simplicity, a serenity I have never seen. It reminds me that you never talk about your father's suicide except in the baldest, most graphic terms—"he blew his brains out," you might say, or "he topped himself"—and that in some respects you have just as many skeletons as me.

It's dark in the library, the curtains drawn, the air thick with last night's cigarette smoke, a litter of glasses on every surface. A voice looms from the darkness, startling me.

"What time is it?"

Rachel, curled on a sofa, a blanket pulled up to her chin, one exposed arm revealing the sequinned top of last night. Her voice is tiny, tragic, a deathbed voice.

"God, Rachel. Did you sleep here all night?"

"Haven't slept." And then, "Hate myself, obviously."

I see that she is close to tears.

"What am I going to do?"

I sit down on the opposite sofa.

"What time do you have to leave? It's still quite early."

"I'm not going. I can't."

"But you have to. Your son will be so disappointed if you don't."

I've spoken without thinking and I watch Rachel sliding her eyes away from me.

"I don't expect you to understand, Catherine," she says, and her voice is crisp with bitterness. "But it's better for Max not to see me like this. This is what he hates. This is why he left."

"Why don't I drive you? I'd be happy to if Lucian will lend me his car. Or I'm sure we could find a taxi, what about that?"

She shakes her head. "Thank you, but no."

She holds out both hands in front of her and in silence we watch the catastrophic tremors. I am wondering if I have the life skills to deal with this naked admission of addiction. Last night I found myself watching Rachel whenever I could. Partly I wanted to see how she behaved around you (with sadness, I thought, and not jealousy as I'd expected), but I also found myself noticing the way she drank. She refilled her cocktail glass from the jug constantly, sometimes when the glass was still three-quarters full.

Her speech was slurred long before anyone else's, as if she'd simply topped up from the day before.

"Strong coffee," I say now, with the voice of encouragement I use when my children don't want to go to school (a big breakfast, eggs and bacon, that's what you need, I'd tell Joe; for Daisy it was hot chocolate, with cream if we had it). "A long shower. Lots of water. I honestly think you can do this."

Rachel groans and slides back down into a horizontal position, and then you walk through the door, dressed only in a pair of jeans, your feet and torso bare. You are beautiful to me, always, and you fill this dark, stale room with instant brightness.

"There you are," you say. Then, "Rach, you need to get going, don't you?"

Rachel closes her eyes and mutters, "Please just go away, both of you," and you look at me, questioningly, so I patch together a quick summary.

"Rachel didn't get to bed last night. She doesn't feel well enough to see Max."

"Jesus, Rach. But we took you to the door of your room and said good night. Did you come back down? Why?"

"Obviously I did. Obviously I'm a mess, a disaster, a complete fuckup. Now please can you leave me alone?"

I watch you kneel down in front of the sofa and take one of Rachel's hands.

"Are you sure we can't work this out? There's still time."

"Let's drive her there. If we leave soon, she won't be late."

"Sure, we can do that," you say, without conviction. "Rach?"

She's balled up on the sofa with her back to us.

"No."

"Want me to text Hugo? And your boss?"

"Wait a minute," I say, but you just shake your head.

"No point delaying; much better to let them know. Trust me."

Rachel turns her head away, too shattered to respond, while you go off in search of your phone. As you leave the room you say to her, in the soothing tones of a consoling parent, "We'll go over and have lunch with Harry and Ling. That will help take your mind off it."

What you're doing is making Rachel feel better about the calamity that is about to unfold, the entirely selfish, entirely unnecessary wounding of her son. How could you get it so wrong? How can you not understand?

I feel close to tears as I walk across the room to draw back the curtains and let in the light. I open one of the French doors and step out into the garden and breathe in the late-summer sweetness. I am thinking of my own son, imagining him waking up in his grandparents' house, next to his sister in their matching twin beds. I am thinking of their dark heads and of the different ways they sleep: Daisy on her back with her arms flung out, Joe scrunched up beneath the covers, entirely hidden, so that sometimes I'd have to check he was there.

Rachel is your best friend, but I can't help feeling you've let her down. You seem to accept her alcoholism without thinking you have a responsibility to help her change. You seem defeated by it; you've given up. I think about my friendship with Liv, the way we've always told each other the hardest truths. When I left you, she stood by me, yes, but she was unequivocal about what she saw as my coldhearted rejection.

"You don't just walk out on people when it gets tough, not without an explanation. You don't just throw someone away when you don't want them anymore."

She knew, though, from the devastation I couldn't hide, that there was something I wasn't telling her, and that in leaving you I had effectively destroyed my own life.

I don't hear you come out into the garden, and when I feel your arms wrap around me, I give a little shriek of surprise.

"I know you're upset with me," you say, turning me around to face you. "But believe me, we've been here so many times."

"I just think we could have got her there, one way or another. I can't bear his disappointment. Or hers."

"Rachel is an addict." I hear how much that word hurts you. "But she's not ready to recover. Not yet. She's a grown-up, Catherine. We can't make her do something she doesn't want to do. All we can do is support her choices."

Thing is, I'm not so sure it is support. I think the technical term is enablement. You all wrap her up in this gilded, lawless world of yours and make a celebration of her choices: friends before family; freedom, not commitment; self-indulgence but never self-sacrifice.

Fifteen Years Earlier

Jack had given me a bottle of tequila for my birthday, which was your drink and his, never mine (a gift to himself, in other words), and so I hadn't got around to opening it. I'd had a shot of Jose Cuervo once and thought it filthy, the kind of thing my parents used to unblock drains. And the tequila Jack had forced me to drink at your dinner party hadn't impressed me either. I was strictly a wine or vodka girl back then, in the days when I still liked to drink.

"The thing about tequila, Catherine," said Jack as the three of us sat in your kitchen looking at the unopened bottle, "is that you have to persevere. It's like learning to drive."

He cracked the seal and placed it back down on the table with a smile that was irresistible.

"Look and learn, baby," he said. "Look and learn."

This tequila was pale gold and it was being served with quarters of lime, not lemon, and the obligatory saucer of salt. Jack went first, knocking back his shot glass as if it were water, then you, and finally the glass was handed to me.

"It's too full," I said, stalling. "It will make me gag."

The truth was, I hated being out of control. I had serious brakes. I could drink just enough to feel happily intoxicated and then stop, cruising through the rest of the night on my semi-high. I didn't chase obliteration like so many of my fellow students, and with you, more than anything, I wanted to feel present and awake.

Perhaps, even then, I knew we didn't have much longer; I'd sensed in some way our brutal end. But here I was on a regular Wednesday night, the exact day scorched into my mind, with the two of you smiling encouragingly as if I were a four-year-old child.

"All right," I said. "What the hell."

I licked salt off the back of my hand and tipped the drink down my throat, quickly sucking the lime you'd handed to me.

"Not so bad, was it?" Jack said, and actually he was right.

"It's almost delicious," I said, surprised.

"That's because your *birthday present*"—ironic emphasizing of words—"cost me a fortune. And it's your duty to share it with us."

I allowed Jack his little half truth. I knew that you would have paid for the tequila the way you paid for everything.

My next shot coming straight on the heels of the first was smooth and effortless, and by the third, I didn't need the salt or lime either.

Here are some things I didn't realize about quick, fast-paced inebriation. Laughter so physical and all-encompassing I was poleaxed by it, literally at times unable to stand, instead sinking to my knees, arms wrapped around my ribcage. Laughter that hurt. Inhibitions? What were they? After my fourth tequila, I was dancing alone, in love with the music and probably myself, the two of you watching me from the sofa. You smiling, Jack just watching. The bottle slowly emptying.

Four Months Before: Lucian

I've been coming to Eastcott Grange since I was thirteen years old, but today I'm struck by its grandeur, this twenty-three-bedroom Victorian palace, a boxy, pillared thing that was built to impress. It still amazes me that the architects were able to use traditional blue lias stone from Somerset and mullion windows and many other celebrated features and still conjure up something quite so ugly. It's an enormous great beast of a place, open to the public for four months of the year, with twenty thousand acres, a formal shoot, ornamental gardens, a forest, even a maze.

"Seriously?" says Catherine as we park up in front of the house. "This place is ridiculous."

She is grinning widely, buoyed by disbelief, and I'm happy to see it, happy that she's here with me, full stop. We have a day left together, a day and a half at the most, and I am trying my hardest to guard against the emptiness I am certain to feel when she's gone.

Harry opens the door himself, which is a surprise; normally it's Filip, his butler. The first thing he does is reach for Rachel and wrestle her into a hug (she's at the monosyllabic, buttoned-up stage of guilt, coupled with a monumental hangover; she didn't say a word on the way over).

"Gather you didn't make it to London after all. Sorry, Rach." His voice is so kind, I worry she'll start crying.

"Bloody Marys are what we need," I say.

We walk through the Great Hall, Alexa's wedges clattering across the black-and-white marble floor, Catherine gasping at the sheer insanity of this room: Doric columns, statues of Roman nobles standing fifteen feet tall on their pedestals. I always think there's a feeling of Dubai here: oodles of money spent re-creating a pseudo-basilica that no one spends any time in. Why would you? I may be biased, but I think my own ancestors got it right with Shute Park. Yes, it's too big, certainly for someone like me, a man with no dependents, but it has a feeling of warmth and friendliness about it despite the size, and I always feel, whenever I return there, that it is my refuge. I've stayed at Eastcott so many times, throughout the schoolboy years and our early twenties, through the inherent stiffness that came with Harry's parents being in residence and the more debauched decades of our late twenties and thirties. But in all that time, a good twenty years now, the place has never once felt like a home.

Two jugs of Bloody Marys are ready and waiting for us in the red drawing room, another stately, unappealing room, all tapestry wall hangings and brittle-thin furniture. Harry hands each of us a glass and then asks Catherine if she'll come with him to find Ling in the kitchen.

"She's really happy you're here," he says. "Why don't the rest of you take your drinks through to the birdcage?"

This is the one place at Eastcott I absolutely love, an orangery that was added to the house in the 1930s and is shaped exactly like a birdcage—or perhaps it's more of a wedding cake; an oval room, anyway—with a domed glass roof. It looks out over the cedar lawn, which is just as it sounds: home to a four-hundred-year-old cedar tree, where Harry and I used to smoke forbidden roll-ups back in the day, a green sheet of sloping smoothness that drops gently to a ha-ha just glimpsed on the horizon.

The three of us sit in pastel-colored Lloyd Loom chairs, drinks in hand, staring out at this indecent slice of rolling green England. Rachel is pristine with blow-dried hair and a freshly ironed white shirt, sunglasses worn inside the only clue that all is not as it seems. She's a past master at the immaculate appearance, her shield against pain, blame, and judgment. If I look all right, then I am all right, the mantra she hides behind.

Alexa says, "Funny how it's Catherine Harry has taken off to see Ling. Not one of us. Should we be insulted?"

"I think they spent quite a long time talking last night," I say.

There's a beat of silence before Rachel says, "And do we think she's actually going to leave her husband? Or is she going to vanish for another fifteen years?"

I offer a casual shrug, but of course the girls know me too well for this. Harry and Jack managed to conceal my shameful quest for obliteration, but Alexa and Rachel watched me unravel, the weeks of dangerous drinking (alcohol abuse the common denominator in my circle), the heart that refused to mend.

"I honestly have no idea," I say eventually, for this is the truth.

"She hides in that marriage, if you ask me," says Alexa. "It's pretty obvious that she has always loved you."

"The question is, what is it she's hiding from?" Rachel says.

"Sometimes I think it's my money she can't stand. And our lifestyle. Too debauched. Too degenerate. Too messed up."

"Rubbish," says Rachel. "Everyone loves what your money can buy, even if they pretend otherwise."

"Catherine's not like that," I say. "She doesn't care about money. Look who she married."

Rachel laughs, and Alexa says, "Bit below the belt, darling," but both of them are missing my point. I used to be so jealous of the man Catherine married. I used to measure myself against him, wholesomeness versus decadence, political passion versus political lethargy, a hard-won education versus the silver spoon. My self-esteem, never particularly buoyant, pretty much imploded when Catherine went back to Sam.

Alexa says, "If you knew why she left you last time, you wouldn't be going round in circles like this. It's ridiculous."

"She got cold feet, that's what happened. And then her mother was ill and she turned to Sam. The rest is history."

"Er, sorry," Rachel says, "but that doesn't explain the way she left you at the time, bolting when you'd gone off to see your uncle, leaving you that nothing of a note and then refusing to see you or ever explain what had gone wrong. There must have been a trigger for it."

"Only that she panicked and couldn't handle the intensity of it all, though the way she left was so cold and out of character, it never really made any sense to me. I've tried asking her about it, of course I have, but she freezes every time."

Alexa shunts her chair closer to mine and rests a hand on my arm, gold bangles dropping down to her wrist.

"Lucian. Darling. As your friend, can I tell you something?"

I nod, even though I know I'm not going to like what comes next.

"I think there's something strange with Jack and Catherine. Did you notice how they didn't exchange a single word last night? Which is pretty weird when you think how close the four of us once were; we were virtually living together for a while. And it made me think of something Jack once said to me at Bristol, soon after Catherine left you. He said she is not who everyone thinks she is. I've never forgotten it. What do you think he meant?"

"Jack loves to wind us up," I say, taking a furious slug of my Bloody Mary so that the vodka and spice burns the back of my throat. "It's his favorite pastime. And you of all people should know that."

I won't have this insinuation in my head, I won't have it. I feel sharp, hot tears forming in my eyes.

"Hey, guys, come on, don't fight," says Rachel, but she's in no position to help, with her brutal hangover and her Hadean guilt, so we sit in silence, glaring out at the well-watered lawn, and I count the minutes until Catherine comes back.

Four Months Before: Catherine

Harry's kitchen is a 1950s time capsule—mustard-yellow cabinets, cast-iron pans dangling from hooks in the ceiling, a rusting Aga that looks about a hundred years old. Ling is standing over the hob, stirring something in a wok, but she turns as I come into the room. There's warmth and familiarity in her smile; already it's as if I'm an old friend.

"Catherine!" she says as we embrace. "I'm so glad you came."

The room smells of ginger, lemongrass, and brave measures of Thai fish sauce. There are glass bowls filled with prawns and chunks of beef marinating in amber-colored liquid, the flesh flecked with specks of green and tiny pale half-moons of ginger. Beside them on the counter are twenty or more jars and bottles and packets with red and yellow labels and the distinctive Thai lettering. She picks up a jar and shows it to me.

"This is red limestone paste; I was surprised to find it. Filip drove me to the Thai supermarket in Bristol this morning—I was so glad, I bought the whole shop."

"You must get homesick."

"It's more that when I saw all these familiar bottles and jars and the crates of Thai vegetables and the huge fat bunches of herbs, I realized I could still eat all the things I love. And that made me feel happy, not homesick. I left my village six years ago, I'm used to living without my family."

I sit on a stool drinking my Bloody Mary, watching Ling as

she tips beef into the wok and leans away from the hot, splashing fat.

"Will they come and visit?"

"I hope so."

She hesitates for a moment.

"We haven't told anyone yet. But we're planning a wedding party. Harry wants to fly my whole family over. I keep telling him, there's a lot of us. You have no idea."

"You've certainly got the space."

Ling laughs.

"Crazy, isn't it? And craziest of all is that it already feels normal. My sister has started calling me Lady Muck. Harry thinks it's hilarious. This morning he brought me coffee in bed and said: 'Cup of coffee, Lady M?'"

Ling somehow manages to roll her eyes and look enchanted at the same time.

"Maybe I'll start styling myself that way. It has a good ring to it, no?"

To me the dining room is hideous, with its patchwork of framed paintings on the ceiling (robust nudes, cherubs with tactfully placed wafting skeins of fabric, that sugarcoated, mock-Renaissance style), gilded candelabras, a long polished table with a fierce, mirrorlike shine. The room is paneled in dark oak on the bottom half and hung with rose-pink damask wallpaper on the top half, where several po-faced portraits also line the walls. All that's missing is a red cord to keep the National Trust hoi polloi out.

Rachel and Alexa lounge in their gilt-edged chairs, entirely comfortable in these ornate surroundings.

"Is there an ashtray, darling?" Rachel asks, lighting up as soon as she finds one, and it feels all wrong somehow, like smoking in a museum. And after only a sip or two of wine, she pulls a face. "It's Riesling, isn't it? Can we have some rosé, Harry, it's a bit too punchy for my hangover," and Harry pulls out his phone, sends a text, and two minutes later, Filip is in the room, carrying several bottles of pale-pink rosé on a silver tray. If you're rich enough, it seems Colton House comes to you.

Lunch is wonderful, more delicious than anything I've eaten in a Thai restaurant, and it also puts Ling right in the center of attention. I see her slowly coming into focus to Alexa and Rachel, I see how she accepts it, this sudden beam of spotlight, without pride or shyness, just the same quiet confidence I noticed before. She tells Rachel, because Rachel asks—probably the first time she's asked Ling anything—about learning to cook in the village where she grew up.

"We were taught by all the mothers and aunts and grandmothers in the village. But there was one woman, Apinya, who was a really clever cook. She grew her own herbs and spices and she always tried out new things, like beef with bitter chocolate or fish-and-orange soup, and even on the days when rice was all we had, she would make something interesting, like spicy fritters with coriander salsa. I miss her food, I am always trying to remember it."

"It sounds such an idyllic way of life," says Alexa. "Why did you leave?"

"I wouldn't describe it as idyllic, exactly. Everyone in my village is very poor, if you saw how we live, you'd be shocked," she says. "We have enough to eat when the crops are good but there's never money for anything else. It's normal to go and work in the city so you can send money back to your family."

The room falls silent. All of us, no doubt, pondering the stark difference between Ling's childhood and her new life here, the equanimity with which she has accepted it.

Talk turns to your party, this time a roll call of guests; nearly all of them, it seems, from our shared past. I catch you watching me as the panic begins to descend, and I wonder if you're starting to understand. Do you see why I always want to run rather than face the past, I always want to hide away? Can you imagine what it is like to feel universally hated for one thing but to deserve that hatred for quite another?

"Charlotte Lomax is coming," Alexa says, firebombing her name across the table. "You'll remember her, Catherine. She used to hang around with us at the same time you did. She's married now, to Johnnie Wilson, that long-haired guy from the year above. He was into the Grateful Dead back then, the hair, the headband, the whole thing."

Memories I don't want filling my brain, a slowly rising bath of self-hate. Charlotte Lomax was probably the worst, a standard-issue Sloane with her shoulder-length blond hair, velvet hairband, and the solid-gold heart that nestled between her collarbones. She was in love with you, so it was said, and when I left you she tried to fill the void. It didn't work; you were beyond help at that point. Rumors on the ground said you were heading for a breakdown.

We may have shared a town, but we never came face-to-face again. I'd see you in the distance sometimes, ten seconds of looking while my heart beat faster, before I veered sharply in the opposite direction. We were at a party together once, for a few minutes, though you didn't realize it. I'd thought it safe, traditional student fare and not your kind of thing at all, post-pub, bring a bottle, at someone's flat in Bedminster, an unfashionable part of town back then. A snarl-up of bicycles in the hall, cheap red wine from polystyrene cups, the atmosphere dense with smoke. I was with

Liv, and we pushed our way through the crowds in search of more wine or faces we knew, and suddenly I froze, for there, standing together by the kitchen door, were the unmistakable backs of you and Alexa. She turned at exactly that moment and gave me a strange half smile, almost as though she had been expecting to see me, before taking your hand and leading you deeper into the room, my cue to leave.

I wasn't so lucky with Charlotte Lomax. It was right at the end of term and I'd almost made it through. My bags were packed and I was leaving for home that night.

"I've put your electric blanket on." I can hear my mother's voice even now; I can picture her changing my sheets and repositioning my teddy bears and unwrapping a scented candle, her one homage to my almost-adult self. I knew about the cancer by then, but we were in denial, the three of us, my mother, my father, and me. I was looking forward to that holiday at home with a fervid longing. I planned to shadow my mother morning till night. Just in case.

I'd gone to the library to pay off a fine, and perhaps because I was so focused on my trip home, I failed to spot Charlotte two people ahead of me in the queue. I'd reached the counter and endured the librarian's reprimand and ripped a check out of my Lloyds Bank checkbook when a voice called out to me: "Catherine Elliot."

And there was Charlotte, glinting earrings, pale lipstick, a bright-blue jumper that I'd slightly envied, I remember.

"I don't know how you can live with yourself."

Her voice was loud, too loud, and several other people in the queue turned to stare. Did they know me? Or her? Or you? Did every single person in the whole of this damned town know what I was really like, deep down, beneath the wholesome facade I'd tried to resurrect with Sam? I couldn't answer her, I couldn't ask what she meant or try to defend myself or do anything other than stand there, by the front desk, paralyzed by shame, rooted in fear. Abandoning you, my public crime, was well documented, but this hinted at something more. Was this it, the moment when the truth would finally come out? All I knew, as my heart banged hard in my chest, was that Charlotte Lomax seemed to be reading my mind. Living with myself was a near impossibility to be navigated each day. I woke to a nightmare and tried, inch by inch, moment by moment, and mostly with Sam's help, to find myself a little warmth; just a glimmer of it was enough back then. It seemed to me, as I stood dumbstruck in the library queue, that Jack had talked to Charlotte Lomax, that my secret was about to come out. I thought of your heartbreak when you finally learned the truth, and hated myself a little more.

I'm so lost in the past that it takes a minute to register the silence around the table, to realize that everyone is looking at me, waiting for my answer.

"Charlotte was never a fan of mine," I say. "Can't say I'd really like to see her again."

"But you're coming to the party, aren't you?" asks Alexa.

"Probably not."

Definitely not now that Charlotte's name has been mentioned. It's unnerving, this sudden scrutiny, this temperature drop, as if a blanket of cool has swept into the room.

"What's the problem?" says Rachel, still in her sunglasses. "Why wouldn't you come? I thought you said your children were in Cornwall."

Where to begin? Not with the truth, certainly. Not with the fact that I have spent so much of my life running from the past, I don't know how to do anything else; I don't know how to stop the running and the hiding and the lying. And I see that you know this, as you sit there across the other side of the table, watching me. There's no smile, not even the ghost of one, but I see something in your eyes that I've not seen before. You know. You are telling me you know. Maybe not the how or the why, but you recognize my shame, and beneath it the disesteem that fuels and exhausts me in equal measure.

And it's you in the end who answers Rachel.

"Catherine has no reason to come to the party unless she wants to," you say, voice sharp, conversation over.

Now

I feel as though I'm living inside a glass box. I can shout as loudly as I want inside this box, but no one will ever hear me. My crying goes ignored, my screams are just a whirlpool for me to drown in. The floor is carpeted in words, walls of letters that spill from my brain, an overflow of black ink. All these questions I cannot ask, all these answers I will not give.

"Do you remember what happened?"

They ask me this most days, and even though on the inside I'm burning, it hurts, it consumes, outside I remain blank. It's not just anguish; I have a physical reaction to this question too. When they ask it, my throat locks and my vocal cords freeze and my brain turns to ice.

Sam comes again today, and it is a relief to see him. He has the children with him, Joe in a new jumper, dark gray with blue sleeves, quite unlike anything he'd pick for himself. I wonder who bought it for him. Sam's mother, probably.

Sam looks thinner than last time, and tanned, although the tree outside tells me it's only the beginning of spring.

"I've started running," he tells me.

Joe, who rarely speaks, says, "He's even signed up for *Runner's World*, Mum. And he sits there for hours reading about compression socks."

I smile, just a small one, to show Joe I understand. Smile and hold his eyes for a moment, the way Greg has taught me. The smile is caught by Sam, who never misses anything, and the happiness in his face seems overblown for such a small thing.

"You're doing so well," he says. "You're making so much improvement every day. Greg tells me the therapy sessions are really starting to help."

Does he? Are they? Can it really help, this relentless churning up of the past, the daily guided walk into the heart of my pain?

I sense the slow build of these sessions and I know, of course, where they are leading. I know that sooner or later we will be taking a pickax to the door that has been closed—not just closed, but slammed shut, bolted, and padlocked—for the past fifteen years. I understand the rules of this game. Death first, the easy one, let's deal with that. And so Greg talks of my mother as if he knew her, as if he knew the way her hair—still deep brown with not one streak of gray when she died—remained resolutely flattened against her scalp no matter how much she blow-dried and backcombed and bouffanted, her word. "I give up," she'd say, slinging the hair dryer across the room. "Helmet head it is."

Greg doesn't know that she was beautiful but in that careless way, grabbing a blob of moisturizer on her way out of the house, smearing it into her cheeks on the drive to work, her only concession to glamour. She didn't need makeup or a bouffant. And she was always laughing, he doesn't know that. He can't hear her laugh like I can, a full-bodied, head-thrown-back guffaw that was at odds with her delicate appearance. He's got me thinking about her, though, I'll say that for him. And I have learned something new. It's all right to let a little bit of her light back in; it doesn't hurt as much as I'd always assumed it would.

"You'll be home soon, Mummy," says Daisy, interrupting my thoughts and leading me back to my family. "And we'll make cakes and go to the beach and sail the boat and everything will be just the same. You'll see."

She wraps her arms around me, my beautiful little glass-half-full girl, squeezing hard, her cobra squeeze, as if she can force her optimism into me by osmosis.

Fifteen Years Earlier

You put on *Sticky Fingers*, an album we'd listened to almost incessantly in our four months together. First song, "Brown Sugar," my least favorite but the one that usually invoked your Jagger impression—a microphone-toting snake-hipped strut. You did it perfectly. Suddenly the three of us were dancing. My balance was off; it was more weaving than dancing, and propping myself against you the moment the track changed. And then it was "Wild Horses," a song I loved so much, transported each time by the raw beauty of Mick Jagger's voice and the sorrow of his words, and I was dancing alone now, no self-consciousness, none at all, as I swayed with my arms above my head and my eyes closed. This song had always been for us, we said, for nothing else could capture the strength of our passion. We were young and sentimental and so newly in love—nothing would ever drag us apart, we thought, not even wild horses.

I was lost in the music and the song and it took me a while to realize you were standing in front of me, trying to talk to me.

"Catherine," you said. "Catherine."

I opened my eyes. I stopped swaying.

"What?" I said, smiling.

But your face was serious.

"I just got a call from my uncle. Didn't you hear the phone?"

You told me he was upset, that he'd broken up with his lover again and you were worried about him. Or at least that's what I imagine you told me, because the truth is I have no real recollection of this conversation.

And then you said you were going to go and see him, and this bit I do remember.

"To make sure he doesn't do something stupid."

We had a sort of argument, I think. I was paranoid about drunk driving and terrified of losing you when we'd only just found each other. Sometimes when you came home later than you said you would, held up in the pub, another drinking session with Jack and Harry, I'd lie in your bed, dreading a knock on the door. I'd picture the accident, your body lying motionless on the side of the road, and I'd lie in the darkness, brushing away silent tears until you came home and climbed into bed with me and made everything instantly great again.

I told you this sometimes.

"Silly girl," you always said. "Why must you think the worst is going to happen?"

But that should have been obvious. My best was so good, so dizzyingly, euphorically, absurdly good, I knew I wouldn't be able to live without it.

Four Months Before: Lucian

There are three crucial elements for a good party, in my view—the people, the booze, and the setting. Tonight we have a tried-and-tested guest list of three hundred, a committed crowd who always arrive with a fierce determination to get the best out of the night. No one will drive, everyone will drink, and most of them will be wearing something brand new: girls in the full kaleidoscope of colors, a sea of red, pink, blue, green, silver, and gold; men wearing suits, black, blue, and white mostly, though there's always the odd exhibitionist who likes to surprise in shocking pink. They will look their best and act their worst; there will be drunken breakups and illicit love affairs, random couplings that really ought not to have happened, and an easygoing, Woodstock approach to drug taking, anything and everything, anywhere and everywhere. Professional partiers, Colton House habitués and old university friends, some of them will even have traveled across continents to be here (Eliza and Georgina Kitson from Kenya, the Buxtons from Sydney, Jonathon and Lydia Maxwell from New York). The setting I lucked out with: two hundred acres of lake, woodland, and rolling green lawns, a purpose-built pool for midnight frolicking, a rose garden in full bloom for the romantically inclined.

I also take the precaution of hiring in a slightly strange character called Andrew Martin to oversee things. His official job title is party planner, though you wouldn't think it to meet him; ex-army and never seen without a shirt and tie, you'd have him down as a hedge-fund manager or a Lloyd's broker, something in the city anyway. The thing about Andrew is that he's really gifted at what he does, no request too bizarre, no detail uncovered; he is so thorough and obsessive that there is never anything left for me to do.

Six months ago he came down here with his paper-thin laptop and his Smythson notebooks and his three work phones and said, "Right, what's our theme?" And somehow or other we decided that this year it should be all about water—a nightclub down by the pool, a fleet of little rowing boats for the lake. As well as building a nightclub (an enormous team of workers and an afternoon's work from start to finish), this year Andrew is also importing a miniature club, which will be stationed down at the lake. As far as I can gather, it's a sort of lamplit coffin-shaped box for thirty with a DJ inside and two bouncers on the door. Andrew is very excited about it. I don't know anyone who gets job satisfaction the way he does (though you could argue that I don't know many people with jobs full stop).

By the time I get up and go downstairs to make coffee, Operation Party is already in full swing. Mary has a team of cleaners with her today, hoovers blasting in all corners of the house, the air pungent with wax polish and bleach. The florist has arrived from Bristol, two hippy-looking girls (they even have flowers in their hair) are arranging a human-size display of lilacs and blue-black roses in the hall, and a local fruiterer is unloading crates of pomegranates, lemons, oranges, and limes for the cocktails. From the kitchen window I see that one of the marquees has already gone up, and outside it a squad of empty spit roasts are lined up, a fearsome-looking tangle of spikes and hooks awaiting their pig carcasses. There must be thirty people on the lawn all fully engaged in party mode, lugging tables and unfolding chairs, shaking out tablecloths, arranging bunting, jam jars of flowers, and bowls of fruit, manhandling hay bales into a neat semicircle around the fire pits.

You'd think that I might feel something, a fragment of anticipation, perhaps, or a stirring of excitement, looking out at all this activity, at all these people working to provide me with the ultimate gathering. But instead I am thinking of Catherine's bag, already packed and stationed like an insult beside the bedroom door. I am reminded so much of last time. And yet I see no future for us, not really.

Last night after Rachel went to bed, Catherine, Alexa, and I sat up in the kitchen talking. Somehow or other Alexa started asking Catherine about her children, and once she started talking, it seemed she couldn't stop, it just poured out of her. The three of us spent a good half hour trawling through all the photographs on her phone. There was Sam, the boyfriend who once inhabited my dreams, older now, hair cut short, a faint tinge of gray around his ears. We saw him playing chess with his son, the vivid glint of a swimming pool in the background, an idyllic sun-bleached Mediterranean scene, a pastiche of family life that must star in so many albums. In another shot he stood resting his hands, dad-style, on a garden spade, his small, pretty daughter waving her own pocket-size trowel, before a neatly turned square of bitter brown earth. There he was again, holding the girl in position at the descent of a zip wire, strong arms wrapped around her small body, dark heads pressed up close. A Cornish beach now, Sam crouching beside a disposable barbecue lined with half-cooked sausages, son and daughter beside him with identical white-toothed smiles.

What struck me most as we sifted through her catalog of family life was the unity between Sam and his children, the very hands-on-ness of him, seemingly a ready-made entertainer primed to kick a ball or build a sand sculpture at a moment's notice. The memory came of my own father teaching me to hunt rabbits with his shotgun, an heirloom I still treasure despite its bitter connotations. When I hold this gun, a Purdey that must be a hundred years old and handed down from father to son, much like the house and the land and the paintings, just its touch, the worn smoothness of its walnut body and the cool steel of the barrel, can transport me instantly to my tenth birthday. Dusk, just me and my dad on the summit of the hill, waiting for the nightly gathering of small game. Somehow we'd managed to get rid of my mother and sisters and spent the day here at Shute with my uncle. Now in the early-evening gloom, it was just the two of us, dressed like soldiers, lying on our bellies, eyes narrowed, waiting. I remember exactly how my heart began to race when the first family of rabbits scampered into view. I knew not to speak, barely to breathe, as I glared through the scope, looking, looking, waiting, waiting, slowly squeezing the trigger just as he had shown me, then pause and pull. Bang. My first-ever kill, a straightforward headshot that made my father whoop.

"Good for you, kiddo! Good for you."

I looked at these photos of Sam, similar age to my father, probably, and I could imagine him guiding his children with that same blend of gentle instruction and encouragement. And I knew in that instant that Catherine would never be able to leave them, nor am I sure I'd even want her to. What, give those sweet-looking kids of hers a slice of the hell that was my last decade of childhood? And Alexa must have seen this too, because she said, "You're really missing them, aren't you?" and Catherine nodded, speechless, clicking her children's faces off the screen of her phone as if any more looking would tear her apart.

I'm not sure either of us slept much, and there was one time, predawn, when I could tell she was awake and I knew that she was imprinting it all on her senses, the feel, the sound of these nights together, just as I was.

"You know what it is I love about you?"

I spoke without asking if she was awake, and she laughed in the darkness.

"Go on," she said, reaching out a hand to touch my thigh.

I began to list her qualities, joking to begin with, but once I'd started, the list grew longer and longer. Silly things first.

"I like the way you throw your clothes all over the floor. I can't bear that whole folding-up and hanging-over-the-back-of-a-chair thing."

"It's you who normally throws my clothes over the floor."

She smoothed her palm from my thigh to my groin and then stopped, a semicolon to what would happen next.

"I'm still listening," she said, and I could hear her smile.

"I like the way you're honest about my paintings. If you don't like something, then you say so. I feel as though I can talk about them with you, I don't get that with many people.

"And I love how you are with Rachel, not judging her, trying to help her, even though she's been pretty awful to you. You take responsibility for things, like you did with Rachel yesterday. It's made me realize the rest of us need to grow up. We're pathetic really, the way we cling to the past."

"Why are you telling me all this?"

And here I paused, afraid to go on but unable to stop.

"Because I don't think you like yourself very much anymore. You used to, once upon a time, but you've changed."

I knew she was crying in the darkness, her face turned away because she didn't want me to know.

"I've always thought I needed Sam to make me feel better," she said, and I understood what she was really telling me. She'd made a mistake and it had changed the whole course of our lives, hers and mine.

It feels like a day of lasts. Last time we'll eat breakfast together, side by side on stools sitting up at the island, Mary's homemade granola and rocket-fuel espressos. Last chance to see her naked under the waterfall shower, to press my mouth against her neck, her breasts, the soft skin on the undersides of her arms. Last time I'll turn her away from me, pressing her against the wall, pressing myself inside her, my hands holding her just beneath her ribcage, warm water that drenches us, those desperate cries that I am addicted to. Last wrapping up of her in a big white towel, another one turbaned around her head; last time to laugh at how childlike she is, with her stuck-together Bambi eyelashes.

My head is full of the words I won't say to her. Don't go. Please stay. I'm going to be lost without you.

Instead we begin a somber tour of my house and land, with its gathering momentum of inappropriate festivity, trailing from the hall to the pool to the lake, hand in hand, like the battle wounded. Catherine hasn't seen the lake since her last visit fifteen years ago, and now it is completely transformed, a whole school of rowing boats, pink, yellow, and green, strung together and bobbing up and down beside the jetty, which has been painted sky blue. Andrew's take on Montauk and Martha's Vineyard, I suppose, over the top but very effective. All the way around the perimeter of the lake, hundreds of dark pink and orange Chinese lanterns have been strung up high on gold-sprayed wooden poles.

"It's magical, it looks just like a dream," Catherine tells Andrew. "You're so clever."

His face, usually serious, eases into a grin. I'm not surprised. I noticed how he looked at Catherine when they were introduced, one glance and then another, harder, longer, his incredulity at her supernatural beauty clear to see. I'd forgotten the effect she has on people, the standard double-take, as if a goddess has dropped down from space.

"The light down here will be gorgeous," Andrew says. "Just LED bulbs in the lanterns, very soft and romantic. We'll have some flares too, just to make it a bit easier for people to see."

We examine the miniature nightclub, styled like a 1920s speakeasy, all fringed lamps and leopard-print bar stools and a tiny, underlit dance floor. To me it feels a little claustrophobic (and entirely pointless), but Catherine loves it. Andrew shows us where he is stationing his burger and slider truck, "very Louisiana," and a small semicircular platform for a female string quartet.

We sit on the jetty, the three of us, legs dangling, while I smoke a cigarette and Andrew checks his phone. It is peaceful here; aside from the hill, it's probably my favorite place on the estate, always deserted apart from a month or two in the autumn when the locals come to fish. As we sit here in silence, I realize I am dreading the onslaught of tonight's mayhem: girls in bright dresses fluttering like moths in Andrew's soft lighting, laughter bouncing out across the water, the ceaseless popping of champagne corks. In other years I've looked forward to these parties; now I'd swap it all for another day alone with Catherine.

I watch as she leans over the jetty and dips her fingers in the water.

"Not bad," she says. "Warmer than I remember."

"It's never really warm enough for swimming. We must have been mad."

"We were."

She smiles at me, at the shared memory, apparition of our past.

"We've got some gorgeous blankets arriving later," Andrew

says, looking up from his phone. "Candy-colored stripes. Got to keep everyone warm when they're out on the boats."

"You've thought of everything," Catherine says, her voice wistful. "It's going to be amazing."

Andrew puts down his phone on the jetty and looks up at her. "You are coming, aren't you?"

Catherine doesn't meet my eyes.

"I'm afraid not, it's a bit complicated."

We limp through a lunch that Mary has left out in the kitchen, Alexa, Rachel, Catherine, and I. Rachel is grimly silent and warding off any attempts at conversation about Max. Today, after a night's sleep, she has woken to the full repercussions of yesterday's catastrophic blowout. Hugo is refusing to take her calls, Max has left her pleading texts unanswered; there is nothing for her to do except travel through the pain, which she attempts to anesthetize with rosé, the only one to drink wine at lunch, cradling her glass between her palms, taking regular sips as if it is medicine, which for her, for all of us, I suppose it is.

Regret and guilt have made her vicious today, and it seems that Catherine will be her target. It's my fault, I guess, for telling the girls that I plan to drive Catherine home after lunch. I see the look that comes into Rachel's eyes, and I know what comes next.

"I thought your family weren't expecting you until tomorrow?"

"That's true. They're not."

"So basically there's no reason why you shouldn't stay tonight."

Her s's are thick and slurred, so it comes out with a distinct "sh." I'm rooting for Catherine, proud of the way she takes a sip of her water and returns Rachel's gaze, calm on the outside at least.

"There are plenty of reasons," she says.

"Such as?"

But Catherine doesn't answer. I'm about to change the subject when Rachel says, "Is it something to do with Jack? I noticed you avoiding each other yesterday."

And there's this horrifying pause when Catherine's face starts to crumple and we all witness her battle to keep herself from crying.

"Catherine doesn't have to explain herself to you, Rachel," I say as calmly as I can. Furious with her, but also shocked by Catherine's expression. She looks . . . defeated, I guess.

"True," says Rachel. "But maybe she could explain herself to you. She's never done a very good job of that, has she? Are you just going to run out on him again, is that what's going to happen? You do know, don't you, how much you hurt him last time?"

"For God's sake, Rach, stop being so bloody horrible. This has nothing to do with you and me." Alexa, who abhors any kind of confrontation, says this with a tremor in her voice. She reaches forward and tips an inch of wine into her glass.

"Well, I happen to think it does. He's our friend, isn't he? We want him to be happy, don't we? The thing I don't get, Lucian," and here Rachel's voice begins to crack, "is why when you could have anyone, the only person you seem to care about is the one who doesn't want you back. Although I suppose I, of all people, should understand what that feels like."

Alexa says, "Oh darling. You're just tired and overemotional; it's been a hellish couple of days."

But Catherine moves her chair away from the table and stands up.

"You know, Lucian is right. I really don't need to explain myself to you. But I'm sorry for the pain you're in today and I get why you're lashing out at me. I'm an easy target. But you're wrong if you think I don't care about Lucian. There hasn't been a single day in the last fifteen years when I haven't thought about him, when I haven't wished things had turned out differently. But they didn't. And there's nothing we can do to change that."

She leaves the room without looking back, and I feel sure that she's crying.

"Thanks for that," I say to Rachel. "Well done."

Rachel buries her face in her hands. Party-ready we are not.

When Catherine walks down the staircase with her bag a little while later, I do take a moment to look, seeing, perhaps for the last time, that extraordinary beauty of hers, which gives me a feeling of vertigo, a sort of head-spinning blood rush and the knowledge that with her, looking will never be enough.

"Ready?" I say as she reaches me, all hair and dark eyes and a small, sad smile, and then in a moment of near comedy I open the front door and Liv bursts through it, colliding with us and the six-foot flower tower.

"Where on earth do you think you're going?" Liv says, looking from me to Catherine and at the overnight bag in my hands. "I've driven like a maniac to get here."

"I'm taking Catherine home."

"You're not really going home, are you?" Liv asks, looking only at Catherine. "You're not going to leave me here on my own, surely?"

And Catherine starts to cry, half collapsing into Liv's arms.

"I'm sorry," she says, tears turning to laughter. "How embarrassing. It's just that it's such a relief to see you."

"Look." I seize the moment. "Why don't you go upstairs with Liv and show her where she's sleeping. I'll ask Mary to bring you some tea."

"All right."

Catherine is smiling as she links her arm through Liv's, and I notice, with a little surge of hopefulness, that as the two of them make their way up the staircase, the overnight bag goes with them.

Now

Greg has this theory about trapped grief and how it's partly responsible for my mutism. He's probably right. Years ago, when my mother died, I was physically unable to talk about it, as if there were a blockage in my throat. Liv and Sam used to say, "You should talk about her. You should tell us how you're feeling."

But every time, I shook my head. "I can't."

And it was true, I couldn't. Because to talk about her was to start crying, to feel the pain of absence, and I didn't want to do that. I knew a better way. Block it, box it off, bury it. Pretend it hasn't happened. So, Greg says, I was learning the patterns of mutism and dissociation even then.

At first my father tried to talk to me too. He'd assumed, I think, that something of our tight-knit triumvirate would continue, that I'd return home in the holidays to our house with its squeaking front door and the apple tree my mother loved, whose blooms we now took as an insult, and we would talk and cry and try to keep her memory alive. This, after all, was what he did while I was away at university, crying with his friends and visiting her grave on an almost daily basis for more tears. He placed a framed picture of my mother and me on my bedside table, the kind of photo that kills you with its portrayal of incidental love. We're sitting on the deck of our beach hut, me slumped on my mother's lap, her arm around my waist, the other hand raised toward my father with its glass of beer. Cheers, the photo says. I looked at that photograph for a long time, burning the image onto my brain: the faded red of my swimsuit with its white frill, my father's blue-checked shorts, my mother's cat's-eye sunglasses. Then I put it away in a cupboard.

"I'm sorry, Dad, it hurts too much to talk about her," I said, stonewalling every attempt at conversation. His brow would wrinkle and he'd do that buttoned-up frowning thing he does whenever he tries not to cry.

Soon, indecently soon in his case, we chose the same route to escape: I carved myself into a life with Sam, and he married an American, an art dealer who was ten years younger than him. There was never any question that Carrie, as he calls her, would move to England. And although he drove to Bristol and took me out for dinner to say, "Carrie and I would love it if you came with us. You could finish your degree in New York," that dinner was really goodbye.

We used to phone each other every week or so for casual information swaps, nothing personal, nothing dark, and Sam and I stayed with them a few times, getting high on yellow taxis and takeaways in cardboard cartons. But really the relationship was reduced to labels, like those paper figures Daisy used to cut out. Here's a father. Here's a daughter. Let's find some clothes for them to wear.

It's never too late to grieve, Greg tells me, explaining yet again the five stages of bereavement. I'm stuck in the first one, apparently—denial. He makes a lot of sense, this psychiatrist who is probably only a few years older than me. I am all about denial.

He uses a technique where he tries to get me to inhabit a difficult memory. Sam has chosen my memories for me since I don't speak, and it happens that today's trouble spot is bang on. Greg describes the twenty-four hours when I rang and rang my parents' house but there was never an answer. Sitting on the stairs with the phone on my lap, ringing the same number again, and then again, and then again, as if I was deranged, as if these two people who had been the center of my world were simply choosing not to take my call. Eventually I got hold of my father. "She's gone into the hospice," he said, his voice breaking on the word. Hospice: even its consonants seem to contain sorrow. A tear breaks free, a solitary one, and Greg is far too professional to comment.

Fifteen Years Earlier

I'd never really had a hangover before, not like this, a savage sickness that seemed more psychological than anything else. I woke expecting to find you curled around me, wanting the comfort of your slow, quiet breathing, your warm skin. The shock of your absence made me fully aware of other things. I was wearing my bra but nothing else. My jeans and T-shirt were scattered around the room—nothing unusual there—but your clothes were not. What were you wearing last night? Jeans, dark-blue ones, a washed-out black T-shirt with Bob Marley's face on it. Those clothes were nowhere. I lay there rewinding my memory, but I couldn't remember getting to bed and I thought you must have carried me. My head was hurting, my mouth was dry, and there was no glass of water by the bed. But worse was the feeling of fear, of paranoia. I needed you so badly right then.

I got out of bed and I realized my body felt bruised. I thought I might have fallen over, perhaps when I was dancing, the last thing I could clearly remember. But I was bruised inside too, and I had a sense that we'd had sex but not the kind we usually had. I felt deeply ashamed. I thought I must have encouraged it, pushed you into acting more aggressively. My instincts had been right: I hated the person I became on tequila.

It was Thursday morning and I thought you must have got dressed and gone to a lecture, which was so unlike you, and that gave me an even more intense feeling of panic. I thought perhaps we'd rowed, that you were angry with me, even that I had disgusted you.

I was vowing I would never drink again, not just tequila but any form of alcohol, as I walked through to the kitchen. Jack was there, standing by the kettle, and he grinned as I came in.

"Morning! How's your head?"

"Terrible. I'm never drinking again."

"Tea?"

I didn't like his smile; there was something off about it.

"Where's Lucian?"

The kitchen clock said 9:30, I noticed. You never got up before ten. Another brutal surge of panic, no breath left in my lungs.

Jack looked at me. "What do you mean, where's Lucian?"

My heart was banging hard against my ribcage. I think even then I knew the answer.

"He went to his uncle's. You must remember that. You thought he was too drunk to drive, but his uncle sounded odd, he said."

"But he came back?" My voice a whisper.

"Well, that would have been a bit awkward. Of course he didn't."

Jack moved forward to kiss me. He aimed for my mouth but caught my cheek.

"You should drink tequila more often. You were wild."

I was crying without tears, just ragged breathing, pacing around the kitchen, clutching my chest. No, no, no. The splintering of my world. The violence of our lovemaking—hatemaking—pressing against my brain, a fragmentary memory or a nightmare?

"You're saying we slept together?"

"Sor-ry. I'm really not buying into you not remembering it. You were unbelievable. I've never had sex like it."

"I don't remember." I whispered it, but now the memories were rushing back in.

Jack and I fucking each other—his word, never mine, a vocabulary to deepen my shame—in your bed. The one we'd lived in, you and I, not leaving it for a whole week once, our own love-in, we said at the time, like John and Yoko. How could this have happened when it was the last thing I'd ever wanted? I would never have allowed it, never, not when I loved you so.

"Of course we shouldn't have done it, but at least let's be honest. I've seen the way you look at me. I feel the same."

No. I knew this wasn't true.

"I didn't want to have sex with you."

I said it quietly, even as my mind was blurring through the details, searching, searching for clues. But I was still drunk, probably, and poisoned by panic; I was frozen into a state of no recall.

"Well, frankly, I find that a bit fucking offensive, Catherine."

This "fucking" of his, imbued with hostility, made me look up.

"Of course you wanted to sleep with me. You know you did."

"I didn't." I whispered it, but now Jack was shouting.

"Bullshit, Catherine! If I must remind you, you were the one who started it. You were the one who started kissing me when we were dancing, and I kept pushing you off and saying, no, no, we can't do this. And then it just got out of hand. We both lost control."

I slid down onto my knees, my body curved over as I wept. I heard Jack sitting down on the kitchen floor next to me, felt his hand on the back of my neck. I thought I might be sick. I hurled myself away from him. I needed to talk to you, make you understand. This was not something I'd ever meant to happen; it was a mistake, a devastating mistake. I was so drunk I didn't know what I was doing. I must have encouraged Jack, given him the wrong idea, but there was no way I would ever have wanted it to happen.

"You know how drunk I was. I didn't know who I was or what I was doing. You took advantage of me."

"Believe that if it makes you feel better. We both know it isn't the truth."

Oh the sweeping hopelessness, the vanishing of my dream, my life, my love.

"Catherine? We need to talk about this. You can't just repaint what happened and put all the blame on me. That's not fair. You wanted it at the time just as much as I did, and you know that, really, don't you? It's not like you tried to stop me."

I did look up at him again then, but I was crying so much it was almost impossible to speak. I nodded instead. I hadn't said no, I hadn't tried to stop him. Jack was telling the truth, I just couldn't bear it.

"I love him," I said.

"We both do."

"What are we going to do?"

Even as I said it, this "we" broke me. I didn't want any kind of alliance with Jack. This shared secret, I knew, would slowly corrode inside me; I would never be the same again. But I was still clinging to the possibility that somehow you and I could stay together.

"The important thing is that he never finds out. He's fragile. I'm sure you know that."

A weighted pause, Jack hovering, circling, with his sentence of destruction.

"I think, like his father, he has a fatal tendency to overreact."

"Oh my God."

"I've known him since he was eight years old, Catherine. And I know what he's capable of. He takes things to heart, he dwells on them. We need to be careful. You know Lucian has never forgiven his mother for being unfaithful to his father. He hates her. And I think it would be the same with us. I think it might push him over the edge."

Jack didn't tell me to leave you; that was my own doing. But I knew as I swept up my things from your room, all those points of familiarity so heartbreaking to me now—your easel in the middle of the room, your chest of drawers with yesterday's twin mugs of coffee on top—that I had to leave and never return; I had to protect you from yourself. I grabbed as many of my things as I could find; I scrawled that horrible note in your sketchpad: *I've changed my mind. I can't do this. I can't see you anymore.*

I took a scarf of yours too, a blue one that still held your sharp, citrusy smell. Did you know? Did you ever miss that scarf?

Jack came out of the kitchen as I wrenched open the front door, clasping my clothes and your scarf to my chest.

"Catherine?"

His voice was low, quiet, perhaps trying to instill some calm in me, but I didn't turn around.

"We made a mistake when we were drunk. It happens. No one ever needs to know about this."

I ran all the way back to the house in Saint Paul's, feeling the real pain in my body now and remembering the grittier details of our pairing. Jack's face above me, the things he said, the things he wanted us to do.

Liv was coming out of the front door as I arrived.

"Jesus Christ," she said when she saw me. Crying, shaking. She took me back inside, sat down beside me on her bed.

"What's happened?"

I looked at my dearest friend and I had no words, not even to her. Just the start of a dark, toxic shame that would wrap me in silence. *Believe that if it makes you feel better*: Jack's words burned onto my soul.

"I've broken up with Lucian," I told her. "And I'm going home."

Four Months Before: Catherine

Liv is staying in the Pink Room, a rose-themed bedroom that is almost absurdly feminine and bears his uncle's decorating traits, I'd say. The walls are papered in a pattern of dark-red roses, the dressing table wears a pale-pink skirt; even the bedspreads are pink, vintage and flower-sprigged. Needless to say, she loves it.

Neither of us says a word while she unpacks her suitcase, hanging up a gold dress (for her) on the wardrobe door and a navy-blue one (for me) on top of it. Once Mary has arrived with a tea tray—silver teapot, china cups that are paper thin, gilt handles—we sit opposite each other on the twin beds.

"You know Harry called me earlier today. Asked me to persuade you to stay tonight. He sounded kind of angsty about it."

"Harry wants us to have the same happy ending as him and Ling. But obviously that's not possible."

"Because of Sam and the kids?"

"Of course. What else?"

"You love Lucian. I know you do."

I nod but cannot speak. There is a real pain in my chest, actual pain, not metaphorical, like the murmurs of a heart attack.

"I think it's the same for him."

"Oh Liv, I think so too. We can't talk about it, not yet, but it's there between us all the time. Neither of us was expecting a second chance."

"But that's exactly it, don't you see? This *is* your second chance, and by leaving now, you're running away again. You're doing the same thing you did all those years ago."

"Hardly the same, Liv. I'm married with kids."

Liv looks at me and says nothing, but it's all there, written in her face. I know exactly what she's thinking. She thinks—or rather, she suspects—I'm hiding something. And of course she is right. The real reason for my desertion of you was quickly shrouded by news of my mother's terminal illness. "Stage four, darling," a new language for me to learn. In those paralyzing months between her life and her death, there was room for nothing else.

Now Liv leans forward. She takes my hand.

"Don't you think it was strange that Harry rang me today? There was something in his voice, a sort of urgency. He seemed genuinely worried about you leaving and how it would affect Lucian."

"He's always been protective of Lucian. You know how close they are."

I am pulled, unwillingly, right back into the heart of a memory that still fills me with shame all these years later. Harry on the doorstep of our Bristol house, pounding the door in an aggressive, un-Harry-like way. He knew I was in, knew too that I wasn't going to answer.

"Catherine, I know you're in there . . . Catherine, please. This won't take long."

I opened the door with unwashed hair and midafternoon pajamas, physical manifestations of my private heartbreak.

"I don't want to talk about it," I told him, affecting a defiance I didn't feel.

"Actually," Harry said, "nor do I. I just want to ask something of you. I want you to promise you'll never go anywhere near him again. Promise me you'll leave him alone."

Leave him alone. Such hostile words. And so deserved. But for a reason Harry would never have guessed at.

The wariness of your friends, the unnerving proximity of Jack and this horrifying secret we share: I have many reasons for not wanting to stay tonight. But I cannot explain any of this to Liv without telling her the truth about why I left you, and I couldn't bear to do that, couldn't bear for Liv to see me the way I see myself.

"Can I tell you something?" Liv says. "I've made a point of staying in touch with Lucian all these years because of you. I always knew how much you regretted leaving him. And how much you missed him. Don't run away again, Catherine. Don't do that to him. Or yourself. You've got a chance, you should take it."

"What about Sam?" I say. "What about Joe and Daisy? I can't just walk out on them."

But already I am thinking that I will tell Sam the truth. I'll tell him that I love you. I'll tell him I don't know how to live without you.

When I come downstairs an hour later wearing the dark-blue dress, you look confused for a moment, then a slow smile, an upward one, works its way across your face until you are grinning broadly, then laughing. I feel this great flood of emotion punching me in the chest.

"You're staying?" you ask, and I run down the last few steps of the staircase, straight into your arms, and you lift me up as if I'm a child.

"Looks like it," I tell you, and then we're kissing, a kiss that goes on and on, much longer than it should, with Liv right behind us and the bar staff pretending not to watch.

"I'm so glad," you tell me, still holding me off the ground, and I say, "Me too, me too." And as always, your thoughts are running with mine, because you whisper, "I couldn't bear you to leave," and I tell you, "I'm not leaving," and although we both know I'm only talking about one night, it feels like something has been decided.

It's a different thing having Liv by my side, and for the first hour of the party we stand together, marveling at the excess. There must be almost as many waiters as guests, girls and boys clearly picked for their looks as much as their waiting skills, dressed in tight-fitting black shirts and black jeans. They rush through the crowd in mock-professional haste and come up to each guest in turn: "What can I get you to drink, a glass of champagne or something from the bar?" We choose champagne, and when Liv exclaims at the taste, I tell her it's vintage Pol Roger, your favorite.

"Get you," she says, eyebrows raised. "Jack's arrived," she tells me a moment later. "His wife is with him."

His overaffectionate greeting locks me down inside as if even my cells recoil at the memory—his lips pressed to my cheek, the smell of his aftershave instantly recognizable after all this time. I force myself to look properly this time; I tell myself to be calm. See the narrow gray tailored suit, Savile Row, I'd imagine. The black shirt, revealing itself to be silk on closer inspection. Sunglasses worn inside, masking those blue eyes. Bright hair, camera-ready smile, his handsomeness a weapon, one that felled Celia, Alexa, even me.

Celia is dressed like some kind of eighties throwback in a rose-colored strapless ball gown, very Diana, very *Dallas*. Actually she looks great, and like Ling, she greets me as though we are already old friends. And I think, as we embrace, that this is what outsiders do, huddling together on the fringes. None of us—Celia, Ling, or I—will ever be fully accepted in your clique of five.

The party is a master class in entitlement. At the poolside bar, we sit side by side on two stools, just watching.

"Look at the clothes," Liv says. "Look at the hair. Look at the jewelry. Everyone here is beautiful, and that's because they have money and time and they know where to go to achieve it."

"It's true. The rich are different," she says a moment later. "Have you heard anyone say thank you yet?"

At our station by the bar we spend a few minutes monitoring a sequence of high-maintenance beauties ordering complicated cocktails we've never heard of, with not a please or thank-you between them.

"Two island margaritas and an old-fashioned."

Mostly they take their exotic drinks without making eye contact with the barman or breaking conversation with their friends.

We watch as you come into the bar, almost absurdly handsome in your dark suit and white shirt; we see how the crowd pulls apart to make room for you, a celebrity in their midst. You catch my eye and smile, but your progress is slow, drawn into conversation with at least four groups of people before you reach us.

"Finally," you say, putting an arm around my shoulder. "Why does everyone feel they have to talk to me? Could I have a martini, please," you say to the barman, and Liv catches my eye and smiles. "And what would you both like?"

You tell us dinner is being served on the lawn and that Harry and Ling are holding a table for us, "Big enough for everyone," you say, which instantly sets me on edge. In your "everyone," I see only Jack.

The marquee is more beautiful than any I've ever seen. Long wooden tables and benches run all the way around its perimeter, simple and almost homely in effect except for the fact that they are ablaze with what must be hundreds of candles, burning from tall brass candelabras and low-level colored glass holders. Each place setting has two tall-stemmed wineglasses for white and red, a champagne flute, a jewel-colored water tumbler, and a gold-patterned side plate. For every table there's a gold-lacquered vase, at exactly the right height, filled with dark-blue and cream roses. I am sitting between you and Harry and opposite Ling, a position of relative safety, though Jack, Rachel, and Charlotte Lomax and her husband are a couple of places farther down, easily within earshot. Charlotte, all smooth brown skin in a backless floor-length dress, dives straight in.

"Catherine! I'd heard you were here. Probably the last person on earth I'd ever have expected to find at one of Lucian's parties. Do you remember Johnnie?"

Johnnie's arm is patted indifferently, but her eyes remain focused on me. Yes, Charlotte, I remember him, the long-haired Golf GTI driver who used to gamble his student loan away at the casino in the first week of term and brag about it loudly in the pub afterward.

"How's your husband?" Charlotte asks, with a voice full of unexpressed laughter.

She doesn't wait for my reply but leans in and whispers something to Jack.

I turn away to find Ling watching me. She is wearing a dress of lemon-yellow silk, her dark hair tied to one side and fanning out across her shoulder.

She leans in, speaks softly.

"It will get easier, the more you see them. No one has the right to judge you."

I'm staggered by her comprehension. This girl, whom I've known only a handful of days, seems able to look right into the core of me.

"Ling," I say, in a quiet voice. "You know, don't you? You've worked it out."

I would like to explain. I'd like her to understand that this horrible dark secret I've carried inside me for fifteen years has eroded my character, my life, it's stolen away the best parts of me. But before I can say any more, she glances at Jack and shakes her head quickly, her meaning clear.

"Let's have fun tonight, Catherine. You and me."

"Deal."

Either side of the table, two waiters start refilling our glasses in perfect synchronicity, as if to emphasize the point.

"They leave us no choice," I say, taking two hefty gulps of champagne.

Ling laughs and raises her glass to me, swallows half its contents.

"Oof." She slams it back down on the table. "The bubbles went right up my nose."

She has two spots of high color in her cheeks, matching circles the size of a ten-pence piece.

"I haven't felt this drunk since I was fifteen," Ling says.

"What happened then?"

"My sister and I went round stealing everyone's drinks at my cousin's wedding. No one noticed until Amara vomited all over the bride."

"The Lady Muck sister?"

Ling nods.

"She lives in Hong Kong. Nannies for an English family—two boys who have taught her all the rude words in the *Oxford English Dictionary*. I miss her."

"She'll come over for the wedding, won't she?"

Harry, overhearing this, cuts in.

"Hang on, you told Catherine?"

He turns to you.

"Secret's out, apparently. Ling and I are going to have a proper wedding. A blessing in the chapel and a big lunch afterward. Will you be my best man?"

I love watching your face. How it changes as you take in what Harry has said, the light that rushes into it.

"I'd be honored."

You reach across me to grip his hand. And then both of you are laughing, a private moment of shared happiness.

"You will be able to come, Catherine, won't you?" Ling says, and I say, "Of course I will."

"Does that mean we have a chance?" you ask, low voiced. And I tell you, "I don't see how we can be apart again," which is the truth.

News of Ling and Harry's wedding starts to spread along the table, and you jump up, demanding more champagne from a passing waitress. There are hugs, kisses, congratulations all round, and by the time I'm halfway down this glass, I realize I'm too drunk. I don't like it. I don't like the slow erosion of clarity, a melting in my brain, a fluidity in my body, sensations that can trigger the harsh adrenaline of recall. Memories I don't want clamoring for recognition. When I want to forget—need to forget—I can do that, though it takes practice, a sort of mindfulness where I focus on the smallest details around me.

You're talking to Liv, and you don't notice me getting up from the table.

"Back in a minute," I tell Ling, and I step outside the tent, forcing myself to register the exact color of the night as the last of the light disappears—midnight blue, I'd call it, though you would know the correct shade. The strip of carpet leading from the garden into the marquee is an ironic red, flashbulb ready, another of Andrew's jokes. And it seems obvious, predestined, that at exactly this moment, when I stand inhaling the night air, Jack returns to the tent alone, so that it is just him and me face-to-face, no Celia, no Liv, no Harry or Ling or you to take the edge off the intensity of this meeting.

"Catherine."

He chucks a glowing cigarette onto the red carpet, crushes it with his foot. His beautiful dark-gray suit is spookily similar to the one you're wearing, you his perennial benchmark. Still copying you, I think, still impersonating you all these years later. Perhaps I should pity him the way I pitied him once before, this boy who would go to any lengths to get your attention, to be just like you. But my head is full of the last time we were together, me standing in the kitchen doorway, Jack by the kettle, the slow and steady collapsing of my world. The shame I always feel is there, but beneath it anger too. Jack made sure I could never see you again.

I think, like his father, he has a fatal tendency to overreact.

Why couldn't Jack have been the one to leave; why did it have to be me? Why did he let me get so drunk? Why didn't he have the sense to stop, to know that the two of us together was something that would break you?

"You haven't told him, have you?" Jack says, eventually.

His voice is softer than usual; he's hard to read. I shake my head.

"If you had, I'd know by now. If you had, he'd probably kill me." He laughs. "Well, maybe that's a bit of an exaggeration."

It's hard for me to look at Jack without the memories rushing back in. They're unshaped, half formed, the way drunken memories often are, but his body is clear, those sharp blue eyes in the darkness, teeth that shone, his arms taut as he held himself above me. When you have a memory you wish to avoid, it's easy to float away from it, easy to disconnect. No, no, you say, I'm not dealing with this. I did it when my mother died. So my father tells me.

"Catherine?"

I do hear Jack's voice, I do understand that he's trying to talk to me. But I have no words. Not for him. And after a while, perhaps a minute, perhaps a little longer, I watch as he walks away.

Fifteen Years Earlier

My mother picked me up from the station and I cried all the way home, staring ahead through the windscreen, allowing myself now to sob like a child.

"I don't understand it," she said. "You were so happy. He seemed so lovely. What can have gone wrong?"

My father placed a mug of hot chocolate in front of me; so sweet, that gesture. In the good old days it would have sorted everything out. Not now, though. Not now I was a two-timing slut. On the two-hour journey from Bristol I had learned the shape of self-hatred, its vocabulary, its dark internal burn.

"Please tell us what's happened," my father said.

"What's happened is that we've broken up and I hate myself. That's it, that's all there is to say."

They knew me so well, my parents, they knew when to leave me alone. My mother slid her hands across the kitchen table and took hold of mine.

"We love you. We think you're wonderful. We *know* you're wonderful."

You rang, of course. You spoke to my mother twice, my father once. On the last phone call my father asked you, politely, to leave me alone.

Then there was Liv, with her daily bulletins, phone calls that always ended the same way.

"Please talk to him, Catherine. It's the least you can do. He's going out of his mind."

But I knew I couldn't talk to you, I couldn't hear your voice, the sound of your breathing on the other end of the phone. The moment I did, I knew I'd lose my resolve.

All I had to do was think of Jack's words.

I think it might push him over the edge.

"No, Liv, I won't talk to him. It's over, I've changed my mind and now we both need to move on."

I spent two weeks at home in the end, shadowing my mother from room to room, to the supermarket, for painfully slow walks around the park. Her back was very bad at that time, and we were at the chiropractor's every other day. I used to sit on the other side of the screen, listening to her low, suppressed moans, those deep gasps of pain that didn't seem right. If I hadn't been so preoccupied with my own tragedy, perhaps I would have guessed at hers.

Just before the fortnight was up, my parents went to the surgery to pick up the results of a recent X-ray. Afterward I would imagine their walk along the high street—past the butcher, where we bought fillet steak for birthdays and our Christmas turkey, past the greengrocer, who held back purple sprouting broccoli for my father, and the florist where my mother bought her peonies—as their last moments of innocence. I was at the kitchen table when they came back, Elizabeth Gaskell's *North and South* open in front of me. From the minute they walked in I knew something was wrong. My father was all bitter and brisk, as if he was fighting back tears (a trait I've inherited); my mother couldn't look at me. How do you tell your nineteen-year-old daughter, your treasured only child, that you are dying? So I collapsed, and the loss of you, the horrifying infidelity with Jack, became a little chip of ugliness on the infinity of pain.

My mother insisted on taking me back to the station herself, her last drive, as it turned out.

"Making mistakes is part of growing up," she said as we stood waiting for my train. "It's not such a big deal. The important thing is to learn from it and move on. Promise me you'll do that."

"You know, don't you? You know what I did."

My mother paused. We were so close, she and I, always able to communicate without words. She would have read my silence and interpreted my guilt. Not the who or the how, but the act of betrayal, she must have understood that.

"What I know is that you are a good person. And you've stopped believing in yourself."

"Oh," I said, and could manage no more. Sometimes my mother's comprehension was a dagger in my chest.

I'll never forget the look we shared before the whistle blew and the carriage door was slammed shut. A few hard seconds of gazing into one another's eyes, a silent information swap, no words needed.

She saw the change in me and I saw the sorrow in her.

Now

The tree is pretty in sugar-almond pink, and I suppose it should lift my mood along with the jam jar of wildflowers—foxgloves, bluebells, clover—that Daisy brought yesterday.

"There are daisies all over our lawn now," she said, and she held out a long, long chain she'd made for me to inspect. I did turn to look at it, I did try to force my mouth into an approximation of a smile, but still she hesitated before coming close enough to hang it around my neck. And it hurt to see that hesitation and to know that I'd caused it, along with Joe's anger and Sam's despair. My children have learned to manage without me, without this silent shell who adds nothing to their lives. And who can blame them?

When Daisy was small, we used to walk up to the common most days, and when spring arrived we'd solemnly inspect the grass for the first signs of buttercups and daisies. She loved the fact that she was named after this prolific wildflower, although I'm not sure she was really; it was just the name we liked most at the time. And as she grew, it suited her more and more, with her wild and generous nature, the girl who loves to dangle upside down from trees and wade barefoot in the world's coldest stream.

My family visit me most days now, preparing me, I think, for my departure, which is coming very soon. Sam gives me information updates in the bright, breezy voice he always uses, dropping in psychiatric terminology as if he's discussing the weekly shop. Spinach, eggs, milk. Trauma, psychosis, mutism.

"We'll need some help to begin with because we don't know how it will be for you, fitting back into normal life with your mutism. So Liv is going to take some time off, and then my mum is coming."

He pauses here, and I think how the old Sam and I would have laughed at this. His mother and me, confined together in a house, day after day? No way, I would have said. Over my dead body. But when you are still alive, breathing, eating, sleeping, only acting like you're dead, no touching, no talking, decisions like this are forced upon you. You make one choice at the expense of many others, it seems to me. It's a strange kind of freedom in this glass house of mine.

For now Sam seems to shy away from the exact moment of "trauma," but he cites other events that led up to it, even the one I dread the most. He is careful and kind when he mentions Jack's name; he will hold my hand, squeezing it hard, though I never respond. He tells me that they will be bringing up what happened with Jack in my next cognitive therapy session; he asks me if I'd like him to be there.

"They know you're not ready to talk, Catherine," he says. "It's more that they want to help you find ways of lessening your anxiety when you think about it."

More bloody breathing techniques, I suppose. There's only one thing that could help, and that is the chance to say sorry. And if I couldn't find the words, then I'd beam them to you from my eyes and you would understand; you'd catch the letters as they fell through the air. It's all right, you'd say. I forgive you, you'd say. Let's start again. When all you have is your dreams, why can't you re-create the perfect end?

Four Months Before: Lucian

There is always a moment when I remember why it is I go to the trouble of hosting this party year after year, three hundred hard-drinking guests trudging through my house and gardens, dropping cigarette butts and smashing glasses and spilling wine onto carpets (not that I care, but Mary does). Tonight the moment comes as I'm walking to the lake with Catherine. Harry and Ling are slightly ahead, hand in hand, a good foot of height between them, her dress an exotic yellow against his summer lightweight beige. They talk incessantly of their planned wedding party, and the joy in Harry's voice, after all the years of loneliness, is gratifying; it lifts me up. I don't know anyone who deserves it more than him. (Apart from me, and I have my own fervent hopes on that score.) Until a few hours ago I really believed that Catherine would disappear back into her old life and I'd never see her again. And although I'd promised myself I wouldn't fall in love with her, I've failed, hopelessly, at that. Tonight, though, there's a shift in her, I see it, I feel it, and I'm daring to hope that perhaps we will end up together, against the odds and after all this time. I'm not sure what Liv said to Catherine when they went upstairs, but whatever it was, it worked. So I am buoyed by Harry's happiness and the projection of my own and by the sight of my guests wandering down to the pool or the lake in technicolored groups, men carrying jackets, girls holding their shoes, laughter drifting out across the evening breeze. This is when I love the party most, the formality of dinner (such as it is) behind us, just the freedom of pure, selfish enjoyment ahead.

We hear the music long before we reach the lake, another of Andrew's genius touches, for the sound of Vivaldi or Mozart or Bach or whatever his all-girl string quartet is playing is instantly transporting, as if we're entering another world. And when we arrive at the lake, I see that everything Andrew planned has come together spectacularly well. In his extra-soft lighting, just Chinese lanterns strung up high around the perimeter of the lake, the moon dominates, turning all his pastel colors luminescent. The sky-blue jetty, the pink, yellow, and green boats glow in its sharp silver light, and the surface of the lake shines, a dimpled sheet of glass. The string quartet are now playing Handel's *Water Music* (Andrew does love a theme), and the banks of the lake are dotted with guests sitting on blankets, drinking champagne. No one seems to be in a hurry to go out on the boats. There's a queue of people waiting for two bouncers to admit them to the miniature nightclub, another crowd gathered around Andrew's champagne bar, styled like an old-fashioned Punch and Judy booth in candy-colored stripes. Friends call out and try to draw us into conversation, but without saying so, the four of us are determined to be on our own. I think it's the shared feeling of secret celebration—Ling and Harry's forthcoming party, the possibility that Catherine and I might have some kind of future.

"Let's go out on the lake," I say.

Harry picks up champagne and glasses while I help Ling and Catherine into the first boat. There are a few girls and boys waiting on the jetty, dressed thematically in shorts and nautical stripes. They hand us blankets and hold the boat steady while we step down into it, though they cannot prevent its sudden dramatic tilt when Harry, all sixteen stone of him, steps aboard. Ling and

Catherine sit together in the bow, their blue and yellow dresses a perfect complement, while Harry and I each take up an oar. Once upon a time we used to do this together at school, rowing the only sport we could ever be bothered to pursue. We were in the upper eights for a while until parties, booze, and girls (for me anyway) took over.

"Like riding a bicycle," says Harry as we glide effortlessly toward the center of the lake. We reminisce about our brief rowing career, the cold, unforgivably early starts on the Thames, the muscle-bound, nondrinking jockiness of the other six.

"It's a miracle we lasted as long as we did," Harry says.

There are a few other boats coming onto the lake now, though unlike us they stick close to the bank, and their lanterns glow from the edges of the night like fireflies.

"Let's rest here for a while," Harry says, balancing his oar across the boat. "Pass up the booze, girls."

We talk about the wedding party for a bit, which is planned for the autumn. Harry had favored a big evening party to begin with, but Ling has talked him into having a lunch instead.

"The thing about a big party," Ling says, "no offense, Lucian, but it's hard to spend time with only the people you want to be with."

"You're right," says Catherine. "We've had to go out on a boat to get away from everyone else. And you don't have a lake, Harry."

Ling and Catherine look at each other and laugh. It's been a revelation to see the way these two have got along with each other. I can tell that Catherine really loves Ling.

And the change in Harry since he met her has been remarkable. He used to be so insular and reserved, exactly what you might expect from someone born to a household where dogs were deified and children ignored. I think if you're a child who grows up without love, you don't expect to find it as an adult. And that's what has set Harry apart—the complete lack of expectation that he would be with someone, someone he loved and who loved him back. I look at him now and I think of all the joy he has ahead—the wedding party, the prospect of children, the transformation of his austere, gray house into a home.

When Ling starts to tell us about a lake where she swam as a child, I find myself hypnotized by her slow, soft voice. She has a gift for storytelling and for making her childhood sound magical, always dwelling on the good things, the beauty, the peace, never the hardship.

"We used to go to this lake on birthdays, rowing upstream in the fishing boats, two hours or maybe three to get there. But it was worth it: that lake had the clearest, brightest water you have ever seen. And the most beautiful birds. My favorite was a bit like a blackbird but with stripes of fluorescent blue. In English it translates to the fairy bluebird."

"I love that," Catherine says, then she puts out her hand and covers Ling's. "You miss it a bit, don't you?"

"Only in the way that we all miss our childhoods," Ling says.

I'm wondering if this is true. For me, yes, up until the age of ten, when my childhood effectively ended. For Catherine, more than any of us: she had the real deal, the insular love bubble, the shrink-wrapped family of three. With Harry, I'd say no. What was there to miss? Those coldhearted parents? A nanny who should have been pensioned off years ago? Harry's happiness is strictly present day, right here, right now.

"One of the best things was the swimming competitions," Ling says, resuming her tale. "We used to row our boats into the middle of the lake and then jump in. We'd swim all the way round the lake."

She is laughing as she stands up, and the boat tips a little. She's over the side, shoes off, dress still on, a small, sharp splash as she lands in the water, before any of us realize what's happening. She comes up quickly, dark hair flattened to her scalp, laughing in the blackness.

"Actually it's not too bad," she says. "Come on."

Catherine says, "Ling, you're crazy, you know that."

She turns to look at me, smiling.

"What the hell," she says, and then she's overboard too in the beautiful dark-blue dress. The moment takes us, me and Harry wrenching off our shoes, our jackets, the boat rocking violently when Harry dives in. Christ, it's cold, but we've drunk enough to be numb to it and we're all four of us laughing at this unexpected turn, the recklessness of swimming in our party clothes, of swimming at all. Harry lifts Ling into his arms, treading water so that his beige suit trousers balloon beneath him. He kisses the side of her face.

"You're not in Thailand now, you know."

Catherine floats on her back, gazing up at the sky. In the moonlight her arms are silvery white; her hair drifts around her face like Ophelia's.

Is she remembering the headiness of that weekend we once spent here with Jack and Alexa, the four of us with nothing but enchantment ahead?

She says, "This is so lovely, I'm so glad we did this."

"We'll do it again," I tell her, and Catherine looks at me and smiles, a silent acknowledgment of our shared future.

"Maybe wet suits next time?" she says, and Ling laughs.

"You're right, it's freezing." She reaches up to kiss Harry's neck, then drops back down into the water. "We need to keep moving." We watch her cut away in an efficient crawl, a quick blur of lemon yellow.

"Don't go too far from the boat, sweetheart," Harry calls, and we hear Ling laughing before she vanishes into the black.

"She's obsessed with swimming," Harry says, staring after her. "We're starting the new pool next week."

More and more boats are coming onto the lake now, voices and laughter and the occasional popping sound as a bottle of champagne is opened, magnified with a strange, watery echo. It is the party I wanted—or rather the one Andrew imagined I wanted; the lantern-lit lake, the boating, the swimming have turned it into something magical.

"We should probably get out," Catherine says. "Some of those boats are quite close. Do you think they can see us?

"Catherine's right, and it's getting cold," Harry says. "Ling," his voice is amplified on the surface of the water, "Ling, let's go in now."

She doesn't answer, and he starts swimming toward her.

"I'll go and get her, you bring the boat."

Something happens to Catherine. She calls Ling's name in a normal voice the first time, then instantly she's screaming it.

"Ling! *LING! LIIIING!*" Her panic is abrupt and infectious. "Where is she? Where is she?"

Both of us shout her name as we drag ourselves up into the boat, so cold suddenly, me rowing toward Harry and Ling, Catherine leaning right over the edge in her sodden dress, water streaming from her hair. Ling! Ling! Ling! It's all my brain knows. Searching the darkness for a glimpse of yellow.

"Why can't we see her? Why isn't she answering? She can't have gone far."

Here at its heart, the lake seems vast and uncertain. And so dark, it's almost impossible to see. Half-remembered facts punch my brain. When you swim at night your body temperature drops quickly. Drowning can happen in an instant, silently, without warning.

Harry is roaring Ling's name; in his voice, the fading of hope.

"We'll find her, Harry. We'll find her. You take the oars," I tell Catherine as I drop back over the side into the water.

I'm so cold now as I plunge beneath the surface—heart pumping at the thought of the weeds, a childhood fear reignited. I open my eyes in the murk, but I see nothing but a flash of beige just ahead of me, Harry's hand turned a luminous white. There is no girl in a yellow dress. I go deeper and deeper, kicking hard, so cold I cannot breathe. I'm up again and down again—my brain pounding only this refrain: Ling, Ling—looking and looking for yellow, but I can't see her, I can't see anything.

When I next come up, Catherine is beside me in the water. She's calling Ling's name, over and over, her voice rasping, raw.

"Keep looking," she says. "Find her, please, please find her."

I push myself beneath the surface again, but this time I'm weighted by hopelessness. We're not going to find her.

I reemerge to the sound of Harry's cries, a howling more animal than human that reverberates through the night. I hear Andrew's voice in a boat nearby.

"Lucian, you have to get out of there. All of you, you must come out of the water."

I watch him leaning out to pull Catherine into his boat, gathering her up as if she's a child. She seems oblivious to him, deranged by sadness.

"Oh no, Ling, oh no," she says, as if Ling is still sitting next to her in the boat, still talking, still alive.

Four Months Before: Catherine

We are rowed back to shore by Andrew, three of us, not four. Wrapped in candy-striped blankets, shaking with cold, with shock. Harry is no longer wailing, but his grim-faced silence is harder to bear. You sit next to him, your hand on his shoulder, staring at the shoreline. No one talks, there is nothing to say. The facts are too harsh to be spoken.

Ling is dead. No matter how many times I tell myself this, I cannot take it in. It feels like moments ago that she was sitting beside me in this boat, sharing a bottle of champagne, talking about her wedding party. Only yesterday, as she stood cooking her beautiful food in Harry's kitchen, I was marveling at the way her life had turned out: one moment working in a busy Bangkok hotel, the next replanted in one of the most indulgent lifestyles in England. Less than an hour ago I was thinking that in just a few days Ling seemed to understand me better than almost anyone. I loved her, and I barely knew her.

"We've got to go back," I say, "we've got to keep looking," but Andrew shakes his head and so do you.

Andrew says, "We're searching the edges of the lake. If she's there, we'll find her."

Harry's head drops forward until it's almost touching his knees. He sobs, just once.

"Harry," you say. "Harry."

In the distance but growing closer every minute is the sound of a siren. Andrew has told us the police and ambulances are on their way; I know we are all thinking the same thing. What's the point?

My recklessness, yours, Harry's, Ling's, it's all I can think of. Me, who never takes risks, who never gets drunk, who fully understands the perils of swimming at night, especially when people have been drinking. What happened, Ling? Did you get cramp, were you too cold, did your body just stop working? Did you slide beneath the water's surface, did you call out to us and we couldn't hear?

"Can you all move back?" Andrew calls as Jack leans over the edge of the jetty to grab our mooring rope. "Can everyone leave the lake now, please."

He is never more in control than in the face of this accident, this fatality, although occasionally he betrays himself with a glimpse of stabbing guilt.

"I should have had a first-aid team on standby," he told me, voice hushed, as we rowed to shore. "I should have considered something like this might happen."

So Andrew feels responsible too.

Harry, stumbling in his blanket, is swamped by Rachel and Alexa and a couple of green-suited paramedics, who lead him away to an ambulance parked just outside the entrance to the lake. Already Andrew is dealing with the police.

"You and Lucian need to go up to the house and get changed," he says. "Now, Catherine." He half shouts it. He has realized, I think, that shouting is the only way to penetrate our shock.

We walk back to the house and you allow me to hold your hand beneath your blanket. I cannot find the right thing to say. I want to help you, to lessen your guilt, but my own is lacerating, for I am convinced that both of us, all three of us, are culpable, that this was an accident that didn't need to happen.

"I can't believe it," I say eventually, and you nod, a sharp little incline of your head.

My brain is crammed with a ceaseless sequence of regrets. If only we'd gone to the nightclub or the pool instead of the lake. If only I'd gone home, as I planned, then maybe Harry and Ling wouldn't have taken a boat out. If only we'd stopped her when she jumped in, if only we'd pulled her to safety straight away. If only, if only we hadn't been drinking. Another drunken night with your friends; another devastating mistake. This time, fatal.

Back at the house, a few remaining partygoers are clustered around the bar in the hall, waiting for taxis or perhaps just rubbernecking. We walk into a buzz of conversation, which drops off in gradients, fading to nothing as people catch sight of us. You walk toward the staircase oblivious to all. I follow you up the first flight of stairs, around the corner, and halfway up the second, just out of earshot of the hall, when you begin to cry. I know this from the stoop of your shoulders and a half gasp, almost undetectable, and I am taken back to that night, long ago, when you stood at the window, turned away from me, telling me about your father dying.

Your room, both of us shaking as we take off our wet clothes. My hands aren't working properly and I can't undo the zip of my dress. We watch each other, both crying now, but quietly. You stop unbuttoning your shirt and reach out to jerk my zip undone, pulling the wet dress down to my waist. Closer now, you kiss each of my eyes in turn, you wipe the tears from my cheeks with the palms of your hands.

"She was so young," you say. "And he was so happy."

"I know."

You start babbling, sentences running into each other, but all I hear is your guilt, and it is exactly the same as mine.

"It's my fault. I should never have allowed the lake to be used. I know how dangerous it can be, I know how cold it gets out there."

"It was an accident," I say. "Of course it wasn't your fault."

But you say, "We didn't look after her," which is the truth.

We shower, holding each other beneath the warm jets of water, your arms around my waist, my face pressed against your chest. While you dress, still shivering, in jeans and the old blue jumper I wore on the hill—only three days ago, the same day I first met Ling—I retrieve my bag from Liv's room and dress myself in jeans and a gray hoodie, clothes that also seem from another life.

Ling is dead and nothing matters anymore. I think of her comprehension at dinner, the way she said, quietly, "No one has the right to judge you," and I wonder, in this moment, why I have ever cared. What could it matter that you find out what I am really like, or if everyone knows it? I am a person who makes mistakes. First Jack, now Ling.

I know as I walk back to your room that there is no more time.

"I need to get back to the lake," you say as soon as I walk through the door.

And I tell you, "I slept with Jack."

"What?" You step backward. "What did you say?" Staccato words, like coughing up blood.

"I slept with Jack. The night we drank tequila. The night you went off to see your uncle."

"Fuck. Jesus, Catherine."

Your hands are covering your face. I don't know if you're crying, but your voice comes out as a wail.

"Not Jack. You wouldn't have done that. I know you wouldn't."

But now, having told this truth, I can't speak, I can't defend myself. I just stand in the middle of your bedroom saying nothing, immobilized by shame. When you look at me again, just a moment before you slide your eyes away, it's as if you're looking at a stranger.

"Why are you telling me this?"

"Because nothing matters now. And everything matters. Because I needed you to know."

"All right, so you've told me. Now I know."

I hate the way your voice sounds: not angry, just cold.

"I was so drunk," I say. "We both were. I didn't know what I was doing."

And still, this isn't what I want to tell you. I want to tell you that I loved you so much, that the sex with Jack was the very last thing I'd ever wanted. That this stupid drunken mistake destroyed my life.

"For Christ's sake, I can't deal with this now. You should go, Catherine. Go home to your family. They need you, and Harry needs me."

I'm so wrung out I can't even cry. I nod my head, praying you'll say something that I can hold on to, just the smallest glimmer of hope that it isn't as I always feared and I did the one thing you could never forgive.

You do look at me just before you leave the room.

"You were right not to tell me," you say in that same flat, cold voice. "I couldn't have forgiven you."

Now

"Let's talk about shame," says Greg, in the calm, measured voice that accompanies much of my day. Greg talking, me listening, or at least that's the ambition. More and more now I find that I do listen.

"It is one of the most powerfully destructive emotions we have. If it festers over a long period of time, then it can become akin to a mental illness. When you feel extreme shame over a particular incident—in your case the night with Jack, the night with Ling—what can happen is that you begin to flagellate yourself, not just for the event but for the person you believe you are: vile, loathsome, irrevocably flawed. This thing you did, this mistake you made, becomes grossly magnified, distorted, twisted. This is when shame is at its most dangerous. This is when shame becomes self-hate."

Violent word, violent emotion. I know all about self-hate.

I gaze back at Greg, I offer him a small nod. I think how he must have assimilated all the gory details Sam has passed on to him—the loss of you, the death of my mother, the sex with Jack—and diagnosed one combustible personal identity. He's bang on, of course. The way I've hated myself is like an illness, a form of self-torture. That night with Jack—fateful, tormenting, a crossroads I must travel over and over again without ever changing the outcome—destroyed two lives, yours and mine. One bad decision, a lifetime of regret.

Greg tells me that those who feel this extreme shame are wont to disappear, to retreat, to hide away. There have been many studies on it, apparently; he quotes a few. Greg always does his homework.

"You began this retreat, this withdrawal many years ago," he tells me. "And it's my belief that your shame and your unfulfilled quest for forgiveness led to you shutting down entirely. The minute you start talking about your shame, the moment you out it—do you understand me—then it begins to diminish. Can you understand this, Catherine? It's vital for your recovery."

I want to look away but I force myself to concentrate on Greg's face, on his concerned eyes, the color somewhere between gray and blue. Shame is an illness. I am sick with shame. To conquer it I must begin talking again.

Four Months Before: Lucian

The place is crawling with police, a brutish juxtaposition against the pastel-colored idealism of last night. The sky-blue jetty is an insult. The pink and green boats turn my stomach. The lanterns that flip and turn over in the morning wind seem to jeer and screech, and those yellow shoes, marooned on the bank, are a vicious, acid-bright reminder that Ling is dead.

I am down by the lake with Andrew, drinking coffee from a thermos that Mary has brought for us, waiting for the divers to arrive.

As I shake out yet another cigarette from the packet, Andrew says, "Think I could have one?"

"I didn't know you smoked."

"Not for years."

We smoke in silence and stand together, looking out at the lake.

"Harry asked to be woken when the divers get here. Don't know if it will be possible."

Harry was knocked out, literally, by some rock-and-roll doctor Andrew called in, who sedated him like a horse. It took four men to carry him up to bed, with Alexa stationed beside him on an all-night vigil just in case he wakes.

"And anyway, isn't it better for him not to see? She's been underwater for five or six hours."

"I don't think we can make that decision, Lucian."

For Harry, of all people, to have lost his wife on my watch, on my land, and after all those years of aloneness is too much. I don't know that I will ever be able to forgive myself.

"Why don't you go and see if he's awake?" Andrew says. "I can deal with the divers."

He wants to spare me everything if he can. I watch as he joins a cluster of policemen on the jetty, a pale-faced, broken man, sick from his cigarette, in a crumpled, up-all-night suit. It's true I don't want to see Ling dragged from the water in her effervescent yellow. And I don't want Harry to see her either. The question mark over her death, the agonizing, unexplained vanishing, is impossible to comprehend. But one thing I know is that the sight of her dead body will destroy him.

In the Blue Room, the one where Alexa normally sleeps, Harry is passed out, still wrapped in blankets (we had to cut his wet clothes from him in the end), Alexa curled up beside him in her silver dress, one slim brown arm draped across the mountain of his chest. I wonder if this was how he and Ling used to sleep. It occurs to me that I never once saw them in bed together, never sat on the edge of their bed drinking coffee and discussing the night before the way you do with your oldest friends. It would have happened, sooner or later, but there just wasn't time.

Alexa opens her eyes, registers me, and her face collapses. Instantly she's crying, silently though, just long black rivulets of tears, last night's mascara working its way slowly down her face. I sit down beside her on the edge of the bed, and she levers up and wraps her arms around my neck, face pressed into my heart.

"I can't bear it for him," she whispers, and I feel the vibration of her words against my sweater.

"Nor can I."

My phone dings with an arriving text and we both shoot our

heads round to check on Harry, but he's out for the count. I take my phone out of my pocket. It's from Andrew.

"Shit," I say. "The divers are down at the lake. We should wake him."

Alexa pushes herself back against the mahogany headboard and sits there, arms braced around her knees, looking sideways at him.

"I don't think we should."

"It's not our choice, Lex," I say, echoing Andrew.

I watch her rest a slim brown hand against his cheek, fingers with giant silver rings, and I am reminded of Ling and her comedy diamond.

"What if he thinks you're her?" I whisper, and Alexa snatches her hand away.

"Oh God."

She wipes her hands across her face, smudging her clown's tears into dirty streaks.

"I never thought he'd marry," she says. "I just thought he was one of those funny old bachelor types who would spend his days drinking port and shuffling around his great big house with his Labradors for company. And until I met Ling I assumed that somehow that was enough and Harry was happy with it. But he wasn't happy, was he? And then he did find a girlfriend, actually a wife, and look what happens . . ."

She breaks off, crying quite loudly now. It can only be a matter of time before Harry wakes. Maybe that's a good thing, I don't know.

"I've spent most of the night lying here thinking about Harry and Ling. I remember after lunch at Harry's place the other day I thought how lucky they were, the way they'd found each other in pretty unlikely circumstances, let's face it. But I've also been thinking about Jack. And me. And Celia. You know about me and Jack, don't you? You know we've carried on our thing right the way through his marriage?"

"God, Lex, I didn't know. I always thought you were still a bit in love with him, but that's all."

"Yes, I'm in love with him. But that doesn't excuse what I've done. Do you remember that night when they had just got back from their honeymoon and Celia went home early? He came back with me. I tried to stop him, I tried not to have sex with him, but I just couldn't seem to help it. I'm powerless where Jack's concerned. I always have been."

I shake my head, for I am wordless. The depth of his treachery. Was Catherine powerless too?

You stole my girlfriend. You betrayed your wife. And me, how you have betrayed me.

"I don't know why I can't give him up. I've tried to so many times. I hate myself for what I'm doing to Celia. Sleeping with her husband behind her back. I feel like such a bitch. Every time I do it, I hate myself a bit more."

"I don't know what to say, Lex. Jack is trouble. And you and I both know that. Remember what he said to you about Catherine? She's not who everyone thinks she is? Well, neither is he."

Alexa stares back at me with confused, troubled eyes, and I want so much to tell her the truth—the filthy, ugly truth. Catherine and Jack slept together. That man you love, the one we have both loved for so long, is bad right the way through. And yet I also want to keep this lethal little bullet of knowledge for myself.

"Why are we even talking about Jack, anyway? We should be focusing on Harry."

Maybe through the waves of temazepam or ketamine or whatever it was the doctor gave him, Harry hears his name, because he shifts in his sleep and the sheets make a soft sighing sound beneath him. I think he is starting to wake up. I need to find some strength to deal with his split-second reality; any minute now he'll be opening his eyes to instant horror, just as Alexa did, only a thousand times worse.

A new text arrives, making us jump. My heart squeezes painfully; I almost can't look.

"Is it from Andrew?"

I nod, reading the screen. **They've got her** is all it says.

An hour later and I have dropped Harry home and am on my way to Jack's house. How many times have I made this journey, but never like this: my heart feels hollow, my brain half dead. And beneath it all, I pulse with fury.

It has been the worst of nights. Harry, as expected, insisted on seeing Ling before her body was taken away. Alexa and I escorted him to the lake, holding on to one arm each, Harry stumbling as though he was lame and dressed, incongruously, in a pair of my tracksuit bottoms, the only thing that came close to fitting him.

Ling was laid out on a stretcher covered in a black plastic sheet with a crowd of men standing by: the policemen who had been here all night and someone who turned out to be the pathologist.

Harry half collapsed when he saw the stretcher, head and shoulders right down, a dead weight, but Alexa and I just clutched him even tighter and somehow we made it. Andrew walked the last few paces to meet us.

"Harry," he said. "I am so sorry."

Harry said, "Please," though it was more of a croak than a word.

The policemen scattered and the pathologist introduced himself. He told us Ling's body had been found lodged in a thick tangle of weeds at the bottom of the lake.

"Are you saying she was stuck there?" Harry asked. "Is that why she drowned?"

"It's impossible for us to know exactly what happened. She'd been drinking, so she probably didn't realize how cold she was until it was too late. Your muscles are the first part of your body to lose heat, which means your legs and arms sometimes stop working. You're trying to swim but you find you can't. Suddenly you don't have the power to swim even a short distance."

"Why didn't she shout out to us? She can't have been far away."

"Often people make no sound at all as they drown. They're trying to save all their oxygen to keep breathing."

"How long? How long would it have taken?" Harry said, and the pathologist looked away for a second.

"Almost instant," he said.

Harry wanted to be left alone with Ling, and though Alexa and I tried to stay with him, he shouted at us to get away, dropping to his knees by the stretcher.

We turned our backs on him, though it made little difference. Even now his shock and heartache at the sight of his dead wife is imprinted on my mind, devastating and ineradicable. I'm worried for Harry, worried where this is going to end. Desperation is something I know. What is there for Harry without Ling? Or for me without Catherine?

Now with her name comes the image of Jack. Jack and Catherine. Oh, I can see it, in perfect, graphic clarity. Her young, pale, naked body sitting astride him, his hands reaching up for her nipples, her dark eyes flashing ecstasy, the piercing lechery of his blue ones. They could not have picked a better way to destroy me. I'm not surprised they decided not to tell me. I wouldn't have forgiven them, then or now.

Jack and Celia's house, just a mile down the road from my own, is like a second home. Or rather, it used to be. They did that clever thing of buying a beautiful old farmhouse, pale-gray stone, leaded windows, thatched roof, and ripping it to shreds inside. So now they have a house that to all intents they have built themselves, only it doesn't look that way. On any other day I would have loved arriving to their immaculate lime-green lawn, the air sweet with the full-blown scent of late-summer roses, a handful of birds surfing the thermals in small, lazy circles. But now I have only two thoughts. Harry has lost his wife. And Jack betrayed me.

Celia hurries across the lawn to meet me, Freddie in her arms.

"God, you haven't been to bed yet, have you? I'm sorry we left when we did, just Freddie—"

I bat away her apology. As if that could matter.

"Do you know what happened?"

"She got into difficulty somehow, might have been cramp or maybe her muscles seizing up because she was cold. That happens a lot, apparently, especially when you're drunk. We were probably swimming for a while, longer than we realized. And then once she hit the bottom she might have got trapped in the weeds and couldn't get back up again. We'll never know."

"That's horrific."

"I knew about the weeds. I should have known something like this could happen. If I hadn't been drunk, I would have stopped her."

"Lucian, this is not your fault."

I shrug, knowing there is no point having this conversation.

"How's my godson?" I say, an effort at normalcy as we walk toward the house.

When Jack and Celia asked me to be godfather, I almost said no.

"You are joking?" I think was my first response, but it turned out they weren't.

"He took another step this morning," Celia says. "If you can call it that."

She is unapologetically posh today: blond hair held back by a silk scarf, pale-pink shirt, navy three-quarter-length trousers; all that's missing is the pearls. But my heart aches a little to see her. Celia, with her unappreciated domestic skills and her firm but fair efficiency, is exactly what I need right now.

In the kitchen, a huge barn-like room with floor-to-ceiling windows across one side, Jack lies on a giant overstuffed sofa, hand clutched round the neck of a beer bottle, TV remote balanced on his stomach. He's watching the Grand Prix, and the furious buzzing—like bees on amphetamines, I always think—slices through my brain.

"Jesus, man, what's happening? Are you all right?" he says when he sees me, though he doesn't bother to get off the sofa.

I tell him what I know. That Harry has gone home, refusing to have Alexa or Rachel or me staying with him, for tonight at least. That we've got Andrew's doctor on standby with a sackload of meds, and the plan is to sedate him through the next twenty-four hours. That Ling got into problems in the lake probably because she was cold. "She might have had an undiagnosed heart problem. I guess we'll find out."

"Right." Jack shrugs and clicks his eyes back to the screen, draining the contents of his bottle and setting it down on the floor.

"Turn the fucking television off."

Jack looks up in surprise, but he picks up the remote and silences the screen.

"Harry's wife just died. Do you even care?"

"I know you haven't had any sleep, but don't take it out on me."

You fucked my girlfriend—your kind of word, your kind of action. I'm not sure whether to cry or slap him. I'm not sure how to cure my heart, broken by Ling's death, scalded by the betrayal of my supposed best friend. Now is not the time. I repeat it in my brain like a mantra. Clearly now is not the time.

"Be nice, Jack," Celia calls from the other end of the kitchen.

"Shut up," Jack says without bothering to look up at her.

Like I say, I'm reevaluating everything. Not just the fact that he slept with Catherine—and oh God, the pain that image brings. But the way he treats his wife. These sudden glimpses of brutality. And I am wondering, right now, why it is that my friendship with him has been so enduring. Was he laughing at me all along, while he shared my house and drank my wine and ate at all the most expensive restaurants on my credit card and then stole the one person, the only person who has ever really mattered to me?

"Would you like some eggs, Lucian? Or something else?" Celia asks.

Anything I eat will taste like cardboard. Cardboard eggs. May as well.

"What I'd really like is a beer," I say, and Jack gets to his feet for the first time.

I cannot look at him. I can barely stop myself reaching out and grabbing him by the throat. Is it true? Did you fuck her? Did you really do that to me?

While Jack gets my beer, I crouch down to talk to Freddie, who is strapped into one of those low-slung bouncy chairs.

"Keys?" I say, pulling my keys out of my jeans pocket, and he snatches them from my hand and holds them up close to his face, deadly serious, frowning, as if he's examining a diamond for flaws. I can see from Celia's expression, rounded eyes, mouth pursed, that car keys were not the right thing to give him.

"Here." Jack hands me a Beck's. "Great party, by the way," he says, chipping the top off another bottle for himself. "Apart from the ending."

I try to take a swig of beer but there's just this great bubble of sorrow in my throat and I can't get it down.

"I know what you're doing and I'm beyond tired, so just fuck off, will you?"

"Oh come on. Of course it's tragic that Ling died, of course we're sad about it, but we didn't really know her, did we?"

"Harry loved her."

"Ling was very sweet, I agree, but we all know it was a marriage of convenience. She needed money, Harry needed a wife."

Celia screams and drops a saucepan on the floor, and the baby creases up his face for a few seconds, like a time delay, and then starts yelling.

"I hate you!" It seems to burst out of her.

"Oh fuck's sake, Celia, calm down."

"I hate the things you say. I hate who you are. You pretend that you're this great guy, this great husband and father, this great friend, but really all you think about is yourself. Harry's wife just died and you don't even care. It means nothing to you. You're disgusting. You disgust me."

"Sweetheart, that's just not true. Of course I care. Why are you getting so upset?"

Jack moves toward her, but Celia screams.

"Get away from me!"

She unsnaps the baby from his chair and grabs him into her arms.

"Sorry about your eggs," she says, rocking him back and forth.

I shake my head. I can't drink the beer or eat the eggs or find a single thing to say. Except the words I have stuck in my head. *I hate you too, Jack. I hate you too.*

Fifteen Years Earlier

By the time I returned to Bristol, the cold wind of disenchantment had blown, and I was universally abhorred for bringing you—it was said—to the edge of a breakdown.

"Something's happened," Liv told me when I arrived back at our flat, a great deal thinner, my skin marked by exhaustion circles, the pallor of many nights without sleep. "No one is talking to us. You for the way you dumped Lucian, me by association."

Liv was outraged by this, but she still stood by me.

"He's broken, Catherine. When I saw him, his hands were shaking so much when he lit his cigarette. I thought he was going to start crying."

At first I just nodded, for speech was impossible.

"Aren't you going to say something? Don't you care?"

"Nothing matters anymore," I said eventually, and my voice sounded exactly as I felt: emotionless, zombie-like, an expression of grayness. Somehow I found the words to tell Liv, "My mother is dying. She hasn't got long."

"Oh Catherine," Liv said. "How can this have happened to you?"

I effectively closed my life down, skipping lectures and hurrying out to my weekly tutorials, furtively scanning the streets like a criminal, ducking into doorways if I spotted anyone I knew. I resigned from the student newspaper; no amount of pleading from Angry Jeff could make me change my mind. At night I lay sleepless in my bed, thinking of you, then thinking of my mother, but only for a few minutes at a time, for the pain was so vicious and extreme I sometimes felt like I was the one who was dying.

I was something different now, a time bomb, a student with a gory countdown to death and bereavement. People didn't want to know. Friends I'd drunk coffee with day in, day out, now crossed the street rather than think of the right thing to say. A close cousin of mine—we were born six weeks apart—stopped calling. I wouldn't see him until my mother's funeral, and even then he had no words. I didn't blame any of them. We were nineteen, twenty. Death was too big for us to handle. It made me think of you, facing your father's suicide all alone. Such irony: the only person who could understand what I was going through was the one I couldn't speak to.

News travels fast in a university town. Not long after my return, I opened the door to find Sam standing there in his big black overcoat and his Nike trainers, worn as sporting accessory, not fashion statement. His eyes were always able to express multiple emotions—strength, understanding, forgiveness. To Sam I could say sorry, over and over again. He opened his arms and I walked right into them. I thought if I held on to him tightly enough, then maybe he could levitate me away.

Four Months Before: Catherine

And I am home. Leaning back against the front door, inhaling the smells of this house of mine, something bacony that Sam must have cooked for supper, fresh paint and coffee grounds, and mud from the stream. In the sitting room I don't bother to turn on the lights, but lie down on the sofa, faded blue and uncomfortable but ours, and instantly reassuring with Daisy's discarded trainer socks balled up in one corner, a half-drunk mug of tea on the floor beside it. Joe's Adidas Superstars, a birthday present, kicked off at right angles, one face up, the other on its side. Thousands of pieces of Lego in a bright-blue plastic box. DVD cases opened up, their discs spilled out across the floorboards. It says a lot, this room. It tells me that Sam, fanatical about returning discs to cases and mugs to the dishwasher and dirty socks to the laundry basket, is losing his grip.

I lie in the darkness picturing what must be happening down at the lake. You'll be talking to the police, and perhaps there will already be a cluster of journalists there. I imagine you trying to console Harry with his insurmountable grief; I think of Alexa and Rachel, swamping him the minute he was hauled off the boat, even Jack on standby, arms folded across his chest: the five of you as impenetrable in tragedy as you are in everyday life.

But mostly I think of you, your face, as I told you the truth about why I'd left. I replay this moment again and again, the words I'd held in for so long a hemorrhaged jet of poison. I see your face, shock first, then immediate withdrawal. You couldn't get away fast enough. I chastise myself for my selfishness, telling you this while you were dealing with Ling's death. But I also see that there was no other way. The drowning of that sweet girl has left us with nothing but endings.

I don't expect to sleep, not tonight, not with Ling and Harry and you, always you, pressing against my mind. But I wake a few hours later, cold and sore from my blanketless, pillowless night, to Daisy's shout, "Mummy's here!" and so there is no warning, none at all, just my small pajamaed daughter and Sam, standing in front of me, long brown legs with their fine covering of black hair.

"I didn't hear you come in."

"Why did you sleep here, Mummy?"

It's hard to answer with her arms around my neck, my face pressed up tight against her hard little chest. And then I realize I *can't* answer, as the trauma of last night—Ling's drowning, your face as I told you about Jack—crowds my brain. No room for anything else. No words, no voice.

"Catherine?"

"Mummy? Mum!"

Daisy sounds urgent, frightened. She needs me to speak.

I snap myself back to the present. I shift her to one side.

"You've gone all brown," I say eventually, gripping one skinny sunburned thigh. "Look at your legs."

Daisy pats my face with her small hands; she traces her forefingers lightly over the skin beneath my eyes.

"Your makeup has come off," she says. "Your mascara."

Daisy is a makeup fanatic, or rather she will be the moment she is allowed. I can imagine her age fourteen or fifteen, glued to YouTube videos, learning how to create the perfect smoky eye. She knows the contents of my paltry cosmetics bag better than I do myself; she also knows that in my world mascara is a rare event.

"Where did you go last night?" she asks.

"I went to a party with Liv."

Now I look up to find that your name is between us, stamped into the burn of Sam's stare, the stiffness of his shoulders, one a little higher than the other, his neck tilted, mouth pinched. We have always been able to communicate with our eyes, Sam and I, and even as I'm answering Daisy's questions—"It was in Somerset, not far from here . . . The house of someone we went to university with a long time ago"—he is telling me that I have done the one thing he always dreaded, and I am telling him, hand clamped around the thigh of my small daughter, that he did this to us too, remember, not just me but him, him and Julia, him and his one-night love affair.

"So this was Lucian Wilkes's party?"

There you are again, your name in the air like the fire particles from a sparkler, at least to me.

"Yes."

This yes, this single affirmation, is to Sam and me something much more. Yes, I slept with him; yes, I love him; yes, it is as bad as—perhaps worse than—everything you have ever feared. But there are things Sam doesn't see. You probably hate me. I doubt I will ever see you again.

"I'll make some tea," Sam says, quiet, flat voice, and I watch him walk away, the squeak of bare feet on bare boards, through the open doorway that leads into our bright new show-home kitchen where the sun glows from all the surfaces, turning everything white gold.

Joe arrives in the doorway, bare chested, one strand of sleep-spiked hair sticking straight up, last year's navy-blue pajama shorts, which now finish well above the knee.

"Mum!"

He loiters at the door with a self-conscious smile.

"Come here!"

I stand up and he runs straight into my arms, and I allow myself a few seconds of breathing him in, hair that smells of the sea, skin that smells of sleep.

"When did you get back?"

"Very late last night."

"I missed you."

This is so unexpected, so unlike him, that I feel my chest tightening, the threat of sudden hot tears.

"Can we have pancakes, Dad?" Joe asks.

Pancakes are Sam's specialty, our celebratory breakfast for birthdays, for homecomings, for cheering ourselves up at the end of a holiday. They will be the last thing he'll feel like making.

"Sure."

I watch him walk over to the fridge and take out milk, eggs, butter, then flour from the larder, stooping to find my mother's chipped beige mixing bowl from the cupboard. Sunday morning in the kitchen, children in pajamas, husband making pancakes, hallmarks of our past. It looks the same, but it feels very different. Any moment now, surely the kids will pick up on the silence, weighted and ugly with things not yet said.

"Want to check on the stream?" Joe asks Daisy, and I find myself smiling in spite of the unspoken gloom. The stream will be the same as it was yesterday and the day before, the same as it was when we first moved in.

"Pancakes will be ready in ten," Sam says, his first words for a while, and they disappear together through the French windows, running the length of our long, sloping lawn, her curls flying, his legs skinny and brown in his too-short shorts.

Sam spins around. The look on his face.

"Why the fuck did you let this go on so long, Catherine? You've always wanted him, why did it take you so long?"

"That's not true."

"You married me because you couldn't have him. It's so fucking bor-ing."

"You don't understand."

"Oh I do. I've been married to you for thirteen bloody years, I know how you've mooned about, wishing I was him or he was me, wishing your whole fucking life away, and never mind the fact that we've got two kids and I've spent years, literally years, trying to make you happy."

Sam is not a swearer; it's one of the things I've always liked best about him. The anger in his face frightens me.

"It's over, Sam."

"It will never be over."

"Sam. Please. There's something I need to tell you. A girl died last night. A friend. I was there when it happened. I was there when she drowned."

"What?"

"Last night at the party. She was called Ling. She jumped into the lake and she never came back up."

"Let me get this straight. You've got a new friend called Ling who I've never even heard of and last night she died?"

"It was horrific, Sam. She's Harry's wife—she was, I mean. She was the loveliest, sweetest girl you could imagine and they'd been married less than a month."

Perhaps it's the mention of Harry's name—Harry, Lucian, for Sam always a toxic association—but I watch his face paling beneath the suntan, the anger rushing back in.

"You're all broken up about some girl you just met? And right here, right now your marriage is unraveling? What's wrong with you, Catherine? What the hell is wrong with you?"

He turns away from me and I am left staring at his back, an

enemy in my own kitchen. There is nothing for me to do except creep away.

Upstairs, I run a bath—our family bathroom with its map-of-the-world shower curtain and Daisy's fruit-scented potions scattered around the rim—and sit in the hot water, knees hunched, thinking hard. The relief of being here again in the comfort of our world, safe in this place where good things happen, where pancakes are made and streams are celebrated and baths are pungent with kiwi-scented bath foam. I am free to cry now for the girl who has died, the desperate end to her fairy tale and the searing conclusion to ours.

"Did you ever love me?" Sam asks, straight off, once the kids are finally in bed, our first chance to talk.

"I still do."

He shrugs this off as if it's nothing.

"Why did you leave him, tell me that. Why did you put us both through all of this?"

"Was 'all of this' so bad? Two children, the years in London?"

"You slept with him, didn't you? Do you think that makes us even?"

"No, I don't think it makes us even. Yes, I slept with him. I'm sorry. It wasn't revenge, if that's what you think."

There's a bottle of red wine on the table, opened but so far untouched. Now Sam grabs it and pours himself a glass. He knocks back a couple of inches, his hands shaking.

"Fuck, Catherine. Fuck. Maybe I hate you."

"What about Julia? What about her? We haven't even talked about that."

"Because Julia doesn't matter, and you know that. I don't love her, I never did. It was a mistake and I regret it and I'm sorry, of course I am. I was an idiot. But it doesn't change anything, not really. You are all I ever wanted, stupid, naïve bloody fool that I am."

I reach out to try to take his hand, but he snatches his away. Another fast gulp of his wine.

"Be honest, you don't really care about Julia. And it's freed you up, hasn't it? It's not like you lost any time in tracking him down."

"I didn't mean this to happen," I say again, and he clicks his tongue, irritated.

"Yes you did. In your head you did. You think I didn't know what you were thinking all those times we saw something about him in the papers, or when Liv or I mentioned him and you'd go deathly quiet?"

It's true. I remember those times, my private agony, or so I thought, when Liv and Sam said your name, Lucian, Lucian Wilkes, and expected me still to breathe.

"Are you in love with him?"

He asks this like he's stabbing little letters of hate into the air. And here it is, my chance to put things right. I'll tell the truth, part of the truth, the only part Sam wants to hear.

"I love you, Sam. I always did. Despite what you think. Despite everything."

I see him looking at me, and somewhere very distant a light comes on in his eyes. Hope, that's what it is. A faint blue flicker of hope.

Four Months Before: Lucian

I thought I'd confront Jack straightaway, but as the days pass, something else is happening. I am transformed by knowledge; I am watching, observing, biding my time. The fact that Jack—my best friend, my supposed brother—continues with his life thinking everything is as normal gives me strength. For me, everything has changed.

Jack appalls me. Not just the devastating infidelity with Catherine—an image that haunts me day and night—but the way he has carried on sleeping with Alexa right under his wife's nose. There's something so malevolent in that. A selfishness, a lack of care. He is not who I thought he was, and each day seems to prove that a little more. Since our last, fraught meeting on the morning after Ling died, Jack hasn't bothered to call, to find out about the police interviews I've sat through, or the coroner's findings (accidental drowning, with alcohol a contributing factor), or even, it seems, to ask how Harry is doing, which is not well.

This morning his butler called and asked us to come: me, Rachel, and Alexa. None of us speaks during the fifteen-minute journey, but I understand that the girls feel just as I do as we stand waiting outside the front door, Rachel brushing tears from her eyes with the heels of her hands. The last time I stood here, Catherine was by my side, but to think of her now is to falter, and I need superhuman strength for this first meeting with Harry.

Filip opens the door, and his face, paler than I've ever seen, is a mirror of our own. He has been looking after Harry for at least five years, and like Mary with me, he sees the inner workings of Harry's life, not just the veneer he chooses to present to us, his friends. The moment we're through the door, Filip says to Rachel and Alexa, "I'm sorry to say this, but Harry has changed his mind. He wants to see Lucian on his own."

Alexa says, "Of course, whatever he wants. How is he?" and Filip just shakes his head.

Walking up the stairs, same dark-blue carpet that dates back to his parents' day, I am reminded of all the years I stayed here throughout my teens. The house still smells of wax polish and leather books, but now there's an undercurrent of Polish cooking too, those little deep-fried dumplings that Harry loves. Little else has changed. Grim portraits on the walls; the giant and characteristically ugly brass-and-crystal chandelier that presents itself, a statement of poor taste, on the first floor. Would Ling have changed the house, given time? Would she have introduced light and warmth into its stark, stately interior, or even the unthinkable, persuaded Harry to sell and move into somewhere more habitable, somewhere more like Jack and Celia's farmhouse? Again, again, the sharp needle of hate.

I am breathing hard and a little too quickly as I turn the door handle to Harry's room. I'm not sure what to expect, but I find him in complete darkness, the thick velvet curtains drawn against the sun-bright afternoon.

"Harry, it's me. Can I open the curtains, just a fraction? It's hard to see."

"I'll turn the light on."

He clicks on his bedside lamp and floods the room with a depressing nighttime glow, and now I see everything: Ling's clothes folded up on an armchair, her hairbrush on the dressing table, and beside it a photograph of the two of them in a tuk-tuk in Bangkok, Ling with her radiant full-beam smile. Harry is lying on the bed dressed for winter: cords, shirt, jumper, thick woolen socks.

I am not sure where to sit. The chair is the obvious place, but now that I've seen Ling's clothes, I'm worried about touching or displacing them, so I perch uneasily on the edge of the bed instead. I'm trying in my mind to form the right words—not how are you, never that, but something that shows I understand, at least a little bit. I think of something Catherine told me, less than a week ago, though it feels as distant as the fragment of a remembered dream: "Until you've lost someone you love, you don't know what it's like. You think you do, but you don't. The absence of that person is everywhere, you can't escape it."

The irony of those words, for that is exactly how I feel about her now. She is nowhere and everywhere and utterly, irrevocably transformed.

"I'm so sorry, Harry. I know how hard this is for you."

Harry nods and turns his face away from me.

"You loved her so much."

He nods again; there's some sort of gasp, that's all. In the silence, I look around the room and see only Ling. The trainers she wore the first time I met her are stationed neatly at the foot of the bed. Her phone in its bright-yellow casing lies on the bedside table. It hurts to see that phone. I imagine Harry scrolling through her messages and photos, looking for something, anything that might bring her back to him for a moment. When Catherine and I broke up all those years ago, Harry barely left my side. I thought it would drive me mad, his overinquiring concern, his constant presence when rage and self-pity and alcohol were the only accomplices I wanted. But it was his acute anxiety, a hunch that saw him tearing across town in the middle of the night, that saved my life. And here I am, in a gloomy lamplit room, wondering how I can save his.

"I'm going to get you through this. We'll take it hour by hour. Minute by minute."

"Not sure I can get through it. Not sure I want to. What's the point?"

This is not the moment for a debate on existentialism, especially when I have my own snake pit of anxiety on that score. Love helps, if you can find it, but not when it's snatched away from you like Harry's. Like mine. My fury hardens when I think of the real reason for Catherine's desertion. I am filled with hate.

Harry sighs, a long, yogic expelling of air.

"I was careless with Ling, and now she's gone. She would have been better off if she'd stayed in Bangkok, if she'd never met me."

"You can't say that. Ling loved you, Harry. None of this is your fault."

"You don't think so?"

Harry looks at me properly for the first time. It's hard to meet his gaze. The truth is, I think we were all to blame; I think the five of us have been cruising toward a fatality of this kind for a long time. Rachel lost her kid a while back—why wasn't that our wake-up call? And why did I let her blow her chance to reconnect with Max, the one thing, the only thing, deep down, that she cares about? Another disaster, and we just allowed it to happen. And why did none of us, even Harry, consider that we had a duty to Ling, who had no experience of our reckless world with its impenetrable rules? For years we never needed anyone else, we thought we were safe in our unreachable bubble, we thought there was a code of honor in a life lived without judgment or counsel; seems to me now the exact opposite is true. Carelessness is what defined us in the end.

"Lucian, I need to ask you something. A favor."

"Anything."

"Ling's funeral. I can't do it. I thought I could, but every time I start to think about it, I realize I can't. I can't think about coffins or flowers or music or prayers."

"You'd like me to organize it?"

"Will you?"

We stare at each other, Harry and I, friends for how many years now—is it actually twenty? I realize, looking at him, that he has aged a decade or more in the three days since Ling's death. He always looked older than the rest of us, with his prematurely balding head, but right now he could pass for fifty.

"Of course I'll do it, I'll do everything."

"It needs to be exactly as she wanted."

I'm waiting for Harry to tell me what Ling wanted, though I can't imagine in the short time they knew each other that they would have got around to making funeral plans.

"It needs to be a lunch party. Forty or fifty people at the most. Thai food. Color everywhere, flowers, candles, whatever. You do understand?"

And finally I get the magnitude of what Harry is asking. He wants me to organize a wedding party for his dead wife.

Four Months Before: Catherine

A veneer of domesticity has returned, fraudulent but vital, on this, the last day before the start of the new school year. Sam sits at the kitchen table, science books spread in front of him, making notes in his spiky, spindly schoolboy writing onto a checkered pad. He wants to be in the garden with Joe, testing out the new football goal that arrived in a forest of cardboard in an Amazon delivery yesterday. Or planting out autumn bulbs with Daisy, gardening her latest obsession, she the girl of serial fetishes.

The children are marking out their last day of freedom hour by hour: Joe, iPod on, mooning about at the bottom of the garden, dreaming of salvation, or perhaps just football; Daisy, beginning and abandoning projects with feverish indecision—an insect hospital created out of twigs and leaves, one floor built, the other left dangling as if the builders had packed up and left, a new story begun in her holographic notebook, enthusiastically titled "The Girl in the Blue Dress" but petering out after just one paragraph. And me? Well, I'm just trying to fit myself back into this life of mine, trying to convince myself it can still work, trying, always trying, not to think about you.

Sam doesn't mention your name again, though it's harder than ever to avoid it, for your party and Ling's death have been all over the papers. I'm not surprised; it has all the credentials for a great human-interest story: the hapless aristo, one of the wealthiest men in Britain, apparently, the glitzy party, the rags-to-riches good fortune and ultimate downfall of a poverty-stricken village girl from Thailand. The papers love a good death. There's a photo of Ling, grainy and indistinct, probably sent in from someone's phone. I recognize the small white teeth, the flop of her dark fringe, the high collar of her yellow dress, but otherwise there is nothing of the girl I knew. "Tragic Ending for Toff's Thai Bride," cries the heading in *The Sun*. Ling is called "poor and illiterate"; I remember her eloquence in describing her life, the gift for storytelling that made it sound not deprived but magical. It makes me think that every story in every paper is founded on virtually nothing: a few bare facts, a journalist's hunch and empathy, or lack of it. There's a photo of you here, the one they often trot out, six or seven years old now, I would think. Your hair is shorter, your face, to my newly trained eye, a little rounder, and you are staring away from the camera, your chin jutted at an angle that makes you look the way they want you to look: arrogant, disdainful, indisputably handsome.

It feels in some ways as if nothing has changed. I am back here again, absorbing your photos like an illness, bearing your silence as my penance. For although I texted you yesterday to ask about Harry and to tell you I'm sorry, have always been sorry, will be sorry, I'm sure, for the rest of my life, you haven't responded. I'm not surprised. I knew the severity of the crime when it happened; I'll never forgive myself for it either.

Last night, after the children were in bed, Sam made a deal with me.

"All right," he said, filling up both our glasses with wine as we sat once again at the kitchen table. "Let's try one more time. But you've got to promise me something. No more mooning about the past. You have to draw a line under what's happened. He's over for you"—never your name, never that—"and Julia is over for me.

Let's not talk about them, let's lock them away and concentrate on what we have: each other and the kids."

I can do this, that's what I tell myself, hour by hour, even while I'm secretly hoping for a text or a phone call from you, just something, anything that might alleviate our brutal end.

"I couldn't have forgiven you"—the last words you spoke to me, forever gouged into my brain. But all there is from you is silence, and I understand why. Now you know the truth, there is nothing left to say. I need to find my own way of letting you go.

The uniforms are laid out on the ends of their beds, pencil cases filled, shiny new shoes by the front door. There's an hour before supper and my family are all in the garden, and I stand at the bedroom window, watching. Daisy is back at the ant hospital, cross-legged but leaning forward, placing each twig with pinpoint precision. I can only see her small, narrow back in its turquoise T-shirt, the cloudburst of knotted hair, hell for me in the bathroom later. When they were small, we loved to photograph the children like this; somehow, the unposed, unaware rear view always seemed to best capture the innocence of early childhood.

Sam and Joe are walking down to the stream, matching shorts and matching walks, both with their necks tilted a little to the right. They are where they most like to be, a world for two, one that requires little effort, nothing so mundane as small talk. They might mention the football, Man U a shared passion, or whatever project they're about to begin, but it won't feel like talking. Sometimes I watch them playing cards or chess or watching a YouTube video or just drinking a mug of tea, side by side at the kitchen table, and I envy them that contented silence. I've never really had that insularity for two, though I had it with you, didn't I, just for a moment?

There is time now to open up the shoebox, to rifle through its contents, shiny pieces of paper ripped from magazines, rough, yellowing pages of newspaper, letters written on sheets of lined A4. The letter I can't usually bear to read looms out at me, and I pick it up and hold it between my hands, vision blurred, but that doesn't matter, for I know every word.

> *How could I have got it so wrong, tell me that? I believed everything you said in the café that day, I thought that you and I were the same, we thought the same, we felt the same. You gave yourself to me and I gave myself to you and that was it, that's what we said, a done deal, no going back, why would we want to?*

You could have written this letter to me yesterday, its message of hurt and reproach exactly the same except that now you know why you got it wrong. Now you know what I'm capable of, and that girl you idolized is as lost to you as she is to me.

You have made your choice, and I have made mine. I know what I have to do as I stand cradling the shoebox in my arms in the middle of my bedroom, holding all that's left of you, it seems to me. The box has to go. I could walk it down to the recycling center at the end of the village and tip all that paper, years of cuttings, crumpled and worn, into the mouth of the big green metal box along with everyone else's Sunday magazines and slashed Inland Revenue envelopes. Or perhaps I could start a bonfire when Sam and the children are at school, your photographs and letters left to burn amid the autumn leaves. No, I couldn't bear that.

In my mind's eye I'm running through all the secret places in this house of ours: the cupboard underneath the stairs, the cellar, which is so damp its walls never quite dry out, the attic that neither Sam nor I have set foot in since the day we moved in. Once my decision is made, I act quickly, pulling down the little ladder into the loft and stashing the shoebox in between all the other unpacked boxes, all those things we hang on to and yet will never use: the old-fashioned glass chandelier that hasn't looked right in any of our homes, my wedding tiara, several pairs of my mother's Gucci shoes, which have always been a size too big for me and are not going to change.

After it's done, I scan the upstairs window to make sure my family are still in the garden, then go downstairs to begin supper. The box is out of sight. The box is out of mind. This is progress. That's what I tell myself.

Four Months Before: Lucian

I'm becoming an expert on pharmaceuticals. Valium, twenty milligrams, not ten, will get Harry through the next couple of hours while he endures his wife's funeral. Alexa and I find the brightest thing in his wardrobe for him to wear, a pale-pink shirt with gray trousers, and walk him down to the chapel, shuffling between us like a crippled octogenarian, eyes on the ground, which is a good thing because it means he misses the hard, inquisitive stares of all the people gathered by the entrance. But I see them, I see the girls, friends of mine, most of them, reaching up to whisper into the ears of their men, I see the men dragging contemplatively on their cigarettes, then darting their eyes over for a quick look at Harry. There are several photographers here too, cameras trained against their faces and a flurry of low-level digital clicks the minute we come into view.

Alexa says, "I'm going to tell them to fuck off. It's a funeral, for God's sake. They're trespassing, aren't they?"

But Harry, who has looked up straight into the eye of the cameras, says in his drawn-out, drug-saturated voice, "Don't bother, Lex."

A girl breaks from the crowd, smooth blond hair, peacock-colored dress and shoes, and I realize at the last moment that it's Charlotte Lomax, the funeral repackaged as fashion opportunity.

"Harry," she says, "I just wanted to say I am so—"

He raises a hand to silence her but keeps his stare downward.

"Thank you. I know you are."

We are in front of the chapel now. The crowd has separated, leaving us a direct path to the door, and there, waiting in a row, are Jack, Celia, and Rachel. Jack is wearing a new suit, by the looks of things, cobalt blue, slim fitting, Helmut Lang I'd imagine—my favorite designer and therefore his—and he's wearing it with box-fresh white Adidas trainers.

Hate doesn't have enough punch for the way you make me feel.

"Harry, oh God, man," he says, rushing forward, sunglasses on. He expertly maneuvers Alexa out of the way and takes Harry's other arm, so that the three of us are making our way to the front of the church, the girls in line behind us. More clicks, more photographs, more papers sold on irrelevant crap, the vulture press doing what it does best.

I hear Alexa gasp and say, "Oh, the flowers," and I know she's crying, which we had promised each other we wouldn't do, but the flowers are tough to take. I rang the Bristol florists we'd used for my party and asked them to fill the chapel with the brightest, most colorful things they had.

"Nothing funereal, and not too weddingy either," I said.

I knew Harry wanted to replicate the wedding party Ling had planned, but I also knew that anything bridal would push him even further down into his private underworld of gloom. Their response was to line up jam jars of gerberas along each windowsill in exactly the colors I'd asked for—hot pink, brilliant orange, acid yellow—and to tie festive little bunches from the end of every pew. They do break your heart, these flowers, they do say Ling, Ling with her fondness for color, her constant smile. I am pole-axed by sadness for this young woman I had scarcely got to know.

There is no coffin here today; Ling will be buried next week, if all goes to plan, beside a favorite oak tree on Harry's estate (utter minefield of red tape to get this sanctioned; I'm letting Andrew handle it). So it's the five of us up front, plus Ling's sister, Amara, who has come from Hong Kong and plans to leave immediately after the funeral. Harry offered to fly Ling's parents over during a god-awful phone call with a Thai translator we'd found in Bristol, Harry's gut-wrenching sobs punctuating a language that made no sense to either of us. But they refused. Hardly surprising. It was enough their eldest daughter was coming, they said.

I tried to talk to Amara when she arrived. I told her how much I liked Ling. How sorry I was she had died at my party, how I felt responsible. It was a tragic accident, I said, and I wished so much it hadn't happened.

But she could scarcely look at me, it seemed.

"My sister was very happy in Bangkok. She loved that job," was all Amara would say before she turned away.

Somehow Harry makes it through the service, and just before the end, Alexa and I escort him, one arm each, out of the chapel, through another photographic assault, and back up to the house, where the scent of Thai cooking fills the air. A sit-down lunch for fifty has been laid up in the orangery—white tablecloths, vivid flowers, that beautiful sloping view down to the cedar tree. It is, I think, exactly what Harry wanted, what Ling had planned, albeit for an altogether different kind of gathering.

"Let's get a drink, for God's sake, before everyone arrives."

Harry shakes his head. "No. I'm done in. I'm going back to bed."

"Please stay," Alexa says. "I was going to sit next to you at lunch; you wouldn't have to talk to anyone."

"No." He half shouts it.

In grief, Harry, famous among us for his kindness, his politeness, is brusque to the point of brutality. He walks off in his crumpled pink shirt and we let him go, Alexa and I, staring after him like troubled parents. Just before he disappears out of sight, he turns and gives us a cursory wave.

"Thanks," he says. "Both of you. I mean it."

At lunch I'm sitting next to Rachel, beautiful in her favorite emerald-green dress and a good bottle in, by the looks of things. I wish I could forget as easily as her, but I'm wrecked by a vision of what this party should have been—Ling in a white wedding dress, Harry happier than any of us had ever seen him. And as always, my head is also full of Catherine. And Jack. For I cannot see her without also seeing him. I cannot remember the velocity of her passion, one touch enough to make her explode, it seemed, or the way we tore each other apart, without thinking: she did that with him too. Jack knows the mind-bending eroticism that is being in bed with Catherine, and how I hate him for that.

"So it's over with Catherine? For good, do you think?" Rachel has always been able to read my thoughts.

I top up both of our glasses with Harry's palest-pink wine.

"Yes, it's over. I should have listened to you and Alexa; I was an idiot to go back there."

"No surprise that you did. You never really got over her."

"You warned me about her, and I didn't listen. You tried to tell me what she was like."

Rachel looks at me, astonished. "I thought Catherine was an angel, according to you? She just married the wrong guy."

I shrug, attempting indifference, and take a deep slug of my Côtes de Provence medicine. It is so shocking—literally, I feel I am in shock—to have fallen in love with Catherine all over again and then to have been smashed up against this brick wall of hate, hurt, and the impossibility of forgiveness.

Rachel touches my wrist. Cool brown hand with her rings of gold and her nails painted pink.

"Lucian?"

I remember now as she looks at me, all booze-exacerbated earnestness, that Rachel's eyes seem to change color when she gets serious. I'm sure it's not the case, but as I return her gaze, I register how her eyes are now a classic navy blue. I tried to tell her about this once, how I could mix a whole palette of blues from the different shades of her eyes, and she just laughed. Now, though, there's no laughter. Just Rachel's worried gaze.

"Promise me you won't fall apart like last time." She touches my wineglass lightly. "Lay off this stuff, OK?"

It's rich coming from her, an addict, but I get the warning. My own potential alcoholism pulses through my veins, the son of my dipso mother after all, preferred poison Pouilly-Fumé by the caseload. She drank without contrition from morning till night, champagne for breakfast if she wanted, the after-hours malt whiskey that turned her into a monster. I see myself doing the same thing, only my passion is more vodka based. And there's a small but insistent voice in my head that I try hard to ignore. This is too much, the voice says. You're drinking too much. When are you going to stop? I tell myself I'll stop the moment it's no longer fun.

When Catherine left me last time, it wasn't fun. There was the discovery of her note, scribbled in some careless juxtaposition on the facing page of my sketchbook next to the drawing I'd made of her a few days before: I've changed my mind. I can't do this. I can't see you anymore.

There was the rampaging through town, stalking her, then, when that got me nowhere, stalking her flatmate, Liv, the next best thing.

"She's gone home," Liv told me. "She doesn't want to be in a relationship; I'm sorry, but she's asked that you leave her alone."

Did Liv know the truth? I wonder now. Has she always known?

This little bullet of hate that lodges within my chest could zap anyone who knew and didn't tell me.

It wasn't just the fact of Catherine leaving that tore me apart. I know that it was also a delayed reaction to my father's death, to my visceral terror of abandonment, of aloneness. My response was to try to obliterate myself, first with alcohol, then with pills. But that was all a long time ago, and it's laughable, really, that Rachel and I are sitting here discussing my drinking rather than hers.

"I'll make a deal with you, Rach. How about you and I quit together? How about you give the coke a rest for a while too?"

As expected, her eyes fill with tears and she shoots her head away from me.

"Don't turn this one on me, Lucian."

Today is not the day for either of us to address our demons, and after lunch we join the rest of the guests on the cedar lawn, with our own personal bottle of wine to finish. Celia comes up to say her goodbyes, and I can tell instantly that something is wrong. It will be Jack, of course, ignoring her, or flirting with Alexa, or perhaps just the same crushing disregard I witnessed at their house.

"Celia, are you all right? I hope you don't mind me asking, it's just the other day . . ."

"No, not really," she says, voice unsteady. "But I can't talk about it."

Tears are imminent, this much I know, and I motion to her to sit down next to us.

"Sit with us for a few minutes. Please."

She shakes her head quickly and starts to walk away.

"You've always been very kind to me, Lucian," she says.

Celia can't have been gone more than a minute or two when Jack and Charlotte Lomax come around the corner and sit down next to us. Now that I know the real Jack, the one he's been so careful to hide, the one who fucks other people's girlfriends and cheats on his wife, I find myself wondering if these two have been having an affair. Why stop at Alexa? Or Catherine?

"Pass the wine, mate," Jack says, and I refill their glasses with the remains of our bottle.

"Plenty more where that came from," says Rachel, stumbling to her feet. The three of us watch her tacking across the lawn, a little too much to the left, a little too much to the right.

"What a dreadful day," Charlotte says. "Poor Harry."

"How's he doing now?" Jack asks.

I tell them that Ania and Filip are stationed like surrogate parents outside his bedroom door. He's not eating, he's not sleeping, it's a struggle to make him drink water. There's a sharp little moment of silence where neither of them seems to be able to find anything to say. I could help them, but I don't. I find that I'm enjoying the mild discomfort of my oldest friend, watching him absorb the heat of my reticence. Does he see it, this gradual, careful retraction of mine? A leisurely snipping away of the ties that once bound us together.

I'm not sure who I am anymore; I just know that I have changed.

Now

Something new is happening. They say the therapy is starting to work, and I think they may be right. For though I am not talking, I am listening. Listening with a fierce greed for any information on you. And if I wait long enough, I find that it comes, I find that someone always mentions your name. I am crying too, and that's progress, apparently. The first time it happened, Liv pointed it out to Alison and neither of them could keep the buoyancy from their voices.

"Oh dear, beauty," Alison said, crouching down beside my chair and taking hold of my hand. "Are you feeling sad today? It's good to cry. You let it out now, my darling."

Today Liv and Sam are here together and they are having—"argument" is too strong; let's call it a disagreement about Greg's slow-burn technique. He is addressing each of the obstacles in my past that he believes contributed to my eventual mutism, ticking them off one by one—bereavement, shame, isolation . . . Oh yes, it's always a fun-packed therapy session.

Liv wants to know if Greg has discovered how much I remember about the night I was admitted here, the events that preceded it. They are trying to be subtle, lowered voices, stationed a few meters away from me, but of course they do not know that I now strain to catch every word.

"Does she know what happened? Do you think she's remembered?" Liv asks, and Sam shakes his head.

"Greg thinks she wiped it out, you know that. He's decided not to ask her about it anymore. Thinks it's obstructive. He thinks she shuts down every time he brings it up."

"That's not fair on Catherine. One of us should tell her. How can she ever recover if she doesn't know the truth?"

"But she is recovering, Liv. You've said so yourself. She's expressing emotion now. The other day she smiled at Joe. It meant so much to him. To all of us."

"If you're not going to tell her, then I am. She has a right to know."

And here the disagreement implodes into a full-blown row.

"Like hell you will! She's my wife, and we will do things the way her psychiatrist tells us to do them. Do you understand, Liv? Do you understand?"

Sam is shouting and Liv is probably crying, but I turn away from them and close off their sound. The information I wanted is not going to come today. Soon Sam and Liv will go, and I will be alone again. I'll stare out through a gap in the curtains at the nighttime sky, navy blue with bursts of sizzling white, just like one of Daisy's drawings.

Fifteen Years Earlier

It was astonishing how we managed to avoid each other in our final year, pinned apart by the same desire. Wherever you were likely to be, I wasn't, and I guess it was the same for you. Even the English department became a safe zone, as you spent all your time at home working on your art. There were occasional glimpses, of course—you and Rachel seen through the window of Foyles bookshop, you and Jack driving along Woodland Road in your pale-blue car, a few seconds of looking before I turned away.

We didn't share the same friends—yours, for obvious reasons, had dropped me; mine and Sam's thought your crowd, with their loud public-school voices and their bottomless bank accounts, were a joke. Different parties (if I ever went to them), different pubs (if I ever went to them); you kept your house in Clifton, while Sam, Liv, and I rented in Saint Paul's.

So there was just the one, devastating confrontation with Jack a week or so before finals. How long did it last—a minute, maybe two before Sam rescued me, taking my elbow and leading me away. And yet in that time, with that smile, knowing, intimate, challenging, he deftly took me right back into the heart of our night together so that I could remember the penetration of him, not you, his hands in a press-up position either side of my head. Memories I refused to examine hammering against my brain.

"Are you OK?" Sam said, catching sight of my face a moment later.

Just a shake of my head was enough for him to put down his glass of wine and take me home. No need to ask me what was wrong; I'd just lost a parent. I had, as they say, the mother of all excuses.

Four Months Before: Catherine

Two infidelities don't make a right. But it helps, no question. We're in total agreement on one thing at least: Sam must not mention Julia, I don't mention you, and so long as that happens, we can pretend we have picked up our marriage where we left off, just the two of us and our kids, bobbing about in our felted cocoon. It works, in a way, this enforced optimism, celebratory dinners night after night, weekend trips planned with a relentlessness and enthusiasm that is exhausting for us all.

Occasionally I'll catch Sam looking at me, and I recognize the hurt in his eyes and know that he's thinking of the day I first came back, when you were right there, imprinted on me, flesh on flesh, bones on bones, breath, taste, tongue, skin that still held your scent of cigarettes and lemons. But mostly we are fine because Sam is also a veteran of faking it. The fable of Catherine and Sam: we can shrug ourselves back into it, and if it seems a little more stretched, a less comfortable fit than before, then we know, from years of experience, that soon it will become like a second skin and we'll both start believing it.

I keep as busy as I can. I've bought myself a pair of Asics trainers and I go out running every day, farther and farther each time. I was no athlete at school, but now I can run for miles, trying to outpace the demons in my head. Fifteen years after it happened, I'm finally facing up to the memory of that night with Jack. I'm forcing myself back into your bed, to that treacherous embrace that makes me cry out at times. I find that I can run and cry at the same time, and if I do it early enough in the day, then my face will recover by the time my family are back home. I keep to the fields and woods, where I see no one apart from the occasional lone dog walker, and I can flash past them, a blur of sweat and tears and acid-yellow trainers that make me think of Ling. Alone in the heart of the woods I'll call your name. I miss you, I'll say to the forest of oaks, or most often: Sorry. Sorry. Sorry. No matter how many times I say it, it will never be enough. I yearn, if not for your forgiveness then for some sign that at least you understand. I made a mistake, a catastrophic one, but not because I didn't love you.

We take our first trip out on *Pandora*, the beautiful blue-and-white dinghy we bought only three weeks ago, though so much has happened since then it feels as if that day belongs to someone else.

"Watch out for the boom."

Boom, jib, port, starboard—it's funny how all these words trip from Sam's tongue. I always think of sailing as belonging to the hairclipped, frosted-lipsticked girls I once knew, the ones who sailed at Bembridge and rode at Belsay, but Sam disproves the point perfectly. He learned to sail on a lake just outside Salford, he can ride Western style, and shoot, and play tennis. He can do all the things you do, only he does them in his own way and with the spiky undercut of humor that is his trademark.

The sailing is a success, and our weekends are mapped out for as long as the weather holds. We celebrate at a pub on the way home with cider for us and bottles of Coke for the children. We sit in the garden and Sam picks up his phone and takes a snap of me and the kids, drinks held high, cheers! I think how this must be the first picture since. Since you. Since Ling. Since everything. Joe says, like he's reading my mind, "I'll take a photo of you and Mum," and now Sam is by my side, arm balanced across my shoulders, casual on the surface, though to both of us it is anything but. For there has been no physicality, none whatsoever, in this resolute reconstruction of the norm. We sleep in the same bed, clothed and clinging to our edges, a great big gap down the middle, room for both children if only they'd come in and save us from ourselves. I feel the pressure of Sam's arm, the warmth of his skin resting against my neck, and I know that it is only a matter of time.

The first time we have sex—how many days later, six, maybe seven?—I do everything I can to still my breathing and switch off my brain. I try to be mindful, to focus on the sensation of Sam's fingers beginning their slow and expert trail across my skin. I try not to look for the scent of cigarettes and lemons or the nobble of cartilage just beneath your ribcage (it's my sternum, you told me when my fingers first found it all those years ago; it's my identity mark). But afterward, afterward, oh God, the despair is tidal, I will not survive it. I lie encased in Sam's arms, staring up at the ceiling, waiting and waiting for the rhythmic flow of his breathing to convince me that he is asleep. I ease myself from his grip and I throw on his discarded T-shirt (Sam's smell: Right Guard deodorant and soap and the faintest whiff of male sweat) and walk out of the room in my bare feet, burglar quiet, even though Sam is so deeply asleep he has begun to snore, and that is another sign that he's happy. And this is what I do. I stand on the landing, staring up at the trapdoor that leads to our attic, missing your box of letters and photos and cuttings, my secret compendium on you, missing you, all that is left of you, even though I'm trying so hard to be someone else, a good mother, a better wife.

This is just the first time, I tell myself, as I stand in the darkness breathing through the pain.

Four Months Before: Lucian

In a surprising, worm-turning twist, Celia has left Jack. She packed up the baby and the car while he was in London, and by the time he got home, they had gone, clothes, toys, everything. She had written him a note that was devastating in its finality.

> *I don't want to be with you anymore. I've been thinking about this for a long time and I won't change my mind. I'm leaving you and going back to live with my parents.*

I meet him for lunch at Colton House, where I try not to express—or even feel—glee at this unexpected outcome. Jack's indignation is hard to take, this the man who continued to sleep with Alexa throughout his marriage, the man who once stole the girl I loved and who sits opposite me now, eating lamb cutlets and drinking wine that I will undoubtedly pay for.

Jack always orders the same thing as me in restaurants, even when, like today, I make a last-minute change—lamb instead of steak. It used to be our standard joke—"I'll have what he's having"—and I found it touching the way he wanted to emulate my taste. Now, though, there is something claustrophobic in his shadowy, mirrorlike perma-presence. Doesn't he have any opinions of his own?

"Celia won't take my calls," he tells me as we drink our way through a very good red. "She's even changed her mobile number, and I can never get past her Rottweiler of a mother. I drove all the way to Warwickshire, and you know what happened when I got there? Her mother wouldn't let me see Celia or even Freddie, my own son, for God's sake. She said I'd be hearing from their lawyers and until then I shouldn't waste my time trying to contact Celia. She said, 'It's over, Jack, you need to accept it'—like, I mean, can't we even talk about trying again? Isn't it actually up to me and Celia?"

"Maybe there's an upside. What about Alexa?"

You've been busy screwing her right through your marriage, after all.

I hate his laugh.

"What about Alexa? Been there, done that. This isn't you and Catherine we're talking about, clinging on to some skewed vision of the past. Talking of which, she's gone a bit quiet. I suppose she's run back to the husband and that's the end of it?"

I seem to have acquired this coating, this superhuman shell, a calmness and poise that makes me capable of almost anything. I can hear this without changing my expression, I can offer a noncommittal shrug, "So it would seem."

But his twisted words of comfort are harder to ignore: "I'm sorry to hear that, but look what happened last time. Girls like her never change."

I look at the man sitting opposite me, I take time to scrutinize his blue eyes (cornflower, the color of insincerity?), and I find no gap, however infinitesimal, in his armor.

I take a little risk, just for fun, just to see how far this liar will go.

"You've never liked Catherine much, have you?"

Earnest cornflower now.

"Mate, I didn't like what she did to you. Running out on you for no reason, leaving you in bits."

What Jack does here—he's been doing it for most of my life—is to remind me of the depth, the length of our friendship.

"We go back a long way, you and me," he says, with another satisfied sip of his expensive wine. In days gone by, to me this meant a mini clip of our best bits: the reassurance to my father that he'd look after me on my first day at school, the actual looking after when the rows with my mother became too much, the replacement with his wholehearted parents. And all along, Jack's action was the thing that effectively wrecked my life and stopped me being with the one person who made me happy. The only question I have is why, but I'm not ready to ask it. More time watching and looking and absorbing the small, everyday betrayals of the man I once considered my closest friend.

Everything he says and does now fascinates. When he smiles at a pretty blond girl walking past our table—she probably smiled first; they usually do—I think, Lecherous bastard, when the old me might have been amused. And when he suggests one more glass of wine—"I think they have a good Gigondas by the glass"—I think of all the wine he has drunk over the years, all the oysters he's eaten, the champagne, our favorite chateaubriand (how many times has he pushed me into ordering that?). Whatever I have, he wants too, wine, food, clothes, even women.

Toward the end of lunch, we get to money, as I had known we would.

"This is awkward," Jack says, "but Celia's parents have frozen our bank account. There will be a settlement, apparently, but until then I'm basically brassic."

"How much? I'll transfer it this afternoon."

"I hate asking, when you've always been so generous. Always helping me out."

"Not a problem," I say, signaling for the bill, impersonating, as best I can, the man I used to be.

On the way home, I stop off at Harry's, expecting to find him wrapped up in his winter clothes in the orangery, an old man in a bath chair. Instead I'm shocked to find the house packed up, the furniture shrouded in sheets, and Harry heading imminently to Thailand, this time with Nat, the Thai translator from Bristol, in tow.

"You should have told me. I'd have come with you. I still would, if you wanted me to."

"I know you would. But it feels like something I need to do on my own. I didn't know Ling for very long, but there was something about her that got under my skin, instantaneously. And I'm not ready to let that go. I'm not ready to let her go."

"Isn't it just going to make it worse, being reminded of her all the time? Being back in her country, with her language, her food?"

"I've thought about that. I've thought about it a lot. And what I've realized is that the pain isn't going anywhere, so I might as well embrace it, indulge it even. I've decided I'll go to Ling's village, I'll meet her family and friends and the lady who taught her to cook, I'll see the river where she swam as a child and I'll understand more about who she was. That's why I'm taking Nat with me."

"Ling would like that. You meeting her family."

"Well, that's the whole thing, really. I need to tell her parents what happened. I want to make them understand how she died. And I need to say sorry to them. You can't imagine how much I want to say that. It's just that . . ." He breaks off, and laughs, though there is no joy in it, no humor. "I'd like them to understand that I loved her and that it should all have been very different."

With Harry gone, my aloneness is complete. I've lost Jack, I've lost Catherine, even the memory of her sullied and closed to examination. And both of the girls have gone to ground. Alexa's absence is explained. When Celia left, Alexa called Jack and offered to come down and keep him company. She was genuinely sad for him, I think, and hopeful that they were free to be together at last. But Jack dismissed her like she was a tired piece of furniture, something of minimal interest, anyway.

"You and I have gone as far as we can, Alexa," he said. "Let's call it a day."

I hated hearing the hurt in her voice, her comprehension of the thing we have known all along: that she meant nothing to Jack, that she was and always has been the stereotypical bit on the side, that the years she spent waiting around, betraying her nature, have been no more than a waste of her time.

"I'm moving back in with my parents for a while," she said, "to work on the book."

A euphemism, I'd say, for mending her broken heart. I wish I had somewhere I could go to mend mine.

Rachel, bizarrely, seems to have vanished, and no one, not even Alexa, knows where she has gone. She hasn't returned any of our phone calls or texts. I even messaged Hugo, her ex, to see if he knew where she was, and his response was brief and unconcerned:

In a ditch, maybe?

And so I am alone in this stupidly large house, which still bears traces of the girl I loved and lost, and knowing the reason why has done nothing to soothe my heartache. It takes me a while before I can go down to the studio, where my sketch of her is still pinned to the easel. I take it down and hold it between my hands, examining it for flaws (mine, not hers). I look and look at the fine nose, the dark arched brows and traffic-stopping eyes. When I'm painting, I try my hardest not to overemphasize; subtlety is the ambition, though I'm not sure I always manage it. With this sketch I realize I've caught Catherine's sorrow, almost by accident. It's plain to see in those beautiful eyes; the difference is that now I understand it.

She sent me a text the night after the party, after Ling's death and her heart-shattering revelation. She told me how sorry she was, that she always had been and always would be; a whole life sentence of being sorry. I read the message and threw my phone across the room. You slept with my best friend. And you told me about it when I was dealing with the death of Harry's wife. I gave her the response I thought she deserved—silence. Now I stare at my sketch of this sad and lovely girl and I tell her I'm sorry too, for not being more understanding. For being so rigid in my hatred of infidelity. Give me time and perhaps I can learn to forgive you. But I will never forgive him.

Four Months Before: Catherine

I'm not very well, I think. I'm spending too much time in my head, lost in my dream world, and it's beginning to get harder to tell dreams and reality apart. If I'm not dreaming and fantasizing, then I'm remembering and reinventing, always trying to get the perfect ending. To make everything right, you have to turn the clock back, the hands spinning through the years fifteen times until we are young again, nineteen and twenty, everything ahead. Our beginning is just right, no changes needed. There you are standing next to your pale-blue car, stubbled, unshowered, with hair that stands on end: the boy who is about to take a stick to my world and spin it round and round until it veers right off its axis. There's a beautiful drawing that appears like magic on my desk while I'm working. There's lunch in an old wooden hut with peeling blue paint, and if I try hard enough I can hear the manic cry of the gulls, I can taste salt in the air.

Now there's a long gilt-edged mirror and a girl standing in front of it, watching, watching as you stand behind her, slowly unbuttoning her shirt, one button, then the next, with hands that do not shake. Your confidence is my undoing, your solemn eyes holding mine in the glass as my shirt falls away, your palms circling my breasts, your almost-smile as you watch me beginning to writhe and squirm, pressing my nakedness back into fully clothed you. Soon you'll carry me over to your bed, you'll run your tongue all the way down my body, starting at my neck, you'll stroke and touch every part of me, you'll somehow take off all of your own clothes without me even knowing how you're doing it, and then you'll be inside me, finally, and it will hurt but I will want you to carry on, and so you do, slowly, so slowly, and now it's the opposite of pain and we're grabbing at each other and perhaps I'm laughing, because all I know is that I want this feeling, this incredible, intense, pleasurable feeling to carry on.

There will be dark nights, months and months of them, when we lie wound around each other flesh against flesh, my hand in yours, palm against palm, lifeline, heart line. You will tell me you love me and I'll say it right back, I'll whisper the words into your ear. There will be light-filled days, there will be coffee and tiny little cakes and an old woman who calls me by the wrong name. There will be Paris, a painting of a dark-eyed woman at the theater, slim white candles burning at an altar. There will be a drawing of a girl kneeling up on a bed dressed in nothing but a loose white shirt that ends just above her knees. How long did it take you to do the drawing—ten minutes, maybe fifteen? Yet you managed to capture perfectly the sweep of my hair, almost reaching my waist, the longest it has ever been. My neck was perhaps a little more swanlike than it really is, a Photoshopped neck, though we didn't have the words for that back then. But it is the eyes you notice, my look of euphoria as I gaze off the page. You know, looking at my eyes, that I am buoyed by the delirium of new love. I am happy, I am confident, I am invincible. Let's stop the clock right here.

Four Months Before: Lucian

Rachel is in rehab. Only this one is in Arizona, some hardcore treatment center in the middle of the desert, no chance to escape even if she wanted to. She calls one Sunday about a fortnight after her disappearance, the first time she's been allowed access to her phone.

"Sorry I didn't tell you," she says. "I wasn't sure I'd go through with it; even when I got off the plane I was considering flying straight back home again."

"So how's it going?"

"Good, I think."

Her voice is cautious, restrained, unlike the old Rachel, who was always ebullient or catatonic, depending on her intake.

"It might actually work this time. I want it to."

She tells me about her days, a 5:30 start followed by an hour's meditation and yoga, then breakfast, then a hike, then a group therapy session before a break for lunch. There's relaxation time at this point, reading books on your bed or going for a walk, and then one-to-one sessions with an addiction counselor.

"And what does the head doctor make of you?" I ask, expecting her to laugh, but she doesn't. Instead she pauses, and a cool breeze blows from across the Atlantic as I realize she is trying to choose her words.

"Already I've learned a lot about myself. What's good for me, what isn't."

"Let me guess, I'm bad for you?"

"It's more that the way I am when I'm around you is bad for me. Does that make sense?"

"Not really. Surely you're not trying to say that being with me would push you into drinking? Rach, if you're clean, I'm going to respect that. You know how much I wanted you to go to rehab. I'd empty my cupboards of booze and fill them with elderflower or lime fucking cordial, you know I would."

"Don't be upset with me. It's just that if I want this to work, then I have to avoid the feelings that make me drink. I think we both know that I've always loved you without any hope of you loving me back. And that feeling of hopelessness I used to get, well, it didn't help. Please don't think I'm blaming you. I'm just trying to give myself the best chance I can."

"So what are you saying, Rach?"

"Hugo has promised me I can start to see Max again if I can just stay clean for two months. I need to give it my best shot. Lucian, you're my best friend. I hope you know that. I just can't see you for a while."

I mainlined an entire bottle of Gevrey-Chambertin after that phone call. I drank it rampaging through my house, clutching the bottle by its neck. In the library I wrenched down Alexa's purple lights from around the old nail, a flashing symbol of inappropriate levity; I took out three bottles from my tequila collection with a sweep of my hand. Dustpan and brush, mop and bucket, shards of glass swept up into newspaper. The undoing of my wreckage took a good half hour and left me stinking of tequila, a sweet yet acrid smell that finally enabled me to weep.

But in some ways it's probably good for me to have this break from my friends, for it gives me the space and time to dismantle my relationship with Jack, piece by piece, slowly and with caution.

I want to know all there is to know about this betrayal of my oldest friend and the girl I've always loved, but I'll find it out my way. Did she start it? With a striptease, perhaps, like she once did for me, the slow unbuttoning, the sliding-down of her jeans, those dark eyes holding mine, the smile she could not suppress?

I force myself into the memory of that night long ago and I remember her dancing, even the exact song, "Wild Horses." I haven't been able to hear it since without thinking of Catherine. She was so beautiful at nineteen, happy, uninhibited. I'd never seen her drunk like that before, but it was funny, it was great. Jack sat next to me on the sofa, watching her too, and I am wondering now if Catherine liked it, being watched by him as well as me. I think, did she always like him a little bit too? Jack with his blatant good looks, all brightness, hair, eyes, teeth. Was she flattered; was there a tension between them, a flirtation I'd failed to pick up on?

It didn't take much for Catherine to be wildly drunk, I remember. At one point she was laughing so much she lay down on the floor.

"Need a stretcher," she said, lying there until I hauled her up and she started dancing again, all rhythm gone now, just lurching with her arms held limply in the air. That was when my uncle rang, depressed after a row with his lover. His voice had sounded strange, and I'd felt the fear instantly. Was he crazy enough to do the same thing as his brother?

Catherine tried to stop me from going. She wound her arms around my neck.

"You're too drunk to drive," she said. "Stay here with me."

"Look who's talking. You'll be asleep in five minutes."

She carried on dancing, if you could call it that, weaving, tilting, so lost in the music I'm not sure she even saw me go.

When I got back the next afternoon, Jack was alone in the house. It occurs to me now that he must have known what I was walking into: that cataclysmic note scrawled on my sketch pad, waiting for me on the bed they'd probably made love in. But you wouldn't have known it from his casual hello, barely flicking his eyes up from the TV screen. He lied brilliantly.

"She went to bed when you left," he said. "And she'd gone by the time I got up."

Night after night Jack sat with me, drinking our way through bottles of whiskey, trying to solve the mystery of her leaving, and worse, her refusal to see me ever again. What could I possibly have done wrong? Never once did he falter; no matter how drunk we got, his story stayed the same. Catherine had gone to bed the minute I left; he hadn't seen her again.

My desire for knowledge of the man I thought I knew better than anyone has become intense, a borderline illness, or perhaps a fully fledged one. There is nothing in my life but this.

Now

I'm better, everyone tells me so. I'm still not talking, but they are starting to think I soon will. There's the same roll call of visitors: Sam almost every day, the children two or three times a week, Liv at the weekend. My father came and I felt bad for him, getting the silent treatment after his sleepless night on the red-eye. He sat in the visitors' chair, talking to me in that loud, self-conscious voice they all used in the beginning, and after a while his conversation ran out. I knew without looking that his lips would be pressed together, brow creased: his not-crying face. I knew he'd be thinking of my mother, of my sweet, nice, uncheckered childhood; he'd be wondering how, after such a glorious beginning, we'd got to here. I'm wondering the same thing myself.

The second time he came, he brought my favorite childhood book with him and began to read. He started on page one, Cassandra sitting in the kitchen sink using the last of the daylight to begin her journal. I'd read this book in the weeks after my mother died, over and over, so that not just sentences but whole pages of text were imprinted on my mind. They are still there; I can anticipate each word, each stretch of dialogue before it comes. And I see the drawings, of course, no need to look. Those wonderful detailed pen-and-ink drawings that remind me of you. He reads the whole book to me before he leaves, four or five hours at a time, and halfway through, I reach out to take his hand; I feel a sort of peace.

I'm still waiting for you to visit; just a minute or two of looking would be enough. And knowing that you had forgiven me, of course. The big one. Sam, with his expert knowledge of his wife, knows how I long for this forgiveness. I think he believes it's the cure-all, the thing that would kick-start me into talking. If he could frog-march you here and have you deliver it, gun held against your head until you spat out the words, then he would.

Of course he's passed all this on to Greg, and our therapy sessions now focus exclusively on that fateful night with Jack. It's comical, really, how I sit here like a wooden block while he tries to therapize me back into blind drunkenness.

"You'd had four or five shots of tequila," he says, "and you were dancing."

He mentions your name, my love; he does this a lot.

"Lucian was watching you from the sofa," he says. "And Jack was next to him, watching you too."

He pauses for effect so that I can feel Jack's eyes upon me; I must allow their particular blue to burn right through my consciousness. He describes you leaving me, going off to see your uncle; he asks me to feel the sensation of being left alone with Jack, for the first time.

"Perhaps you didn't mind him staring at you at first? There's nothing wrong in that. Everyone likes to be admired, especially when we're young.

"Were you surprised when he made his move?"

Like I say, he's a good psychiatrist. He knows his stuff. He knows how to get results. It may have taken time, but he has achieved exactly what he wants. My mind filled with nothing but those images I spent so many years trying to avoid. No more running. No more hiding. Time to face my past head-on.

Four Months Before: Catherine

Liv is here for the weekend, and it feels like a celebration. She is godmother to both children—how could I have given her to one and not the other?—and we spend the first hours of her visit around the kitchen table, drinking tea and inspecting the things she has brought. She is an expert present buyer; she knows what the kids want before they know it themselves. For Joe, a vinyl record player—she waves away our concern: "It cost nothing, don't panic"—and several of her own perfectly chosen LPs, *Scary Monsters*, *Parklife*, and *(What's the Story) Morning Glory?* It makes me wince a little to see those album covers on our kitchen table, to remember the impromptu parties from our past, fueled by vodka and her infinite record collection. For Daisy, there's a trio of intensely colored notebooks, turquoise, electric pink, and orange, and a glittery new pencil case tightly packed with felt tips, another spot-on present. Daisy zips and unzips the pencil case for a few moments, examining the contents with a satisfied smile, then retires into a corner of the kitchen, lost to us for the rest of the night. Her pleasure heart-achingly simple.

Once the kids are in bed, we open Liv's expensive Italian wine and skate across the safest topics. Liv asks Sam about his job and he tells her funny stories about his new friends in the science department, who to me are still a blur of names I struggle to remember. I tell her about the local school, country mothers versus town ones (less makeup, dirtier cars), the three of us treading carefully to avoid all paths that might lead to you.

The next morning, Sam is taking the kids sailing.

"Last sail of the year," he tells us, which brings an inadvertent stab of sorrow. End of summer, official end to the season of you.

I've told Liv very little about our ending, just that it was over and you didn't want to see me again. Now, though, with the door closing behind my family and a fresh pot of coffee on the table between us, the moment for small talk has dissipated.

"What happened?" Liv asks.

Outside we can hear the car doors slamming, one, two, three, the engine starting up, the car sliding away.

Even now, when it no longer matters, when nothing matters, it's hard to say the actual words. There are whole seconds here, and I'm clinging on to them, these last moments before Liv understands who I really am.

"I told him the truth about why I left. I told him I slept with Jack."

I keep my eyes on Liv's face, watching for horror, but instead I find confusion and doubt. She doesn't believe I'm capable of such a thing.

"How? How could that have happened? You wouldn't do that, I know you wouldn't."

I'm trying these days to own these feelings of shame, to conquer them, even. I'm trying to admit—first to you, now to Liv and also to myself—that I once was a person who became so hopelessly drunk she committed an act of betrayal. A person who slept with your best friend. Someone who did the one thing you could never forgive.

"We were drinking tequila, we were drunk. I was so out of it that most of the evening is a blur. Lucian went off to his uncle's house, only I don't remember him going."

"Are you sure? Didn't he tell you he was leaving?"

"I knew that he was worried about his uncle and I didn't want him to drive. I thought he was too drunk and I was scared he might have an accident. The next thing I know, I'm in Lucian's bed having sex with Jack. I don't know how we got there. I don't remember how it started. To begin with, I thought it was Lucian."

"Hold on, this isn't making sense. You thought you were having sex with Lucian but it was Jack?"

"My memory of that night is so patchy, Liv. There's so much I can't remember. But I do remember the sex. I know it happened. I know it's true. I wish more than anything that it wasn't. I remember him doing things I didn't want to do. It was strange, almost as if he wanted me to think he was Lucian. I should have stopped him, but I didn't. I knew it was Jack and I just lay there and let him do what he wanted to do. I've been so ashamed, Liv, so disgusted with myself. I've hated myself, if only you knew how much."

I'm crying now, but from relief. To tell this secret of mine, finally; to admit that my life has been scarred by shame.

Liv shifts her coffee cup aside as if it's too much of a distraction. She reaches across the table to take hold of my hand.

"Tell me everything you can remember about that night. I think you've spent so many years blaming yourself for what happened, you might have lost sight of the truth."

Now

Today Greg spares no punches. Today he delivers me right into the heart of my dread, to the exact moment when my life shattered. He describes the events of that night in the same calm, clinical voice he has used all along. He takes me through it moment by moment, from the first tortured kiss to the last. But I have no need of his words. This moment of betrayal, I have lived and relived it so many times. The memory is crystal clear.

You are in bed with me, on top of me, kissing me, crushing me, holding me so tight I can barely breathe. This kiss, this suffocating kiss, means I cannot see you or speak or ask you to wait. Please. I am still asleep. You are screwing me, that's the word, I get it now, literally a screw that turns and turns deep in my flesh. I don't like it. I reach up with my hands to stroke your back. To soothe, to slow, perhaps to stop you, and now your breathing changes gear and you are sighing, sighing, right into my mouth and I don't like it. You are panting, huh, huh, huh, huh, a sound I've never heard before. Smell, touch, taste, sound. This doesn't feel right.

"Need to fuck you."

A word you never use.

"Turn over," you say, and I don't want to, and also your voice doesn't sound like you.

"Don't want to."

My own voice, when it comes, sounds thick and blurry, drunk, still half asleep.

You pull your mouth away, you lean above me on your hands. In the darkness I can see your face, and now I know fully the thing that subconsciously I have always known. It's not you but Jack, on top of me, inside me, all over me, and this is what I wake to. I am crying as he pushes and grunts, quiet tears that streak all the way down my cheeks. He bends his elbows, his face close enough to mine so that he can kiss my tears, he can lick them with his tongue.

"You want it," he says, pressing deeper, so deep it hurts. "You love it when he does this to you."

Those words will stay, they'll never go.

I don't say no. No, it isn't what I want. I don't push him away. And that will never go either.

Jack is talking again. With his thumb and forefinger he pinches my nipples, first one, then the other.

"Do you like it when he does that?" he asks.

He thrusts his tongue into my mouth, an invasive one-sided kiss.

He slides both hands beneath my buttocks, lifting me further into him. Deeper and deeper he goes. He moans. He wants me to do the same, but I am silent, waiting for my ending.

"Tell me what you like," he says. "Tell me what he does to you. I'll do it too. I'll do whatever he does."

A strange thing happens. The girl I was floats from my body like a soul and hovers somewhere above me, watching, waiting as my body is mauled and pounded and obliterated by your friend. There's no feeling now, no pain, just the absolute quiet of my watchful, disconnected self. This girl, the one on the ceiling, remembers the end, remembers the juddering and the sighing and the slamming into the body that lies on your bed. That horrible final yell. The silence that follows.

I am not crying in this therapy session, though my hands are gripping the arms of my chair so tightly that my knuckles have turned white. Greg has left his chair and is crouched down beside me, telling me to breathe.

"Breathe, Catherine, you must breathe."

There's a sharp pain going right through my chest, like a javelin's been hurled into it, but I don't tell Greg this because I cannot speak. Instead I take the breaths, deep ones in, then out, in, out, longer each time, and I listen to his soft, calm voice leading me away from your bedroom of old and back into the warm white light of our cottage.

This is how Greg closes every session, returning me to my safe place, to Sam, to Joe and Daisy. Every day he gets a little closer to bringing me home.

Four Months Before: Lucian

I'm in my studio, working on an oil portrait of Catherine. I was tempted to mess around with the colors—I tried a pale violet for her skin, a deep rust for her hair—but in the end I've gone for a more literal representation. Black-brown hair, creamy skin, those sorrowful eyes, her wonderful mouth. I am completely absorbed. I have this feeling I had once before, that I'm bringing her back to life. I felt it a long time ago when I painted my father for the first time, working from an old photograph. It was as if the painting was smiling at me, the way he used to, the smile a half laugh, as if he was permanently ready for amusement. How did a man who loved to laugh end up taking his own life? How did a girl who loved me so much end up sleeping with my best friend, my brother?

So completely focused am I on this painting that I don't hear the studio door open, and I am astonished to find Liv walking toward me.

"Oh God," she says when she sees the portrait.

I shrug. What is there to say? Yes, I still love her. No, I'm not over her. I don't see that I ever will be.

I watch Liv putting her hand up to her temple.

"She feels exactly the same about you."

"Why are you here, Liv? To tell me that?"

"No, no. Something else."

She begins pacing around my studio in tight little circles.

"Catherine must never know that I'm here," she says.

"Fine. It's not like we're talking anyway."

"Lucian?"

She stops pacing. She stands a few feet in front of me.

"I'm going to tell you the truth about Catherine and Jack."

Liv cries throughout her replay of that night, though the tears don't interrupt the telling, they just run down her cheeks and occasionally she brushes them away with her hands. She tells me that Jack got into bed with Catherine when she was asleep and started having sex with her. She says that at first Catherine thought it was me; only when she was fully awake did she realize it was him. She didn't push him off, she didn't stop him, she didn't say no. She just wanted it to be over.

There is in me an anger that burns and consumes and suffocates. I'm grateful to Liv for telling me the truth, but I also want her gone. The magnitude of my former friend's treachery has fallen upon me, a heavy, dark blanket of hate. There is nothing else.

"Why didn't she tell me? I would have understood."

"She thought . . ." and here Liv hesitates and seems to change her mind about whatever she was about to say.

"Go on."

"She thought if you found out you might do something stupid. You know, like your father."

Oh Catherine, how well you know me.

"What will you do?" Liv asks before she leaves.

I shake my head, barely able to communicate. "I'll talk to him. We'll have a little chat."

There are hours of planning before I'm ready to confront Jack. I send a text inviting him over for cakes and fine wine, our standard *Withnail* joke, and I ask Mary to make something for supper even though I'm one hundred percent sure neither of us will be eating.

I walk around the ground floor of the house, thinking, obsessing, trying to stay calm. I go down to the cellar, scanning the shelves until I find the wine I know he loves so much—it can only have been a few weeks ago that Jack, Rachel, and I sat here drinking my uncle's Château Lafite. All this preparation, all this care, it feels a little like putting together a last meal: Mary's famous chicken pie, the Baccarat glasses that Jack always envied, his favorite wine. I want him to feel comfortable and relaxed before I go in for the kill, hitting him with my sickening new knowledge. I want to see the whites of his eyes as he begins to comprehend how much I know, which is everything. I'm not sure yet what I want from him—an apology isn't going to cover it. What, sorry for all the years of heartache, for the premeditated obstruction to my happiness, for the way he destroyed Catherine, with her tragic, shameful eyes. "Hate" isn't strong enough; "loathe," "despise," none of them quite fit. A new word is needed for the way I feel about Jack.

A fire is laid in the library, the wine is uncorked, decanter and glasses ready, and still there are several hours before he is due to arrive. I'll spend them on Google Earth, a new habit of mine; late to the party, I know. Thing is, I remember every detail Catherine told me about where she lived: the exact location, last house on the very outskirts of the village, a little thatched cottage with blue-painted windows. "A gingerbread house," she said, "so pretty it's almost an embarrassment." I like to zoom right in on this house, on its roof made of straw, now faded to gray, and its yellowy walls and the bright-blue front door, exactly as she described. I like to look at the thin, straggly garden with the band of bright water at its bottom and wonder, was she out there today, was she wading through the stream with her kids, was she sitting at the table drinking tea, was she stooped over the vegetable patch pulling up a lettuce for their supper?

And suddenly looking is no longer enough; now I need to see this little house in the flesh.

My heart is beating faster as I drive to the village and see the cottage for the first time. I park up and sit behind the wheel, watching. Catherine is probably in there. The temptation to knock on the door—a good strong blue; manganese would be the closest—is intense, but I tell myself no, not yet, not until I've seen Jack. When I've dealt with him, then I'll come back and I'll tell her, sorry, sorry for not understanding, not guessing the truth, not forgiving you anyway, you, the girl I have always loved.

It's an addictive thing, looking at the embarrassingly pretty house—she's right, it's Hansel and Gretel on steroids—and soon enough I find that I want to draw it. I pick up my sketchpad—there's always at least one in the glove compartment or the back seat of the car—and begin to draw. I hold up my pencil to measure the diameter of the diamond-paned windows and the exact spacing between them, three up, two down, just like she said. The roof takes longest, the detailed shading of straw, the faint hint of its net covering, the pronounced jut above the cottage walls, as thick and prominent as a wodge of icing.

When I've finished the drawing, I title it *Your Gingerbread House* and I rip it out of my sketchpad and decide that I will drop it through her letter box and to hell with the consequences. I want her to know that I've been here, I hope that she'll see the drawing and understand what it means: I know what happened to you and I'm dealing with it. It may have taken fifteen years to get here, but we'll have our vengeance, we'll free ourselves from the monstrous legacy of our past.

Four Months Before: Catherine

It is your drawing of the house that snips the final thread. I find it face up on the doormat, instantly recognizable, as is the title, in your beautiful artist's script: *Your Gingerbread House*. I throw open the door like a wild woman, already crying, and search the streets, head swiveling left and right, but you have gone. Now I can look at the drawing more carefully, the tight pencil strokes of our thatch, the diamonds of the windows so exact, as if you've counted every one. It is fairy-tale perfection, a house to disappear into, and it reminds me instantly of one of the ink drawings in my favorite book. And of course, you made me one of these drawings before, the seaside restaurant where we had our first lunch, and I still have it, stashed along with the photos and clippings and letters, my hidden keepsakes of you.

There's no thought as I pull down the staircase to the attic and climb up to retrieve the shoebox. There's crying and looking and touching and holding as I sit downstairs on the sitting room floor surrounded by you: magazine articles, bits of lined A4, photographs, like an exploding time bomb from our past. Paris. Bristol. The beach. We look so young and so happy; this time my heart cannot be mended.

The front door opens and Joe and Sam come through it—Daisy is at a friend's house, I hadn't forgotten—and it doesn't really matter that they find me like this, because I have tipped over the edge, there's nowhere else to go. I need to be caught and Sam knows this, with his firm, clipped "Joe, go into the kitchen and start your homework. I need to help Mum."

And then he's kneeling on the floor beside me, picking up newspaper cuttings that have turned yellow with age, and a photo of you in your university bedroom, bare-chested and smiling at me in a way that must hurt.

"Jesus Christ, Catherine." Those are his first words, but there's no anger, just sadness. "This"—his hands are full of you, cuttings, photos, letters—"is madness."

"I'm sorry," I say. I do say that. To Sam I have always been able to say sorry.

"You should have told me. Catherine, you should have said."

I didn't tell him, because I couldn't. I had no words. My punishment for what had happened was never telling the truth. My punishment was a life lived in silence.

This is what silence does to you. It poisons you with a slow and suffocating creep, you and those around you, husband, children, the lover you may not have. It burns from the inside out with the chill of liquid nitrogen. It steals not just your thoughts and words but your feelings too, so you are left like a wooden block trying to impersonate appropriate emotion. You can switch it on like an electric light, but you won't fool anyone. You try anyway; every day becomes like your own private street theater as you learn the roles of wife, then mother, and act your way right through them. When you allow silence in, when you keep a secret, not just keep it but hold it under as I do, pushing down with both hands, then you also feed the shame that surrounds it. And shame is deadly. It makes a mute of you, it chokes down your unsayable truth and wraps you in a firewall of hidden anger. And this is your life.

"Why did you leave him when you loved him so much? Why would you have done that? I don't understand."

"I left him," I say, "because of Jack."

Four Months Before: Lucian

I am expecting to feel nervous when Jack arrives, but as I watch him getting out of his shiny black Jeep, with his bright hair and his expectant smile, I am filled with quiet, deadly anger. We embrace by the front door, the back-slapping hug of old, though now it sickens me, and Jack inhales the air.

"Something smells incredible. Don't tell me it's . . ."

"Yep. Mary made the pie."

"Mate, this is so nice of you. I've been feeling a bit low the last few days without Celia and Freddie. I could do with cheering up."

He follows me into the library, fire now properly ablaze and chucking out heat into the room. He sees the two empty bottles by the fireplace, my uncle's decanter filled to the top with his favorite wine.

"Look at that! This is a treat, a real treat."

We sit opposite each other, a chesterfield each, in front of the fire that is already far too hot. Jack pours our wine—always the perfect host in my house—and updates me on his sad little life, no nearer to a settlement with Celia, fast running out of cash. "You only have to ask, you know that"—words like sawdust, an adder tensing, waiting, retracting.

I watch Jack swallowing down the first few sips of his wine.

"God, that's good."

Sticky Fingers is on the sound system. Not a coincidence; the soundtrack of rape. There are ten tracks on the album; "Wild

Horses" is the third one in, there's seven and a bit minutes before we get to it—I counted—and when it starts, when Catherine appears, young and so very beautiful, dancing with her arms held above her head, the last time either of us was truly happy, there is no more time.

I stand up, because it's easier this way.

"I know what you did."

Jack looks up at me, confused by the gravity of my voice.

"What are you talking about?"

"Catherine. I'm talking about Catherine. And what you did to her."

He does look a little scared then, just for a moment, before he's on his feet apologizing.

"Mate," he says, "I am so sorry. We were so drunk. We didn't mean it to happen, it just did."

This "we" is the only ignition I need.

"You raped her. You raped her when she was asleep."

"I did not! Who told you that? Catherine? That's a fucking lie. Catherine was drunk, we both were. But she wanted it just as much as I did."

I know better than anyone his inability to resist a final taunt, the last word his holy grail. And yet. The match is struck.

"You knew how much I loved her. You of all people. And all these years you've said nothing; you let me think Catherine left me for Sam."

"The reason we didn't tell you is because we knew how you'd react. It was a mistake, that's all, a stupid drunken mistake."

There it is again, the expert needle that is this word "we." Jack and Catherine. Imprinted on my brain.

"Catherine would never have had sex with you if you hadn't forced yourself on her."

"Believe that if it makes you feel better. But she and I know the truth."

Fury is weightless. I cannot feel my body as I walk around the coffee table so that I am facing him, my back to the blazing fire. He does look afraid as I step toward him, no thought of what I'll do, just violence in my veins.

"Calm down, for fuck's sake," he says.

I raise my hands, an instinct to hurt. I grab the tops of his arms, squeezing so hard he shouts out.

"Why do you need to be me so much? Everything I've had, you've wanted for yourself. Even Catherine. You took her because she was mine. Because you couldn't bear me to love someone more than you."

In those blue eyes fury, but also mortification.

Yes, you twisted bastard, I know exactly who you are.

He shoves me hard in the chest and I lose my grip, arms flailing as I try to steady myself. He pushes me again, a violent thrust with the flat of his hand, and this time I'm flying through the air, flying backward, and my head strikes the beam above the fireplace, a piercing, a splintering, and just one moment of sharp, sharp pain, while Mick sings of the tears that we'll cry and the living that we'll do after we die.

Fifteen Years Earlier

You wrote one more letter; it arrived a week or so after my mother had died. I'd stayed on for a few days after the funeral, but the house without her in it was cold and dismal and I couldn't wait to get away. I returned to Bristol and spent the remainder of that year hidden away in the little terraced house I shared with Liv and Sam in Saint Paul's. When I remember that time, I always think, poor Sam, Sam who had two fully working parents, who was only twenty and was mad about football and astronomy and mixing up weird fizzing concoctions in the chemistry lab. His only mistake was to love a girl who was crippled by loss.

I was alone in the house when your letter arrived, and from the moment I saw the envelope with my name and address in your sloping, looped handwriting, my heart began to pulse. I'd lived without you for almost a year by then, I was getting used to you not being in my life, yet I ripped open that envelope with hands that shook.

Inside, a drawing of a flower, a peony, a close-up of its bloom, the petals packed tight like the leaves of a cabbage. Peonies were my mother's favorite; her coffin had been covered head to foot in a hundred pale-pink ones. No better symbol to pierce my heart. But that wasn't the thing that made me cry; it was that you'd remembered me telling you she loved them.

Catherine,

I am so sorry that you've lost your mother. I remember how much you loved her. Whenever you talked about her you smiled, did you know that? I spoke to her once on the phone when we were going to Paris and I needed your passport. Her voice was light and warm and full of laughter, just like yours. "Really?" she said. "A day trip to Paris. Now that sounds interesting."

People like her don't just disappear, I hope you can believe that.

It's like that song, the one you used to love: there's still plenty of living to be done after you've died.

Lucian

Four Months Before: Catherine

Sam is a better man than I deserve. I say that a lot and it's true. For it's Sam who has urged me to make this journey to your house as the light starts to drift from the sky; it's Sam who made me see the one thing I've always refused to accept.

"You were drunk, Catherine. That doesn't make you responsible for what happened. You woke up and found Jack having sex with you. That's rape."

This word "rape" falls all the way through me. Rape. An act of violence. A crime. When I told Liv about the night with Jack, I knew full well that it wasn't what I'd wanted; I could picture my nineteen-year-old self lying motionless on your bed, awash with tears my tormentor kissed away.

Yet Jack was so clever. Quick to manipulate my panic and confusion, my half-formed memories and hungover brain. He convinced me that not only was I complicit in the betrayal of you, I was the initiator. How I have hated myself for that.

"I didn't say no," I told Sam, for this was my greatest shame.

"And you didn't say yes. Call it nonconsensual if you want, it boils down to the same thing."

"I was so ashamed. That's why I didn't tell anyone. I felt I deserved it because I'd got so drunk I didn't know what I was doing. If I hadn't been so drunk, I would never have allowed it to happen."

"Getting drunk isn't a crime. What he did is. He's a sick bastard.

He preyed on you when you were asleep. When you were drunk and defenseless."

"When I last saw Lucian, the night Ling died, I told him about me and Jack. I told him we'd slept together."

"You really believed that? That it was sex and not rape?"

"That's what Jack told me the next day. He said I'd started it, that I'd been all over him. And I was so sick and ashamed I chose to believe him. It didn't fit with my memories of it, though; the thing I remembered most clearly was just wanting it to be over."

"Oh Catherine."

Sam took hold of my hands, the two of us standing there in our newly painted sitting room, surrounded by the history of you. In Sam's face now, comprehension. At last I am understood.

"Go and find him, Catherine. Go and tell him the truth, just like you've told me."

"Why are you doing this, Sam? You hate him, don't you?"

"I hate what happened to you. It wasn't your fault, and you've spent your whole life regretting it. You've made yourself ill with it. I think you'll feel better once he knows the truth."

I am buoyed up by the anger Sam hands me, and afterward I will not be able to recall a moment of my journey to your house, not a road or a tree or a passing car, so preoccupied am I with my justice. Jack took my life from me and now I'm taking it back. I'm turning the hands of the clock myself: once, twice, fifteen times. We will be that girl and boy again, only this time we'll get it right.

Now

"Big day today, my darling. You're going home."

Alison is helping me to get dressed in jeans and a T-shirt and a pair of silver flip-flops, which are brand new; she snips off the plastic loop that holds them together. She trims my toenails and paints them carefully, three even stripes to each nail, no smudges, a brilliant orange.

"Daisy chose that color for you," she tells me as she works. "She says it used to be your favorite."

I know what she's doing; they've all been doing it, day after day, night after night, trying to prepare me, trying to rehabilitate me back into family life.

Greg was here, sitting on the scratchy brown visitors' chair first thing, hoping to convince me that I've made enough progress to survive in the outside world. I'm not speaking yet but I soon will, he says. He's sure of it.

"You lived through all those memories, Catherine. You won't have to do that again. You can focus on the present now, on Sam, Joe, and Daisy."

"How about you say hello to your man when he comes, darling?" says Alison, sticking to her theme. "It would mean so much to him. Promise me you'll try, won't you?"

I feel as if I'm standing on the edge of a cliff, waiting to jump. The moment I speak, I allow the truth to come rushing back in, I let go of my dream world, of you and me, the girl and boy who drift from beach to café to bed, marooned in memory, but beautifully so, I like to think. I try to speak, I do, but what happens is that my throat becomes locked and my chest feels tight and my voice remains stuck in my mind, stuck on two words I do not wish to say.

Greg comes back for one last pep talk before I leave.

"Now, are you feeling all right about going home? I'm going off in a minute, so I just wanted to take this last chance to say goodbye."

I give him a small approximation of a smile, a bit like your smile, your minimal, down-turned one, your defining characteristic, it seems to me now.

"That's good, Catherine," Greg says. "I'm so happy to see you smiling. It would change everything if you'd start speaking, just a word, just one word to give us all something to hold on to. Think of Joe and Daisy, think how it would turn their lives around if you'd speak to them. Can't you do it for them, Catherine?"

I turn my face away and stare out of the window at the apple tree in the corner of the garden. When I first came here, it still had a few squashy brown apples clinging to its branches; once or twice I saw them fall to the ground. I've seen that tree naked and gray through winter, and the cloudburst of saccharine color that marked its springtime flowering. When I first came here they thought I'd lost my mind, though those weren't the words they used.

"She doesn't remember the accident because she disconnected from it. We call it dissociative amnesia."

Now they've worked out I live in my head because I want to, because it's the only way I can stay with you. And they don't keep beds here for that.

Sam comes around the corner with Alison. She's holding a

huge bunch of flowers, crimson roses and sprays of white lilac; he's always been good at flowers.

"I'll miss her beautiful face, that's for sure," Alison says.

"You've been so good to her, Alison. To all of us."

"Hey," Sam says to me in his method-husband-to-wife voice, and I flash him with my eyes, a silent acknowledgment. "Look at you in your outside clothes."

"There's no rush," says Alison. "None at all. Why don't I make you a cup of tea and you can talk to Catherine about what happens next."

"Good idea," says Sam, sitting down in the visitors' chair.

"The kids are so excited that you're coming home," he says. "Liv is with them and they've decorated the whole house: flowers, bunting, great big banners everywhere."

I manage another small smile. My daughter's handiwork, I can imagine it well. Sam clasps his hands together, fingers interlinked, and rests them on his knee. He's wearing black jeans and a black T-shirt, his roadie gear, we always used to say. His arms are tanned from hours in the garden, or perhaps from being on the boat. His face is leaner than it used to be; he looks healthy and handsome. We sit in silence while my other world tugs at my brain, tempting me. It would be so easy to slip and slide backward until I can find you again.

"Well," Sam says, "this is it. I guess we're ready to go home."

He gives me one more look and then he says the thing we've both been waiting for, the thing he always says.

"If you could just show me you can talk, Catherine, it would change everything."

Four Months Before: Catherine

It is a strange feeling drawing up to your house, seeing Jack's black car parked up next to your navy-blue one and now mine completing the row. It's symbolic, really: it's been about the three of us, you, me, and him, all along. I am not nervous as I stand at the front door, waiting for you or Mary or even Jack to answer. This new anger, this quest for justice, has propelled me into a place I'd forgotten. Strong. Calm. Invincible.

Through the door I can hear loud music, instantly recognizable to me after all this time, and it fills me with hope. I know you couldn't listen to that album without thinking of me. And then I hear shouting. Jack's voice first, then yours. I hear your anger, your rage, and for a whole minute, perhaps two, I freeze, not sure what to do. But then I barge open the door, and beneath the music I hear wailing, a horrific sound. Not you. Him.

"No. No. No!" he cries.

I'm running toward the library as Jack runs out of it. There is blood on his face, his shirt, his hands.

"Need an ambulance!" He screams it as he races toward the phone, and I am filled with instant fear. Please, that word is in my head. Just please.

At first I see nothing. The room is empty, that's what I think, as I listen to Mick Jagger's ragged vocals and remember how once upon a time, you and I knew every word to every song. And then I do see you, lying on your back so close to the fire I think your flesh might burn. There's a lake of blood beneath your head, and your neck is twisted so that you're facing me, but I don't think you've seen me. You haven't seen anything. I know you're not breathing even before I kneel down and cover your body with mine, checking and checking for the faintest rush of warm air, the way I used to hover over my babies in the middle of the night, just to make sure. There is no breath. And when I find your hand, limp, too limp, pushing my thumb into the base of your wrist, there's no pulse either. My face is against your shirt and I catch the scent of lemons, I cling to the fading warmth of your skin. My love. My love.

Jack is back in the room.

"Catherine," he says. "Help me."

But I don't want to help him. I don't want to see him. This man who stole my life and has now taken yours. I press my face against your chest, I hold you so tightly, but there's nothing I can do.

"Catherine." Jack says my name again. His voice is close. "Please, listen to me. I'm not going to hurt you."

I feel his hand on my arm, trying to pull me away from you, but I will never let go.

"I'm so sorry, Catherine. I'm so sorry."

I hear that he is crying, perhaps the last thing I recognize, but his words, his tears have no meaning, just sound, like the background wash of the music that still plays, songs that belong to another time, another place.

You've left your body and now I have left mine. I watch, as before, from my place on the ceiling. I see the girl cradling the man, I see her dripping tears onto his face, streaks of salt to wash away the red, I see her wrapping her arms around him, holding on. Lucian, she says. Lucian. She begs him to stay. Please don't leave me.

And now another voice is in the room, the one she trusts, the one she needs. Sam has come to find her.

"Jesus," he says, and that one word contains all her horror. He says it just right. "I knew I shouldn't have let you come out here on your own. I was so worried about you. Is he dead? Catherine?"

She hears him kneeling beside her. She feels his hands stroking her back, her shoulders, her hair.

"Let go, darling," he says, the first time he has ever called her that. "Let go of him now. Catherine? You need to let go."

His voice breaks on her name.

"What happened?" he asks, and Jack's voice answers but the words come out as sobs, almost unintelligible to her and perhaps to him.

"He fell . . . we fought . . . the nail . . ."

Sam gets hold of the girl now; he pulls her away from the body, drags her up until she's standing, flopped against him. There is blood all over her face, her neck, a bitter black pool on the navy of her T-shirt.

"Baby," he says, for this is what he used to call her. He has found the right name. "Baby, can you hear me?"

She does not speak and her eyes are dead, a dead person's unseeing eyes. His voice is raised, threaded with panic. Catherine! Catherine! Answer me. Talk to me. He is rocking her gently, back and forth. And now Jack is standing next to her but she does not see, she does not care.

Sam has wrapped his arm around her shoulders and he begins to lead her from the room, but at the last moment she stops still. Outside, the sun has dropped down behind the hill and blood drains from the sky, first pink, then steel, now black for her vigil. And it seems to her, as she turns to take one final look at his broken body, that even the air is weeping.

Now

The question rises up, as always, but this time it passes from my brain to my throat to my mouth and then the words are out there and I see the look of dread as Sam hears them.

"He died. Didn't he?"

No method voice now, just a broken whisper as Sam tells me what I already know.

"Yes. He did. I'm sorry."

There are no words for this, no words, but we sit together with your death between us, and it's almost comforting, almost as if we're sharing the loss, just like we did when my mother died. The past doesn't matter and nor does the future, there's just this moment of acceptance. No sound, just space. Pure white, like one of your canvases.

"Should I tell you what happened?" Sam asks after a while.

I nod and then, because I can, I use my voice.

"Yes."

"There was a fight between them. It was over you. He fell back against the beam, and a nail went through his skull."

He pauses, framing what comes next.

"He knew what happened to you, Catherine. He understood."

So this is how your forgiveness is delivered to me—by a man who spent a lifetime hating you and loving me. Not forgiveness, I know now, but understanding. And sorrow at all those lost years.

"And Jack?"

Finally I speak his name without fear or shame.

"Jack has lost everything. His wife, his child, his best friend. There was an investigation, of course, and talk of manslaughter, but they went with accidental death in the end."

Death, the word echoes, but I won't let it bring me down. I'll stay right here in the bright white space you have created for me. In a while I'll reach forward and touch Sam's hands, gripping together so tightly on his knee.

"It's all right," I'll tell him. "We will be all right," and I'll watch the light come into that handsome, healthy face and I'll feel glad that I can fix him.

But not quite yet. First I'll turn away and look out at my tree for the last time, looking but not seeing the branches swaying in the breeze with their tiny buds of green. I'll sink back into the place where you are, the place where we were young. There will be salt in the air and on our tongues and you'll be smiling at me, if you can call it that, and you'll ask me to tell you my life story and I'll say I don't think my life has really started yet.

And you'll say: "Perhaps it begins right here."

Acknowledgments

I would particularly like to thank my amazing agent, Felicity Blunt, for championing this book; with her early guidance it became the story I wanted to write. Thanks also to Melissa Pimentel and the brilliant translation rights team at Curtis Brown.

I have loved working with the very talented editor Francesca Pathak at Orion: thank you for your enthusiasm, understanding, and absolute connection with the story. Thank you to the whole Orion team for working so hard on this book. Thanks also to Celine Kelly for her early editorial suggestions. I am also very grateful to Abigail Scruby at John Murray for her editorial wisdom.

A huge debt of thanks to Dr. James Stallard for sharing his expertise on dissociative disorder, his reflections on Catherine's case, and, coincidentally, a couple of brilliant plot suggestions. Researching Catherine's condition, I also drew from the invaluable resource *Shame and Guilt* by June Price Tangney and Ronda L. Dearing. The artist Tom Hammick, whose work I love: your gorgeous painting *Carmen and the Bull* was an inspiration for one of Lucian's.

Lucinda Horton and Harriet Edwards, dearest friends, inspirational writers, cofounders of our writers' group: simply, without you there would be no book.

Thanks and love to Jane and Anna, my sisters, first readers, and everything in between, for your lifelong commitment to the cause. Jake, Maya, and Felix, you have grown up to this book and turned into such amazing people along the way. You make me so proud.

And last but most, John. You support me in everything but especially my writing, and this book has always been for you.

About the Author

Clare Leslie Hall is a novelist and journalist who lives in the wilds of Dorset, England, with her family. She is the author of *Broken Country* and *Days You Were Mine*.